# THE FATHER OF FLESH

## Other Books By Nicholas Paschall

*Ghost of O'Leary House*

*Grimlocke Chronicles*

*Dead and Proud of It*

*Lust of the Damned*

*Rise of the Hunters: Birth of a God*

## Available Through Darkwater Syndicate

*Travails for Teyuna:*
*Book two of the Broken Gods series*

*Shadows and Teeth, Volume 3:*
*Ten Terrifying Tales of Horror and Suspense*

*Postcards from the Void*

# THE FATHER OF FLESH

BOOK ONE
OF THE
BROKEN GODS SERIES

NICHOLAS PASCHALL

The Father of Flesh
Published by Darkwater Syndicate, Inc.
8004 NW 154 Street #623
Miami Lakes, FL 33016



www.DarkwaterSyndicate.com

Library of Congress Control Number: 2017931995

ISBN-10: 1-946378-07-0
ISBN-13: 978-1-946378-07-1

# Dedication

This novel is a direct result of a conversation I had with my father over what makes someone afraid. It was a long discussion had over margaritas before a James Wan movie. We debated what made fear something that manifested in your heart, where it could bring bile to the back your throat, make you look away from the page, or put down the book entirely because it's just too frightening. I took his advice for this book, and searched in the darkest corners of my soul for suitable material to present.

I would also like to thank Tricia Nelson for reading some of the earlier drafts for me. My wife and I have become inured to horror, and so I can't tell what's scary anymore.

This one's for you, Dad!

# Table of Contents


| | |
|---|---|
| Chapter One | 1 |
| Chapter Two | 11 |
| Chapter Three | 21 |
| Chapter Four | 31 |
| Chapter Five | 41 |
| Chapter Six | 51 |
| Chapter Seven | 61 |
| Chapter Eight | 71 |
| Chapter Nine | 81 |
| Chapter Ten | 91 |
| Chapter Eleven | 101 |
| Chapter Twelve | 111 |
| Chapter Thirteen | 121 |
| Chapter Fourteen | 131 |
| Chapter Fifteen | 141 |
| Chapter Sixteen | 151 |
| Chapter Seventeen | 159 |
| Chapter Eighteen | 169 |
| Chapter Nineteen | 177 |
| Chapter Twenty | 187 |
| Chapter Twenty-One | 197 |
| Chapter Twenty-Two | 207 |
| Chapter Twenty-Three | 217 |
| Chapter Twenty-Four | 225 |
| Chapter Twenty-Five | 235 |
| Chapter Twenty-Six | 243 |
| Chapter Twenty-Seven | 251 |
| Chapter Twenty-Eight | 261 |
| Chapter Twenty-Nine | 269 |
| Chapter Thirty | 279 |

Chapter Thirty-One 289
Chapter Thirty-Two 299
Chapter Thirty-Three 309
Chapter Thirty-Four 319
Chapter Thirty-Five 327
Chapter Thirty-Six 337
Chapter Thirty-Seven 345
Chapter Thirty-Eight 351
Chapter Thirty-Nine 361
Chapter Forty 369

# Chapter One

Lying on a cot in his nameless village in the rolling hills of the Guangxi province, Kwan moaned in agony. He was sick, far sicker than he'd ever been.

The night before, he'd been walking the perimeter of his village, lantern held high so that he could see through the smothering darkness. They'd just had a birth in their community of seventy—now seventy-one—souls, and there were creatures that stalked the night hungering for young, unspoiled flesh.

Kwan had turned a corner and was heading back into the center of the village when he saw it sliding out of the village well.

It was vaguely humanoid in that it had two legs and stood upright, though the legs were malformed. Thicker than normal legs with corded muscle, the pallid things ended in a total of three toes, one long toe on the right leg and two stubby ones on the left. Its skin was a pulsating pink that seemed swollen with fluid, straining against its hide as if it were about to burst. It had eight tentacles instead of arms, three sprouting from one side, five from the other, each ending in a four-fingered hand. Veins throbbed visibly as the creature clambered out of the well, leaving behind a trail of viscous fluid that shined a brilliant fuchsia and brown.

Most horrifying of all was its face. The head had twisted until it was completely upside down, flesh bubbling up to replace the neck and lower jaw. An open maw dominated the upper torso; it didn't seem to be able to close. Saliva dribbled from the lipless mouth in great rivulets over the face; the eyes looked about wildly before they'd focused on Kwan. On its hunched back it had two multi-jointed arms that ended on pitted orbs, one of which turned as if regarding Kwan. Kwan had pulled the Soviet pistol from his belt and raised it as quickly as he could.

"Demon!" he'd shouted, alerting the village of the creature in their midst.

His yell had appeared to startle the demon. The pitted orbs had convulsed at the end of the limbs, spewing into the air clouds of noxious gas that rolled with the gentle wind, washing over Kwan as he aimed his pistol at the creature's head. Firing off two shots, the bullets tore through the exposed flesh which bled chunky rivulets of fat mixed with pus. But the wounds quickly opened and split, forming mouths where the bullets had pierced, gaping toothless things that clapped open and closed as if they'd been taunting Kwan.

The creature had stumbled forward in an ungainly fashion, whipping its tentacles about to gain better balance. Kwan, who'd been coughing from the cloud it had discharged, had run behind it, almost slipping in the slime trail, and fired another round into the area where he thought the monster's spine would be.

The beast had swiveled in place, its body flexing as if it were made of rubber as it rounded on Kwan. The gurgling mouth atop the beast had discharged a great deal of spittle as it had roared at Kwan before rushing at him, dropping to the ground and clambering toward him on its eight tentacles as a spider might crawl along its web. Far quicker than Kwan had expected, the creature had set upon him, clubbing him with its thick, fleshy tentacles. One of the hands had grabbed Kwan by the hair, yanking him off his feet.

He'd unloaded the rest of his bullets into the creature's swollen belly, hoping to drive it off, but all that resulted in was more of the foul-smelling fat rolling out of the wounds which had quickly sprouted into mouths.

By then, several other men had been awakened and run from their homes, farming implements in hand to do battle with the demon. Kwan's neighbor Chang had stuck the beast in the back with a pitchfork, tearing away one of the stalks with a savage twist. This had enraged the monster, leading to Kwan being beaten harder, being drug along as the monster turned its attention to Chang. One of the Ho boys had a rifle, and had fired several shots into the "head" of the creature, rupturing its forehead and the rolling eyes, effectively splitting its only human feature in half.

The creature had dropped Kwan by this point. He had lain in the slime that oozed from the creature's legs as it began to grapple Chang, lifting him off the ground. Kwan had witnessed the maw expand, the ruined head splitting vertically to allow the jaws to open further as it rammed Chang's shrieking form into the toothless hole. Tentacles had battered everyone away, preventing them from coming to Chang's aid, as the creature straightened up and swallowed Chang whole, its bloated belly distending as a human outline pressed from within the strained envelope of flesh.

Everyone had gasped as Chang, who could be easily seen through the demon's thin skin, screamed from within. Lumps like serpents moving across the abdomen and grabbed onto Chang. His screams became an agonized gurgle as one of the tentacles audibly snapped his jawbone, breaking teeth as it forced its way into Chang's throat and deeper. Chang's screams, muffled as they were, had only grown in intensity with each passing moment.

Kwan, struggling with a broken arm, gripped his lantern and had swung up into the crook between the creature's legs, shattering the glass and dousing it, and himself, in flaming oil.

The creature howled again, this time with fresh pain as the fires licked all over its body. It shuffled backwards as its legs burned out from beneath it. The other villagers caught on and fetched oil canisters from their homes, splashing the creature's shapeless form with oil to fuel the flames that were crawling up the stinking mass. The split maw had spit up a chunky soup of raw bloody matter, as well as an internal tentacle popping out to lob Chang's bloody broken pelvis, before retreating to the well, dropping itself into the underground river that flowed beneath the village. With steam running from the well like a factory's smokestack, the villagers had tended to Kwan as best they could, putting out the flames that had climbed up his arms.

One man, the village doctor, had examined the mutilated hips and buttocks, all of it covered in scratches and burns, the sphincter torn and dribbling some of the yellowed fat that had apparently been pumped into Chang before he was torn into pieces. The doctor didn't have long to evaluate the remains as they'd quickly begun to dissolve into a frothy mess of fat and molten bone.

Kwan had been given the next few days off from tending to his fields to try and recuperate from the attack. His broken arm ached horribly but had been set and wrapped tight with a splint, and his burns throbbed with even the slightest of movements.

Now, as he sweated in the cool bedroom of his home, all he could think about was the well, the running water and what lay beneath it. He imagined great things in his fevered dreams; villages of bruised skin and gaping maws with impossible architecture, all centered around a pyramid. Hundreds of the shapeless demons, no two alike, moved about the homes, the cavern floor thick with their slime, the air their stench, stretching beneath their feet like rubbery skin. The trees in the place—if they could be called that—were also made of the same pallid flesh, the branches ending in pitted orbs that would occasionally discharge spores and fluids that the others would flock to, lapping it all up in abject pleasure.

What haunted him the most was the low gong that rang through the cavern which signaled a halt to all activity. Kwan wiped his brow, his bones aching as he *felt* this strange dream's gong ring in his mind. He got off his cot to go and relieve himself, his body feeling sluggish as if he were ill. Stumbling to his chamber pot, he squatted over it and sighed as he did his business. Looking down at his arm, his eyes widened. The skin of his left arm seemed to ripple, as if it were melting wax.

On the verge of a scream, Kwan finished his bathroom break in record time.

* * *

The next few days saw Kwan getting sicker. He refused to have the village doctor come and see him and he barred his windows and doors from the inside, sealing himself in as if it were to be his tomb. His neighbors grew worried, so on the third day, the Ho boys brought their tools and with the help of the village carpenter, An Wong, they took to task the job of dismantling the front door to Kwan's home. It took them little time as, for some reason, the wood seemed to have rotted.

As they pulled the door free, revealing boards nailed over the entryway, they were assaulted by the stench of rotting meat and feces. An stood by as Bai Ho and Jin Ho emptied their stomachs into the nearby bushes that straddled the porch. After they wiped their faces clean An passed them each a white cloth to affix over their noses, just as he began to tie one over his.

"The smell will be tolerable if we cover ourselves," he said. They each quickly wrapped the strips of cloth over their faces, now resembling bandits of old. Bai, partly due to frustration, took the crowbar they'd used to pry open the door and smashed one of the wooden boards apart. It crumpled like wet paper, falling with a squishy splat to the ground, causing the men to all look down at it.

Covering the wood was a thick layer of fleshy growths, pulsing with life and dribbling yellowed fat like molten butter from tears on the ends of the board. The smashed wood, much to the men's growing horror, began to mend itself, strands of fleshy veins growing out to reconnect the splintered wood, pulling and knitting the flesh and wood together as a bone might heal, only this took half a minute instead of months of recuperation.

"What in the world...?" An said, low enough that the Ho boys barely heard him. An had served in the army during the Japanese invasion, and had seen horrible things done to his fellow countrymen. He'd endured, and come out stronger because of it. To hear him startled frightened the young men.

A low sucking noise came from the darkness within the home, drawing their attention to the partially opened doorway. Through the remaining boards and the waning sunlight, they could see Kwan moving in the darkness, shying away from the light.

"Kwan!" An shouted. "We're here to help! Come, let us take you to Doctor Jingshu! He can help!"

"No... help... leave now!" Kwan's raspy voice growled, the words sounding odd as if Kwan were speaking with his mouth full.

An looked to Bai and Jin, who nodded, and they began tearing away at the fleshy boards, kicking them off to the side into the bushes so that they could enter the wooden structure. Their sandals met with a mushy, muddy flooring of the same pulpy flesh, veins pumping fluids through the strange membrane. Looking around, they saw the flesh had grown over the walls and ceiling, and that in some places it split off into small limbs, each with three or four fingers, which opened and closed of their own accord. Jin nearly squealed when an eye opened on the wall next to him, the pupil spilt into a three-pronged crosshair, purple with flecks of gold.

Kwan was over by his cot, leaning over it as if he were eating. An took a careful step forward, crowbar in hand.

"Kwan?" An said trying to get the man's attention, his voice barely above a whisper.

In the dim light, Kwan was barely visible, but when he stood up all three men shouted in surprise. He no longer had arms, only a long fleshy tentacle extending from where his head had been, a lamprey-like mouth underneath it. The body was riddled with sores and openings that all opened and closed like a gasping fish, letting out wheezing noises as Kwan struggled to rise to his feet, his legs thick and powerful now.

"Told you... to leave!" Kwan shouted from the orifices, a multitude of voices crying a symphony of obvious pain. He lashed out with the tentacle, slamming An in the chest and knocking him to the ground.

Where the tendril had struck, there was now a tear in An's cotton shirt, the ripped fabric sticking to the tentacle, slowly being absorbed into the mass. Kwan charged forward, spittle flying from his spiral mouth as he hissed angrily.

Bai reacted first, choking up on his crowbar as the tentacle reared at him. He swung, knocking a foot off the stubby end of the tongue-like muscle with his tool. He didn't notice how the tentacle reacted until it was too late, when it twisted and came at him again, this time with the split forming a two-fingered hand. It gripped him around the chest, crushing his biceps into his frame with a horrid snapping noise. Bai screamed as his bones splintered beneath the strength of the monster that Kwan had become. His scream cut short as he was stuffed into Kwan's distended jaws. What they had thought to be small teeth lining the mouth proved to be flexible nodules the size of a big toe, which wriggled about, moving Bai's body quickly down the gullet and into Kwan, who bulged in the midsection as he consumed the young man.

An pulled an old pistol from his belt and fired into Kwan's groin. A low hanging tendril that had once been Kwan's penis flopped out as the pistol shots blasted holes into Kwan's legs and crotch. The tentacle lashed forward like a viper, biting into An's arm with a fleshy barb that began pumping… *something* into An. It made his right arm numb and heavy.

Bringing his pistol to bear, he shot the tentacle in half, liquid fat spattering out in a torrent before the tentacle reshaped, sealing itself up. An ripped the severed half off his arm, which was taking on a waxy look and swelling painfully. He looked at Jin, who had yet to move as he watched all this unfold.

"Go!" he screamed at him, waking him from his stupor. "Get help! Bring fire like we did with the demon!"

Jin nodded before turning to go, falling flat on his face into the writhing floor. Looking down, he gasped at the sight of the floor, pulpy and pallid, having grown up over his sandals and onto his pants. Sucking at his legs like a child at his mother's teat, the floor was slowly pulling him into it, as if it didn't have a bottom.

"I can't move!" Jin cried, tugging at his right leg with visible strain. "S-something just bit me! Oh, spirits, something just bit me, and I can feel it pumping something into me!"

"Kwan!" An cried, raising a hand to cover his face. "Why are you doing this? We are your friends!"

"Friends…? No… not friend… offerings… offerings to Father!" Kwan cried out as the last of Bai's sandals slid down Kwan's gullet, disappearing within the man-monster. "He will be… pleased. So very pleased…"

Bai's screams grew muffled as the muscles contracted, pushing his lower half against the wall of skin separating Bai and the foul air. A writhing tentacle wriggled from below him, striking as fast as a serpent before pushing into him, despite Bai's screams of pain.

"Kwan, no! Don't do this!" An pleaded before the head-tentacle reached down and grabbed him, lifting him up high into the air. An raised his pistol and fired three rounds into the top of Kwan's shapeless body. The rivulets of fat that drained from the wounds quickly formed into miniature tentacles, which writhed happily from their sprouting points above the bullet holes.

An screamed in agony as his right arm twisted, snapping with the sound of dry timber popping in a bonfire, as the swollen limb curled. He looked over at it and in what little light there was, he could see that his fingers were purple and straining, looking like over-stuffed sausages, while his wrist had split open, bleeding out a watery slime in place of blood.

An watched, horrified as his biceps began to swell, ripping his sleeve before popping once more and growing longer, distending away from the bone within, which felt as if it were on fire.

"Soon… you will all see… soon," Kwan said, gently rocking An in the air as if he were a toddler, despite the man's screams.

The rest of the villagers heard the screams and had come to investigate, stopping at the door to peer in at the strange battle taking place. The elderly, who had survived so many wars, told their children to pack their belongings quickly. Those that listened ran home while their elders watched in morbid fascination as blue and red veins extended up from the floor and jabbed into Jin, piercing his flesh like a knife before visibly joining with his circulation.

Jin's screams, louder than An's by far, began to wane as he lost what little blood was left within his body. Most of it was being replaced with a viscous fluid that was pasty white and pink, his body bulging where the veins connected. An was slamming his pistol down onto Kwan's vice grip, trying desperately to free himself.

The villagers cried out as they heard a sickening snap and a final cry from An, watching as his shadowed form bent at an awkward angle, his back clearly broken. A low grumbling from within the cabin made all the villagers shudder with just the one raspy word.

"Run..." Kwan hissed, Bai's howls of agony doubling in intensity, broken only by his retching sounds.

# Chapter Two

"... and so if you open your textbooks to the third chapter, you'll see we are going into Central America around three thousand BCE."

The room was dark, a single projector illuminating the room as a hundred students scribbled down notes. The room was built like an auditorium of old, with seats rising in concentric rings around a central platform where a podium stood. A crooked old man stood on a low stepstool up on the dais, conducting the day's discussion. He paused to advance the slide machine, in the meantime adjusting his thick glasses. His bushy eyebrows bobbed as the next slide came on screen, depicting an image of ruins amidst jungle.

"Now, you may not realize it, but there was plenty of activity here during this time. Tribes forgotten by man were building great cities dedicated to their gods, some sacrificing captured warriors in bloody rites atop pyramids, as seen here."

Hopping down from the stool, the old professor slowly walked with his gnarled hands held behind his back. He looked over the class with wide eyes, looking all the larger by the thick lenses of his glasses.

"You there!" He pointed to a random student, who jerked in his seat in alarm.

"Y-yes Professor Nickels?" she replied, earning snickers from the people around her.

"Tell me the name of one of the earlier tribes that settled in this region, without looking at your textbook!"

"Uh, the... Zohapilco?" she guessed.

He clapped his hands and laughed before wagging a finger in her direction, looking as though he were chastising a young child caught stealing candy. "You've been reading ahead! *That* tribe is not for another five to seven hundred years from when I'm talking about! Bonus points for being prepared for next lecture though."

The girl blushed and sank a little lower into her seat as the class chuckled along with the professor. He cleared his throat to get their attention once more, his bullfrog voice carrying across the room.

"The truth is nobody knows for certain. We have very few artifacts. We have some ancient corn that we uncovered, along with some broken pottery, but that reveals very little of the people who lived here. Foundations indicate they were skilled stoneworkers, and that they knew how to build large structures, as represented by the pyramid behind me."

Professor Davis Nickels walked back to the podium and pressed a button, flipping over to the next slide which showed a system of caves adorned top to bottom with cave paintings. The art depicted crude figures with spears around a flowering plant, or perhaps a vortex of water.

"Now, what you see here are some caves close to the site in question. The art shows these men, or women, dancing or moving around this figure. Who can guess what it is?"

A dozen hands shot up and Davis laughed. "It was rhetorical, I'm sorry. The answer is correct with each guess, as well as wrong. We simply don't know. It could mean anything! But with the way these ancient people acted, one can surmise that it was something religious in nature."

The girl he questioned earlier piped up. "What do you think it is, professor?"

All the eyes in the class swiveled between her and Davis, who fixed his stare on her. He spoke in a distant voice, as if remembering something long-since forgotten. "I have an idea... nothing more. But I worry if I'm right..."

The class grew silent as the old man stared off at nothing for several moments before he turned to the girl. "I believe it is religious in nature, though not in reverence. I believe that the people of this region believed something foul lingered in their lands. And I believe this was an artist's rendition of the people dealing with their demons, so to speak."

The class was furiously scribbling down his words, earning a chuckle from him. "Now, pencils down as I have an announcement to make. The rest of the class is going to become essay based."

The class groaned and he held up his hands.

"I know, essays are the devil's work and I am but his minion, but you are all graduate students and as such you will be faced with miles of paperwork if you wish to take over my job once I finally keel over. Now I am going to assign three essays, each worth thirty percent of your grade. The final ten percent will of course be your final exam, an in-class essay. I know most of your other classes offer to let you work at a much more relaxed pace, but I'm from an older generation, where you really must keep your nose to the grindstone until you're down to bone."

Davis reached into his vest pocket, fishing out a golden pocket watch to check the time. "And with that, I'll release you all early, seeing as my throat is tired and the next segment is best done in one sitting. I'll see you all Thursday, read up to chapter six!"

Davis turned and retreated to the podium, where he turned up the lights and clicked the ceiling mounted projector off, before shuffling some papers about and sliding them in his satchel. He stepped down from the stool only to come face-to stomach with the young girl he'd questioned earlier. He looked up, smiling genially.

"Yes? I'm sorry, you'll forgive me for not knowing your name quite yet…" he said, offering a hand.

The girl adjusted the books in her hand, her pale skin glowing beneath the lights of the classroom. "Oh, sorry! I'm Huan, Huan Zi."

"Oh, an old kingdom Chinese name, how very nice to hear one in this modern age," Davis replied in clipped Mandarin. Huan looked startled for a moment before bowing slightly.

"I didn't realize you spoke Mandarin," she replied in the same tongue. "My family speaks Cantonese; do you know that as well?"

"Of course," he replied in Cantonese. "I learned while doing a dig over there in nineteen thirty-one. Found some amazing relics, great excavation."

"Oh my, how old were you?" Huan asked before covering her mouth, clearly embarrassed.

Davis smiled at her. "Calm yourself, I was nineteen at the time. Yes, I'm old, but I'm still spry. Now, what can I do for you?"

"I was told that you go on digs on occasion and that you bring graduate students along with you, offering them credit for your classes and some recognition in your field work?"

Davis nodded happily. "That I do, though I don't have anything prepared for another year or so."

"Oh," she said, crestfallen. "Do you have room for another volunteer?"

"Always!" Davis chirped in English, reaching to his satchel and fishing out a form. "Just fill this out real fast and leave a phone number and I'll call you when I am ready, all right? I'll speak with your advisor and take you under my care since you're showing an interest in my work."

"I went to see the exhibit with the relics you pulled from the Ubaid ruins in Iraq. How did you get a permit to go into such a… an unstable country?" Huan asked as she walked over to the podium, pulling a pen from her jeans.

"Simple, I went down to Mexico and then called up the Iraqi government. I spoke with some of Saddam's people and bartered a few relics I had in exchange for the chance to explore the ruins. I offered half of what I pulled out of the ground to them, with them getting first choice."

"You mean what I saw was only half of what you collected?" Huan gasped, looking up from the form.

"About a third. I keep a few trophies for my personal collection," Davis replied.

Huan hummed as she scanned the form over. "A release of liability? Why would you need that?"

"If we're to go to ruins and delve deep into caverns and such, I have to make sure I'm not liable should the worst happen," Davis replied with ease.

"Oh," she said before signing the bottom and filling out her information. She handed him the form and smiled, clutching her book to her chest as she began to walk off.

"Oh, and Miss Zi?" Davis said, carefully sliding the paper into the folder with the other filled out forms.

"Yes sir?" She turned, looking at him.

"Bear in mind that in addition to credit for a dig, I offer a single artifact found to you, providing you do your thesis upon said artifact about its properties and history," Davis said, smiling as her face lit up.

"Really?" she exclaimed.

"Really. For the work I'd have you do, it's the least I could offer," he said. He looked around, as if hiding something. "Just make certain not to brag about it, okay? It's not exactly above the board, so to speak..."

She squealed and hopped from foot to foot. "That's so exciting! Please, bring me on your next dig!"

"I'll see what I can do," Davis said. "Now run along, I'm sure you have better things to do than talk to an old man."

"Thank you Professor!" she said before racing up the stairs.

"You're welcome Huan," Davis said, watching her as she darted out of the classroom. "You're welcome."

* * *

Unlocking his office door, Davis heaved a sigh as he took the mail from the slot and began rifling through it. He had a home to go to, this was true, but all his home was used for was to hold relics from the past and to host dinner parties. He paid a lovely woman named Rebecca to come and clean up three times a week, something he felt was beneath him. Walking into the room he looked up and smiled.

*Being the oldest Professor has its advantages...* he thought.

He had a large room that he didn't share with anyone besides his assistant, Lawrence Wilks, who had a small desk next to the door. Davis dropped the mail on his desk and slowly made his way over to his own, a large thing that he'd had shipped from the Ukraine after he'd discovered it in the ruins of a castle rumored to be haunted. He'd taken great care to preserve the artifact, and was often caught polishing it when he had nothing better to do.

The desk in question seemed as if it'd been carved from a single tree as there were no seams or pieces that could come loose. Great reliefs jutted out, demonic faces leering at anyone who dared look, while the rest of the desk was covered in ancient carvings of some forgotten language. Davis had ordered and placed a glass top for his desk so that he could write and work without worry of damaging the precious thing, his computer sitting on the edge with a large monitor that allowed him to better see what he typed.

The chair had come from the same find. High-backed with actual skulls built into the armrests, the chair was warped and bent at odd angles that forced anyone seated in it to sit up straight. He'd had it outfitted with padding and painted over with lacquer to preserve the foreboding chair, and loved the results.

Placing his satchel on the desk, he hopped up into his seat and sighed as he heard the whispers enter the back of his mind, praying for release.

"Sorry my friends," he murmured back, rubbing the skulls soothingly, "but not today."

Sitting up straight, he pulled his keyboard over to him and logged into his computer. While it was booting up he glanced around his office, smiling at the relics he'd collected over the years.

Hanging from the wall was an Ubaid sword within a verdigris-ridden sheath of spoiled copper, the blade peeking through in a few spots. He loved showcasing it to students from its plaque on the wall. It'd served in many battles, Davis imagined, its last one four years ago in the ruins against servants of a great evil.

Below it was a small bookcase with a vase from the Song Dynasty, a jade tortoise from India that served as an incense sconce, and a chunk of green stone taken from the temple steps in a lightless cavern where Davis had seen the horrors that the universe had to offer. Below these items were books of mythology from all the continents as well as several on the history of the Catholic Church. Behind him was a window that allowed him to look out onto the rotunda, where the fountain gurgled happily into a large pool while students sat at tables eating their meals, chatting about exams and deadlines and the various things students were wont to chat about.

Turning back to his computer, he smiled when it greeted him with a pinging noise and opened to his e-mail. He scanned over several documents that had been forwarded to him from colleagues all over the world, but one stood out to him. Leaning in, he clicked on an e-mail labeled: "Old God Evidence." Opening it, he saw still images taken from what looked to be a village on a hill, covered in what resembled pink flesh. Several trees were engulfed in the mass and now seemed to be sporting human hands instead of leaves, while blurry images featured various humanoid figures that were not of this world.

Looking at who sent the e-mail, he frowned. Doctor Shen was a medical professional who had served the People's Republic of China for years and was a consummate politician. He rarely did anything out of the kindness of his heart, and hated Davis with a passion, seeing as Davis had killed his brother Xian on an expedition into a tomb cavern nearly eighty years ago. Xian had become afflicted by a sudden madness and had become a threat to the entire archaeological team; Davis did what he had to and shot the man in the head, ending his life.

Much as he'd regretted shooting Xian, Davis never doubted it was the right thing to do—the tomb they'd explored bore an ancient curse, and Xian's erratic behavior stemmed from it. Still, justified or not, the act never sat well with Shen. That was not the only souvenir of Davis's visit either—to this day Davis spent every January twenty-second in horrible agony thanks to the curse, and always made certain he could remain in bed for the duration of its aftereffects.

Clicking on another image showed that the village well seemed to have become a gaping maw with a circle of eyes, possibly as large as soccer balls, and that they were staring straight at the camera. Their pupils were violet and split the eye into three segments, causing Davis to shudder at the very thought of what could be the source of the corruption. Looking to the text of the e-mail, he began reading it softly aloud.

*Professor Nickels, it has come to my attention that since your time in our country you have become an expert on the occult and all that it entails. As such I will defer to your expertise on what this could possibly be, as our own experts agree that it belongs in the field of the paranormal. I've stationed military around the site and ordered them to halt the growth of the matter on the ground using mortar-fire and napalm. The creatures you see seem to be vulnerable to light and fire, and have taken great lengths to shroud the village in darkness. The enclosed photos were taken by a drone that was equipped with a powerful light to allow us to see the spread of this infection. I ask you not as a friend, but as a colleague, to come and find the source of the problem and put a stop to it.*

*Sincerely,*
*Minister Xao-Ming Shen*

Davis studied the images for a few minutes before getting up and walking over to his bookcase, his gnarled finger tracing the spines of the books before selecting one and pulling it off the shelf. It was a green book, withered with age. It bore no title and was apparently written by hand. Opening it, Davis flipped through the pages and read the passages silently, looking for any indication as to what paranormal manifestation it could possibly be.

After nearly ten minutes of searching, he gave a despondent sigh and closed the book.

The text was a copy of a book written by a possessed monk from the third century detailing the old gods and what they wished to do with Earth and the souls that lived here. He was certain it would hold the answers he sought, because whenever events such as these cropped up, consulting the book often pointed him in the right direction. This time, however, it turned up nothing.

His thoughts were derailed when the doorknob of his office turned, and a young man wearing a green vest with brown slacks walked into the room, a book bag slung over his shoulder and a coffee from the campus Starbucks in hand. He was well groomed with short blonde hair and light blue eyes.

"Professor Nickels!" Lawrence exclaimed, depositing his backpack on his desk. "I was unaware you would be in this early. I would have thought you'd still be with your graduate students..." His voice dropped an octave, sounding overly conspiratorial. "...teaching them the theories you have on how the ancient people of the world worshipped forgotten gods."

Davis smiled at the sarcasm in his assistant's voice. "Dear Lawrence, I must say I'm surprised at how closed-minded you are! Here you are, looking through my collection for the third consecutive year and yet you still don't believe. The evidence is right in front of you!"

"That's what the bible-thumpers say about Jesus, you know," Lawrence said as he took a seat at his desk. "Anyway, I have the papers from your Introduction to History class ready for you; most were duds but a few showed promise."

"Those must wait," Davis said as he opened his e-mail, addressing the Dean of the University. "I'm going to be traveling for a while and will need you to take over my duties teaching the lower years the basics while I am away. For the graduate students, send out a mass e-mail with the assignments I gave you, and tell them to do self-study, and when to turn in the papers."

"Sir?" Lawrence asked, clearly confused.

Quickly typing up a letter to the Dean explaining that an emergency had cropped up and he was going abroad, he sent it before opening his browser to a travel site. Punching in his destination, he paid with his saved credit cards information and shut down his computer. Then, sliding out of his chair, he grabbed his satchel and marched to the door, not looking at Lawrence once.

"If you need me," he said, "I'll be in Boston at their university. I'll have my cell phone with me and I'll be gone for the foreseeable future, so carry on as if I were here."

# Chapter Three

Stepping off the plane, Professor Nickels adjusted his clothing. The flight from Austin had been a long one and his joints ached, his muscles twitching and straining with each movement. Reaching into his satchel for his prescription meds, he fished out an orange bottle and shook out two pills. He bought a bottle of water from a vendor and took the tablets, chugging the entire bottle to wash the taste away before tossing it in a nearby trash can. Walking slowly through the terminal, he made his way out of the airport to the taxi line. He hopped into the back of a waiting cab, smiling at the black man in the driver's seat.

"Where're you going, sir?" he asked, looking at Davis through the rearview mirror.

"To Boston University, if you would."

"Main campus?" The cabbie asked as he adjusted his rearview mirror.

"Yes. Take the direct route, as I've seen the scenery before and would like to give you a big tip," Davis replied with a warm tone. "No hurry, but I've seen all the sites I wish to see."

"Fair enough," the cabbie said, pulling out of the terminal loop.

Meanwhile, Davis opened his cell phone and dialed the number to B.U.'s library. After two rings, it was answered by a young voice, probably a student worker. "Hello, university library, how may I help you?"

"Yes, my name is Professor Davis Nickels and I'm calling to reserve a study room in your library for one of your rarer items."

The man on the other end was silent for a moment. "Rarer items? I'm sorry Professor, but our collection of rare books is strictly controlled and only certain people can access them."

"You'll find my name on the list," Davis said with a smile. "Go ahead and check, I'll wait."

"Okay, let me look." The man sounded unsure. Davis could hear the clicking of keys coming through the line. "What do you know, you are on the accepted list. Which book do you want to see?"

"The *Grimlocke Chronicles,*" Davis said without hesitation.

"Oh, um… we don't usually let people read that book, it's, uh, it's one of the oldest texts that we have."

"I'm on the list, aren't I? I need it for a research project I'm working on and would hate to go over your head for this. I know the rumors about the book being cursed, I've read it before."

"You have?" he asked in genuine surprise.

"Yes, and I'm still quite alive and sane as you can tell. So please have one of the locked rooms ready for me within the next hour and bring the book out upon my arrival. I'll leave my wallet with you as I know that's protocol."

"O-okay, I'll just look in with the head librarian to double-check and then we'll get you set up, professor."

"That sounds great, Jeremy. I appreciate it," Davis replied.

"You're welcome—wait—how did you know my name?"

"Oh," Davis faked a surprised tone. "You must have said it earlier."

"No, I would have remembered that. How did you know my name?" he asked again, sounding agitated.

"I'll see you soon, Jeremy, and you best have the room ready for me," Davis said before handing up.

"You sure sound like an interesting guy," the cabbie said as he drove through traffic.

"I like to think I am," Davis replied. "I teach archaeology down in Texas, though I taught here for a brief period."

"Really? I don't hear any accent," the cabbie said.

"That's because I move around a lot, going from dig to dig. Getting financing is tough sometimes, but it's always worth it in the end," Davis replied, staring out the window.

"I hear that! Payday is coming and I am looking at a fat check this month!" the cabbie exclaimed with a laugh. "Gonna take my lady dancing and have a blast!"

"Ah, youth. Enjoy it while you can young man, enjoy it while you can," Davis said with a knowing smirk.

They drove in silence the remainder of the way to the university, with the cabbie taking a few back roads to get them there quicker. Traffic snarls were always a trouble in Boston and the fact that the cabbie could see them coming by a mile was a handy trick. Davis was contemplating how best to approach the subject at hand when the cabbie pulled to a sudden halt. Looking up, Davis realized he was at the university steps leading to the main building, which was flanked by two much larger, sprawling wings.

"Ah, here we are then," Davis said, reaching for his wallet and pulling out a slim card. "I trust you accept credit cards?"

"Of course. That'll be seventy dollars and ten cents," the cabbie said, taking the card and swiping it into his reader. As he was handing the card back, Davis passed him a twenty-dollar bill.

"Your tip, under the table so to speak," he said, grinning. The cabbie smiled back through the rear-view mirror.

"Thanks old man, you're all right!" The cabbie laughed. "You need help getting out or anything?"

"No, I'm not that old yet!" Davis laughed back, thankful that his medication had begun to kick in on the ride over. "Now, you have a wonderful day, and drive safely."

"Sure will, man; I sure will. You take it easy old timer, and have fun doing what you're doing!" the cabbie said as Davis exited the vehicle, pulling his satchel along with him.

Davis waved the cabbie off and turned to examine the buildings with a critical eye. They hadn't changed much in the forty years since he taught here, though several new buildings had been erected that he didn't remember. Walking slowly up to the front steps, he took them carefully as his knees were hurting. Once he reached the top he opened the door and stepped inside the air-conditioned lobby, where many students were milling about.

"Slothful!" he exclaimed as he walked through the crowd and down one of the hallways leading towards the library.

He exited the building and walked across campus, the many trees and blue-green grass enchanting to behold. The weather was cooling down and his muscles creaked with each step, but he persevered. The library was within sight. Notwithstanding that he was an expert in his niche, he knew he'd be able to dig up the answers he sought within the library's walls. Sometimes, he mused, what separated the professionals from the amateurs was not knowing the answer but simply knowing where to find it.

A chilly puff of air met him as he walked through the automatic door leading into the library. He headed for the desk, staffed by a young man with green-tinged hair and a shirt bearing the name of some music band, large circular earrings in his ears and a pierced lower lip. All in all, he looked out of place in an institution of higher learning, but Davis told himself that times were changing and people were evolving in how they presented themselves.

"Hello," Davis said, greeting the strange boy like an old friend. "You must be Jeremy."

The boy looked nervous and clicked something on a computer in front of him. "And you are Professor Nickels, then?"

"Yes sir, I'm glad that we've been introduced. Now that the pleasantries are out of the way, allow me the chance to look at the book I requested. I assume the room I asked for is ready for me?"

"About that... the head librarian said that he'd like to speak with you before letting you look at the *Chronicles*," Jeremy said, glancing at a black phone sitting on the desk. "Do you want me to call him down?"

"Yes, please do," Davis replied before moving to the side to allow a student to walk up and check out a book. Jeremy did this while speaking in hushed tones on the phone, and the young woman who checked out the book gave Davis an odd look as she walked away.

*Oh, good,* Davis thought bitterly, *my reputation precedes me. The last head didn't care when I came in, why should this one?*

Jeremy hung up the phone and smiled at Davis. "Professor, if you take the second elevator up to the fourth floor you'll find the Dean of Library Sciences waiting for you."

That surprised Davis, who merely nodded and walked over to the elevators Jeremy had indicated. The dean was waiting for him? How very odd.

“What could the dean want with me?” Davis wondered aloud as he rode the elevator up. “I’m on the approved readers list after all, so I shouldn’t have to go through this…”

The doors slid open to reveal an atrium with long sofas against the walls and a desk sitting beside a pair of large double doors. A woman in a spotted purple shirt sat behind the desk, glasses perched at the end of her nose with red hair pulled into a bun as she typed away at a computer.

Davis walked up and cleared his throat, hoping to catch her attention.

She seemed to ignore him for a moment before holding up a hand, one index finger raised as she finished typing out another sentence. She finally turned and looked over the desk at Davis. “Are you the visiting professor?”

“Why yes, I am. My name is Professor Davis Nickels; how do you do?” he said giving a stiff bow in her direction. She raised a well-manicured eyebrow and sighed.

“Dean Reynolds is a very busy man but has requested to see you before granting you access to our special archives,” the woman said without introducing herself. “If you’ll head through the double doors, he’ll be waiting for you.”

“Why, thank you! And I hope you have a pleasant day!” He said, saluting her with two fingers. He walked up to the door, pushing it open, grumbling about incompetent secretaries beneath his breath.

The room was large and lavish. Deep, dark wood chairs sat before a desk with red velvet and gold filigree, a small plaque sitting on the clean desk bearing the simple title of “Dean of Library Science.” There were several bookshelves lined with books, but judging by the thin layer of dust on them they didn’t see much time before hungry eyes. A man was standing behind the desk, bald save for the edges of his head like a friar of old, though his hair was black with streaks of silver, showing his advanced age. He was pouring a short crystal glass full of amber liquid, not bothering to look up at Davis as he entered.

Davis took this as a sign to approach and perhaps take a seat in one of the two chairs before the wide desk. The man turned on his heel and set the decanter on a shelf without offering a drink to Davis, which bothered him slightly. Not that he would have accepted, but manners would have directed at least an offer. Already, this man annoyed him.

The man adjusted his plain black tie and picked a piece of lint off his matching black suit, before pulling up his rolling leather chair and sitting down. "Please, have a seat, professor," he said in heavily accented English. It sounded as if he were Russian, or someone from one of the former Soviet countries that had been engulfed in civil wars for years. Davis eased himself into a chair and leaned back into the seat's padding. Surprisingly comfortable!

"If I am to understand correctly," the man said with little aplomb, "you wish to access the occult section of our collection, specifically an older text that is considered a prize by many."

"Only to those like myself who research the occult," Davis replied before smiling sweetly. "Or practitioners of the dark arts themselves."

The man frowned before leaning back in his seat, sipping his drink as he studied Davis. "I've heard of you, you know? The globe-trotting archaeologist that always seems to find a seemingly forgotten tomb or catacomb that everyone else has overlooked. Your work in the catacombs of Paris is the stuff of legend; fighting off cultists while gathering artifacts at the same time."

"People who devote themselves to dark entities are rarely strong or smart. They usually have one or two leaders worth noting."

"And you handled them both with a knife you… liberated from their own ritual, if the stories are to be believed." The man took another drink, staring at Davis with dark eyes. "Do you still possess the knife?"

"That I do. It had been used to sacrifice over a dozen children to some nameless entity that I never was able to discern," Davis replied. "Why?"

The man set his drink down before running a finger along the rim. "As you very well know, our university holds the largest collection of occult material in the Americas. From pottery to books, scrolls to weapons, we have it all. But you've been spending the last fifty years…"

"Eighty-two," Davis commented idly.

"…swinging in and scooping up treasure for your own collection and donating the rest to your university's library. Now, I could outright purchase many of your finds using our generous funding from our private benefactors, but you and I both know that you've kept the best of your stash for yourself. The knife, for example… I would like a chance to have my researchers study and catalogue it."

"Why?" Davis asked.

The man leaned back in his chair. "Because that knife belongs with us and you know it. I would love to buy it from you," he offered before frowning as Davis shook his head, "but I doubt I'll be able to offer a substantial enough amount for outright purchase."

"So you want time to study the dagger in exchange for me to study the *Grimlocke Chronicles*?" Davis deduced.

The man nodded. "And they said you were growing slow in your old age! I know you're on the approved list, so that means you're safe to read from the book, but I have final say on who sees it."

"So how long do you wish to examine the dagger?" Davis asked, clearly uncomfortable with parting with the blade. "It has several paranormal properties that I'd rather keep in check, if it's all the same."

"I assure you, my researchers are well versed in how to handle possessed, cursed, dark, or otherwise paranormal objects. We won't even try to remove the curse, just find out how it works so that we can record it in case you suddenly die and your goods go up for auction. I would hate to see a truckload of anomalous artifacts being distributed to the masses due to an estate sale."

Davis chuckled at the thought. "Yes, I can see how that would be dangerous. So, if you'll have someone come and pick up the dagger from my assistant? I'd rather not mail it."

"Understood, make the call here and now and I'll grant you the access you want," the man said, swirling his drink back and forth.

Davis pulled out his cell phone and dialed Lawrence's number. On the fourth ring, he answered. "Yes sir?"

"Lawrence, I'm going to have a visitor come down from Boston. They'll have a note from me to take possession of the Mar'tuck dagger. You'll have to fetch it from the house, feel free to store it in the office until it can be passed over."

Lawrence was silent for a moment. "Sir, I'm not exactly comfortable touching that particular relic. I know what effects it can have…"

"The effects only occur when skin contact is made, so handle it with a cloth and keep it in the briefcase I keep beneath its case in my viewing room," Davis said, looking over at the dean and rolling his eyes. "It isn't that hard, Lawrence, just please have it ready. Thank you!"

He hung up without another word and looked at the man expectantly. "You know, I never introduced myself."

"Your reputation precedes you. Plus, I was a student here when you taught. It's strange, you don't look a day older than you did thirty years ago. Odd, isn't it?" The man said, putting his drink down. "But forgive my manners, I'm Dean of Library Sciences, Harvey Reynolds."

"Pleasure to meet you again. I must say, I don't recognize the face, and I'm normally quite good at remembering my students," Davis said.

Reynolds shrugged. "I sat in the back and took notes. I got a B in your class as I wasn't a stellar student. I remember you issuing the challenge for anyone to list every U.S. president for an A in the course. I also remember you laughing as people tried to recite them and failed."

"It's a test I've discontinued due to laptops and wireless Internet," Davis said with distaste. A knock on the door caused Davis to jump in surprise. A young man opened the door and peeked inside, his shoulder length black hair falling around his face to frame his gray eyes. He was slender and in a button up white shirt with black slacks and suspenders. The glasses hanging from his collar danced as he walked into the room confidently.

Davis frowned as Reynolds accepted a stack of paperwork from him before turning to face Davis once more. "Professor Nickels, this is my assistant James Walker. He'll be accompanying you to your reading, and if you will accept my invitation, he'll also come along with you on your next dig that is bound to occur from this research. I assure you he's well versed in the old languages of Asia and Asia Minor, and is an expert in the field of paranormal research."

Davis frowned, looking the boy up and down. Reaching into his satchel, he fished out a form and laid it on the luxurious countertop, setting a pen on top of it. "Read and sign, and you can come."

# Chapter Four

Seated in the wide room behind a locked door, Davis was doing his best not to glare at the younger man with him. James had proven to be quite knowledgeable, answering several of Davis's questions point blank. He knew about the Sons of Ash and the Sisterhood of Serpents, as well as the standard old gods that all slumbered beneath the waves of the Atlantic and Pacific. He hadn't known of some of the rarer items of interest, and had almost no knowledge of demonology or diabolism, which was perhaps a good thing.

James was leaning against the carpeted walls of the room, arms crossed while listening to some music through earbuds hooked into his phone. It was just loud enough that Davis could hear it, which grated on his nerves a little. He wasn't a fan of music in any form, as it led to dancing.

And Davis was a terrible dancer.

His mind drifting elsewhere, he wondered how he would look through the book with James present. Would he be able to commune with it as he had in the past, or would he have to flip through the thousands of pages in a vain attempt at finding a clue to what the Chinese government was facing?

He thought back to his old colleague Shen and the experiences they'd had when they dug through the Mongolian steppes in search of burial caves. The blind creatures that ran through those caverns, their saggy skin a pale white with long black talons, had howled with the most unholy shrieks Davis had ever heard. They'd been easy enough to put down—simple gunfire to the head—but the nightmares that lasted for the week afterward led to a bout of incurable insomnia.

Davis had been paid generously then by the new regime, and had been allowed to gather a trove of artifacts for his own collection. He'd of course gone over the books and scrolls, selecting the best from the lot before saying he needed nothing else. The Chinese treatise on known demons and how best to battle them was only surpassed by the book he was waiting for. He should have checked that book, but his grasp of reading old Chinese was weak, and he preferred to consult this tome occasionally.

The book had a nasty habit of killing those who read from it, those too weak of will to survive the horrors within.

"Have you read from this text before, James?" Davis asked without turning to face him.

James walked up to the table and looked down at the diminutive old man. "No," he said finally. "I haven't been granted access to this book. Dean Reynolds has expressed worry that the book could harm me, or worse, corrupt me."

"Your knowledge, or lack thereof, of diabolism is something the book would find appealing," Davis commented.

"Wait, what?" James asked, removing the earbuds with a sudden tug. "Did you say the *book* would find *me* appealing?"

"Well, not the book itself, it's just made from leather and flayed human skin. The spirits that possess the book would be very interested in you."

"Great," James groaned, running a hand through his curtain of hair.

Davis looked up at him. "Do you know how long it takes Jeremy to retrieve the *Grimlocke Chronicles*? We've been here for fifteen minutes."

Jeremy had escorted them to the room and left them alone, stating he would return with the book in question.

"No clue, I'm only a graduate student here," James quipped. "I've never actually seen the book."

"You have a strong stomach?" Davis asked, humor in his voice.

"Yeah…" James said, trailing off.

Davis nodded. "Good. I don't relish the idea of you vomiting anywhere near me, as this room is quite stuffy as is. It hardly needs the stench of your bile and whatever you ate adding to it."

"I'm so glad we've become friends," James grunted.

Davis ignored him as the door opened, revealing Jeremy carrying a large leather-bound book, easily three-feet tall and two-feet wide. The book's waxy veneer was made even more disturbing by the crumbling edges and crude stitching done over the work, as if performed by an amateur surgeon. The pages were thick, making the spine of the volume a solid six inches. James let out a low whistle as Jeremy grunted, carefully hoisting the book and sliding it onto the table. Breathing heavily, the sallow-skinned youth leaned on the table while fishing out a pair of white felt gloves, tossing the package across the table.

"You wear those while handling the book," Jeremy said between gasps. "We don't really catalogue this book, but no marking within it. You have a notepad?"

Davis lifted his satchel and pulled out a small moleskin notebook, along with his pen.

Jeremy nodded before looking at James. "And what's he doing here?"

"Ask the dean," Davis said, pulling on a felt glove, frowning. "These never seem to fit right..."

"I thought it was just going to be you in here. I don't know if I can allow him to look at it too," Jeremy said. He was clearly torn by the idea, as it was obvious he didn't want to carry the volume back anytime soon.

"Like I said, take it up with the dean," Davis said. "Now be gone! Back to the front desk with you, to better serve the students of this fine campus!"

Jeremy rolled his eyes before walking out the door, closing it with a slam.

"James, be a dear and go lock the door," Davis said, reaching across the table and grunting as he dragged the book closer to him. Spinning it in place so the book was right-side up, he stared at the greasy leather for a few moments before reaching forward and opening to the first page. Printed on it was a great drawing done in dark red ink, which many had speculated to be blood. Davis stared at the picture, waiting for the effects of the tome's powers to take hold. Going any further before allowing the first page to test you was a death sentence. James walked up behind him and stared into the book, eyes widening.

"Oh my god," he exclaimed, horrified at what he saw.

He had a right to call out to God as the pictures of humans twisted in agony, flesh merging together while being peeled apart by nightmarish creatures, slowly animating as if they were part of a flipbook. Davis stared on dispassionately, knowing this was just a trick the book could pull. The relic had been studied by many before him and they'd all discovered that the image never moved, it just projected the events that the picture showed into the mind of the reader.

Davis could smell sulfur and blood, hear the cries of men and women as well as the horrible howls of beasts unimaginable. His skin prickled, goose bumps crawling up his arms as he watched the final figure, a looming giant larger than any building, come into view.

A great horned skeleton with leathery wings and green bones, this entity swept the page of any remaining mortals. Whipping a hand through them in a gory display of evisceration that had the remaining horrors howling in pleasure, it lifted the gathered gore and supped on it while the demons cackled madly.

Then the skeleton turned on the monsters, gathering them by the handful and crushing them, thick black ooze dripping between exposed bone. The skeleton leered, a baleful blackness seemingly sucking light from the room as the lights above flickered. Slowly, the skeleton nodded once before receding into the mists of the picture, demons crawling back into the frame as more humans seemed to be sketched back into place, the picture growing still once more.

James turned to the trashcan and emptied his stomach while muttering prayers to God. Davis sighed, shaking his head.

"If you're going to be joining me on my venture you'll need a strong stomach, boy!" he barked. "Now finish up and go take that trash bin outside, I don't want this room stinking of your last meal."

James vomited until he was dry heaving, and this was where Davis drew the line, sending him out of the room to go finish his business in the bathroom, sending the trash bin with him. Davis couldn't help but notice the strands of black hair coming from James's temples slowly turning stark white. He felt no pity for the boy. After all, that was how Davis's own hair was silver by the time he was thirty.

* * *

By the time James returned, Davis had flipped through several pages, examining descriptions of forbidden places and forgotten gods of unimaginable power and immense size. He looked up from the tome, smiling grimly as the student closed the door, locking it.

"I told you not to vomit," Davis said in a teasing voice.

"Yeah, well, I tried! Just… the picture, it came alive! What… what was that *thing*, that giant skeleton?" James said, pulling on his strands of whitening hair. More strands were growing pale, leaving the boy looking as if he had taken to getting a bleach highlight job.

Davis shrugged. "Who knows? I've always seen it as the guardian of ancient lore. Anyone that tries to flip beyond it will die a most horrible death. Every time you open this book you must watch it. Some think it's a warning."

"A warning?"

"You do know the history behind this book, yes?" Davis asked, his finger running down the page, tracing some drawings of a bisected human filled with insects. "Who wrote it and all?"

"Yeah, um, some German monk by the name of Grimlocke," James said, pulling up a chair to sit down next to Davis.

"Not a monk, a diabolist. His real name is lost to history. He worshipped the ancient gods and revered them in pagan rites, traveling through Europe and Asia, locating sites and doing his best to activate them," Davis said. "The book resurfaced in the third century, found in the smoldering ruins of the Library of Alexandria. It killed five scholars before they decided it was better left it alone, and sent it to Rome to be contained. It was there they learned how to read it."

"So how did we get a hold of it? Shouldn't it be in a Vatican vault somewhere?" James asked as he ran a hand through his hair.

"You'd think so, wouldn't you? But the book twists the minds of men who are susceptible to the ether, convincing them to do horrible acts. I hear many voices in the back of my mind when I read from its pages."

"You? You're connected to the mystical energies of the world?" James said doubt heavy in his voice.

Again, Davis just shrugged. "I know a few parlor tricks and how to converse with unclean spirits. The dagger Dean Reynolds wants to study so dearly houses the souls of three serial killers who used it to take their own lives, not to mention countless others who were slain by the blade while in the hands of such maniacs."

"Wow…" James said, stunned to silence.

"Just remember, after my venture you'll be the one carrying that back up here. Just… don't touch it with your bare skin," Davis warned before waving a hand over the large crisp page. "Now, onto more depressing subjects. We'll take shifts reading from the pages to reduce the chance of madness setting in. Say, thirty minutes each?"

"Oh, um, sure. What is it we're looking for?" James asked.

Davis stared at the page, reading of the Ba'agor, a horrible creature that was constantly decaying and regenerating due to its consumption of human entrails. He looked up for a moment and smiled. "We're looking for anything that resembles a monster or old god from Asia. I have my notebook, so you write down anything you find. And don't read anything aloud. That is a surefire way to catch the attention of one of them."

"Of who?"

Davis just stared at him before returning to the text, shaking his head. "Some occult expert you are…"

The two fell into a tense silence as Davis flipped from page to page, taking notes when he found something pertinent. James watched from his seat, arms crossed, hair growing paler as the seconds ticked by. His eyebrows were already a frosty white, and his eyes were becoming a sparkling blue, his skin growing paler. Davis prayed that the exposure to the book hadn't planted a seed of corruption within the boy. He might need to depend on him to accomplish something someday, and he didn't want the lad snapping under the pressures they were no doubt going to face.

"So…" James said after ten minutes of silence. "Have you encountered any? Old gods I mean."

"I'm alive, so the answer is no. I've encountered shrines and followers, as well as servants of certain old gods. They were terrifying enough to deal with, so I'd rather not have to deal with the actual beings they represent."

"What have you encountered?" James said, making quotation marks in the air for the word "encountered."

Davis leaned back in his chair. "I dare not speak their names as they still slumber, but in a recent expedition I encountered a collection of bones made animate by the foul energies of an entity trapped beneath some Mesoamerican ruins. The indigenous tribes in the region had done a great deed by sealing the monster away, and taught the bone guardian not to attack them should they need to descend into the depths."

"How'd they train it?" James asked, clearly interested.

"How, I couldn't say, but what the training did was make you invisible to the undead creature should you be smoking a combination of herbs. How the swarming bits of bone could detect it, I have no clue, but I'd discovered descriptions of the forgotten prison of the minor god in other ruins that made mention of using said herbs."

"So it just let you pass?" James asked.

Davis paused, thinking of the student he had with him who'd been sacrificed to the monstrous collection of sharpened bones. It'd been necessary, as Davis had gone deep into the caves below and checked on the seals holding the god in check. "Yes. Yes, I was able to pass without injury."

"Wicked," James smiled.

"You could say that," Davis smiled, looking over at James before returning to the book. "Now, here's something… be useful and write this down as I read it."

James took the pen and notebook, looking at the good professor expectantly. Davis cleared his throat. "Of the Orient, there are four which dominate the region; the union of flesh, blood, bone, and soul have been split as the original god has been severed, each quarter stored away so that it could not heal from the most grievous of wounds. I have located the sanctuary to the Blood Mother, for she is the one who pumps the essence of evil throughout the greater god once they are whole. She rests behind layers of protection, the likes of which I have never seen. Her guardians seemed to know my intent and let me pass. I was able to sense her pain in the ether, and hear her voice crying out for her siblings and lovers."

James was furiously scribbling away, proving to be an able scribe if anything. Davis continued.

"She showed me her glory while I slept in her sanctum, a place of stone weeping sanguine tears into a great pool. I supped from the mixture and felt vitality and youth restored to me, as well as a new source of darkness welling up deep within. My dreams were filled with images of her siblings and their spawn, the Father of Flesh and the Brother of Bone laying close to one another in distant China. The Mother of Blood did not know where the Sister of Soul resided nor what became of her. I fear for the worst, for if I cannot unite all four great ones then how shall I resurrect the glory that they once represented?"

Davis fell silent and leaned back in his chair. Pulling out his cell phone, he opened his e-mail, retrieving the images of the creatures Shen had sent him. In the shots, they looked to be monsters shaped without reason or rhyme, as if they were boneless.

"Boneless…" Davis said softly, so soft that James looked at him with a quizzical eye.

Davis shoved his phone, a photo of one of the creatures taking up the screen, towards James. "Describe what you see here!"

"Oh… oh my God, I don't know! What the hell is it?" He asked, not daring to touch the phone as if the image would spring to life.

"That's what I'm trying to figure out!" Davis exclaimed. "This is a picture of a village in rural China. Their government has determined it is paranormal in nature, and their authorities on the subject seem to believe I would be able to come up with what they are and better, how to handle them."

"So they want you to go and kill these things?" James said, doubt evident in his voice.

Davis nodded with a grim smile. "The minister who recommended me is an old… friend, who knows I've faced far worse situations than whatever these things are. I believe them to be the guardians of one of these gods that Grimlocke spoke of. He found one of them and learned of two others' tombs, so it's safe to say he tried to visit them. We need to learn all we can before I come up with an idea of how to go about this task."

"What task?" James asked as Davis got up, motioning for the boy to trade places with him.

"At best, reducing the number of guardians an old god has around its sepulcher," Davis replied. "At worst, finding the tomb and resealing it before whichever fractured piece of this nameless god can awaken."

# CHAPTER FIVE

Two hours and three trips to the bathroom later, and the duo had yet to find anything beyond Grimlocke's casual mention of the old gods of the Far East. Instead, James had been given a crash course in the various servants of the numerous old gods and the purposes they served within the hierarchy of demons in the supernatural world.

"So let me get this straight," James said, leaning back in his chair enough to where he could stare at the ceiling. "The old gods are all beings of incredible power—both supernatural and physical?"

"That's correct," Davis replied as he skimmed a paragraph on a frog demon that would infest a human host and make them perform violent acts of cannibalism. "Though they aren't all equal in power."

"So they vary in power and strength, and you're telling me they used to *battle* each other over humans? What were we to them, money?" James asked, looking back at Davis. His hair was now fully white and dusted across his shirt in a ghostly brush. It'd taken him a full hour to become as pale as could be, but he looked like a well-versed diabolist now—pale, wide sunken eyes, thin… if he encountered James on the street he'd steer clear of him, knowing what he knew of the world.

"No," Davis said, focusing back on the subject. "Not money, livestock. Each old god had territory carved out in the world and had their own followers that thrived beneath their unholy masters."

"How could they thrive? You said that the old gods treated them like *cattle*!" James exclaimed.

"Because the old gods protected their followers from plagues and natural disasters in exchange for human sacrifices. Any human that pledged himself to an old god in an ancient rite would forfeit his soul to said entity upon death. It's said, at least in this damned book, that pockets of worshippers still abound in less civilized areas of the world, with worshippers performing this ritual on themselves to gain the blessing of their patron."

"Or matron," James said before staring at Davis. "You know, Mother of Blood…?"

"The old gods are pretty much gender neutral, so you can assign either to them, but I'm used to referring to them as male," Davis heaved a sigh.

"That's chauvinistic, professor," James said with a smile. "I bet you don't have any graduate students that are hardcore feminists, do you? Your students let you get by with it because you're old."

"Possibly, but I imagine my graduates know me well enough that I don't worry over what genitals you have, just whether you can do your job or not," Davis replied, turning the page. "I've met many women who were grand explorers of forgotten ruins and sites deep within jungles no white man has ever walked before. I've also known just as many who've accidentally killed themselves by eating a local plant that was in fact poisonous."

"So your male graduates are better?" James pressed.

Davis shrugged. "I have more of them than I've had of women so it's hard to say. I've had fools and geniuses, people who thrived on luck and others who lived on finely-honed skill. Like I said, if you can do the job I don't care about you in any way, shape, or form. Just do as I ask and we'll get along fine."

"Whatever you say…" James grumbled, folding his hands behind his head and closing his eyes.

"That's the spirit!" Davis exclaimed before flipping a page. As he skimmed through the handwritten notes he came across a drawing that made him pause. It was a charcoal sketch of a creature with no discernable structure, a slumped figure with five fleshy tendrils sprouting around a hollow maw in its chest. The stomach was distended and legs muscular, one ending in four claws, the other one large claw. Two arms jutted up from the creature, if you could call them that. They resembled taut muscle, segmented so that they could move about around and over the beast. Each limb ended in a pitted ball.

A side note was scribbled into the leathery page.

"Breathe deeply, for the Children of Flesh convert man into their most perfect image. If they are pressed for time, they will swallow men whole and convert them slowly. This does not slow them down, rather, it seems to make them excited. I was barely able to escape with my life for, unlike the Mother of Blood's Sanguine Sanctuary, these creatures are hostile towards all manner of man and beast. Their contagion cannot spread through water, though they are capable swimmers, traveling far to gather more children for their Father's family."

Davis groaned internally, leaning back in his seat, rubbing his left temple gingerly. Capable swimmers meant that these things were based out of an underground lake, or cavern connected to a river. The image of the well with eyes came to mind, as Davis could imagine a creature made entirely of muscle climbing up from the dank recesses to bring fresh meat for the... what would he call this group? A colony?

James looked over at Davis, raising an eyebrow in piqued interest. "Find something?"

"I think I found our culprit," Davis said, shoving the book towards James, who grabbed it halfway. Reading the loopy script, he whistled low.

"Wow... these are something else. Anything on this Father of Flesh guy?" James asked.

Davis stood up, popping his back in satisfaction. "No and we have no time. We need to move out now. Go gather Jeremy so he can return the book to the archive."

James stood, stretching for a moment before walking towards the door and unlocking it. He returned minutes later with Jeremy, who had a smug air about him. "So you're both sane," Jeremy said as if impressed. "Though one of you seems worse for the wear."

"Go to hell, just get this thing out of my sight!" James growled.

Jeremy nodded, grabbing the edge of the book and pulling it from Davis's grasp, causing the dark murmurs to fall silent, their echoes rattling in the back of his mind. "Thank you for not damaging it, professor."

"As if I would harm such a treasure," Davis replied, not paying attention. He gathered his satchel and pulled out his phone. Tossing it to James, he smiled. "My e-mail is open. Reply to the dear minister that I'll need three plane tickets to Hong Kong where we can meet him. Tell him we leave in two days."

"Three tickets? Why three? You have someone else in mind who will go on this crazy venture of yours?" James asked as he began rapidly entering the text via the keypad on the phone.

"Why yes, I do." Davis smiled.

* * *

Walking through the airport terminal after being inspected *twice* by security, Davis had in hand his folder of graduate students. He flipped through the loose leaf pages in search of that one liability waiver he had in mind. James walked beside him, the two of them moving at a brisk pace, weaving through the crowds as the headed towards their flight. Davis smiled when he found it and pulled the paper from the folder, sliding it back into his satchel carefully. Pulling out his cell phone, he dialed the number at the bottom of the page and waited for someone to pick up.

"Hello?" answered a tired voice.

"Huan? It's me, Professor Nickels," Davis said, smiling at a fat man he'd almost tripped.

Huan immediately sounded more alert. "Professor? What can I do for you?"

Davis grinned. "You can begin packing for an excursion into the wilds of rural China, as I've found myself in a predicament where your language skills, combined with your thorough knowledge of archaeological recovery, will be very handy.

"But... what about my other classes?" she asked, suddenly sounding worried. "I can't just up and abandon them, they'll fail me!"

"Now, don't worry about that. Stop by my office and pass along your class information to my assistant, he'll take care of the rest," Davis said, knowing that the rest of the faculty would kowtow to his request. He brought in too much money for them *not* to.

"If you're sure... all right, I'll be ready! When do we leave?" she exclaimed.

"Thursday, probably in the morning. We'll be taking a cab there so don't worry about using a car." Davis said, stopping at the terminal where the plane was. "Now I must go. Be ready by Thursday!"

"Yes sir!" she chirped before hanging up.

Davis slid his phone into his pocket before checking his watch. Closing it, he shook his head. "We should be boarding soon; I bumped us up to first class."

James looked down at the professor. "Really? I've never flown first class before."

"A real surprise there..." Davis mumbled before clearing his throat. "When we get to Austin, you can stay in my home. I have several guest rooms and you can make use of one, unless you want a hotel."

"No, your home should be fine," James said a bit too quickly.

Davis narrowed his eyes at him. "You're not to go through my collection, do you understand? I don't want to wake up and find your cooling corpse on the floor of my viewing room."

"I understand," James said.

"Good," Davis nodded before smiling at the announcement that they were to begin boarding. "Let's get going. I want to relax and a plane ride is a great time to nap."

Boarding the plane, James took his seat and immediately began to fiddle with the options, asking a passing stewardess if there was drink service on this flight, and generally being a nuisance. This didn't stop Davis from reclining his seat, fluffing his complimentary pillow, and closing his eyes for a much-deserved nap.

* * *

Davis opened his eyes to a bleak landscape, a darkened shroud hanging high in the air where winking stars glimmered like diamonds. Looking around, he saw that he was in a rural countryside at the bottom of a hill. There was a path cutting through irrigated sections of rice, and three small huts that appeared to be deserted. Walking by one of them, he could peer inside and see that most of the items were scattered about haphazardly, as if the tenants had fled without time to pack. Looking down, he stared at a hand-stitched doll with buttons for eyes, dressed in a simple brown dress.

Thunder crashed overhead, followed by a flash of lightning, revealing the bloodstains all over the doll and the entryway to the home. The lightning faded, and it was all swallowed up in the darkness of the night once more.

Folding his hands behind his back, Davis closed his eyes and listened. The rushing wind coming down from the hill smelled of sweat and grime, while in the distance he could hear whispers echoing across the ether. He could not make out what they were saying, but he knew that they were in anguish.

The souls he kept in his own personal collection had taught him that sound long ago.

Walking slowly up the hill, Davis noticed when the ground grew soft and slippery, like mud. Holding a hand out, he didn't feel any rain, nor did he smell the recent scent of a shower. Ignoring it, he pushed onward, walking up the hill until he finally caught sight of a tall tree next to a larger hut.

*It would seem I've reached a village,* Davis thought to himself. *And the voices are growing louder. There must be hundreds trapped somewhere close by to cause such a stir!*

Slowly making his way to the tree, another crack of lightning illuminated the sky for several seconds, making Davis back up. The tree was not a tree at all, but a warped pink and white pillar of twisted flesh, great limbs extending out with smaller branches forming baby arms or, in some case, larger arms. A great eye blinked in the center of the mass, staring at Davis through a three-slit violet eye, while several maws opened and closed where the roots seemed to be, twisting up and out of a thick covering of greasy flesh that served as the ground, bits of hair rising as if it were blades of grass in messy clumps.

Davis sucked in a shuddering breath. He was *in* the village in China! But how was he here? He'd just been on a plane mere moments before, getting ready to take a nap. Was this a dream? A nightmare?

"Neither," answered a voice that Davis had not heard in several years.

Turning, he looked at the young man standing but three feet behind him. Nude save for a black tarry substance covering most of his body, the bleak man was pallid in complexion, muscular, and clutching a sword in a cracked sheath in one hand, a battered shield in the other; both from a certain set of Ubaid ruins that Davis had visited every twenty years for the past century.

"Hello Joshua," Davis offered a weak grin.

"Hello professor," the wraith said in a sibilant hiss. "It's been a while."

"It has. Your vitality has served me well for the past four years." Davis said, as if offering a condolence. "Plus your death was able to keep the Darkness Given Hunger more time to sleep. The bindings on it are ancient and weak, and need to be kept well fed."

"So you fed *me* to them out of the goodness of your own heart while accepting the boon granted by the old one? My life energy, my youth, my very memories! You make me sick..."

"An understandable feeling, I assure you. But it will come to pass, eventually your strength will wane and you will slip away from this state and on into the next in the afterlife."

"Heaven, you mean?" Joshua asked, a smile gracing his features to show off sparkling white teeth, surrounded by black tar that seemed to wriggle and move of its own accord.

"No, more like being consumed by the old one I left you with. Every time I do that rite of bringing a warrior down there they linger on in memory, sometimes visiting my dreams to warn me of what awaits me in the afterlife."

"Oh," Joshua said with a wide grin. "But this is no dream, and I am no figment. This is what you will be seeing in a matter of days. Welcome to one of the greater provinces of China."

Joshua's sword slowly crackled to life, green flames dancing along the patina sheath encrusted over the blade. Funny, it looked better than the one from life, hanging in his office.

The light revealed that Davis was far from alone. Several smaller… things had approached him. No two looked alike, but they all had an extra limb overgrown with tumors and corpuscles, ragged bits of skin hanging off arms ending in wicked claws. All three bore a tentacle sprouting from the shoulders, which was covered in flushed pink flesh dotted with a single large eye like the one in the tree.

"Can they see me?" Davis asked, eyes never leaving them as their tentacles snapped and whirled above them, flitting about like waggling tongues.

"They can sense your spirit, as that is what they truly crave, but no. They cannot see you." Joshua said as he walked closer, holding his sword up high to illuminate the area past them, leading deeper into the village.

"Why am I here?" Davis asked, looking at Joshua.

Joshua didn't meet the man's gaze; he instead looked up at the sky with a wry smile. "Because *he* senses you. He senses everyone who will stand in his way and he's preparing for it."

"Who?" Davis asked, looking off in the distance where Joshua was looking.

A third flash of lightning showed a massive creature, standing upon three legs with five great tentacles of flesh, each limb the size of a skyscraper. Eye spots the size of fire engines dotted the sides of the great beast and, from this angle, Davis could see a mouth lined with flesh nubs the size of small cars perched atop the corpulent being. It seemed too immense to stand on three legs, rolling folds of fat stretching the skin too thin while in other areas the pink flesh was cracked, bleeding out a yellowish-gray material in rivers.

Flying creatures like eyeless, earless bats flapped around the titan, feasting on the succulent flow of fluids until one of the arms on the torso, human-sized wriggling limbs that all seemed panicked, thrashed out and grappled the bald creatures, pulling them *into* the gigantic monster's frame in a disgusting display of osmosis that made bile rise to the back of his throat.

Joshua was suddenly behind him, leaning over his shoulder. "He knows of you, you know. He can smell the stench of power that has been bestowed upon you over the years, the scent of lingering souls trapped in items you should have destroyed long ago. And now he has seen you. He still slumbers, but soon his bindings will break, and he will be the first of many to emerge."

"H-how long?" Davis asked, turning to look at Joshua.

But he was gone, a soft chuckle on the wind rolling past.

# CHAPTER SIX

Davis stirred from his disturbing vision feeling chilled to the bone, his mind racing and his hands shaking. Reaching into his satchel, he carefully removed the orange bottle and shook out two pills before bothering one of the flight attendants for a bottle of water. James looked over from his seat near the window and chuckled.

"You've been out nearly the entire flight and now you have to take your medicine? How *old* are you anyway?"

Not in any kind of mood to deal with James, he merely ignored him while waiting for his water bottle. The stewardess, an attractive woman possibly in her thirties or forties—it was all kind of a blur to Davis at this point—passed him the bottle, asking if she could get anything else for him.

"Yes," he gasped, taking the two pills and guzzling a few gulps of water from the bottle. Once he had his medicine, and while ignoring the worried looks from everyone around him, he fought to make a smile and forced the words from his mouth. "Do you have anything warm to drink?"

"Warm? Like coffee, or would you prefer hot chocolate?" The stewardess asked, uncertain of what to make of Davis. He knew he must have looked like hell; the few times he ever had a vision he always looked horrible afterwards, the effect of the mystical experience draining his body of its strength.

Davis shook his head to clear his thoughts and smiled, this time genuinely, still fighting to speak as his tongue seemed to stick to his teeth. "Both are bad for me but I think I'll take the hot chocolate if you have any to spare."

"I'll see what I can do," she reached down and patted his forearm before walking off. James leaned over, causing Davis to jump in surprise.

"You okay, professor? It's not like you to be this—I don't know—*normal* around me. Earlier we were trading quips like you were in your thirties," James said. "Now you look like you've gone through the ringer and can barely make a sentence. What's up?"

Davis drank deeply from the water again, finishing the bottle, before looking at James. "I just don't like flying, all right? It always makes me ache so I try and sleep through it."

James nodded, the half-truth working on him. "And the pills? That prescription bottle is in Spanish."

"I visit Cuba for my medical needs," Davis said, tucking the bottle back into his satchel. "Now it's easier, what with the United States easing up on travel there."

"Why not just get your medicine here?" James pressed, running a gaunt hand through his ivory locks.

Davis clenched his teeth and fought a sudden jolt of pain shooting through his chest to his right arm. Flexing his fingers, he heaved a sigh of relief when he felt the weight on his body drift away. Looking at James, he smiled and merely shook his head.

"You don't want to listen about an old man's medication regimen. You're young, you don't have to worry about that until you're... half my age," he said after a moment's hesitation. Thoughts of Joshua invaded his mind, how he'd left him sprawled out on the sacrificial dais after clubbing him with his own sword, left to die at the ever-expanding slime that was the old god trapped thousands of feet below the surface of modern-day Iraq.

*It's been four years... I'll need to start grooming a new warrior for the next sacrifice,* he thought to himself, eyes drifting to James, who had yet to take his eyes off him. *Perhaps James? No... he won't linger after this task. I imagine he'll have spent enough time dealing with anomalous entities and want to return to Boston.*

"So, you're okay?" James asked, a tinge of worry in his voice.

Davis hated that sound.

"Yes dammit, I'm fine!" he said in a low voice. He turned just as the stewardess brought over a large mug of steaming hot chocolate. "Oh marvelous, simply marvelous!"

"Here you go, I made sure to add double the chocolate for you. You look like you could use a pick me up, if you don't mind me saying so," she said, straightening up as she handed him the drink.

"Oh by all means, if I look a fright then please alert me. My young companion here was just asking me how old I am and what my medications are," Davis said, smiling as he heard a few gasps from around him, the stewardess adopting a shocked look. "You putting in the extra effort is what will really help these old bones, not the pestering questions of pretentious children."

The stewardess looked at James with a frigid glare. "Is there anything you want, *sir*?"

James managed to clear his throat before answering, his voice cracking a bit. "N-No, I'm f-fine!"

"Good!" The stewardess exclaimed, turning a softer eye to Davis. "Would you like a blanket, hon? You look like you might be cold."

"That would be lovely, Delores, thank you," Davis said, sipping his hot drink, savoring how it seeped down his throat and into his belly, the warmth spreading through his frigid limbs and chilled bones.

"How did you know my… never mind, I'll just get you that blanket," Delores said, walking off to the small room where the flight attendants kept the spare… well, *everything*. James leaned back over, whispering harshly at Davis.

"Why did you do that? Now everyone in first class thinks I'm an ass!" James was looking around at some of the passengers who were staring at him, muttering to their friends and family around them.

"Relax sonny boy, the worst that'll happen is you'll get a stern talking to." Davis slurped his cocoa happily. "Besides, asking me my age was a tad rude on your part, don't you think?"

"Well how else would I know? It's not like you know my age or anything, we get to know each other by—"

"Twenty-six, this November," Davis commented as he continued drinking, stopping James cold mid-sentence.

"How did you…" James couldn't complete the thought as Delores returned with a thick blanket, which she insisted on "tucking" around Davis's legs and lower back.

"Now, is there anything else I can do for you, sir?" she asked, clapping her hands together.

"No, Delores, you're doing a fine job. You eased an old man's ailments today," he said, winking at her with one bushy brow.

She giggled. "Sir, it's already nighttime. We'll be landing in the next half-hour, so you'll need to finish off your drink and rest up before we begin the landing procedures."

Davis smiled before downing the rest of the steaming drink, handing off the warm mug to her. "There you go, dear. Now I'll just try and relax. Landings are rough on these old bones."

"You do that, sir," she said while shooting James a final glare. As she sashayed off to help another passenger, James leaned over again.

"How did you know how old I am?" he demanded.

"Lucky guess," Davis lied, reaching into his vest to pull out his pocket watch. Flipping it open, he whistled before closing it, stashing it back in his vest.

"Lucky guess? That's the best you have?" James said with a laugh.

"No, that answer is the best *you* have. I have my secrets which I don't share as often as other old men," Davis said. "Now if you'll excuse me, I'd like to get a little shut-eye before we land."

* * *

It was already dark by the time they left the airport, the cool autumn night filled with the scents and sounds of the city. James had been kind enough to take Davis's satchel along with his own suitcases, as the old man wasn't feeling too well. He didn't want to take his medication again, not in front of James at the very least, so he hobbled along citing the altitude change as his reason for being in pain.

*Not too bad to tell a half truth, is it?* Davis thought as he walked through the parking garage, keys in hand. *I mean, the altitude does make my joints hurt, but being separated from the earth for so long… I need to get ready for a Pacific flight!*

"Now if you see a white Jeep Renegade, that should be my car," Davis said as they searched through the parking lot. "I can recite to you the entire Declaration of Independence but I can't remember where I parked!"

"Found it!" James said, pointing forward.

Davis looked where he was pointing and laughed; he'd almost walked right by it.

Unlocking the doors with the press of a button, he offered James the driver's seat. "If you can drive stick, you can drive us home."

"Seriously? You've known me for less than twenty-four hours and you're trusting me to drive your car?"

"Jeep. Things pretty sturdy so I'm not worried about me or you, and I have good insurance so whoever you hit will be covered," Davis waved away the concern, walking around and stepping up into the passenger seat. "Just turn on the heater, I'm freezing!"

"It's like seventy degrees out, how are you that cold?" James asked, pushing his suitcases and Davis's satchel into the backseat. "I mean, this is Texas and you're dressed in layers!"

"Just get in and drive, smart ass, before I decide to ditch you here," Davis snapped, prompting James to hurry into the driver's seat. He adjusted the mirrors before buckling himself in and turning the ignition, the engine roaring to life.

"Wow, this is *so* not my Prius..." James said, taking a firm hold of the steering wheel.

"Yeah, you kind of need a bigger vehicle in Texas, especially here in Austin," Davis said, buckling his seatbelt.

"Why? Do you haul anything big around?" James asked, slowly pulling from the parking space and down the slope leading out onto the highway.

"No, you'll see what I mean," Davis said with a chuckle.

Within minutes of getting on the highway James was cursing at the other drivers, yelling at them loud enough that it made Davis's ears ring and the windows rattle. James spewed foul language that would make even a Marine blush.

"See? I told you..." Davis said, motioning out to the four-lane highway where everyone was speeding along, cutting each other off and slamming on their brakes at the slightest cause. It was clearly making James frazzled, but the Jeep was new and still had good brakes, so luckily nobody was killed by the irate northerner. He took directions from his phone to get to Blackmore Manor, a historical landmark in northern Austin which Davis owned. In the years since purchasing it he had repurposed the old building to become a mansion for him and a museum for others.

When they pulled up to the gates of the manor, James just stared at the three-story building in awe. The house was impressive—built with three balconies facing out towards the street, two on the second floor and one on the third, and a wide porch that surrounded the entire building. A gothic-styled wrought iron railing kept the flourishing vegetation from growing over and onto the porch. Full blooms of purple sage bushes were spaced evenly along the sides of the house, running all the way back to what looked like a garden, complete with a fountain. The light was too dim to see further than what the headlights washed over as they rolled past the gate and into the circular driveway.

"Here we are," Davis said with a contented sigh. "What time is it?"

Checking his phone, James frowned. "Around eight thirty. Don't you have that pocket watch?"

"I do. Dinner should be ready, and I believe it will be served in the west dining room, if I know my assistant as well as I think I do."

"Wait, your assistant works for you here as well?" James asked, exiting the vehicle. "I thought he was a teaching assistant or something."

"He is, but he's more than that. I'm allowing him to catalogue my finds for his thesis in exchange for him acting as a live-in servant for the time being. Between that and the healthy salary I offer him, he happily jumped at the chance."

Davis smiled as he fished his satchel out of the back seat, looping it over his shoulder. The porch lights flickered on, the double doors leading into the foyer opening to reveal Lawrence, the dusky blonde dressed in a T-shirt and jeans with an apron tied over his chest and around his waist.

"Professor? You arrived in time for dinner," Lawrence called out.

"I'd assumed so," Davis called back as James walked from the other side of the Jeep, hands full of luggage. "I brought a house guest, so if you could prepare the guest room with one of the balconies I'd be most pleased."

"Easily done sir," Lawrence said as he walked forward, taking the suitcases from James in an overly forceful manner. "I assume this is the man here for the dagger?"

"The very same," Davis said, cutting off James before he could speak. "I trust you've studied it and the writings I have concerning it?"

"I spent the better part of the afternoon typing them up into a file while also testing the knife on several subjects. As expected, they all expired within minutes of touching the blade. Blood tests are still being run but I doubt it was poison."

"Wait, blood tests? You have a laboratory in there or something?" James laughed, a laugh which fell short as the two other men looked at him as though he were stupid. "You're not joking…"

"Of course not!" Davis exclaimed. "I have three separate laboratories where Lawrence and I experiment with the paranormal properties of items I retrieve from the field. Speaking of which, Lawrence, this is James. James, Lawrence."

Davis waved between the two casually as he walked up the steps and through the open door, sighing as a blast of warm air rolled over him. He shrugged off his shoes and stuck his feet into a pair of thick slippers before pressing further through the foyer. James walked in after him, rolling up his shirt sleeves due to the heat. He looked back at Lawrence, who didn't seem disturbed by the temperature and merely walked past him with his luggage over to a set of stairs leading James where the student assumed his bedroom to be.

"I'm going to change before dinner, Davis. It's a little warm in here for me," James said.

"Follow Lawrence, as I doubt he'll wait for you," Davis replied, walking beneath the overhang, past a column where three items were displayed behind bulletproof glass. Davis ran a finger down the glass over a chalice decorated with skulls and Celtic symbols. Whispers leaked out, even from behind the enclosure. The violin above it whined softy as Davis inspected it. To hear the voices of these artifacts…

"Sometimes it's a little much, even for me," Davis muttered. He pulled his hand back, silencing the whispers and walked through the oak door into a small dining room. A large table sized for eight people dominated the chamber; from each wall hung paintings by local artists.

"Always good to support the arts..." Davis mumbled to himself as he dropped his satchel onto the table, allowing him to retrieve his notebook from the time spent pouring over the *Grimlocke Chronicles* in the insufferably stuffy room. Taking a seat at the head of the table, he flipped through the pages, nodding at passages he'd scribbled down as well as the work that James had done.

"Give the boy a decade and he'll be a decent researcher... shame he's to waste his talents up in Boston," Davis said before he flipped to a near empty page, a simple drawing sitting in the middle of it.

Angry and red, this looked as if it were drawn by a bloodthirsty sociopath. It was all jagged angles and line breaks marking through each other. A circle was drawn with a three-slit iris in the middle.

It was the eye from the photographs, from the vision.

"How did you get in here...?" Davis said, grabbing the page as if to tear it from the notebook.

Instead he found himself no longer sitting in his dining room but at a table in a small home, lit only by the sunlight pouring in through the holes in the roof. Seated across from him was a monstrous amalgamation of flesh, a human head split down the middle with four tentacles slithering out like serpents from the fissure.

Like all the others he'd seen, this one had no visible neck, merely a build-up of muscle that left the figure slightly hunched over. Two arms sprouted from its left side while one larger arm emerged from the right. All three were resting upon the table, a total of twelve overstuffed, fatty fingers slid into talons of clear keratin. The sweaty look of the creature made the scene even more uncomfortable, especially with the strange twitches that seemed to rock its body every few moments.

The four tentacles slid apart, revealing a lipless maw beneath it all, the fractured pieces of what was once human being pulled taut over pink flesh.

"You..." the creature hissed and gasped, a horrid squelching noise akin to a fish gasping for breath. "You will come... you will... be one of six... you will... open the first gate... with blood of... the ancient!"

The heavy breathing that seemed to rock the monster's frame quivered with every word, but the message was clear—as well as over—as soon as Davis realized what had been said. He was back in his dining room, a crumpled sheet of blank notebook paper in his gnarled hand.

The door opened, revealing James in a tank top and jeans, clapping his hands together gleefully.

"What's for dinner?" James said, stopping when he saw Davis's expression. "Whoa professor, you don't look so good… you okay?"

Instead of telling the boy that he was fine like he wanted to, his vision faded to gray as he slumped over the table, unconscious. He was dimly aware that James was calling out to Lawrence about something but he just felt so sleepy at that moment, he could barely manage to stay conscious long enough to hear the worry in James's voice.

# CHAPTER SEVEN

Davis could hear the worried voices before he could see anything. Something wet and warm was lying over his eyes, which felt pleasant enough. He was content to stay wherever he was, but his rumbling stomach and the arguing between two people made this option something of a chore. Heaving a sigh, he reached up and pulled what was revealed to be a wet rag from his face, discovering he was in the sitting room connected to the west dining room. Standing near the door by a long glass case holding a variety of knives and daggers used over the centuries, were Lawrence and James, each pointing toward a book while trying to speak over each other.

"Gentlemen!" Davis croaked, gathering their attention. "What in the world are you arguing about?"

"Oh, you're awake professor!" Lawrence exclaimed, turning to lower the glass cover over the case, locking it for good measure.

James look displeased.

"Yeah, you had us worried," James said, glaring at the back of Lawrence's head. "What happened?"

"A vision, nothing more." Davis said, swinging his legs to the floor from the plush sofa he'd been laid out upon. The floral pattern clashed terribly against the wooden floors and half-dozen African tribal masks scattered across the walls, but he loved this furniture. "Is there any dinner left?"

"Yes, of course!" Lawrence said, turning. "Let me get you some. James will keep you company while I bring you a bowl of turnip stew."

"Thank you Lawrence," Davis said. Looking down at his hands they seemed more wrinkled than ever, the arthritis aching where he held the warm rag. He reached into his vest pocket and pulled out his watch, opening it. Frowning, he closed it and slipped it back inside before looking up to James.

"How long was I out?" he asked, smiling slightly at James as the pale youth pouted. "And what's wrong with you?"

"You've been out for around an hour, and what's wrong is your assistant is stingy!" James exclaimed. "I just wanted to examine a few knives in the case with markings I recognized and he told me no. When I asked why he had the gall to tell me I didn't know what I was getting into."

"So?" Davis asked, eyes darting from him to the book and back.

"Oh," James looked slightly embarrassed at this. "I went to your library and grabbed a book that would have the symbols, to show him I knew what they were. He and I were arguing over the properties of the Celtic throwing knives when you came to."

"Oh yes, that pair. They're enchanted to leech the life energy from whoever holds them, in exchange for making the blades sharper and more accurate. The Celts believed a year or two of life given in return for an advantage on the battlefield was a fair trade."

"Oh," James said, looking down into the case. "So why do they have symbols of Mawat on them? Isn't that an angel of death and destruction?"

"In Christian mythology he is. They adopted him into their teachings just as they did the Winter Solstice and Ishtar, marking them as holy days to convince pagans to join their ranks in a more seamless fashion. Mawat is an old god, though not a terribly prominent one. He's supposedly three-faced, though from what I understand that could just be a metaphor. His followers revel in slaughter and mass sacrifices under blood moons, which are their holiest time of year. They used monoliths to better calculate the time when the moon would be painted red by Mars so that they could coordinate their campaigns around the time, ensuring they always had prisoners to kill for their patron."

"Wow, um… I didn't know all *that* about Mawat," James said, rubbing the back of his head.

Davis shrugged. "Not many do. He's a forgotten god for a reason. People like me do what we can when we learn of some fool trying to awaken him, using lethal force if necessary. I gathered those knives in Germany in nineteen fifty-seven from an underground sect of Nazis that were following Himmler's last commands of waking the old gods."

"Wait, Nazis?" James asked.

"Yes, do you think they all vanished overnight? Many of them were arrested while others were children that survived the capture of Berlin. They grew up listening to the rhetoric of Hitler's regime and joined the underground movement to bring about what *they* thought would be the dawning of a new age for the Aryan people."

"What were they doing?" James asked, walking over to take a seat in a chair across from Davis.

"They were gathering orphans, legally and illegally, from all over Europe and bringing them into a secret bunker where they'd constructed an altar from the teeth of former prisoners of the death camps in Poland. How they got them I never learned, but it was gruesome to behold. They were ritualistically slitting the throats of each child on the blood moon every hour, allowing the blood to fill in urns, which they poured into an engraving they'd made that would grant them knowledge of where Mawat was, physically."

"And you got there before they could start?" James asked, hopping in his seat slightly.

"God no, we got there after they'd bled the fourth child. They still had seventeen left. The cultists fought like madmen, using firearms and old weapons to try and stop us. But in the end, we killed them all and disposed of the blood safely. We collapsed the bunker and the scriptures used to create the ritual were split between four parties, myself included, so that nobody would ever have the full manuscript again."

"Wait, you have some actual diabolist literature?" James asked, now intrigued.

"Don't get too excited, I keep all I have in a secret room in the house," Davis said, leaning back on the ornate sofa. "I have a good deal of dark manuscripts and cultist material hidden there."

"Shouldn't that be, I don't know, handed over to Dean Reynolds so we can study it? We *are* the premier occult research facility in the world."

Davis chuckled. "So you think. I've worked with many of your alumni and, like yourself, they don't know much beyond the basics. It's kind of sad really, Lawrence knows more about the mysteries of the universe than you, and he doesn't even believe in most of them."

"What?" James exclaimed. "Then why do you let him examine your collections?"

"Because I do what the professor is unwilling to do," Lawrence said from the doorway, a tray bearing three cups of steaming tea and a bowl of vegetable-laden broth in his hands. "I assumed you would want tea with your evening meal so I came prepared."

"Very wise as always Lawrence. Will you be joining us for a robust discussion over what we've learned?" Davis asked as Lawrence walked over and laid the tray down on the table between James and Davis.

He took a seat at another stuffed chair and relaxed into it. "I have some time before the blood tests on the subjects are finished so I can stay and offer my opinion over a cup."

Davis reached forward and pulled the bowl of stew into his lap, taking a silver spoon and digging into the meal with vigor. Lawrence reached forward and grabbed a cup of tea before motioning to James.

"It's Earl Grey, so I hope you enjoy it. We don't have sugar in the house but we have honey. I assumed you liked your tea with some sweetness to it."

"I actually don't drink tea, I prefer coffee..." James said, trailing off as Lawrence stared at him with disinterested eyes. "I guess I can try it."

They all sipped tea in silence, Davis's slurping of stew being the only sound in the room as the other two sat watching each other. James was the first to break the silence.

"I'm sorry about earlier, I just recognized the symbols and thought I could study the knives a bit before the professor woke up," James said.

Lawrence took a long sip of tea before sighing. "I suppose I shouldn't have been so abusive towards you. A curious mind is something to be encouraged, not punished. But keep in mind that most of the items that are kept in this house are cursed or possessed by malignant spirits. Those knives shaved a year or so off my life during the brief time I handled them."

"What was it like?" James asked. "Feeling your life being drawn from you, that is."

Lawrence pondered for a moment. "Have you ever given blood? Donated or had some taken for testing?"

"Of course," James answered.

"The feeling of blood leaving your body, the chills that runs up the arm? That's what it feels like, but it starts in the hand and extends up to the shoulder of the arm holding them."

"Eww… that sounds horrible!" James exclaimed.

"It is. The fact that Professor Nickels faced someone with both in his hands is mindboggling. He told you the tale I suppose?"

"Most of it," James nodded.

"Did he mention that they discovered stashes of raw opium in the bunker? Or that most of the cultists were on the substance? The draining effect would be nothing to someone hopped up on a numbing agent like that."

Davis set the bowl on the tray. "I didn't mention that because we never were able to discern if they were in fact using the opium, or just selling it."

"What happened to it?" James asked.

Davis shrugged, picking up his cup of tea. "We collapsed the bunker on top of it and then had the land sold to a growing company that needed a new factory. I assume that there is a layer of cement over the remains of the bunker now, as well as several tons of rotting opium."

James seemed surprised but didn't say anything, instead drinking his tea in silence. Davis and Lawrence spoke at length over the possibilities of what could be waiting in China, even going so far as to venture a guess at what exactly would prove most effective against the slumped over monsters.

"My Sharps Buffalo gun has always been my favorite, but I fear bringing it underwater won't work well for me," Davis said, setting his empty teacup on the tray. "Perhaps I should bring one of my weapons from the collection?"

Lawrence hummed and stared down into his tea. "You do have several interesting items with anomalous properties that could prove helpful if battling something susceptible to light and fire."

"You've been combing through the pieces, what have I got?" Davis asked.

"Several tools of war. You have a mace from sixteenth century England that supposedly glows in the presence of evil and inflicts wounds that cannot be healed. I tested this on a dog and found that its broken ribs, even when set right, wouldn't heal. I eventually put him down after eight weeks."

"That would be helpful… these things will most likely qualify as evil," Davis said, drumming his fingers on his knee.

"You also have several swords that inflict damage to the nervous system when striking a foe, all from ancient Sumer. I've theorized they had problems with something that was difficult to kill but easily driven off by pain."

"Sumer does have legends of dragons and chimeras…" James muttered.

"Things that would have been around during Sumerian times. I believe they worshipped an old god aptly dubbed Maker of Pain. Perhaps these swords were used in religious ceremonies?" Davis offered.

Lawrence rolled his eyes. "Whatever they believed in, the weapons could prove useful. There are also holy symbols that could be of use."

"Offer one to James here, I have my own talismans," Davis said.

Lawrence turned to James. "I'll go over a selection of weapons for you tomorrow in the morning. Does that sound good?"

"Sounds perfect!" James exclaimed, clearly excited. "Would it be too much to ask that I look over your notes on some of the artifacts Professor Nickels has collected?"

Lawrence shifted uncomfortably in his seat. "I can forward you a copy via e-mail when I have them typed up, but for now they're written in a shorthand script I made for myself. I'm afraid you wouldn't know what I was saying."

"Oh," James said before looking at Davis with hopeful eyes. "Are there any artifacts you're going to bring with you?"

"A few I generally use on every expedition, as well as a few more modern pieces that I find useful. Shen said the monsters were harmed by fire and napalm, and honestly, what isn't? But taking that into account I have a few ideas of what I'll bring with me. Shen will most likely prepare a private flight for us, as he'll be expecting us to come armed."

"So this is more of a hunt than a dig?" James asked.

"Oh no, we'll be digging. But we'll be doing it fast while fending off monsters that will be trying to eat us. I have a feeling we'll also be going down into a river in search of underwater ruins. I hope that whatever ruins we find are in a cavern somewhere as I loathe swimming for too long."

"Are... are you going to be able to do this professor?" James asked, looking down at his hands. "You didn't look so good on the plane after you woke up and you just passed out an hour ago."

"Just the stress of the job I'm afraid. Lawrence will be taking the teaching workload off my shoulders while I'm gone, so that's a relief." Davis said, smiling at his assistant who gave him a tight smile in return. "But the prospect of dealing with so many unknowns makes me uneasy. I would usually research an area and all the legends surrounding it for months before even considering the actual trip. We only have two days until we leave!"

"That *is* a bit stressful I suppose," James agreed, taking a moment to sip his tea. "So since the dean offered me up to you like a lamb for the slaughter, what exactly do I get out of a dig with the famous Professor Nickels?"

"The form you signed had a liability clause in it, as well as a promise of one artifact of my choosing. Normally I would require you write your thesis on the properties of your find and the history behind it that can be determined from the area we found it in. Since you aren't my student you're free of that duty."

"Wow," James whistled. "I get my own relic?"

"One of my choosing," Davis nodded.

"Wicked!" James exclaimed before setting his teacup down on the tray. "Thank you for the meal, but I'm going to go to bed. I couldn't sleep at all on the plane, and it's nearly one in the morning."

Lawrence looked at his wristwatch and frowned. "I'd hoped to compile another few page's worth of notes on the Inca spear, but I suppose that can wait for tomorrow. Professor, do you wish for me to phone Mr. Stewart?"

"Mr. Stewart?" James repeated, stretching to get the kinks out of his back as he rose from the chair. "Who's that, some colleague of yours?"

"He's my lawyer," Davis said grimly. "I contact him to update my will before every expedition. Lawrence, I think that would be a wise idea. Do you still believe you are up to the task?"

"I think so sir, though I won't know where to begin," Lawrence answered.

"Graduate with your doctorate and publish a book or three before you go back. You have sixteen years before it has to be reset." Davis said with thick voice. "I've clearly outlined what needs to be done and how to do it, so just make sure you keep it up."

"This won't be needed professor," Lawrence smiled, reaching over to pat Davis's withered hand gently. "You'll make it back just fine. Just pace yourself."

"Of course. I think I'll retire as well," Davis said. He stood up and rubbed his right hip. "Don't stay up too late Lawrence, okay?"

"I'm not about to promise that professor," Lawrence said. He stood up and gathered the tray, following behind James into the dining room. "Goodnight sir!"

"Goodnight," Davis called back, watching the two young men leave. He pulled out his pocket watch and stared at it, flipping it open with his thumb. The golden piece of clockwork ticked in his hand, each tick deafening to Davis. He closed it with an angry motion and stuffed it back in his vest.

"Stupid thing..." he muttered, stalking out of the room into a small study.

The room was adorned with Aztec weapons and armor on the walls, great stretches of tanned hides depicting battles in basic paints, faded by the wear and tear of time. The lone bookcase held dozens of books on the Mesoamerican cultures and societies. A small desk sat with a rolling chair, a lone typewriter sitting on the blank expanse of black wood. Behind it was a long display case, holding three spears atop velvet cushions.

Made from hard wood and topped with colored feathers and jagged obsidian spearheads, the weapons all held a unique look to them. They looked as if they had been made days ago, yet showed signs of battle from the sweat stains on the hafts, and chips in the volcanic stone that had been made from striking an enemy with too much force.

Opening the case, Davis reached in and withdrew the shortest of the spears, one that was still two heads taller than him when held. He felt stronger, braver while holding this weapon. The various aches and pains he had all over his body seemed to fade to dull throbs while he held the tool of war. Tilting it down, he palmed the wide spearhead and ran a finger over the nearly imperceptible carvings in the stone. He didn't know what they said, but he knew that they were from a civilization much older than the Aztecs.

These had been tools used against servants of old gods buried deep in caverns in Mexico, beneath the polluted capital, back when the land was fertile and managed by the war-like peoples of the various valleys. In his research, Davis had learned the surrounding tribes that the Aztecs had conquered all paid homage to a god of war and hate. How they battled it, Davis couldn't fathom.

But they'd won, and this spear had been used in that victory.

"You'll be coming with me," Davis whispered to the spear. "You'll feel the tides of war once more."

# Chapter Eight

The morning came far too early for Davis, who stretched in his bed when the sun fell upon his face, peeking through the curtains. Fighting the lethargy in his limbs, he rolled out of bed and walked over to his coffee maker perched atop a long dresser. Filling it with dark roast before setting it up to percolate, Davis blinked back some crust from his eyes. The smell of coffee was already enough to make him more alert, allowing him to look around his room for anything else he might want to take with him.

His room was ornately decorated: a king-sized four-poster bed with emerald trimmings over black wood; he had a mountain of pillows he slept with, usually building a little nest with them before dozing off to sleep. His medication had ensured a vision-free night, for which he was thankful. He had three comforters as he got cold very easily, and was often wrapped up in them even during the height of summer.

The walls were lined with various firearms, a large armoire sitting next to the bed holding the ammunition for each rifle and pistol he owned. Clips and boxes of bullets were stored in the cool environment so they would not go to waste. It took him quite a while to find a man willing to make solid metal slugs for his Sharps Buffalo Rifle, its heavy depleted uranium rounds capable of dropping a charging an elephant from a hundred yards, from further away if he used his scope. The fact that it was bolt action made Davis always pack a second, smaller firearm, as well as a few pistols.

He kept the bullets for his forty-five Magnum in a box with a talisman from an African tribe, the strange wooden amulet said to bring great pain to evil entities. The copper slugs, each bearing a cross shaped incision on the tip to make the bullet explode within the body for more damage, were doused in this magic before being drizzled with holy water.

Waiting for his coffee, Davis opened the armoire and began loading copper slugs into empty magazines, his arthritic hands moving quickly as he slid each blessed bullet into place.

Next he inspected the magazines for his light automatic weapon, an old Israeli model with an extended stock and loaded with .640 rounds. These were neither blessed nor cursed, merely on hand for Davis to use against people who tried to harm him. When set to semi-automatic, a burst of fire from the hollow point bullets ripped through anyone in his way. He rarely had problems with cultists once he opened fire with this gun.

The last time he'd used it had been in Paris, when a coven of demonologists with a sizable cult was attempting to summon a greater demon of Shalim, an old god dedicated to hunger and relentless violence. They were partially through the ritual when Davis and his team had found them in the catacombs, an easy feat as they were chanting in Latin. Two skilled priests took on the demonologists, who used every trick they could to slay the "interlopers", while the cultists had brandished knives and clubs.

The shrill cry of Davis's Uzi had torn through five of them before they knew what was happening, leaving five rapidly cooling corpses in bloody pools and some twenty-odd cultists being shot at by the Ravens, a paramilitary organization within the Catholic Church that tried to curb paranormal activity within Europe. They all wore masks, leather armor and white or black robes, while preferring crossbows and blades over guns.

It made sense as they were rarely called to deal with meager cultists, but actual demonic threats that were unleashed in each area. Blessed weapons were the only thing that left lasting damage and, even then, the demon would regenerate from even the most grievous of wounds given time and darkness to dwell in. The Ravens had been hunting demons and occult dangers for nearly fifteen centuries; they knew what they were doing.

Coming to from his memories of that night, Davis smiled as he grabbed the box of bullets for his rifle, fifty caliber rounds that were heavier than your average round. Each one was depleted uranium, allowing for the already powerful gun to pack a punch capable of sending a greater demon to its knees. Davis was good enough with the weapon that he could fire off ten bullets a minute, taking targets as far away as a thousand feet. He'd used it more times than he could count, the weapon proving as resilient as Davis himself. Grabbing a spare satchel, he loaded in two boxes of bullets, six magazines for his pistol and six extended magazines for his Uzi, before slipping the automatic weapon and pistol into the leather bag.

Setting the satchel down on his bed, he breathed a sigh of relief. Between his firearms and the spear, he felt more at ease about going to this dangerous locale. Shedding his robes, he walked over to his drawers and pulled out a pair of jeans and a long-sleeved shirt and vest from his closet. Once dressed, he poured himself a cup of coffee, patting the Inca spear where he'd left it for the night, and walked over to the double doors leading out to the balcony, the highest one in the manor. Smiling at the breeze, he sniffed the air, taking in the scents of flowers, fresh air—and rotting flesh?

Opening his eyes, he looked around down below to see where the scent of rot could be coming from. Walking by his front gate were your standard Austin residents going about their day, while below his flower beds bloomed despite the gradual weather change to a colder season. Confused, he sniffed again and looked out over his garden and across the street.

A homeless man in a yellow rain slicker, face unshaven and eyes shrouded by a ball cap, stood motionless on the far sidewalk. He wore threadbare jeans and a tattered shirt. When Davis looked at him, his stomach turned as though he'd smelled sour milk. The man wasn't moving and, in fact, looked like he was staring up at Davis.

How long had this man been waiting for Davis to walk out onto his balcony? And how did he know this was going to happen?

"Who are you?" Davis muttered, sipping his coffee. He stared at the man for several moments, daring him to move.

He didn't budge an inch, even when someone bumped into him. They apologized and he said some words, which apparently were frightening enough as the young man that bumped him ran off without so much as a glance back. The dirty man was mumbling something, though at this distance even Davis's improved eyesight couldn't make out what he was saying.

Slowly, one arm rose and pointed towards the rising sun. People walking around him looked at him oddly, but he didn't seem to care, or notice, that they were there. He pointed east for several moments before simply vanishing when a passing truck obscured Davis's view of him. Davis hummed into his coffee, turning to go back into his room.

Coffee mug slapped from his hands, the yellow slicker squeaked as the bum stepped forward, fists clenched as smoke rolled off his body, his brief jump through the ether leaving him standing on the balcony with Davis. The man was breathing ragged breaths, his eyes violet with the same haunting glimmer as the creatures he'd seen in his vision. He smelled horrible, like week old fish left out on a hot summer day, and looked even worse up close. Beneath his skin muscles seemed to slither about, creating lumps and bumps that stretched the sweaty skin about. One of his eyes seemed to inflate, leaking yellow ooze out from behind it as one of the muscles passed under it.

"You… are the one… Chosen by Fa'theli?" The bum asked in a choked voice, as if the very action caused it pain.

Davis's eyes widened at that and he quickly decided his next action. Kicking out into the creature's knee, he crowed in victory when the knee bent and split within the jeans, yellow fat draining out of the torn holes and spattering the smooth marble balcony. Racing around the bum as he fell to the ground, Davis could grab the haft of the spear just as his leg was snagged by something with a terrible grip.

Looking down, his Davis panicked. The yellow slicker had paled considerably, taking on the appearance of a bat wing save for the part that stretched out to grab his ankle in a vice grip. The hood had slipped over the ball cap of its own accord and melted over the face, leaving a toothless hole and two boneless arms, fingers rapidly elongating and twisting together to form fleshy tentacles. It dragged Davis closer, to where it could loom over him. Sickening drool dribbled from the gaping maw, dozens of tongues growing along the inner walls of the tunnel leading deep into the beast.

"Nowhere... to hide... chosen... the gate must... be opened... cannot allow you to... stop..." the creature said in a wet, sucking voice. "Six must... blessed they be... will defeat—"

Davis chose not to let the monster continue, instead swinging the spear up and into the monster's left bicep, severing the arm, which fell to the ground below and began to dissolve into a pool of congealed fat and grease. The beast seemed shocked, so Davis pulled back the spear and swung again, aiming for the meaty lump that served as a head.

He sunk the sharpened obsidian halfway into the creature, cutting into the mouth hole with a savage thrust. Grappling with the pole, the creature howled in agony as fat dribbled from the wound in runny rivers, the spearhead obviously growing hotter by the second. It brought up its remaining arm and used the two tentacles to grasp the exposed haft, ignoring the sizzling noise that erupted when it laid its tentacles on the polished wood. The tongues waggled obscenely from within the mouth, beckoning him to come into the horrid tunnel.

Davis sawed the blade back and forth in the creature's head, causing the wailing to intensify and a foul odor of burning fat to fill the air. The tentacles released the haft, black burns on their pale flesh showing the muscles moving beneath the thin membrane of translucent skin slowly knitting and stretching over the exposed tissue.

The membrane of skin twisted, stabbing down into his shoulder with the force of a charging bear, and Davis screamed in pain. He didn't hear any cracks and thanked the gods for that, and yanked the blade clear of the head before slapping it away from the body to prevent reattachment. The creature howled in agony, smoldering skin smoking from the top of where its head once was.

Bringing the spear down in a slashing arc, Davis tore through the tenuous envelope of skin, severing tendons and slithering muscles while cauterizing the wound with the fiery edges of the spear, which was now glowing a hazy red from prolonged contact with the creature. The "cloak" of flesh was now cut diagonally, both sides twisting and writhing as they slowly morphed into new, potentially useful shapes.

Davis backed up and regained his footing before hacking into the creature's wounded left shoulder, twisting the spear at the right moment to cut out a chunk of flesh, drawing it out like one would scoop out a ball of ice cream from a tub. The wounds weren't closing or changing, and the creature obviously didn't have many defenses to speak of other than preternatural strength and regenerative qualities that made it nigh impossible to kill otherwise.

Standing on two thick legs, the creature was now missing the top of its head and an entire arm, as well as a good section of membrane hanging from its shoulder like a rack of rancid ham. It stepped forward, a slushing sound filling its mouth. Davis ducked as the creature spewed a nasty mix of molten fat and bile over him, staining his carpet. The smell was horrible and it was all he could do not to vomit on the spot. Instead he rushed forward and slashed the knee he'd kicked earlier, sending the creature toppling to its side in a dramatic flailing of alien limbs. Davis stood over it and stabbed it repeatedly in the abdomen, searching for a heart of sorts, leaving ragged holes of burnt tissue and bubbling fat dribbling down its chest and sides. The cloak slithered out from underneath it, having formed a thick, knotty tendril that cracked like a whip.

Surging down at Davis, he blocked with the shaft of the spear, bringing another scream from the frothing hole as the tendril left behind a sticky, burning layer of flesh on the haft. Jabbing at the base of the tendril, Davis met with success as he severed it, watching it fall over the edge of his balcony and into his garden. He paid it no mind, knowing Lawrence would clean up the mess, instead choosing to deal the deathblow to the monster by tearing out its chest.

"You… cannot kill… me chosen… of…" the creature moaned before the spear was rammed into the mouth, stifling a horrid screech as the spear sluiced through the spongy tissue like a scalpel through raw chicken. Severed chunks of tongue rained down as the monster thrashed about wildly.

The creature shuddered, falling silent and still, the severed piece of chest dissolving into a greasy pool while the body began to bubble and melt like an ice cube tossed in hot chocolate. Thinking quickly, Davis grabbed his coffee mug and scooped some of the flesh into it for Lawrence to examine. The boy was a miracle worker when it came to discovering secrets best left unknown.

Rubbing at his injured shoulder, he popped it back into place with a grunt. Then, looking over the edge of the railing, he frowned at what he saw. The tendril and arm were spreading into a thin fleshy sheet over the grass of his yard, just like it'd done in the Chinese village. Walking back into his room, he picked up the service phone.

"Yes sir?" Lawrence answered after a single ring, sounding bored as always.

"I just got attacked by a servant of an old god," Davis panted, leaning on the spear. "It's dead and melting. I have a sample for you, but I need you to go burn some in the front yard. Some limbs fell and it's now trying to contaminate the entire garden. Please see to that."

"Yes sir," Lawrence deadpanned before disconnecting the call.

Davis looked over at the melting mound of skin and muscle, fat popping out in dribbling bubbles from between skin sloughing off. How had the creature known he was chosen? There wasn't a person alive that knew that. And it told Davis that he couldn't kill the entity that was presumably sending these monsters abroad. If they could travel so easily and knew of him, then they were already expecting him, just as he thought.

"This doesn't bode well," Davis muttered to the room, a sudden knock catching his attention. "Enter!"

James, dressed in jeans and a sleeveless T-shirt that revealed a tribal tattoo on his right arm, walked in. "Were you yelling up here? I heard you from my room."

Davis sighed. "The disadvantages of having a large home," he said, waving in the general direction of the melting monster. "I need more coffee before I can deal with this nonsense."

"What the hell is that?" James cried, walking closer to the puddle, sliding a little on the carpet where the grease had soaked in.

Setting up the filter with coffee grounds, Davis replied: "I assume we're facing the Father of Flesh's minions. For creatures that have an aversion to light, this one didn't seem terribly bothered by it. Though it originally looked like a homeless man, maybe the camouflage helps protect it somehow?"

"God, it stinks!" James said, stepping out onto the balcony. "How did you kill it?"

Setting a new mug beneath the coffee pot's dripper, he hefted up the spear. "Tried and tested to be useful against evil entities. I have two more, and we're bringing them."

"Okay," James said, excited. He looked over the railing for a moment before shouting out. "Dude! Lawrence is burning the front yard!"

"I told him to," Davis yawned. "Couldn't be helped."

"Couldn't be helped? What, you have weeds that you just can't get rid of?" James asked, backing off the balcony as black smoke rose from the grounds.

"In a sense. A limb I severed from the creature fell there and began to contaminate my yard. Knowing what it does, I asked Lawrence to deal with it," Davis calmly explained.

"Oh," James deflated a little. "So… Lawrence was going to show me some weapons today… do you think he'll do that after torching the yard?"

"How Lawrence's mind works is a mystery, but I would hope so," Davis said, bouncing on the balls of his feet. The coffee was brewing far too slowly.

"Wait, how did the creature get up here?" James asked, looking out at the balcony. "Did it climb?"

"No," Davis said while pouring himself a cup of coffee. "Like many creatures of the dark side, I believe some of the entities created by the Father of Flesh can access the ether, allowing for teleportation. I pray this is only effective over short distances, or the blockade around the village is pointless."

"I think it's proven pretty useless as one showed up *in the United States!*" James exclaimed, looking down as the body popped a final bubble, becoming a gelatinous mess. "Huh, no bones."

"I surmised that, yes. When they call him the Father of Flesh, they aren't just exaggerating. He, and probably all his minions, are composed of fat, muscles, tendons, and skin. I've seen some hair growths and claws, so they can apparently use things like fingernails to generate harder material."

"When did you see this?" James asked.

Davis took a quick sip of his coffee, mind racing as he didn't want to reveal his visions to James. "In the *Grimlocke Chronicles*," he lied.

James nodded, excusing himself to go and finish dressing for the day. Davis just stood there in his tousled outfit, sipping his coffee.

"Today," he said, looking down at the greasy residue sinking into his carpet, "is going to be long, I can already tell."

# Chapter Nine

Wincing as Lawrence wrapped padded gauze around his shoulder and chest, Davis sipped his cooling coffee as James listed off the demands that Shen had e-mailed to them, stating that supplies would be given when they arrived. Davis was barely paying attention, though he was listening for Shen's casual remarks about which artifacts they could keep and who got first choice of treasure.

"He said we can have twenty-five percent of any items recovered after they've sorted through them! That's insane!" James argued, holding his tablet in front of him. "We're the ones who are flying across the globe to solve their problems! We should be paid better than that!

"And we will," Davis growled, Lawrence's ministrations causing the soreness in his shoulder to spike for a moment. "Send him a reply that we'll do it for forty percent, with first choice of find in exchange for six of trained soldiers to work with us. Otherwise we'll tell him to kindly find another paranormal expert willing to risk their lives."

"You want I should type that out word for word?" James grinned.

"Make it sound more disinterested, mention I have classes to teach and gathering a crew this quickly is a strain on my old heart," Davis smiled, patting Lawrence's hand as he slipped in a pin to hold the gauze in place. "Thank you."

"It was no problem, sir. I often wonder how you handle yourself without me when in the field," Lawrence said. He stood, his jeans stained gray from his time using copious amounts of apple vinegar to clean up the fatty tissue left behind by the monstrous creature. "Shall I activate the Siren Stone, sir? Keep in mind it only has a few charges left in it before we will need to power it back up."

The Siren Stone had been something found in the Ubaid ruins after Joshua had been sacrificed. With their master fed and asleep once more, the creatures of the crypt had been fine with him wandering the corridors and halls, paying him no heed, even when he used a scalpel to take samples of the gelatinous creatures.

It'd been in a room filled with skeletons, all with holes in the backs of their skulls as if someone had taken a large spike and hammered it into the cranium in one fell swoop. They numbered in the hundred, and each bore a symbol carved into the bone of the slumbering god deep beneath the ruins. After experimenting with the stone (poking it with a silver rod, taking thermal images of it, checking for radiation) he'd taken it, a foot in height and slightly phallic, and stashed it in his satchel. He'd forgotten about it until he'd researched the Ubaid writings he'd taken photographs of while down in the unexplored regions of the complex.

The Siren Stone had been made with the express purpose of preventing minions of old gods from entering an area, sealing all entrances and exits in a flash of golden light. This kept out true diabolists and demonologists as well as the dark creatures they cavorted with, something that had brought a smile to Davis's face. It was a tad ironic finding it where in the ruins of an old god's lair, but it was a potent item.

The only drawback was that, like many artifacts, it was powered by souls. When he found it, and handled it for a time, he could sense six beings, lost and confused, within the stone. Lawrence had studied it intensely and had determined the ritual needed to transfer a soul into it through experimentation with apes.

They'd paid a good deal of money for test apes during that trial period, as well as for an industrial wood chipper for "leftovers."

The garden looked amazing thanks to the mulch though, so Davis hadn't voiced any complaint.

"Perhaps that would be a good idea," Davis said slowly, standing up from his perch on the edge of the bed. He walked over to a coat rack that held numerous necklaces, some ending in large colorful gemstones, others in small wicker figurines of men. Fingers dancing over the numerous trinkets, he made a triumphant noise as he snatched up a golden chain. Its pendant was a symbol fashioned out of gold with several emeralds set into the strange icon. He slipped it over his head and sighed in content, running a thumb over the surface of the pendant as he motioned for Lawrence to select a new shirt for him to wear.

While Lawrence rooted through the closet, Davis croaked out orders. "James, send the new demands to Shen, don't forget his title, and then call Dean Reynolds and say I'm going to borrow you for three months."

"Three months?" James squawked.

"What, you think we're going to find all the relics in one neat pile after dealing with the monster guarding them?" Davis sneered, shaking his head. "Yes, three months. Tell him you'll get a relic of your choice and that you'll chose one for his collection in payment for me borrowing you."

"That's… fair, I guess." James said, tapping a few points on his tablet. "What should we do about armor? That one that attacked you seemed to just bludgeon, so Kevlar will be useless."

"Include a request for padded Kevlar armor as well as equipment and men to go underwater for an extended period. All of them must speak English, as I assume you don't speak Cantonese."

"I know English and Italian," James smiled.

"You should learn, China is only growing as a world power," Davis commented before focusing on Lawrence. "I'll need you to go and gather Ms. Xi's information and talk to her professors. Just use the standard forms. Also, tell the dean that he'll get twenty-five percent of whatever I find for the university's collection or auction. Give Ms. Xi this address and tell her to come equipped for a two-week excursion."

"That'll leave just fifteen percent of the findings though," James said, doing the math in his head. "If the Chinese accept, they'll get sixty percent! How can you accept, let alone suggest, that lousy of a pay-off?"

"Because dear boy, I don't do this for the money! I have tenure at the University of Texas here in Austin and a dozen other schools clamoring for me. I'm paid well and have substantial savings that've been earned through wise investments and earlier expeditions. Money is hardly going to keep you warm at night, but the knowledge that you may have saved the world will help you sleep a little better at night."

James stared at Davis before shaking his head. "I assume your student will be getting a relic as well?"

"Of course! I told you that all graduate students who come along with me on my hunts are granted a piece. You'll get to skip out on the research I will require of Ms. Xi, seeing as you wish to spend your career in Boston."

"Well that's where the greatest collection of paranormal objects in the world is, and I'm studying the paranormal! That's the place to be!" James argued.

"That's neither here nor there," Davis waved it aside. "Now send the e-mails while I prepare. How good are you with a firearm?"

"A gun? I don't know, I used to go hunting with my uncle when I was a kid," James said with uncertainty.

"So a Winchester .243 for you and whatever you and Lawrence have picked out for close quarters," Davis said, walking to his armoire. "I think I have some rounds that are silver…"

"Will that be helpful?" James asked.

Davis shrugged. "Silver harms certain anomalous creatures. This rifle should let you shoot things in a precise method, blowing off eyes or severing thin limbs."

"You don't have anything with more power?"

"Not that I'd trust with you," Davis said, looking at James with a firm glare. "You just said you don't know how to use a gun, so I'm giving you something basic. We'll shoot any outlying creatures before moving in. Hopefully we can get the Chinese military to lend us some flamethrowers."

"Flamethrowers?" Lawrence asked, looking back from the closet. "I'll be sure to send a request…"

"The fleshy growths on the ground spread, forming eyes and small limbs," Davis explained, recalling his vision. "You saw what just the severed arm did to the yard, Lawrence! We'll need some serious firepower to burn away the nastiness infesting that village."

"I'm sure the Chinese can provide flamethrowers," James muttered, rubbing his chin. His frost colored hair looked wispier than before, and reflected the light in strange ways that Davis found fascinating.

"I'm going to be bringing the spear over there," Davis nodded to his Aztec polearm, "and three guns. I'll also pack some trench knives and an assortment of tools that can be used for climbing, picking locks, or marking paths in a maze."

"Being a little paranoid?" James asked, turning to leave the room.

Accepting the shirt and vest from Lawrence, he turned and frowned at James. "You can *never* be too prepared."

James held his hands up in surrender and walked out of the room. Lawrence helped Davis get dressed, not that he needed it, and then used a lint roller over the professor's clothes.

"Sir," he said as he cleaned a smudge of grease from Davis's pant leg, "James… is he a diabolist?"

"Not that I know of. He just looked at something that puts my collection to shame and didn't have a stout enough heart to handle it," Davis smirked.

"I know his current condition is because of his exposure to the *Chronicles*; you've told me of others who've actually died from reading the book," Lawrence continued. "My question was whether you trust the young man?"

"I barely trust you Lawrence, and that's just because I've known you for so long," Davis chuckled, patting Lawrence on the shoulder. Lawrence stood back up and looked down at the professor, chewing on his lip.

"I don't like this, grandpa," Lawrence said, emotion creeping into his voice. "I don't like this at all…"

"What have I told you about calling me that, boy!" Davis hissed, snatching the lint roller to run up and down his arms. "If anyone found out we were related you'd be fired in an instant!"

"I know… it's just I worry about you. You're getting older, and now that I've been around all those horrid items, I've begun to… hear things," Lawrence said, eyes darting to the doorway.

"Whispers, you mean? From just over your shoulder or inside your head?" Davis snapped to attention instantly.

"Like they're just behind me…" Lawrence admitted, his light blue eyes showing his fear and confusion.

"Don't worry, that's the Nickel bloodline at work. We come from a long line of practitioners, so it's only natural that you sense things every so often. The key is that you don't try and communicate with them. I have enough cursed junk in this building to fill an asylum with ghosts and spirits. I don't want a haunting!"

"Yes sir," Lawrence said, finally regaining his cool demeanor. "Now will you be needing anything else from me, or shall I take my leave to handle your courses while you prepare?"

"Go," Davis said, straightening his cufflinks. "And be safe."

Lawrence paused by the door for a moment before nodding slowly. "You too…"

* * *

The rest of the afternoon was spent with Davis combing through his museum for pieces of weaponry that would prove fruitful should James be forced into close quarters. He'd found the boy staring at a violin and bow stored upright in a glass case. They'd gone and looked over what he had that would prove useful. The mace that had been suggested proved to be too heavy, and several other choices required years of practice to master. When James found an old scimitar beneath a dusty case Davis had nearly dropped the crossbow he was holding with joy.

"That," he'd said as he'd walked over to open the case, "is a Persian blade from the eighth century. Not only was it forged by a renowned blacksmith, it was cursed by him as well!"

"Cursed?" James had repeated.

"Yes, oh my yes. You see, the blacksmith tempered it with the blood of his wife and three daughters, and tested it on his son once it was complete. The price for making the blade was to be killed by it, as he knew he would never make anything as good again."

"So I should leave it?" James had asked.

"No," Davis had insisted, having reached into the case and grabbed the brass handle, engraved with prayers to Allah, before having handed it over to James. "The anomalous properties of the sword are well documented. The weapon cannot be knocked from your hand unless you fall unconscious or wish to let go, and the weapon never goes dull. It's sharp enough to slice through fourteen inches of reinforced steel plating with minimal strength and grows stronger when it is causing anguish."

"Can these… things feel anguish?" James had asked.

Davis had considered this for a moment before commenting. "I would say yes; my spear caused the creature upstairs great pain. That would qualify as anguish, I assume. The sword also, just so you will remember this, glows softly when magic is around."

"So you think we'll encounter a diabolist there? Or a demonologist?" James had asked, curious.

"It's a possibility. These creatures can, and I imagine will, revert into a human form to perform tasks that their monstrous bodies just cannot do. The one that attacked me was originally an old man in a yellow slicker."

"Huh," James had said while examining the scimitar's thin blade.

Now, at half past two, they were staring at the Siren Stone, both with frowns. James was looking at it as if it were about to bite him, while Davis was listening to the whispers in his mind, the voices pleading to be set free. He could picture the people, all women, and their final moments of life before being stored in this horrid receptacle. They were in constant torment as they felt the pull of the afterlife but were anchored within a foot-tall stone on a raised dais behind bulletproof glass.

"Lift the glass, if you would," Davis commanded James, who didn't argue for once. He merely stepped forward and lifted the glass case, before setting it gently on the floor.

"How do you activate it?" James asked, staring at the stone in wonder.

"Can you hear them?" Davis whispered suddenly.

James looked over at Davis whose eyes were locked onto a central rune on the stone, which was a dull blue from paint long since faded.

James shook his head before clearing his throat. “Um, no? I mean, I feel *something* about the stone isn’t right, maybe even dangerous, but no voices or anything. Why, do you?”

Davis shook his head, looking down at the ground. “Just murmurs. I’m more in tune with the ether than you are, apparently.”

“I would hope so after all you’ve been through!” James laughed, easing the tension in the room. “So how do we turn it on?”

“From what I could tell from numerous brown stains and a hole on the top, blood sacrifice to turn it on, blood sacrifice to turn it off,” Davis said, pulling a bowie knife from his belt. “You want to cut your finger or should I do it? Because if I do it you have to lift me up to bleed over it.”

“Just give me the knife you damn runt,” James smiled, snatching the blade from Davis’s gnarled grasp. “So a cut across the thumb?”

“Make sure three drops fall into the small funnel on top. You should be able to see it if you step close to it.”

James glared at Davis once more before walking up to be flush with the dais, looking down at the top of the stone. Sure enough, a funnel leading to a dark hole was atop the Siren Stone. He looked back at Davis, a frown on his face. “Now I hear voices…”

“In your head or outside it?” Davis immediately asked.

“Just over my shoulder, it feels like someone’s blowing on the back of my neck… and I’m getting a headache in the top of my head!” James said before slicing his thumb with the knife, cutting a little deep and dribbling blood messily over the funnel, offering more than the requisite three drops. A wail of a young woman dying ripped out from the stone, rattling the glass in the windows and display cases before all fell silent again. James popped his thumb in his mouth and handed the blade back to Davis, who carefully sheathed it.

“Did the shout mean that it’s active?” James asked, waving his hand about. “Damn, that was a sharp knife!”

“I sharpen all my knives,” Davis said, clearly distracted. He looked back at James. “And yes, it does that every time.”

“I can see why you didn’t want to activate it!” James exclaimed.

“What makes you think I didn’t want to activate it?” Davis asked, looking at James with a stern eye.

"You hesitated when Lawrence mentioned it earlier, like you didn't really like the idea. It's cool, I can see why. Everything seems kind of muted now. I definitely don't feel anyone behind me anymore."

Davis just nodded, the screams of the remaining women rising in tenor as the stone churned out the magical field. His talisman was growing warm beneath his shirt, almost making him want to grab it and let it heat his clammy hands. Instead he looked at the glass case on the floor and nodded to it.

"Put that back over it please," Davis whispered, his bullfrog voice croaking out the request.

James nodded, obviously having forgotten about the glass. He squatted down to pick it up, grunting at the weight, while Davis merely stuck his hands in his pockets, wiping the sweat from his palms on the cloth within. He thought for a moment about his pills, and shook his head slowly. That would raise questions from James…

"Better wait on that…" Davis murmured.

"You say something, professor?" James asked as he angled the glass case over the stone, trying to line up the grooves of the dais with the edges of the glass.

Davis cleared his throat and shook his head. "Just some thoughts, nothing important. Now hurry up, I have but a few hours to teach you how to use that sword and we can't waste them in here!"

# CHAPTER TEN

The clock struck five when a powder blue Mini Coupe pulled past the main gate into Blackmore Manor, parking behind Davis's Jeep, quickly getting blocked in by Lawrence's blue Cadillac. Davis watched from his bedroom's balcony as Huan got out of her car, dressed in shorts and a tank top, revealing a floral tattoo on her right shoulder in dark ink. Scowling at the vain markings, Davis fiddled with his talisman as he watched James walk out to Huan, running a hand through his white hair to tuck it behind his ear as he stretched out a hand to greet her. His sleeveless shirt showed off his lean arms and ribs, his tribal tattoos stark against the pure white skin of his arms.

Lawrence was getting out of his vehicle, a book bag slung over his shoulder that looked fit to burst at the seams any moment. He motioned for everyone to enter the manor, and they happily moved into the foyer, closing the great doors behind them with a dull clang. Davis popped one of his pills into his mouth, savoring the bitter taste as he swallowed the horrid thing. Sometimes he couldn't stand the taste of his medication, other times he reveled in it.

Today had been a strenuous day of sword training with James, who showed marginal skill at handling the Persian blade, at least enough to handle any hostile entities that would come to close to him. They'd set the scabbard onto a belt with pouches for several surveyor's tools for the young man to carry, along with a sling to hold his rifle off his back. He had a large pouch for his silver bullets, and Davis had gone through the time to instruct him on how to safely clean and dismantle his gun before reassembling it.

Now that the boy could defend himself somewhat, they'd have to explain the situation to Huan. Davis had sent a text informing Lawrence to share the basics of the expedition to Huan, to make sure she was still all right with the idea of traversing the rural grounds of China to do battle with servants of an old god. He'd texted back that she was okay with the idea. Davis left his room and made his way to the stairs to the second floor. He could already hear the muffled chatter of the young girl and James, both clearly excited about… something.

Rounding the corner to face the landing above the first floor, he peered over the bannister at Huan and James, who were staring at a suit of samurai armor kept behind a display case, the Oni mask within leering back at them.

"Careful with that," he called out, catching their attention. "That suit is cursed to stir blood lust in whoever wears it."

"Really?" Huan asked, far more excited than she should have been. He'd expected the standard skeptical behavior from Huan that he got from his other graduate students, but she was a breath of fresh air. "So you keep it locked up to prevent people from wearing it?"

Davis nodded as he descended the stairs. "The anomalous properties of the armor were first documented in the fourteenth century, when its last three wearers went on killing sprees unlike any other samurai before them. A group of priests exorcised the armor, but found that a foul spirit was bound to it. They could contain it long enough to have the wearer disrobe until he was safe. After that it was stored away until the Second World War, when American soldiers found it in Okinawa. I purchased it for a modest sum when I learned of its paranormal properties and have kept it under lock and key ever since."

"So has Lawrence studied it?" James asked, looking over at the young man as he lowered his back pack to the ground, rubbing his lower back from the strain.

"I studied it for a brief time but found it wholly unnerving," Lawrence replied. "I ended my research once I discerned its properties and conducted no experiments with it, as that would involve human test subjects."

"Experiments?" Huan said, raising a hand to her mouth. She looked the picture of innocence with her blue-streaked hair pulled into pigtails, her eyes wide with fascination. "You experiment with the cursed objects?"

Lawrence heaved a sigh, obviously having explained himself to many before her. "It's so I can understand the limits of the curses or magical properties of the item. I use lab animals, never humans, I assure you."

A lie, Davis knew. Two winters before he'd invited several homeless people into the manor and allowed them to handle, one at a time, a golden scarab that was said to judge a man's worth by weighing his heart on a scale against two feathers. All the homeless people had died and the trees had been fed a fresh batch of mulch. Davis knew that if the police ever came and explored his backyard, he would be in trouble.

Thus, why he routinely had dirt and new patches of grass laid out over the area, allowing the bone chips to sink deeper into the soil. His closest neighbor was over five acres away through thick woods, and he didn't have anything to worry about when it came to noise pollution, so using the wood chipper in the dead of night was a simple matter that Lawrence had quickly grown used to.

Snapping back to reality, he held his hands out wide and smiled. "I'm glad you could make it to my quaint abode, Huan."

Looking up, she beamed at him. "Thank you for having me, professor! I can't believe you got me out of my other classes so easily!"

"Everyone on the faculty knows me and my need for students when going out into the wilds of the world," Davis said. "They've become accustomed to me hijacking their more promising students for my own nefarious needs."

Huan tittered, looking over at James, who merely shrugged before sticking out a hand. "I'm James Walker, from the Boston University."

"Really?" she asked, sounding fascinated.

"Yeah, I'm on loan for this expedition," James said with a wan smile. "Has... has the professor told you what we'll be doing?"

"Mr. Wilks told me that we would be exploring some underwater regions for ruins of an ancient Chinese site of religious importance. He said that I was selected because of my fluency in the local dialects and my skills as an archaeologist."

"How are you with a gun?" James asked, before Davis could ask her anything.

"A gun? Well my father was Army, so he taught me how to use a pistol when I was young. I still go target shooting occasionally," she replied with an uncertain voice. "Why does that matter?"

"Because this unknown site is guarded by some nasty critters that might—no, *will*—need to be put down," James said, stuffing his hands into his pockets. "One attacked the professor this morning. We'll be outfitting you with some gear so you'll be armed in case we need to fight."

"I-I didn't know we were going into hostile territory…" Huan said, looking between James and Davis.

Davis smiled. "Liability agreement, remember? I'm your academic advisor now, so you're kind of onboard. I'll pack a Desert Eagle for you with some extra clips. I have heavier lead loads with extra gunpowder packed in each round, so they should pack a punch."

"Who are we going to have to look out for? Bandits? Grave robbers?" Huan asked.

Lawrence snorted and knelt to where he'd deposited the backpack.

"Show her the images, Lawrence," Davis said, growing irritated by having to repeat this information.

Over the next five minutes Huan paged through drone camera images of the creatures in the Chinese village and the spread of fleshy matter over the area. She saw the well with its eight eyes and the homes and trees covered in the material, forming a village of living, bloodless tissue. Her questions were limited as she seemed to accept the premise that there were hellish monsters rather quickly. This made Davis wonder.

"Huan," he said, gathering her attention, "have you ever heard of anything like this before?"

"When I was a child, yes. My grandmother was from China, in a remote village far from the more heavily populated provinces. She said that monsters would emerge from wells and steal newly born children from their mothers, infecting any who dared cross their path with a sickness that made them turn into monsters as well. She said her village was attacked twice, and those that were infected were dumped into the well, kicking and screaming."

"This didn't pollute the water?" James asked.

She shook her head. "The well was over an underground river," she said. "The currents carried the men and women away. That was how I lost my uncle."

"He was infected?" Davis asked, suddenly interested.

"Yes, he was slashed by one of the monster's tentacles, which injected poison into him," she said, looking between the three men. "I never gave the stories much thought. I mean, we have vampires and ghosts and whatnot, right? But seeing these images, I know my grandmother wasn't just telling old stories to scare unruly children. She was warning us of dangers in the world that we had no protection from."

"Well I have items that offer a measure of protection," Davis said. "Do know how to fight?"

"I studied gymnastics and Tae Kwon Do for eight years. I'm a black belt," she said proudly.

James whistled and took a minute step back.

"Okay, so you know how to use a spear?" Davis asked, a gleam coming to his eye.

She shrugged. "If it's balanced I can learn in a few hours."

"Follow Lawrence and he'll show you two spears. Choose one and then go into the backyard and practice on some trees. Don't worry, you won't break the relic; they're made for battle."

"If you say so," she said, following Lawrence who headed to the west dining hall silently.

Once she was out of the room, James whistled. Davis raised an eyebrow at him only to earn a sniggering laugh from the boy.

"That girl is devoted to you, professor," he said, slapping his knee. "I think she might actually be in love with you!"

"Nonsense," Davis said.

"Nonsense? You just showed her evidence of a more dangerous Bigfoot and she took your word it was real. You said we'll have to fight and she just nodded. You said to go train with a fucking spear in the backyard and she just nodded. The girl idolizes you!"

Davis pondered the statement for a moment before shaking his head. "Irrelevant, so long as she can follow orders she'll be suitable for the group."

"Yeah, she'll follow orders all right," James muttered before turning to once again fiddle with the scabbard attached to his belt. "I swear I have this thing on wrong!"

"For the last time, you don't!" Davis exclaimed, exasperated.

* * *

Dinner was served at seven, just as it had been the night before. This time it was a potato soup with roast beef and onions.

Huan and James had spent the afternoon practicing with their respective weapons. Huan was well on her way to becoming a serious threat with the spear, while James could wield the blade in a stiff manner that left several openings for any trained swordsmen to take advantage of.

But the monsters were hardly strategists, despite their ability to think, as the speech from the one earlier in the day had proven. Whether they all shared this intelligence or it was relegated to certain members of a caste or breed, Davis couldn't tell. He didn't have enough knowledge, which infuriated him.

He hated going into a situation ill-informed.

Huan was now wearing a large black shirt that billowed around her, while James had changed into a sleeved red shirt, both having showered after their work-outs. They seemed amiable with each other, which pleased Davis, as surly teammates often led to fatal results. Davis cut into his slice of roast beef while listening to the two debate the history behind the monsters and the region of China.

"The Nanling Mountains are notorious for the lack of maps, the villages of the district numbering in the hundreds! Of course, something could be in the region the Chinese government has overlooked," Huan said, motioning with her fork at James, who was rolling his eyes.

"The Chinese have had empires when the rest of the world was playing with dirt, they would know if there's something dangerous in the region. They're calling us in because they don't want to risk exposure with troop movement. The Russians are watching them like hawks, if a division of soldiers suddenly moved near one of the borders they'd be prepped to invade within hours."

"The border doesn't even run along Russia, dolt!" Huan shot back with a smile. "If anyone would have reason to be nervous it would be India. And they have the Himalayas protecting them from any kind of incursion."

"And yet I would wager troop movement towards India would raise suspicions as well! The Chinese don't want this cat out of the bag, and they're doing their best to keep it under wraps!"

"Why would they worry about people seeing this? There are satellites that have no doubt picked up the activity already!" Huan exclaimed.

"No," Davis interrupted. "The creatures are shrouding the area in darkness. They're vulnerable to light and fire, which is probably how I handled the one that attacked me today so readily."

"What was it like?" Huan asked, leaning forward.

"It was human in appearance, at least at first, but then it lost its coloring and become a hunched over blob of flesh with two arms ending in tentacles and two squat legs," Davis described, setting down his fork and knife. "It was greasy and would regenerate any wounds that weren't burned off it. When it took significant damage to the main torso it collapsed under its own weight before melting."

"Melting?" Huan repeated.

"Yes, the creature appears to be made entirely of sinew and muscle, with watery fat acting as blood. Once it loses control, it begins to break down and melt into a greasy mixture that Lawrence will be studying tonight."

Lawrence nodded his head from his seat, cutting through a piece of roast beef as if they weren't discussing anything of importance.

"So the creature can appear human?" Huan asked, sounding concerned.

"Yes, though I believe that it is uncomfortable in that state, as it was barely able to speak above a watery whisper," Davis agreed.

"And they can change shape? Do you think it's a defense mechanism for direct light?" Huan asked, spearing a piece of beef.

"That could be a possibility," Davis admitted, cross that he hadn't thought of that. "Most minions of old gods have a way to trick those around them, to better infiltrate societies."

"Old gods?" Huan asked, earning a groan from Lawrence and James.

"Now you'll get him started on his crazy theories," Lawrence grumbled.

"And he won't shut up about it until our ears fall off!" James moaned, stabbing his slab of roast a few times in anger.

Davis ignored them, knitting his fingers in front of him and leaning on the table. "Well, by old gods I mean the primordial beings that were on our world when it was new. They existed alongside amoebas, helped them evolve into fish and then amphibians, and created various races of creatures to serve under them."

"Why?" Huan asked.

"All entities need sustenance to survive," Davis said, bringing up a piece of meat to serve as an example. "The old gods all feast on life energy, what you and I call souls. They created complex life forms to worship them, venerate them and, eventually, die for them. When they did, their souls would go to the old god they swore an oath to, and it would grow in strength."

"So how many old gods are there?" Huan asked, elbows on the table, hands folded to rest her chin upon.

"Originally? Who knows! But now there are only a dozen or so left, with one very prominent one in the forefront, devouring souls of those he deems worthy enough, and allowing a lesser god to feast on the ones he rejects."

"Which god is that?" Huan asked, nose crinkled in thought.

"Yahweh, the Abrahamic God. He has three massive religions pledged to him and they swell him in power, bloating him to the extreme. The other half of the coin is his counterpart, the one deemed a fallen angel."

"You mean Lucifer?" Huan asked.

"That's not his real name. He was first worshipped by Assyrians and called Pazuzu," Davis said, popping the piece of beef into his mouth to chew for a few moments. "Whereas most old gods are content to let their followers grow and occasionally battle with each other, Pazuzu wants to slay all life as we know it, and claims the souls of those sacrificed to him. His followers are able to circumvent the cycle, and have led to numerous old gods dying out by taking their cults and sacrificing them in orgies of sin and blood."

"So Satan is an old god, as is Yahweh? And what proof do you have of this?" Huan asked, trying not to sound rude.

"Tablets from cultures we don't even have names for, witnessing the sacrifices going on while breaking them up. The cult leaders will tell you what you want to know if you squeeze them just right."

"You mean torture," Huan said, disbelief heavy in her voice.

Davis nodded. "Whatever it takes to learn the truth. Don't believe me? There's an organization within the Catholic Church, paramilitary in nature, called the Ravens. They battle against the old gods of Europe, and will often call upon others to aid them in keeping the ancients asleep."

"Why are they asleep?" Huan asked.

"Because they're full," Davis said, his bullfrog voice gravelly as he answered her question.

The rest of the meal was eaten in silence.

# CHAPTER ELEVEN

The following morning, they had three virtual tickets to Hong King from Austin, with several layovers. Huan and James were cheery, dressed in cargo shorts and T-shirts, whereas Davis had adopted his Kevlar flak jacket disguised as a safari jacket, covered in pockets. With a bulletproof helmet perched over his head (disguised as a safari hat), the three sat in the back seat of the Jeep as Lawrence drove them towards a private airstrip. It was roughly thirty minutes away, with the flight leaving at five in the morning.

Davis clutched at his talisman beneath his button up shirt for a moment, murmuring a prayer while fighting away the throbbing in his chest.

He glanced at his students, who were sitting side by side, Huan on the outside so she could watch the terrain pass them by, while James got to watch Huan. Even without using his tricks, he could tell the gaunt boy was smitten by the Asian beauty. If he were eighty years younger, Davis might have flirted with her, if only to pass the time.

Sadly, he didn't have the energy anymore to tease his young charges like he once did. Pulling out his cell phone, he checked the e-mail from Shen one last time, just to make sure that their weapons and gear would be handled with care. He'd e-mailed the so-called "Minister of Paranormal Events" the list of items they would need when they arrived, as well as what they were bringing with them. Nothing was too specific or extraordinary, just tools for digging, weapons against the creatures and scuba gear to go down into the well.

Why the well? Davis had studied the photos that Shen had sent over and over, trying to determine which area would be ground zero, or which creature was patient zero. The military had the entire village surrounded and were using incendiary weapons to keep the crawling flesh from spreading. It had covered the entire village in knotty growths and eyes, small arms sticking out and moving of their own accord to feed toothless mouths anything they could grab.

The only thing *not* contaminated were the stones of the well. That, combined with the knowledge that the infection could not spread through water meant that the original carrier of the contagion came from the well. It was the only entrance to the village that wasn't covered and it was the only structure that wasn't infected, the stones of the ancient well proving resilient against the slippery grip of the meat trying to stretch up and over it.

This had only been confirmed when Shen replied that villagers who escaped before nightfall stated that something came from the well and fought several people before retreating. They'd used oil and fire to drive it off, but not before it infected one of them. The victim had rested in his house for a few days, refusing to come out.

"Even nailed boards over the doorway into his home," Shen had reported, citing a transcript of the relocated villagers' testimony. "He was so sick he moaned loudly, we could hear it at night while we slept."

This had prompted Davis to bring an extra gun, one that was specifically designed to kill a man through sheer, overwhelming firepower. A sawed-off ten-gauge shotgun that he had used on occasion, it was his solution to anything paranormal that was bearing down on him. Anything within twenty feet of him shot by the small cannon would lose a limb. In a dig in Alaska, the camp had a grizzly bear run in from the woods to get at their food. The ten-gauge had blown the head off the creature's body from fifteen feet away, severing it at the neck and saving the Inuit who was serving as their guide.

Damn thing packed a punch, but the kickback was hellish for Davis due to his small frame. He usually had to ready himself to shoot it and not get thrown to the ground, wasting precious seconds lining up the shot just right. It had never disappointed him though.

If the first villager infected was still in the village, it would be the oldest one and the best source to take tissue samples from as any human elements would almost certainly be subsumed by the old god's corruption. A tissue sample could mean the difference between death via some unknown threat or victory over the creatures that the slumbering god created as a form of defense. The fact that they attacked diabolists, as Grimlocke wrote, meant that the sleeping god felt particularly threatened. The severing from the original god must have been painful to the Father of Flesh. Perhaps this one was on the verge of death, or at least as close to death as any of these things could get.

"Professor?" Huan said, interrupting his thoughts.

"Ahem, um, yes?" Davis cleared his throat.

"Why did you choose to take up the Minister's offer to aid China against this threat? The way you talk about him makes it seem like you don't get along," she said, causing James to look away from the window to listen to the answer.

"And how would you know that he I and don't get along?" Davis asked.

"You always hesitate when you speak about him, and never refer to him as a friend. He's always a colleague, or merely Shen," Huan said. "If you respected him you would call him minister, or speak of him fondly."

"Most perceptive of you Huan, if I were grading you right now I'd give you an A," Davis said, shifting in his seat. "Shen and I were once involved in a dig in the mountains of Tibet, about three thousand feet up in the Himalayan mountains. We'd gotten a hint that there was a temple built into the side of a mountain and after a year and a half of searching, we found it. We climbed the mountain and set up a base camp. The Sherpa guide with us wouldn't set a foot within the cave, citing the ground was holy and that any man who entered with ill intent would suffer a most horrible curse."

"So you and Shen entered?" James asked.

Davis nodded. "Shen had a brother, Xian, who led the way. He was the youngest of us and felt like he had something to prove, I guess. After passing under an archway carved to resemble a spider he began to act irrationally, screaming how the spiders were pouring from everyone's mouths and crawling towards him. He pulled his sidearm and, in a fit of desperation, fired a wild shot that struck the wall. I pulled my .45 and fired two shots into him, both in the chest. It knocked him back and he was dead before he hit the ground."

"Oh my God!" Huan said.

"Jesus…" James agreed.

"I know," Davis said, trying his best to sound like the event rattled him. "I relive it every now and then and wonder if we could have done anything different. If I could have shot his arm and made him drop his pistol, if I could have found a way to subdue him without killing him. But I can never think of a way."

"You were just trying to protect yourself, right?" Huan asked, her voice wavering as she pressed for details. "What was it like?"

"I was trying to protect the entire expedition. There were twelve of us in a narrow tunnel, if he shot off another round it would have been exceptionally dangerous, possibly lethal, to someone in the group."

"So," James said after a moment. "If one of us gets infected by this flesh thing, will you shoot us as well?"

Davis frowned. "We're going to be wearing hazmat gear, so the chances of infection will be low. But if you become a danger to the group, I would be forced to handle you the same way. I would expect the same from you if I became a threat. Do you understand?"

Huan looked amused while James's gaunt face was set in a frown. Huan spoke first. "I understand professor. If… If you become infected, I'll end your suffering."

"Thank you Huan," Davis said with a smile before nodding once to James, confirming the young man's choice to do the same if it came down to it.

James merely looked out the window, silent for a while. When he finally spoke, his voice was strained. "What *if* you get infected? The report said it took days for the infection to completely overcome the villager. Maybe we could cure you somehow?"

"If that seems reasonable, then we'll try that. I wouldn't execute you the moment I suspected infection, barring you showed a remarkable level of aggression," Davis agreed. "We'd stop and try to treat the infection as best we could. That's why we need the tissue sample, to better understand how the Father of Flesh creates minions."

"And why," Huan said, surprising Davis. "I mean, if he's hidden away why would he suddenly become active enough to attack a village? What happened?"

"That… is a very good question," Davis said. "I'm a little disappointed for not thinking of it myself."

"Perhaps seismic activity?" Lawrence offered from the driver seat, looking in the rear-view mirror. "The region where the village is has had seismic activity in the past. Perhaps it stirred the Father of Flesh in his sleep and made him feel threatened?"

"That makes sense, especially if connected with my theory that he is in an underground cavern close to the waterways that the village gets the well water from," Davis said, stroking his chin. "We'll have to be careful when we descend into the well. The *Chronicles* noted how the infection can't spread through water, but the creatures have proven capable swimmers, as well as adept at climbing sheer surfaces. I'm sure if the Father feels threatened he'll do more than send his Children after us."

"What do you mean?" Huan asked, James looking intrigued.

"I worked on a dig in southern Iraq not too long ago. There was an old god slumbering there and I actually found it, I think," Davis said.

"I thought you said you've never seen an old god before?" James asked.

"Like I said, I think it was an old god. In the lower sections of a forgotten temple there were creatures composed of caustic goo that would use bones of past explorers and sacrifices to form humanoid shapes to fight. Gunfire did little to deter them, so a student of mine engaged them with a sword and shield he'd liberated, dispatching them while I shot chunks of skeleton away as best I could."

"And what, the old god woke up?" James asked.

"Oh nothing so horrible!" Davis said, waving his hand. "No, we came upon a section of temple in a large chamber that was composed of nothing but dark slime, churning about as if it were the water of the Mediterranean."

"So that was the old god?" Huan asked.

"I believe, and this is only a theory, that what I witnessed that day was the cocoon that the old god had wrapped itself in to feel safe while it slumbered," Davis explained. Upon seeing the confused looks from his students, he turned a bit in his seat. "Look, the old gods thrived on bloodshed and sacrifices. But when mankind had formed a covenant with them they grew fat on the offered souls. They were interred by their followers in sepulchers designed to keep them safe. Then, the followers were culled by men and women who'd found a way to infuse themselves with the power of the old gods."

"How do you know this?" Huan asked.

"I don't, really. It's just a debate between believers of the old gods' existence. I've encountered cultists, diabolists and demonologists in my career," Davis said, leaning back in his seat. "Many I've interviewed and they confirm some rumors, disproved others."

"What's the difference between a diabolist and a demonologist?" Huan asked, looking between Davis and James.

Davis motioned to James, who rolled his eyes. "A diabolist is someone who has communed with an old god and received direct commands from the entity. If they survive and understand what was imparted upon them, they form a cult and begin doing the bidding of the old god, usually sacrifices and oaths to tie their souls to it."

"And a demonologist?" Huan asked.

"They're even worse as they've usually been imparted with power from the old god that grants them the ability to create and command the god's minions," James continued. "They take cultists and warp them into monstrous versions of themselves that will defend the cult no matter what."

"A basic introduction to what they are, but good enough for now," Davis commented, earning a glare from James.

"Do you think a cult may have started all of this?" Huan asked.

"If they did then they're all dead now," Davis chuckled. "The Children of Flesh are volatile beings that show little to no mercy to *any* living thing. The fact that the only way to get to the temple or complex is by going underwater, that would make the cultists the first to be converted, so to speak."

"Why do *you* think this is happening professor?" Huan pressed. "Why now?"

"I don't know, maybe the Father wants to try and wake up and reunite with its counterparts? Maybe it's dying? Any theory is as likely as the next right now..." Davis said, looking out the window at the passing scenery. They stopped at a red light, Lawrence cursing his luck, when Davis saw it.

An Asian man in a yellow slicker, haggard and filthy, standing at the corner of the street, next to the crosswalk sign. He was alone, and staring right through the tinted windows at Davis. He held up a hand, and brought one bony finger to his cracked lips before he took a step and began approaching the Jeep.

"Lock the doors," Davis whispered before speaking louder. "Lock the doors!"

Lawrence clicked the button locking all the doors between looking back at Davis. "What is it, sir?"

"Do you see that man?" Davis asked, staring at the shabby form sluggishly walking towards the Jeep.

"Yeah, looks like he's homeless," James said. "What's the big deal?"

"That's what the demon looked like before it attacked me yesterday, before it changed shape," Davis explained. He pointed at it through the glass. "Look at it, out in the sunlight. It's moving as if it's drunk, or hurt. That isn't normal."

"He does look a little tipsy..." James commented.

"He's just a homeless guy professor, he's probably coming up to ask for some change." Huan said, reaching for her purse. "I have a few ones I can give him, here, lower the window."

Davis didn't respond, instead he yelped as the entire Jeep rocked from side to side. The homeless man had reached the vehicle and was trying to open the door, shaking the frame as if he were ten men. His face was slack and eyes blank, a line of yellow drool coming from his gaping mouth.

"Still think he wants some spare change?" Davis growled before slapping the back of the driver's seat. "Drive!"

"Yes sir!" Lawrence said, slamming down on the gas pedal and speeding through the light, ignoring the screeching of tires as other motorists did their best to avoid the Jeep. The door rattled and a horrible noise akin to a large fish slapping onto a dry dock was heard. Looking out the window, the homeless man was running alongside the Jeep, one arm still on the handle, tugging forcefully.

"Shit!" James cried out as the Jeep tilted a fraction of an inch, forcing Lawrence to turn slightly. "What're we going to do?"

Reaching into his vest, Davis took hold of his .45 Magnum and pulled it out. Popping a bullet into the chamber, he turned so that his back was against James. He looked back at him. "I'm going to be shooting, so you two cover your ears."

James nodded, then wrapped Huan in a hug and both covered their ears while kneeling in the seats, their heads between their legs. Lawrence swore as the Jeep tilted again.

"Lawrence! Next time the Jeep tilts roll down the window," Davis ordered.

"You sure?" Lawrence asked, sounding uncertain.

"No dammit, just do as I say!" Davis said, lining up his shot.

The Jeep tilted once again and the window rolled down quickly, revealing the man to be sprinting next to the speeding car. His face was waxy and appeared to be melting as he slowly began to change.

Davis didn't give him the chance and shot him in the head, which exploded like a ripe watermelon from the high caliber bullet ripping through the boneless skull. The body staggered, the arm holding onto the Jeep letting go as it slowed down, yellow fat and pus oozing from the terrible wound. It was on all fours in the middle of the street, sans head, its yellow slicker moving around it as if there was a violent wind.

The Jeep put enough distance between the two that Davis felt safe. He looked over at his two students and patted Huan on the back. "You can get up, that was it. Lawrence," he said, addressing the driver. "You can raise the window now. I think we lost it."

"Are you certain?" Lawrence asked, looking back at Davis, who was popping another round into the chamber. He tucked it back into his vest and smiled.

"No. I know they can move through the ether with ease if given the chance, but I just left it headless on a busy street. There are going to be people panicking when it starts to regenerate and it will, and this I guarantee, be violent towards those offering it aid."

"How do you know?" Huan asked.

"How mad would you be if I just shot you?" Davis asked calmly.

"Mad, I guess…" Huan replied.

"Well this thing is a direct manifestation of a creature so old the concept of firearms is out of its realm of thought. Essentially it saw me shoot fire out of a metal object that destroyed its head in one clean go. Now its cover is blown and people will be swarming around it, calling nine-one-one to get police there."

"And?" James asked.

"And, like I said, it'll be mad. Corner an angry animal and you have a recipe for disaster. This is worse because the animal is nearly impossible to kill!" Davis explained, looking out the window at the passing cars and the greasy stains of tissue dribbling down from the top of the Jeep onto the glass.

# Chapter Twelve

Walking from the Jeep, they made their way to the private hangar where a large white jet sat, waiting for them. Davis was looking for the plane's markings when he noticed the guards. Two tall, muscular Asian men with sunglasses walked up to the group, each holding out a hand out to stop them.

"This is a restricted area," the one on the left, who had a scar running down his face, said.

"No visitors allowed," the other, his face decorated with a wispy mustache, said in accented English.

Davis cleared his throat and in his best Mandarin replied, "Forgive us for our intrusion, but we were told our flight would be in hangar four. I am Professor Nickels and behind me is my crew of workers who will be aiding me in the task Minister Xao-Ming has requested me for. If we are in the wrong facility, then we will happily leave."

To say the two guards looked stunned would have been an understatement; Scar held out a hand, motioning for everyone to come on through while Mustache walked along with them to load their baggage into the hold of the plane. Scar looked down at Davis and bowed. "I'm sorry professor, we did not expect someone of your… stature when we were informed you would be coming to use the plane."

Davis nodded, bowing at the waist slightly. "It is understandable my friend; you were guarding property of the Republic of China. You expected a tall white man I presume?"

Scar looked a little uncomfortable while nodding. "It is rare to see someone of your size in this country that is not afflicted by a disorder."

"I can assure you all I am afflicted with is age," Davis said with a laugh. "Now, we have a few more crates in the Jeep. Do you think you could get them for us Mister…?"

"Shang Lao," the guard said, bowing again.

"Thank you Mr. Shang, just be mindful of the passenger door, it's a little loose," Davis said.

The side was dented in as if someone had been kicking it repeatedly, while the handle was nothing more than wrenched metal twisted into a useless form. Lawrence said he'd call the insurance company and have them handle it, but Davis wasn't worried about that.

He was worried about the ever-growing pain in his chest. His prescription bottle was in the pocket of his khaki vest, with enough medicine to last him two weeks if he needed. The fact that he'd be in China meant he'd be able to get refills on his medicine in nearly any major city, so he wasn't worried about that. He was worried about the frequency at which his body ached, and how short an amount of time his medication lasted him.

Between that and his pocket watch, he knew something dangerous was on the rise. Pulling it out of his vest to check once more, he smiled slightly. The reading was better than it'd been this morning… tucking it back into his vest, he tugged on his clothes to make sure everything felt right.

He'd heard Huan and James chuckle about his attire numerous times now, but he didn't care.

All the pockets on his vest and belt held items that had saved his life countless times. He'd abandoned his backpack after the Ubaid expedition and just found a better flak jacket. All his clothes were lined with polymers that resisted cutting, making any slashing objects less effective against him. If these creatures used their talons to fight, then Davis would be safe.

Well, *safer*.

"The crates that are on the left are filled with, um, *sensitive* items so be certain not to drop them," Davis said as Shang walked towards the Jeep. "And be certain that everything is loaded properly! My cohorts are mere students so they are bound to have stored things in an inferior fashion!"

Shang laughed. "Such is the folly of youth!"

"Like you would know sonny," Davis chuckled, turning to walk towards the plane. It wasn't nearly as big as the jumbo jets, but it looked like it would be spacious enough for them to relax in for the duration.

Looking over at James and Huan dealing with Mustache, he smiled as Huan tried to apologize for her "friend's" foolish talk. Apparently, James had said something offensive thinking the men didn't speak enough English to understand. Davis walked over to the group and cleared his throat.

"Is there a problem here?" Davis asked, this time in English.

"Yes," Mustache said, practically growling. "Young fool call me name. I no like being called name!"

"By the old gods, what did you do James?" Davis asked, looking at the teen with a stern eye. He was rubbing his arm, looking down a little. Huan, who was shooting him glares, stepped up and spoke in Mandarin. "This dolt dropped the bags in front of Xian. He here and said he could load the stuff up. When Xian said he would *organize* our gear in the hold once it was there, James said it was the same thing and then called him an idiot."

Davis wanted to bury his face in his hands but instead tapped Xian on the elbow, bringing his attention down to him. "Listen, Xian, is it? My friend here is rather uncouth, a typical example of the spoiled child the west produces. He feels like he is entitled to everything and offers no aid, as if you are a servant."

"Indeed," Xian replied in Mandarin, earning a strange look from James, as he couldn't understand what the two were talking about.

"But why get upset over what an overblown child says about you? Just end the situation quickly and be the bigger man. You were going to sort our goods, right?" Davis smiled.

Xian narrowed his eyes at Davis. "Yes."

"Then let me help you carry the bags up, to show you not all westerners are lazy," Davis said, walking over to one of the larger bags. He bent his knees and grabbed hold of the bag containing the spears and rifles, and struggled to lift it. He didn't have to fake the struggle long as Xian moved quickly to take the sack from him, easing it out of his grip with a tight smile.

"It would be my honor to help you, venerable elder," Xian said, a smile forced onto his face. He hefted the bag up as Shang came over with three duffel bags in each hand, hefting the gear about as if he were a pack mule. Davis looked over at James, making eye contact, and mouthed the words "Shut up" to him. James made a motion to zip his lips closed.

After five minutes, everything was loaded, and another ten minutes had everything strapped down and sorted. They pulled a rolling stairway up to the jet's entrance, Xiao climbing the stairs and opening the jet up before lumbering in, a veritable bear of a man entering a darkened cave.

Davis was pleased with the plane when he saw the interior. Lined with seats with small tables in front of them, there was a wet bar near the tail of the plane next to a bathroom. The overhead compartments were stuffed with fluffy pillows and blankets.

"This is wonderful," Davis said, looking over at Xiao, who was in the cockpit. "You are the pilot?"

"Yes," he replied in clipped English. "I am pilot. Fly long time, in many wars. Know route over ocean."

"We'll stop for refueling I assume?" Davis asked, nervous of what he was about to go through.

"Yes, Hawaii will be refueling station," Xiao replied without looking at him, settling into his seat and flipping a few switches. "Now go, I have much to do."

"Okay, I'll leave you to it. Thank you for understanding back there and helping an old man," Davis said, turning to leave.

He barely heard the belated "You're welcome," come from Xiao as he walked into the main area of the plane. Shang had moved behind the wet bar and was already mixing drinks, much to James's and Huan's approval.

"Shang? You're a bartender?" Davis called out to him, cocking his head curiously.

Shang shrugged. "A decent one," he replied with a grin. "I dabble in many things. Most of us do in the Department of Paranormal Events."

Davis took a seat at the bar, climbing up the bolted barstool with ease and plopping himself down on the cushioned seat. "Department of Paranormal Events? It's amazing, I've worked in the occult field for decades and never heard of you."

"That is because we are good at our job," Shang said with pride as he shook a martini shaker. "I've personally seen ghosts, demons, things that could only be called monsters, and everything in between. I've been undercover to try and root out cults, and I've been the one to kick in a door to capture necromancers doing their business."

"Have a lot of problems with necromancers?" Davis asked, eyebrow raised.

"I'm sorry, but that's classified," Shang replied before pouring a martini and sliding it across the bar to Davis. "Here, you looked nervous about the flight. This should ease your nerves."

"What's in it?" Davis asked.

"Cherry Moscato with aged rum, poured over ice," Shang said. "It helps my grandfather whenever he must travel, and you look to be about his age."

Davis sniffed, pulling out his orange bottle, shaking two pills from it. "Really, how old is your grandfather if you don't mind me asking?"

As Davis threw back the tablets and took a sip from his drink, Shang leaned back against the rail behind him, head tilted up as he thought for a moment. "I believe he will be one-hundred and nine this year."

Davis snorted, setting his admittedly delicious drink down. "He is close to me in age after all."

"How do you do it? My grandfather claims the herbal remedies he uses are far better than the surgeries that many people have to cure their ailments," Shang said, fixing up two more drinks for James and Huan.

"Diet and exercise mostly, with a healthy dose of willpower and a stubborn refusal to give in to the Reaper," Davis said with a smile, hopping down from the stool and grabbing his drink. "We'll talk later Shang."

"I'm sure we will professor," Shang replied as Huan walked up and began speaking in rapid-fire Mandarin with the giant man. Setting his martini glass on one of the tables, he crawled up into the seat and settled himself next to James before taking another sip.

"I saw you with those pills again," James said in hushed tones. "Huan's back was to you but I think she may suspect something."

"Like what?" Davis asked, enjoying his drink.

"That you're a junkie for painkillers, I don't know!" James whispered. He ran a hand through his ivory locks. "Look, you can outpace both of us and we're in our early twenties. I haven't even gotten you to admit how old you are, and you knock back those pills like they're candy, man! Is there something we should know?"

"Fine, if you must know we'll wait for Huan to get back so I don't have to repeat myself," Davis said, sipping his drink slowly. He was already feeling tipsy from just half the glass.

Huan sashayed over with two tall glasses of what smelled like whiskey and soda, handing one to James before plopping down on his other side. She drank her drink through a straw but James took several deep glugs of the concoction before setting it down on the table and letting out a gasp.

"Whoa, that is spicy!" James exclaimed, much to Shang's amusement.

"Yeah, Shang used cinnamon whiskey for these, said they bring fire to the belly." Huan laughed.

"Now the professor has something he wishes to share with us, don't you, sir?" James said with a cocky smile.

Davis grumbled, a slight blush coming to his face from the drink. "About ninety years ago I… interrupted a ritual meant to empower a cult's leader with the powers to become a diabolist. The interruption made the ritual fail and caused massive backlash over the room, killing most of the cultists and wounding me. I was taken by my companions to a field hospital and treated, where they learned I had no apparent injuries despite the constant pain I was in."

Huan covered her mouth while James took another sip of his drink.

"Ever since I get flashes of pain that are worse around certain events, and certain times of year. I take pain medication to fight the damage that was done that day. What you see me take occasionally? Morphine tablets."

"Should you even be drinking while you're on that stuff?" Huan asked, looking at his martini glass, which was practically empty.

"It's not recommended," Davis said. "But then again almost everything I've done in my life hasn't been recommended."

"Professor! This is your life! What if you… you… I don't know, need to be of sound mind to do something?" Huan argued.

"Are you saying I haven't been of sound mind while teaching class? Because I always take a tablet before class," Davis said.

"Well, no. You're usually more chipper than anyone else in the room," Huan admitted.

Grabbing his martini glass, Davis downed the last of it before smiling. "Then don't worry about it."

* * *

The flight over the Pacific was smooth the entire way, even when landing on a private airfield in Hawaii. The two Chinese agents refueled the jet as James and Huan slept. Davis flexed his hands open and closed so that he could work the kinks out of them.

The refueling took maybe an hour, during which Davis watched his two students rest on the wide seats together. Somehow, while drinking their cinnamon whiskeys, they'd grown closer and were now spooning on the seat, Huan holding onto James's arm over her shoulders. It brought a smile to his face, as he hadn't had the *urge* in nearly sixty years, something most people would lament.

He found it liberating in a way. He'd had five children in his time with his wife, and two of them survived to adulthood. Those two children grew distant from their father and started families of their own. Only when they needed money did they think to call him. But he always caved and wired money to them when they claimed they needed it for rent or food.

It was out of this service that Lawrence had come to know Davis. He'd arrived with suitcase in hand and a note from his mother, explaining to him that Lawrence was his grandson, one of many. In her note, she pleaded with him to not do as the boy wanted and to turn him away. This had made Davis curious enough to allow the boy to stay for a week.

Lawrence made Davis an offer at the end of that week: to become his personal assistant in everything. He would stay home and catalogue the things discovered by the tomb-raiding old man, and in exchange he would get room and board. He said he felt obligated because of the way his mother would call Davis for money at the drop of a hairpin. He wanted to work off his mother's debt, as well as learn about the Paranormal from his grandfather.

How could Davis argue with that?

That had been some twenty-odd years ago, and like Davis himself time seemed to stand still for the lad; he was forty-two as of this past August and he didn't look a day over twenty-five. With Lawrence around Davis was allowed a chance to speak with someone concerning the things he investigated. The only real downfall in his grandson was that he didn't accept the theories on old gods. Like his father, whom Davis had never met, he was a devout Jew. He celebrated all the holidays and even managed to get Davis to join, after a decade of trying.

Davis himself was Jewish, so he knew the old traditions well enough from his own childhood. He'd told Lawrence the facts in regard to his god, but Lawrence wouldn't hear of it. The young man looked at his religion as something of pride, as he knew how much his people had gone through over the centuries. He didn't take it too well when he pointed out that Yahweh had shifted his focus to the Christians as they'd gained more militaristic power over the years than the scattered Jewish people. It was an agreed upon subject that they didn't discuss anymore.

Xiao pushed his way into the jet and stomped to the cockpit while Shang closed the door, twisting the lock to seal it closed.

Walking back slowly to not awaken the two, Shang gave Davis a raised eyebrow. "Are they dating?" he asked in Mandarin quietly.

"Not that I know of, I just think your drinks proved to be enough to convince them they were," Davis whispered back.

"Would you like another?" Shang offered, nodding over towards the wet bar.

Davis waved him off. "Not now, maybe later. I'm going to just relax and meditate for a little while."

"You meditate?" Shang asked, sounding surprised.

Davis chuckled. "Not all westerners are poorly-educated slobs, you know?"

"I didn't mean it that way I… just didn't know you meditated," Shang said, turning to head to the wet bar. "Carry on, professor."

Leaning back, Davis closed his eyes and began to regulate his breathing, in through the nose, out through mouth. Opening his mind's inner eye, he peered through the ether to see what was around.

Monsters.

Around him, outside his own mind, were creatures of sweaty flesh and slithery tentacles, all seemingly staring at him despite their lack of eyes. Two of them stood out from the rest, standing nearly seven feet tall, they had bony arms that extended above them that ended in pitted spheres. They even had faces, upside down human heads with no lower jaw and all the hair missing, their eyes wide and unblinking.

"You… come to us…" one of the two said, causing the crowd of monsters to hiss and gasp, wriggling about in an orgy of clammy flesh rubbing against fatty tissue.

"You… stop us…?" the other asked, the eyes blinking slowly, the gaping central maw perched above the upside-down head gurgling as if fluids were building up in there.

"I'm coming to find out what you are, and how to prevent you from hurting more people," Davis said, focusing on keeping his mind on the situation at hand.

"No… you come for… riches, just like… the other…" the first one gasped.

"No matter… you are…" the second one began before stopping and turning its body slightly as if listening. The eyes rolled madly back to focus on Davis. "You… are our… freedom!"

And with that the ether was clear, the apparitions gone like dust on the wind.

# Chapter Thirteen

The harsh landing was what pulled Davis from his meditation, knocking him onto his side, the cushioned seats making the fall a less unpleasant one. He blinked his eyes blearily, adjusting his glasses as he looked around the cabin. Shang was cleaning up the tables even while the plane was moving down a rough runway, showing that the large man had an amazing degree of balance and grace that belied his size.

Across the aisle were his two blushing students, sitting far apart from one another and looking everywhere but at each other.

*Ah,* Davis thought, *the follies of youth!*

Clearing his throat, Davis croaked, "Now I think this should be our final landing. Let's get ready when we disembark."

"Get ready?" Huan and James echoed.

"Yes, as in fully kit yourselves out with your gear as if we are going to enter hostile territory within the hour," Davis said. "I think my dear colleague decided that I couldn't be trusted not to dally while in Hong Kong and has had us land on a modified airstrip close to the village."

Shang merely snorted. "You are most perceptive, professor. What gave us away?"

"Other than the landing feeling like we're rolling over gravel? The lack of *real* airline staff. Not that you haven't been lovely, it's just most planes have more than two agents working the flight. Add to it that I saw no markings on the jet when we were getting in and the fact you work in Minister Xao-Ming's office makes me believe this was a partial kidnapping."

Shang smiled, nodding his head. "You came willingly, that's all that mattered."

"You're hard to read Shang," Davis said with a proud smile. "As is Xiao. I assume everyone in the department is?"

Shang stared at Davis for a moment before slowly nodding, as if he didn't understand. Sighing, Davis closed his eyes as if in concentration for a moment before a smile spread across his face. "You have no grandfather. At least alive, that is."

"Wha… yes, I told you remind me of him," Shang said, taken aback.

"When you were a child and he could barely walk, yes. But then he fell and hurt his back, before coming down with pneumonia. The injury combined with the sickness did him in, didn't it?" Davis asked as Shang's face went from shocked to neutral in an instant.

"I don't know what you're talking about," Shang said before walking towards the cockpit.

"How did you know that professor?" Huan asked, standing up and stretching, her shirt growing taut over her lithe body. Davis noticed how James's eyes lingered on her chest.

"I know things, my dear, it's how old people operate. Now, let's get ready to disembark!" Davis said, standing up. His body crackled with pain, forcing him to steady himself on one of the tables. "Damn…"

"Professor?" James asked, looking at Davis with concern while Huan came over and placed a hand on his shoulder.

"Fetch a drink from the bar, something sweet. Amaretto will do," Davis ground out while reaching a shaky hand into his vest for his pills.

"Right," Huan said, running back towards the wet bar, searching for the bottle.

"The pain, is it getting worse?" James asked.

Davis grunted. "With age my boy, only with age. If some monster doesn't punch my ticket to the afterlife, this pain surely will."

"You need to think positive professor, you never know when they'll develop something stronger than morphine," James said as Huan came over with a brown bottle with a golden label. James unscrewed the top and handed it to Davis, who chugged a bit of the sugary sweet liqueur before passing the orange pill bottle to James.

"Two pills," he said, pressing it into James hand.

James looked at the label and his eyes widened, but he obeyed, shaking out two pills before screwing the cap back on. He gave them to Davis, who quickly swallowed, chasing them with the Amaretto. Davis took the bottle with tremors in his hand, tucking it into his pocket.

"Thank you my boy," Davis said, slumping back in the seat. "You can take the drink back; I won't need it."

"Are you sure?" Huan asked.

"Certain my dear, very certain."

"What is going on here?" Shang exclaimed, looking at the scene before him. Davis gave him a weak wave of the hand.

"Oh nothing, I just needed to take my medicine and I needed a drink to down the pills. They're all kinds of nasty."

"What kind of medication? You should have told us in case there was an emergency while we were in flight," Shang said, sounding annoyed.

Davis shrugged as he stood up on wobbly legs. "My medication is none of your business, and I take exception to your rudeness! How dare you demand something like that from an elder? Did your mother teach you no manners or were you raised in a barn?"

Shang was taken aback for a moment before his face went slack. He went rigid, arms at his side and bowed once more. "I apologize for my candor; I was worried for you and overstepped what is decent. Please look kindly upon me."

"Thank you Shang, I held hope that I would be able to call you by your given name, should we become friendly enough. This may very well lead to such an event, I must say. You may call me Davis from now on," Davis said, shocking Shang and Huan.

James just looked confused. "What do you mean? Isn't his name Shang?"

"That's his surname. In Asian cultures the surname is given first instead of the common name. It is only when you become friendly that you allow someone to call you by your given name, in Shang's case it would be Lao," Davis explained before patting Huan on the hip. "Huan here is several generations American, so that has changed for her. Huan is indeed her given name, correct?"

"Yes sir," she said, looking down at him with a measured glance before focusing on Shang. "Shang, I am so sorry if we've offended you."

Shang relaxed from his stance, standing at his full height. "I must say, I never thought I'd meet a white man who would know our ways enough to offer his name first out of respect for our traditions. Thank you, Davis, you may call me Lao if you so wish."

"I will in private, but in mixed company I'll keep it professional Shang," Davis said with a nod.

"Then I will do the same, professor," Shang replied, turning to walk back to the cockpit.

Speaking in a low voice, he said, "Don't tell either of them anything about me, especially what medication I'm on. They're working for Shen in a department where I could easily qualify as a danger."

"Sir?" James said, standing up from his kneeling position.

"They work for the Department of Paranormal Events. I hadn't realized it until a few moments ago that Shang was gathering information on us while we were drinking, listening to you two flirt and me tell tales of adventures past."

"We weren't flirting!" Huan growled, glaring at James.

"Yes you were dear, but you were drunk so it doesn't count," Davis replied absentmindedly before continuing. "They must be on assignment to monitor us so they can learn how we go about analyzing the paranormal. We must be very cautious..."

"Why?" James asked.

"Because," Davis looked over to the cockpit where both Shang and Xiao were looking back at them. "They may not need us after all if we don't prove useful. And tools that aren't useful often get destroyed."

"Oh," Huan said quietly, the thought sobering enough that she was no longer fixated on James and the flirtations they'd exchanged during the flight.

Shang left the cockpit and unlocked the pressurized door, popping it open to let sunlight and the fresh scent of mountain air flood in. Davis recognized it instantly, even after all the years that had passed. These were mountains in China, far from cities and the like. Small farming villages would be nearby, with a rock quarry or two within a day's travel. The entire countryside would be a hue of emerald from the grass blowing in the wind. The chill of fall had not set in yet, and so the villagers would most likely be out working their fields.

"Let's go," Davis said, patting the table once to signal his students. They all stood and walked out of the plane, headed down a rolling staircase had been pushed up against the jet. The airstrip was roughly three football fields of cleared land, with small rocks here and there. A herd of cattle were off in the distance, one man with them.

"Move," Shang said, not exactly aggressive but very much an order. Davis descended the stairs and walked around to the back of the plane, where he found six men, all dirty and tired looking, standing by.

Davis turned and looked at Shang, a question in his eyes. Shang cleared his throat and shouted in Mandarin. "Allow them to grab what they need, bring the rest to the tents at base camp."

The men all backed up as the lip of the hold slowly opened, like a yawning beast, revealing all their tools of war and discovery. Davis went and grabbed the bag containing his rifle and spear and took both out, slinging the satchel over his shoulder and choosing to use the spear as a walking stick. The painkillers were still clawing their way into his bloodstream and so he still shook from the ache radiating from his chest.

Davis spent minutes grabbing boxes of ammunition, sliding them into his side satchel along with flares, a flare gun, and several powerful glow sticks. He watched, and directed, James and Huan as they selected what they wanted to carry with them. He'd allowed his modified Uzi to be strapped to Huan's back, her pert chest holding a strap for her Desert Eagle. She had a pouch of loaded magazines at her side, and they'd practiced replacing them quickly.

She was a fast learner.

James strapped his blade to his side and slung his rifle over his shoulder, the old Winchester proving to be just large enough for him. A bag of .243 bullets was tied at his waist, all coated in silver melted from crosses soaked in holy water. They were perfect for nearly any supernatural enemy one encountered, so long as it might be considered foul—the blessings only added to the pain and damage if the beings were also unholy.

He was sure the Children of Flesh qualified.

Shang stood by the entire time, arms crossed as he studied their movements. Davis could see the calculations going on behind his eyes, taking a mental inventory of things they were packing. He smiled inwardly at how Shang would scowl when he packed an unmarked bag into a pocket or pouch. Huan and James were far easier to read so Shang took to "helping" them when they were loading their weapons or packing away gear into a backpack. Huan had a tall backpack that reminded Davis of his old bag; the thing had been over a hundred pouches and packages; it'd been his best friend for over four excursions. He'd retired it after the Ubaid ruins…

*I do that a lot…* Davis thought to himself. *Weird habit to form, but I tend to stop using a method of my madness every time I bring someone to those ruins.*

The thought of that dig brought up the memories of the vision with Joshua, the student he'd left to the Darkness Given Hunger, a horrible old god that was imprisoned by the Ubaid using magic most arcane. Joshua was still together enough to come and taunt Davis in his current predicament, showing him the beast that lurked somewhere deep beneath the ground, hidden in the mountains.

"How long has the contamination been going on?" Davis asked genially in Mandarin, perking Huan's ears.

"By our guess it was active for twelve hours without our supervision and has grown at a growth of three feet in diameter a day. We burn away the veins that stretch out to create more covering, so the spread has been contained. The creatures themselves seem to flourish at nighttime and move around most when the sun is down. Otherwise they have some sort of artificial dusk they've extended over an eight-mile radius."

Shang recited this by rote, as if he'd been briefed only moments ago. Davis looked at him, tucking a sack of exploding caltrops into his satchel. "And do we have all the gear I requested?"

Shang nodded. "Several armed soldiers to act as an escort, all armed with flame throwers and wetsuits will be here within forty-eight hours. As you advised, they will have high caliber firearms instead of automatic weapons," Shang said. "Many protested this, but once we… *engaged* three of the hostiles as they walked down the road around three in the morning, we learned of their regenerative qualities."

"How many men did you lose before you thought it a good idea to listen to me?" Davis asked, his tone harsh.

Shang was quiet for a moment before he licked his lips. "Eight."

"And I imagine you only drove the creatures away instead of slaying them, am I right?"

"Correct," Shang said, no emotion in his voice.

"Is Shen going to be joining us or will he be resting in Hong Kong while I handle the dirty work?" Davis said, pulling his ten-gauge from a bag, strapping it to his thigh so he could pull it at a moment's notice.

"The Minister is too important a figure to risk to on a Class III containment issue," Shang said, as if that explained everything.

James stood up and glanced at everyone. "It would be lovely if I knew what you were saying!"

He stomped out of the plane and motioned to the men to go ahead and take the equipment left behind. Davis smiled at the young man who came and grabbed a crate full of dynamite. "Careful with that," he told him.

The boy nodded and carted the explosives off. Davis turned and smiled at Shang, who was still staring at him. "So tell me this," he continued in Mandarin, "what exactly is a Class III containment issue?"

"I can't reveal the specifics of what our program does—" Shang started before Davis slammed the butt of his spear down on the metal flooring of the cargo hold, a loud clang issuing forth and silencing the Chinese man. Huan looked on with an icy mask, like she didn't care for what was being said.

"I know you can't reveal specifics to me, but answer me this: have you seen *this* type of containment issue before?" Davis growled.

Shang shook his head slowly. "No," he said. "We've had several breaches where villages in the region would have creatures come up from the wells and attack new mothers for their children. This is the first instance of an infection taking place. We didn't even know they were able to do this…"

"What have you labeled them as?" Davis asked, curious.

"*Shui gui*, though we know they aren't spirits. Our experts have analyzed some residue they left behind and found them to be physical in nature," Shang explained.

"Plus the eight men that they tore apart, that makes them different than most ghosts," Huan said with a sly grin.

Shang growled and took a step closer to her. "Watch your mouth girl! You'd best leave the conversation to the experts on the matter!"

"Seeing as she is my student and I have brought her up to speed on what these lovely little creatures are, that would mean you should be the silent one," Davis said. "But we need you to tell us how much your people have screwed up, and how much we're going to have to do to clean up after you." Davis added, taking a step forward and placing the tip of the obsidian spear just below Shang's ribs.

Shang looked back, not moving. "You kill me and you'll never make it back to the States alive."

Davis gave a feral grin, eyes lighting up in the darkness of the cargo hold. "Funny, I don't think you know *what* would happen to me should I kill you. You'd be dead after all. I can always come up with a story and might get away with it. But you… Shen's already deemed you worthless if he sent you to work with me."

"What do you mean?" Shang asked, confused.

"Oh, he didn't mention that I'm the one who blasted a hole through his brother's head all those years ago? I was here before your organization was formed boy, and I've been facing nameless horrors before your *mother* was born!" Davis hissed, pressing the blade into Shang's clothes, a slight sizzle coming from the tip of the obsidian. "Don't presume to tell me what will happen should I do something! If I deem your death a necessity, you'll learn about it once the bullet, or blade, goes into you. You need me, I don't need you."

Davis pulled his spear back and leaned on it before smiling like a harmless old man. "You'd best remember that sonny, and remember it well. Should I find either of my students treated... *poorly*, I'll vent some anger out on you and your little agency you've got set up here in the outback of China. Do you understand me?"

Shang gulped before nodding. He looked at Huan and gave her a quick bow before rushing out of the empty cargo hold. Huan walked up to Davis and laid a hand on his shoulder. "Thanks professor. I forgot how sexist my people can be..."

"Stupid people have stupid ideas... women can be just as useful, dangerous, ignorant or weak as any man," Davis said with a derisive snort. "Keep an eye on James, and don't let them know you and I can speak Cantonese."

"Why?" Huan asked.

"Because that's how they're going to talk about us when we're around," Davis replied. "The less they know about us gives us more ammo should we need to shoot our way out of here, so to speak."

"I must say I wasn't expecting this when you called me, professor..." Huan said. "Not that I'm complaining. Who would turn down a chance to actually save the world?"

Davis looked out into the daylight as they strolled from the cargo hold. "Who indeed?"

# CHAPTER FOURTEEN

The camp was perhaps a half mile from the airstrip, the six men having loaded the various crates and bags into the back of a mule drawn cart. They walked ahead of them as Davis, James and Huan followed Shang and Xiao, who were speaking in hushed tones between themselves, their dark sunglasses having been slipped back on due to the sunny day in the rural mountains of China.

The air was crisp and clean save for the faint scent of rot on the wind and a looming darkness on the horizon, a cloud of black ash hovering in the sky, swirling about as if it were in the middle of a hurricane. The fields and hills around them were all tilled and planted with lanes of rice half submerged in water. They passed by an orchard where large containers were being filled with loquats, several boys on ladders pulling ripe ones off the branches and tossing them down to their sisters, who carefully placed the fruit in barrels and crates.

After fifteen minutes, they turned off the road and began climbing a hill roughly a football field away from the darkened area beneath the churning cloud, which turned out to be the village. Shang and Xiao broke away from the group and jogged ahead. Meanwhile, a balding man with a cane snapped off orders to unpack the cart. Judging by his ornamental garments, he was likely the man in charge.

He had a stern face, wrinkles and creases formed from years of war and rebellions. He seemed to be sneering at Davis and his students, especially when he looked at Huan.

"Well, you must be the great Davis Nickels!" he said in rapid fire Mandarin, spreading his arms wide as if to welcome the group. "As you can see we've set up a command base here just south of the village."

Davis looked around at the various tents and tables, and several supply crates with padded armor, gas masks, and cheap automatic weapons still inside. Soldiers were camped at the base of the hill, closest to the village, and they seemed to be actively doing… something. Across the camp near a large supply tent there were four computers set up and plugged into a generator, a small satellite dish opened and laid down onto a table. Pulling his phone from his pocket, he smiled.

Full bars!

"Yes, I am *Professor* Davis Nickels. Feel free to call me professor…" Davis said, staring at the man, waiting for him to introduce himself.

"Ah, how rude of me. I am Pho, secretary for the Department of Paranormal Events. I was sent here by the minister himself to oversee the work that you do," Pho replied, bowing slightly at the waist. His fake smile and glimmering eyes reminded Davis of the bureaucrats he was forced to deal with in the States whenever he brought an antiquity home.

Davis sighed, "So it would be you my assistant has been e-mailing?"

Pho nodded. "Yes, we have been going over the agreement with each other. The minister informed me this morning that he would not be able to relinquish forty percent of relics found."

"Oh?" Davis said.

"Yes, he spoke with the other ministers and they believe the treasures of our nation are paramount to understanding our past and making steps into our shared future. I was told I could offer up to fifteen percent. I trust you find that acceptable?"

"Funny how the agreement changes after we already flew across the world…" Davis muttered before clearing his throat. "The deal was forty percent, Secretary. I have the confirmation e-mail from your office in my inbox dated before we left. Now if you want to change the deal, we can simply leave you with your interesting problem and take our theories elsewhere. I'm sure once this spreads beyond this province the new Secretary will honor the original agreement and not try to rob us because he thinks we're stupid."

Pho's eyes bulged for a moment. "The offer of fifteen percent is most generous; I would suggest you take it."

"Anything less than what was promised and I won't solve your little problem over there," Davis said, pointing his spear at the darkened village. "And I already know you know *some* ways of handling these things, but not permanently. I've killed them before," Davis added, thinking back to his balcony incident.

"You have actually fought them?"

"Received a hearty punch for it, but I was able to kill it with a little know-how and the right equipment," Davis said, nodding to the spear he was using as a walking stick.

"Then you'll most kindly offer us the spears for analysis to recreate their effective uses in battle," Pho said, spreading his hands wide once more. Shang walked up behind Pho and stood there, arms crossed.

"Pho, you really don't seem to get this, so let me spell it out for you," Davis said, switching to English so James could listen in. "If any of my equipment or my comrades are bothered, touched, moved, or otherwise used without my express permission, I'll kill the man or woman who did that. This is your warning. Now, you can order the villagers to load all my gear into *our* area, not your main tent, or I can kill a man. You choose."

Pho scoffed, his eyes full of mirth before noticing that Davis had quickly pulled his sawed-off ten-gauge from his hip, angled it directly at him. "Y-you would dare threaten the secretary of the minister?" he cried in outrage.

"Like I said to Shang earlier, if the minister sent you down here to work with me you're expendable. I killed his brother and walked out of this country with *all* the treasure from a dig he and I shared. Now I come here again as an expert in a situation you are likely not ready to deal with, and you try to shortchange me? I think we'll stick with our forty percent and be fair about it. Now show me something useful, like some pictures of the village that are more recent than three days ago."

Pho frowned but nodded. He turned and barked orders to the villagers, directing them to unload the cart near the tents by the computer stations. Pho hobbled over to one of the computers where a young man with glasses sat, typing away at the keyboard. He seemed to be controlling a camera… no, a drone.

"This is Wu Chiang, our field expert at remote reconnaissance," Pho said, clapping the young man on the shoulder.

James leaned over to Huan. "What did he say?"

Davis replied in English before Huan could. "This guy is their greatest remote controlled toy operator."

The man narrowed his eyes at Davis, who merely adjusted his own glasses perched on his bulbous nose. Pressing on before Pho could say anything else, he stepped up and looked at the screen. "All right Wu, what kind of tool are you using here?"

"Um," he said, looking at Pho who nodded, "I am using a modified stealth detection drone propelled by five rotors, mounted with a small camera that feeds back to this computer."

"Where is it located right now?" Davis asked.

"At the northern edge of the village, measuring the new growth for today. The military requests that I do this daily."

"Do they burn it back every day?" Davis asked.

"Yes?"

"Then count it every few days to see if the growth is accelerating. If it does, then start monitoring every hour after the burning. Something is either regenerating or it is creating more flesh to spread out from matter within the village. Does the drone have a spotlight?"

"Yes," Wu said, sounding a little afraid.

"Then let's go in and look at what's been growing since I've been traveling," Davis said. "Just a quick pass over, let me get some shots of the buildings and their placement, a good look at the well, and the locations of the creatures."

"All right," Wu agreed, maneuvering the drone lower to fly into the shrouded region. It plunged into darkness before its lamp lit up like the light of the sun, blazing down upon a world that had not seen light since its formation.

And this was a world that had no need for light. Eyeless creatures shuffled about paths of bruised and calloused flesh, buildings completely encased in the pale, waxy meat that was dominating everything else. In random spots on walls and the ground there were violet eyes of varying size, blinking when the light passed over them, small humanoid arms growing from woodwork reaching out towards the light with three-fingered claws.

"It's a shame we don't have audio," Davis said, crossing his arms.

"Why?" Pho asked, eyes widening slightly at the sign of learning something new.

"Well your boss was right, this is old god related," Davis replied, shaking his head. "I've been told that these creatures have been seen for many years, and have a penchant for stealing pregnant women, newborns and new mothers. That make sense to you?"

"We've often speculated on that," Pho said, looking down at his cane, tapping it once on the stone. "It comes from the water and attacks all that we have on payroll. We had a few captured diabolists that we released into this area so they could start cults. That provoked a response."

"Really?" Davis said, pulling a pad and pen from his satchel and passing it to Huan.

Pho smirked before continuing. "Yes, eight days after the first diabolist was released we confirmed a connection was made to an old god. The tracer we had surgically placed on the inside of his ribcage allowed us to monitor his physical state and where he was. Our plan was to let him build a cult and then do what a diabolist always does."

"Sacrifice humans to their old god?" Davis asked, confused.

"No! Encounter agents of an old god and try and create some lines of communication by attempting to become a demonologist," Pho continued, only to be interrupted once again.

"Okay, from the cults I've observed, they usually have a diabolist as the leader as they can receive messages from the dreaming gods. A demonologist is someone who can bend the minions of an old god to his will and do whatever they do with minions like that. The difference is stark and the fine line is that the demonologists have a fraction of demonic or otherworldly energy within them. We know they have a link, but we, and by we I mean the whole of occultists in the west, have never found what that link is!"

"While in containment all the diabolists, at one point or another, said their goal was to commune with certain old gods. We never could get the names from them, but they were all within Central Asia. But I digress, these ones were trying to become demonologists."

"If you say so," Davis said before nodding for Pho to continue.

"For security's sake, we'll label them Diabolists One, Two, and Three," Pho explained, looking over to Shang with a question in his eyes. Shang nodded and turned to head towards a large tent. "One was released and began forming a cult by day two. By day one-hundred and eighty-one she had over a hundred cultists all swearing allegiance to her. That was when event one happened."

"Event One," Shang began to recite from the pages of a manila folder. "Happened on day one-hundred and ninety, in a remote village that has been removed from the map. One was staying in the village, assembling a temple for the old god she paid homage to, when one of the entities emerged from the town well."

"How do you know this?" Huan asked while scribbling down notes, James looking over her shoulder.

"Every time her heartbeat elevated beyond a certain point, one of our satellite arrays would zero in on her and record the event. When the recording started, we could see one with her followers, as well as the entity. Large, bipedal, with three head tentacles surrounding a large opening that led into the chest and belly. Thick legs dragged the creature towards one, who was growing more and more excited at the sight of it."

"Tell us what happened Shang," Pho said, smiling thinly at Davis.

"The creature… *ate* one and then retreated into the well, where it swam for three miles to a set location beneath the Nanling Mountains. The radio signal grew weaker over the next six hours before it stopped."

"So these things devour people?" Huan asked. Davis closed his eyes and clutched at the talisman hidden in his clothes.

"We've learned that those who are devoured are regurgitated later as numerous smaller versions, which move in packs," Pho said, turning to point with his cane at a tree next to a fleshy building.

Davis blinked as he saw three of the small ones move beneath the light, tentacles lined with fingers as they reached for its glare, all intent shoving the drone into their gullets.

This was where Davis had been taken in the vision by Joshua, the tree on the screen offering him nearly the same vantage point as Joshua's flaming sword had. These... monsters that were climbing over each other trying to reach the drone may very well have been the smaller beings he'd assumed were children when he'd first seen them. None of them bore an eye, and the eye on the tree was closed for reasons Davis couldn't explain.

"What's going on?" James asked, pointing at the monitor. Everyone looked at Wu, who was lazily circling the village taking pictures through the camera. Wu stopped at the harsh English and looked at the screen, which showed the well, where eight violet eyes circled what used to be stone. Now it appeared as a sucking maw that three-legged hunchbacked creatures climbed in and out of, their one tentacle held up in the air carrying gooey material down into the well.

"Are those... what are those?" Pho asked, stepping closer to the screen and Wu. "Bring the drone around to look and shine the light down the hole. What is that?"

"That *should* be the well sir, it seems they finally consumed the rocks it was made of," Wu stated, shining the light down into the throat of the well, the walls dribbling down long lines of fat and pus from open sores and scratches created by the smaller workers carrying supplies underground. The light shined on several of them standing on what looked to be a *pier* that was constructed from the stolen boards and bricks from the buildings. Where the pier headed other than down into the flowing water was anyone's guess, but the boards being slid into place congealed together, the skin splitting open and stretching over to connect to the stone and wood around it.

"They're making a ramp to...?" Wu said, looking up at Pho.

"I don't know... what do you think it's for, *professor*?" Pho asked, looking to Davis with a snort. "You are the expert here, so let's hear it!"

"So... the diabolist was eaten and tracked to somewhere under the mountains, this village has been taken in a maneuver like how man conquers lands, building upon the foundations of the old to bring life to the new," Davis said, rubbing the shaft of the spear with his gnarled fingers slowly.

"That's almost poetic," Pho snorted.

"That's the point. When you're dealing with an old god, you can't think of things like we do. They think in a way that can barely be described as thinking. But imagery and symbolism seem to ring true to them, for some reason. They like things symmetrical, they have certain things they cannot stand and they defy their own desires in ways one would deem insane."

"And so you really don't know why they're building a pier at the bottom of the well?" Pho asked, clearly disgruntled.

Davis adjusted his glasses. "I don't think it's a pier. That would insinuate boats. I think it's an addition to the well which is becoming an entrance into their world. Call it a chute if you must."

"A chute? A chute for what?" Pho asked before looking down at Wu, who shrugged.

"Well I know from experience these things can see even if they don't have eyes. I imagine that they're planning to retrieve more materials for their growing home, while also seeing to the problem that has been bothering them daily."

"What are you saying Nickels?" Pho finally growled, slamming the table with his cane.

Davis didn't flinch, he just looked up. "They're going to wait for night and then they're going to attack. That chute is for the spoils of the battle to be funneled down to where they can be ported to their home. Do you have the flamethrowers my assistant asked you to get?"

"We… we ordered them today, and overland transport should have them arriving tomorrow," Pho answered.

Davis turned and walked over to one of his crates, knocking it on the side with his spear. "No worries. I planned on you failing, so I packed an extra condom just in case yours broke."

Huan chuckled while Pho glared. "And what have imported into my country?"

"Six-hundred and forty thermite grenades," Davis said with a careless shrug. He picked up one of the tennis ball sized bombs and tossed it underhanded to James, who yelped as he didn't know what it was. Everyone backed away from him, causing James a minute amount of worry.

"Don't pull the pin James," Davis said in English before looking at everyone else. "That is a container that activates the thermite and issues a small explosion to spread it."

"Thermite?" James said, eyebrows raised. "You brought thermite onto the plane with us?"

"Only enough to melt the plane," Davis replied. "But I imagine these are going to serve as the primary weapons of war for the inevitable attack that will be coming tonight."

"And you know this how?" Pho asked, this time with sincere curiosity in his voice rather than spite.

Davis closed his eyes and opened his inner self to the ether, where tortured souls wailed within the bodies of the Children of Flesh, chained to the living nightmares. He could feel fifty some odd souls in the village, as well as a dark swell of energy pulsing through the village like a heartbeat. The flesh on the ground and buildings was connected to something greater.

Davis opened his eyes, wincing at the light. "Because if I was a soul-swilling demon, I would take as many as I could from the growing number of them close by. The chute will be for bodies that the smaller ones will take to the main nest."

"How can you be so sure?" James asked, eyebrow raised.

"Because old gods have simple demands. They want souls to satiate their hunger, they want followers to carry out their commands, and they want a safe location for their physical form to rest while they wallow in the opulence of being fed souls like peeled grapes."

# Chapter Fifteen

The group had dispersed, Pho and Shang going off to the main tent, a sizable portable building in almost every aspect. The villagers, all dirty and tired, went to their tents to drink rice wine and trade stories of happier times.

Davis stood beside seated Wu's shoulder, ordering him to maneuver the drone around to the edge of the village closest to the military presence. Several larger Children had gathered, some standing as high as seven feet even while slouched over, great drooling holes and thick tentacles on their sides making them seem more comical than anything else.

James had taken a spot on the hill, a jutting outcrop of rock, and set up a sniper's position. He'd laid his box of silver bullets and.243 on the sun-warmed rock, taking a break to fetch a meal of rice and pork from the villagers before settling in at his post once more.

After telling Wu to monitor the Children should they begin mounting an attack, Davis returned to his tent. He sat down at its center and lay his spear across his lap as he entered a meditative trance. He would need guidance for the task that lay ahead. It was all for naught however, as the very air was permeated with the foul presence of the Father, preventing him from calling out to the spirits for aid. After twenty minutes of fruitless searching, he instead turned his attention to another form of spying on the enemy ranks—farseeing, the art of projecting your mind from your body to survey your surroundings.

Taking a copper bowl from one of the villagers he filled it with clear water before pricking his finger to allow three drops of his blood to fall into the still surface. After muttering a few arcane words, he found himself thrust out into the world, his spirit moving through the air with ease as he traversed the land, floating like a specter to the village. Following the drone's light so he could see, he looked over the three largest Children, each slumped over with prodigious arms ending in three-foot-long clawed fingers, smaller tentacles sprouting from extended forearms to match the eight that grew from their sides and back. Each tentacle was lined with human fingers like the legs of a centipede, and every creature was moist with sweat, great folds of fat rolling over the titanic stomachs that jutted from their frames. The way their legs were designed, it looked as if the Children could move faster if given the proper motivation, folded up like overgrown frog legs with wide trowel shaped feet ending in a hard talon that acted as a single toe.

The legs were heavily muscled, and lined with red spots that Davis assumed were heat sensors. Where the head would be instead there was large drooling orifice, a tube leading into the stomach of the creature, ringed with powerful constricting muscles and folded, two-fingered arms that looked as if they would aid in pushing a human down the gullet. Hovering close to the creature, Davis could see a single violet eye sitting in the back of the "throat," staring back at him.

Marginally smaller were the four-legged Children that pranced around their larger kin, their dozens of flailing tendrils whipping about their backs. Distended stomachs dragged along the ground as the creatures moved about, their gullets sealed by a simple flap-like jaw. Each one was different than the last, though they all seemed to bear the same basic anatomy. Several of the four legged menaces had arms growing from their backs, two or three of them, all poised to grab someone and force them down into the stomachs of the Child's throat. Being as large as Mastiffs, they could reasonably hold a human within them if they kept them from moving.

Davis was certain the Children had a way of making that happen.

The gathering mob of sweaty, sticky monsters was worrisome. Several eyes from the small three-legged gatherers peered up at the drone in either awe or hate. The creatures all reached up plaintively at the light, slippery fingers and slickened tentacles writhing bonelessly in a sea of limbs all too gruesome to fathom as they fought for dominance, all trying to reach a little higher to grab onto the hovering machine. Davis smiled and pushed on, moving to peer down the well. The eyes surrounding it instantly locked onto his divinations and peered through them into Davis, causing an involuntary shudder to run through his body. Without the drone and its torch nearby, there wasn't sufficient light for his farseeing ability to detect anything. But what he could see was the flesh that had grown thick over the stone, the small clawed feet of the laboring Children leaving grooved cuts along the skin that bubbled with fat and grease.

Pulling himself back through the bowl, Davis stared down into the dirtied water with distaste. Even using divinations around the Children of Flesh wasn't safe! Standing up with the bowl, he opened the tent flap to throw the water out, splashing it directly into James's face with a wild sputtering.

"Oh! James… how can I help you?" Davis said, setting the bowl down on the ground inside his tent.

Wiping grimy water from his white hair, he glowered at Davis for a moment before sighing. "I was just coming in to ask you a couple things."

"I'd assumed that, I was trying to be polite and prompt you to just ask your questions," Davis said before tossing James a hand cloth. "And for God's sake, clean yourself up man! I don't want you dripping all over my tent!"

James wiped his face and patted his hair, grumbling the entire time. He came into the tent and sat down on the ground, his legs crossed. Davis turned and walked over to his satchel, reaching in for a bottle of water.

"So how long have you worshipped an old god, professor?" James asked, causing Davis to pause.

"Pardon?" Davis said, eyes flicking over to his spear.

"You heard me," James said, a cruel smile in his voice. "The way you act; the things you can do… all classic signs of a diabolist."

"Ah, but you seem to forget the one clue that truly marks a diabolist," Davis said, pulling the bottle of water out of his pack and turning to face his inquisitive student. "I don't have a cult, nor do I make sacrifices. Diabolists are dedicated to one old god and revere him over all others, and will do anything to grow closer to that god."

James frowned before pulling up a shock of white hair, shaking it. "Why did this happen to me and not you then? You should have been affected by the book like I was!"

"For one, when I first read the book I *was* afflicted with the same condition you have. For two, just because I can resist the foulness of the book doesn't mean I'm a diabolist, it means I have mental fortitude!"

"But you can read minds, and access the ether!" James accused.

Davis smiled. "And how would *you* know that unless you could also access the ether? Anything you care to admit, James?"

James flushed at the veiled attack. "I have nothing to hide! I'm a student of the occult, and my research has made me sensitive to the ether."

"Pull the other one James, you and I both know that is a load of bullshit," Davis hissed. "I am no diabolist, that I can assure you. But from facing them over the years I've learned a trick or two."

"Like reading minds?" James asked.

"Like reading surface thoughts, like names. If I fluster someone they think about a lot more and I can pull those thoughts as well," Davis replied. "Now how is it you can sense the ether? I know from experience you need to be exposed to it just to gain access, let alone sense its channels being opened by a practitioner."

James looked down at his hands, staring at the damp rag. "My father was an occultist… not in a cult or anything, mind you, but a collector of cursed items. He liked to put them in display cases and stare at them for hours, never touching them without a velvet cloth in his hands."

"Smart man. Not very wise, but smart," Davis noted.

"Yeah, well, not smart enough. He had a fiddle made by some mad worshipper in Italy in the eighteenth century, carved from some unknown wood with profane writing along its edges. Something, I don't know, *possessed* him and forced him to pick it up one night and come to the living room to where we were all sitting and playing. I was about ten, my sisters were nine and five. My mother was knitting while we played a board game."

"Oh my…" Davis said, dreading where this story was going.

"He came in the room, naked, bleeding from hundreds of slashes he'd made all over his body, pentagrams and arcane symbols no sane man would ever make, that seemed to slide along his skin as they steadily bled onto the carpet." James said, a distant look on his face robbing him of the ability to focus. "I remember him smiling, that wide smile that only a lunatic can manage, someone detached from humanity… *Honey,* he said to my mom, *you've gotta listen to this!*"

Davis rubbed his hand over his face, crossing his arms as he listened to James tell the story in a detached, emotionless voice.

"He put the violin to his chin and drew the bow across the strings, and a noise belched from the instrument, a horrid noise of crying children. I covered my ears instantly, as the simple noise disturbed me more than anything I've ever heard or seen, well, besides the *Chronicles…*" James said with a small smile, nodding and looking at Davis for a moment, tears welling at the corners of his eyes while he spoke. "That's what saved my life I think. As he began to play a very excited piece, the horrible crying children growing louder, my hands muffled enough of it so that I didn't suffer the same fate as my mother and brother."

"What happened to them?" Davis asked, knowing this violin's history.

"They stood up and began dancing, dancing in place while wailing and crying. Their skin had begun to peel like the skin of a snake. As they continued to shed the lights in the room grew dark, the smell of sulfur and brimstone filled the air, and the violin grew louder as if it was echoing in a grand hall!"

"He played the *Devil's Trill…*" Davis said without meaning to.

"I'm not surprised that you know of the song," James said, his tone bitter. He went back to telling the story. "An entity walked out of the darkness, tall and slouched, with prodigious muscles and a long serpent tail that coiled around my father, growing slick from his blood. The horned head of the creature bowed as father continued playing, swaying gently back and forth as the speed of the song increased to a fervent pace. Minutes crawled by, blood filling my palms from my ears as I continued to try and keep the song out."

He held out one of his alabaster arms, the veins ever present beneath his translucent skin. "My mother sloughed off all of the skin of her arms and face, leaving muscles straining to continue moving per the dance. My brother stumbled, breaking his ankle… but he continued to dance from foot to foot, just now he stood on the fractured stub with his foot hanging on by torn tendons and bleeding muscle, bits of skin falling from him. He was in shorts and a T-shirt you see, so the skin had peeled off from his legs too, great strips of chalk white paper rolled at his feet. Blood flew from him like rain, spattering the creature, the furniture, the game board… me! I tasted his blood accidentally when it fell in my empty mouth. That was when I realized I was screaming."

Davis shook his head sadly. "And what happened then?"

"The tail curled in and rammed straight into… into my father's backside, raising him up like he was a star on a Christmas tree; dad still played with the maniacal smile, blood oozing from his rectum as the tail sank deeper into his anus, lifting him higher and higher, higher than where our ceiling had been… the monster reached out with its giant hands, palms up. And my brother and mother just danced onto them, leaving bloody footprints and strings of muscle behind.

My mother wailed something, but I never got to find out what it was… Blood had filled my hands and was slipping through my fingers. As father finished his sonata, the devil stood up straight, revealing that the tail wasn't a tail at all, but a serpentine penis. It unfurled its wings, gossamer in nature with what looked like silver threading between black bones. It bowed to me and then, in a deep baritone that was smoky and thick, it asked: *Forse vi preoccupate per la mia canzone bambino?*"

"Do you like my song, little boy…?" Davis translated, Italian being the fourth language he'd mastered.

James pointed two fingers at his temple. "I *heard* him! He said that to me despite my *cupped ears* which were *overflowing with blood*! The fucking demon then stepped forward as its penis flexed and pushed further up into my father, as my brother and mother lay in his gigantic palms panting for breath… He looked down at me with glowing red eyes, eyes that still haunt my dreams. *Spalancate il mio bambino,* he said to me, and damned if I didn't sit up straight and open my mouth as wide as I could."

He choked up. "That was when I heard my mother give out a cry. He crushed them, wringing them between his fingers so the blood could pour out and over me. It filled my mouth, pulpy and thick, and I swallowed all that I could. It was like someone upended buckets over me, a torrential rainfall of crimson splashed all around me, soaking through my piss-stained pants and my shirt, my socks and my hair, getting into ever crevice. *Ora vi battezzo nel nome del diavolo,* he whispered to me, like he loved me. Like he *cared* for me."

"It baptized you in the name of the devil? That's… that's a very profane rite that the demon gave you."

"I started to pass out, a belly full of my mother's blood and sticky from the fluids dribbling from his hands. I let go of my ears and fell to the floor, inhaling my brother's blood. The last thing I remember before passing out was a horrid hissing noise accompanied by the worst pain I've ever felt on my chest."

"On your chest? Oh… oh no…" Davis said, watching as James lifted his shirt, baring his chest. There, in the middle was a scorched mark, cracked scarring of pentagram, an angry red color as if it were freshly cut and just now healing.

"It bleeds every so often, and when it does I hear the song, the song of screeching children to the tune of some horrid sonata. Sometimes I hear *his* voice, whispering in my ear. He whispers foul things, and chuckles when I try and think of something else."

"He's waiting for you," Davis said.

"Yeah, I figured. Anyway, I woke up in a hospital. Apparently, I'd almost died from blood loss. There were thick wads of cotton in my ears muffling my hearing, but an investigator told me that my home was a crime scene, and that my family was missing. That I was found naked and alone, branded like common cattle. They wanted to know what happened. I happily told them, and that sealed my fate."

James was crying now, rocking back and forth as he stared down at the floor of the tent. "I was committed to a sanitarium back in England, loaded with medications that left me near comatose, locked away for the next eight years. When I finally awoke, clear headed and frightened of everything, I discovered I was being discharged. I was of age. That was when I found out I had an estate worth millions, and I heard your name."

"Because I bought that violin for one point eight million dollars at auction," Davis said. He remembered when he was showing James the weapons, how distracted he'd seemed. How poorly he'd trained with his saber that afternoon. Davis sat silently, staring at James for a moment as the young man silently wept.

He eventually looked up at Davis, glaring.

"You can see why I would assume you to be some kind of diabolist then, can't you? You tap into the ether, you can read minds, you know all about old gods… and you have that damn violin on display like you're fucking proud of it!" James growled, tears dripping from his face. "How can you just let something like that sit? Just break it!"

"It can't be broken. The curse on that was said to be cast by a potent demonologist that followed Pazuzu… he claimed the devil needed music, claimed that he needed to make a sonata for the devil. So, he cursed the violin to teach the heretical song to any that would hold it for too long, while also allowing a portion of Hell to ingrain itself in the wood. The dark energy is what possessed your father and started the ritual, the monster that came was but a reflection of Pazuzu, one of many that drift through the ether waiting for something to summon them. If I destroy the violin the curse will drift to another one and imprint itself into the wood. It will look like an ordinary violin though, not like the occult relic I have trapped behind bulletproof glass."

James smiled wanly at that, looking down at his hands. "I knew your name before I ever met you. I'd wanted to come and learn from you, but the rumors persisted that you were a diabolist, a man who sacrificed his students to sate some ancient being best left forgotten."

James pulled the trench knife from behind his back, where it must have been tucked into his belt. "I told Huan to carry the knives you packed on her at all times. I was going to confront you later, but now seemed as good a time as any. If what you say is true and those *things* are going to come out from beneath the shadows when night falls, then I wanted to know. I wanted to know so if it could be done, I could slit your throat. But you're right… you're just a man… an old man who knows some tricks…"

Davis smiled as warmly as he could, thoughts of Joshua flitting through his mind. "No need to spill innocent blood today, not when it might be spilled in a few hours anyway."

James chuckled, head facing his lap. Davis walked up to him, his hips meeting James's shoulders. He laid a hand on James's head and ruffled his hair. "Stay in here if you like, just make sure you've dried those tears before coming out. Huan will have a field day with you if she found you crying."

Davis stepped past him and out of the tent, his mind swirling with the story he just heard. Someone baptized by an old god? People like that were prized by cultists, often brought into the clan and taught the ways of becoming a demonologist. If James held the potential, Davis may need to get rid of him…

# Chapter Sixteen

Davis stood outside his tent connecting his phone to the wireless internet that the Chinese government had set up in the rural mountains. After waiting a few minutes for the device to sync up, his inbox filled with messages, half of them from Lawrence.

"What has he discovered, I wonder?" Davis said aloud, flipping to the oldest message and opening it.

"Professor Nickels," he read aloud. "I have made some interesting discoveries with the sample you were able to retrieve. For the sake of our discussion, I will refer to these entities as the Flesh. First and foremost, the Flesh has an aversion to light akin to most nocturnal hunters; they can be present in the sunlight, but are uncomfortable. The fat that you collected became volatile in UV testing."

His ears perked to the sound of James shifting around inside his tent.

Davis continued: "This leads to the second quandary that the Flesh represents. Each aspect of the Flesh is capable of infesting and altering carbon-based life forms and turning them into a mockery of what they once were. After injecting a mouse with a milliliter of the fat, the mouse began showing symptoms within the hour. It is now hour three and I am the proud owner of a minion of an old god. I have begun testing on dear Mortimer the mouse to see what I can glean from extended trials."

Davis closed that e-mail when he noticed Huan walking up, dressed in her Kevlar-padded armor, all a dull gray in color. She had a gas mask slung around her neck and one of the spears over a shoulder, her pistol strapped to her hip along with a bandolier of the thermite grenades. All in all, she looked like a modern warrior princess.

"I see someone is already getting ready for my predicted battle come sundown!" Davis said a little loudly, alerting James to her presence.

"Yeah, I figure I can go and watch the drone for a while and try to figure out what to aim for," Huan said.

"I must say, you're taking this in stride. You weren't surprised about the Father of Flesh or his minions, or the nature of our little expedition. Normally I have to break in a graduate student into the life of paranormal entities."

Huan smiled, cocking her hip to the side. "Believe it or not I traveled a lot with my father growing up. My mom died giving birth to me so it was just me and my father for years. He did his best raising me. And we always could afford to live in good homes. We never stayed anywhere long though, and when I turned fourteen I found out why: dad was a monster hunter."

"Really?" Davis exclaimed.

"Yeah, he usually stuck to your average grave digging ghoul or run-of-the-mill cultist. They were a dime a dozen in California," Huan explained. "Well, for my fourteenth birthday he took me along on a hunt that was supposed to be a younger vampire, freshly turned."

"I assume that you found something more?" Davis asked.

Huan nodded, nose crinkled in disgust. "We found a nest. Everything holed up in a storage building, a hole in the pavement leading to the sewers where they could move around unseen. They were ghastly things, all pale skin and atrophied limbs as thin as rails. I remember their long fingers, how knobby they were, and the teeth. It's not like in the movies; they have a mouth full of serrated teeth that would put a shark to shame."

"I have a good deal of vampire relics recovered by hunters. They're all carved from bone, mostly human," Davis said.

"Sadistic fucks, I'll say. Anyway, the things were horrible, lurking in sewage and climbing along walls like damn spiders. A bullet to the head was enough to knock them out of the fight for about three, three and a half minutes. Long enough to blow out their hearts with a good shot from a shotgun. After the fifth one came around we decided that we'd best turn around and retreat. Dad said that he'd killed four more than he'd set out to for the night and that was enough."

Huan reached into her body armor and fished out a necklace where a large triangular tooth hung from a leather thong, a whole drilled through the root. It was an inch long and a half inch wide. "While we were turning back a vampire leapt down from the ceiling, fluid as water, and sank his fangs into my father's neck, spindly fingers gripping his shoulders and lifting him to block me from shooting him."

"What did you do?" Davis asked, enthralled by the tale.

"I raised my shotgun and unloaded three rounds through my father into the fucking parasite, throwing it down to the ground. Then I took it out of this world with a blast to the head. I collected teeth from all the dead ones, and took my dad's wallet. He had contact information for the bounty, and collectors who'd like some genuine vampire teeth. I keep this one close to my heart as it's one of the ones that ended my dad's life."

"But… you shot him!" Davis exclaimed, shaking his head. "Didn't you kill him?"

Huan shrugged. "Maybe. But he was dead as soon as those teeth ripped into his neck. The amount of blood that sprayed down the monster's gullet, drooling out from between its teeth like strawberry jam running down a wall on a hot summer day. His blood pressure had dropped and he was cold by the time I touched him not a minute later."

The front of Davis's tent zipped open, revealing a red-eyed James who came crawling out. "You killed your own father?"

Huan smiled at him. "Yup! I had to do it, and like I said, he was dead anyway. What I did was an act of mercy more than anything else."

Davis studied her for a moment, shrewd eyes looking her over. No child could so callously talk about their parent's death especially if they had a hand in it… "Tell me Huan, do you remember the noises that your father made as he died?"

"Are you kidding? I dream about them every night!" she exclaimed.

"So you have nightmares?" James asked.

Huan shook her head. "Not really, just memories and strange things like talking fish and clowns."

"Ah," Davis said. "Huan, you should go and check out the monitors. We need as much intelligence on the Children's movements and we only have a few hours before dusk."

Huan leaned forward with a smile before saluting. "Sure thing professor!"

As she trotted away, Davis turned to James. "Keep an eye on her, she might be... unstable."

"Wow, you think?" James laughed, shaking his head.

"I'd rather be wrong and paranoid than right and dead, so we just keep an eye on her and make sure she doesn't show any... *issues* during the coming firefight."

"Sir, to be frank I think I'm going to have issues after this fight," James said, walking off towards his own tent. "I'm gonna get ready. Per my phone sunset is in roughly two and a half hours."

"A wise action then, I'm going to check over Lawrence's e-mails while we're waiting," Davis said.

"What, you're not going to get ready?" James asked.

Davis smirked, waving down at his vest and khaki pants. "This is all I'll need, in addition to a gas mask and my grenades. I'll be bringing my rifle and pistol, along with my spear and knife."

James pulled the trench knife from where he'd had it tucked under his shirt. "I've never used one of these before."

"They're brass knuckles built into six inches of sharpened steel, use them like they were intended. Wear gloves with them so you don't come into skin contact with the Children and you'll be fine."

James just looked at the knife before slipping his fingers through the knuckles slot. "Huh..."

"Now if you'll excuse me, I'm going to finish my research. Or, more precisely, my assistant's research," Davis said, pulling the flap of his tent back and walking beneath the padded canvas.

Grabbing the haft of his spear, he leaned on it heavily. He flipped open his pocket watch and frowned.

"Not much time left before it starts..." Davis grumbled, looking at the multiple hands. "And so much... this will be a nasty fight."

Clacking his pocket watch closed and tucking it into one of the inner pockets of his jacket, he pulled out his cell phone and set it down on a crate, activating the dictate mode to read out the e-mails to him. He went to the next e-mail, turning as the feminine voice started up and began to read out the text of Lawrence's hard-earned research.

"As predicted, fire is an absolute way to deal with the Flesh. I have used a syringe filled with various narcotics, poisons, and acids and found that they fail to hinder the beast in any substantial fashion. Only the acid seemed to do anything, burning away a reasonable amount of flesh before the fatty substance it uses for blood absorbed the remnants of the caustic fluid," the voice recited. "I heated a steel file to the point where the metal would burn paper, then applied it to Mortimer's leg, successfully severing the limb. That limb did not grow back, unlike the acid burn, which had caused a crater that had formed into a second mouth."

"Pause," Davis said aloud, stopping his phone from going further. "So heat *is* the way to remove them from the picture… my spear generates enough to ignite so it will prove useful. I'd hoped my Buffalo rifle would prove useful as well, but it'll just result in further mutation. The trench knives might serve to cut off a tentacle. Small arms fire will just create more mouths…"

Davis thought for a few moments on what could be done to reduce their numbers. The thermite grenades were limited in number and while they would probably reduce one to ash, the problem would be the seconds it would take to cripple them. The one Davis fought on his balcony was handled in an effective, if sloppy, manner. Any severed limbs would spread to create the flesh growing over the soil and grass of the field between the village and the military camp at the base of the hill.

"Resume," Davis ordered, sitting down on a prepared cot.

"In related news, a report of a monster sighting was made here in Austin. It killed four people and consumed another before retreating into the sewers. We may have to deal with an infestation here in the States after you help the Chinese with their own problem."

Davis shook his head. He knew the one he blasted off the Jeep would do some damage, but he didn't think it would be able to slink away like that. Maybe these weren't alpha predators like he'd originally thought? The ability to look human and their preference for hunting at night was making them seem more and more like ambush predators than anything else. Davis looked up when he heard the dictating phone mention breeding.

"...appear to be asexual in nature, with an inherent desire to attack and consume prey that is up to their size. A second mouse, designated Daisy, was introduced into Mortimer's cage. He sensed her, despite his lack of eyes and summarily attacked her, clubbing her with three tentacles he'd sprouted around his secondary mouth. The loss of the leg had been accounted for with Mortimer shedding five percent of his mass in a transitional morph that made him a three-legged creature with a more bulbous body, comprised of two mouths and five tentacles in total. Daisy was stunned long enough for the tentacles to wrap around her frame and, well, stuff her into Mortimer's primary mouth. The secondary mouth flattened and closed through the aid of two tentacles, which curled over the maw. Mortimer took Daisy into himself and, upon being seized and weighed, showed that he was nearly double his original weight."

"What does this have to do with them being asexual?" Davis muttered.

"Mortimer kept Daisy within his frame, crushing her with several rings of muscle while inserting internal tentacles through her throat and up her anus. Mortimer lost another three to five percent of his mass injecting Daisy with his own fluids, which seemed to pacify her. At this point she had, upon inspection, been wrapped in a thin membrane of flesh and was vomited out. Mortimer lost interest in her, but appeared to have gained some mass through the transition. Her spilled blood and torn muscle took four minutes to be broken down by a base substance that is like ammonia. Used a syringe to withdraw a sample for testing. After the chemical broke the tissue and blood down it was absorbed and made into liquid fat. Mortimer's primary mouth was open and all of this was visible using a flashlight and a tight gloved grip. I could feel his body expanding and growing in my hand, and he became noticeably stronger in his struggles, forcing me to release him."

Davis's phone paused for a moment before making a clicking noise, indicating the e-mail was done. Davis stood up and pressed for the next e-mail to start, just as James opened the flap of the tent and slouched in, dressed in padded Kevlar, goggles and gas mask hanging around his neck. Davis shushed him before he could speak.

The dictation program started up again, the smooth feminine voice repeating Lawrence's greeting from the first e-mail.

"This is e-mail is written after observing Daisy in her thin membrane for a total of twenty-two minutes. At that time, the membrane peeled back through no visible means other than internal muscle, revealing a new Flesh creature, two tentacles, five legs, no tail and a mouth where the neck once was. The smaller Flesh creature that Daisy had become is devoid of any rat anatomy and moves with an awkward gait. The tentacles are noticeably thicker and longer than Mortimer's, and Daisy is much faster. Beneath where she had lain while within the membrane, the peeled back envelope now lay on the shredded wood that made up the bottom of the cage. After three minutes the wood beneath it had been fully integrated into this new creature, which I've dubbed *bedding*. On the bedding there has formed a sunken pit approximately four millimeters deep, which has begun feeding a cloud of black spores into the air, striking the sealed top of the enclosure, forming a cloud that has forced me to now peer through the glass and now take only visual observations for fear of what the spores could actually do if exposed to the air."

"Pause," Davis said, turning to James. "These are Lawrence's tests with the substance I retrieved from the Child of Flesh that attacked me on my balcony. He injected it into one of our test animals and created a Child of Flesh that has shown us how they reproduce, fight, and feed. However gruesome, I'll have to insist with Pho and whoever oversees the military group that anyone being consumed must be executed to *try* and prevent more Children from forming."

"And if one of us is to get eaten?" James asked, staring at Davis.

Davis licked his lips. "We'll stick together and try to focus on one Child at a time. If one of is getting consumed... we'll use a grenade on the Child to kill it."

"Isn't that dangerous?" James asked.

"Would you rather we kill each other?" Davis asked, clearly annoyed at the line of questioning. "I'm hoping that Lawrence has sent something along that will show me how to disinfect someone. I know an old incantation that can halt demonic influences, but not one that removes them."

"Do you think it would work?" James asked.

Davis shrugged. "It's Assyrian and was made specifically for battle against an old god and his minions in the days of old. I'll just have to test it out on anyone showing signs of infection."

"Well hopefully we won't have a chance to test that. And the ground flesh, the bedding? That's a separate creature itself?"

"Apparently," Davis replied with a sigh. "We'll have to use flamethrowers to cleanse the village completely, before descending into the well to try and locate where these things are coming from."

"That sounds like it'll be fun…" James said with a frown. Davis just chuckled, earning a look from the devil-blessed young man.

"It's just… I think that *finding* the spawning grounds of these creatures will be the easy part. The hard part will be surviving the storming of the beach, so to speak."

"Our own D-Day… what fun!" James groused, earning another chuckle from Davis, who patted him on the back with a knotty hand.

# CHAPTER SEVENTEEN

Davis sat on the slope of the hill, a series of sandbags encircling him to create a sort of light fortification that mainly served as a place to house his arsenal, as well as his students, during the coming battle. And with the sun setting behind the Nanling Mountains, its last streaks of light allowing the bleak hold of darkness to stretch across the valley, the attack was likely imminent. Davis had his spear, five thermite grenades on a bandolier, his shotgun attached to his belt at his hip, his Buffalo rifle sitting over the sandbags and his pistol set under his vest in a chest holster. Tucked in a sheath on the other side of his hip was his trench knife, just in case the situation got desperate.

Huan was giggling to herself as she stared through a M4 carbine rifle liberated from the soldiers at the base of the hill, its heavy slugs almost comparable to Davis's rifle in power. She had her Desert Eagle and trench knife as well, along with a staggering eight thermite grenades. She assured Davis that she knew how to use them, and demonstrated with one on a small tree some twenty feet away, lobbing the orb like an oversized baseball with startling accuracy, the brilliant flash of magnesium igniting followed by a black cloud of smoldering wood, the thermite eating through the dry wood like a pressure washer fired into notebook paper.

James was still holding his Winchester .243. He'd taken a night vision scope for it. He also had a handful of grenades and his trench knife, along with a Benelli M4 tactical shotgun, one used by police in the States and, apparently, in the Chinese military. The shotgun was capable of tearing holes through oak trees at thirty yards and held seven three-inch Magnum shells, enough to punch through any model of personal armor or bulletproof glass. Davis was a little leery about James carrying the shotgun around, at least until he learned all the trained soldiers at the base of the hill had modified M14 automatic guns and the tactical shotguns as well, along with thorough body covering, including goggles and gas mask, long sleeves and gloves. The men must have been toasty warm beneath all the rubber protective clothing. At the very least, all that padding would make it more difficult for the Children to ingest the soldiers.

The commander, a young lieutenant that looked small compared to his heavily armored warriors, was armed with a rifle Davis didn't recognize, along with a headset that allowed him to communicate with his men directly into their hoods. Using their flares, they'd formed three sets of concentric arcs thirty, sixty, and ninety yards away from them, the sparkling red light illuminating the growing bedding that was creeping across the grass, eyes popping up from the rolling tide of flesh to peer at the lights curiously.

Looking through his night vision scope, Davis mumbled a forgotten curse as he noted there were now seven of the larger Children, as well as twenty to thirty smaller ones, not counting the swarm of three-legged workers that were dismantling the village. They'd stopped their task and had gathered behind their aggressive cousins, their lone tentacles growing curved nails, sharp and wicked looking. They skittered to and fro, crawling over each other like hamsters as they seemed to be preparing for the signal to attack.

That was when the valley began to vibrate from a horrid squelching howl, akin to a blender full of fruit turned on high. Looking through the scope Davis felt a sudden sense of vertigo, his head aching as his eyes throbbed within their sockets. A warm trickle of blood seeped from his ears as he fought to remain standing behind his sandbag wall. Looking to his sides, James had dropped his rifle and was holding his hands over his ears while Huan's smile only grew as her ears steadily flowed with red. Yet, unlike James, she held her ready stance.

As unnerving as that was, Davis was dismayed to see the effect this call had on the soldiers at the foot of the hill; they were all stumbling drunkenly, leaning on their weapons as they fought to remain standing. The lieutenant was shouting orders into his headset all while tottering on unsteady legs.

While the Chinese forces all staggered about from the stunning roar, the Children of Flesh began loping across the ninety yard markers, the smaller ones running on four to six legs like demented deer while the larger ones slouched across the battlefield, their heavy arms acting as an extra set of legs as they moved. The workers moved in between the nine foot mountains of muscle, weaving between their steps as if daring the behemoths to step on one of them. All the while, the roar continued to issue forth from somewhere in the valley, echoing along the hills and reverberating in Davis's teeth.

Growling, Davis lined up his rifle and sighted one of the smaller five-legged beasts, built like a headless dog with three large tentacles rising from its shoulders. A gaping hole served as its mouth and dribbled a viscous fluid as it sprinted along. Davis lined up the shot and pulled the trigger, the loud crack snapping his students out of their stupors. The five-legged Child bucked and rolled as the bullet tore through the upper lip of the mouth and into the shoulder, blasting a tentacle free in a display of flowing fat and fleshy gore that seemed to stun the creature, allowing one of the behemoths to trample it beneath its bulk as the herd charged forward.

Davis could see James scooping up his rifle and sighting one of the creatures, aiming carefully.

"Shoot off limbs!" Davis shouted as Huan fired, blowing a gaping hole through the right leg of one of the behemoths, causing it to stumble as the leg gave way beneath the weight of the creature's frame. Another sharp crack widened the hole, causing the leg to rip free from the stump as the behemoth trudged on without it, the stump sealing over and sprouting a mouth framed by three boneless arms.

The soldiers seemed to be regaining their senses as the frontrunners passed the second flare, many of them opening fire into the coming storm of muscle and sinew, small holes erupting along the bodies of the smaller Children, causing whip-thin arms to sprout from each hole after a few seconds. If their automatic weapons were doing anything, it was hard to tell.

James blasted off the leg of a four-legged Child, the creature rolling forward from the sudden loss of limb. It lay still as flesh began to stretch and knit over the wound, the remaining front leg shifting to be in the middle of the torso, the mouth and tentacles rising to the top of the creature as it morphed to become viable once more, six thick tentacles moving to pick itself up off the ground.

Wherever limbs or fat dribbled out, the ground began to grow out new coverings of bedding, which spread beneath their clawed feet at a rapid rate. Knowing that the bedding was the least of their worries, Davis fired his Buffalo gun and lanced the upper torso of one of the behemoths, splitting it in half from the stomach down to the chest in an eruption of fat and pus that caused it to slow down. It struggled for a moment before the split down its chest spread to create a wider maw for the monster.

They continued firing, their shots slowing the oncoming horde of unnatural monsters until the sound of loud popping filled the air, several pops and speeding shells flying in a lazy arc over the line of soldiers. A group of ten soldiers, five loading and five firing mortars had joined in as the majority of the enemy forces had crossed the sixty-yard flare. Explosions of earth and rock peppered the hides of the smaller, more agile Children as the behemoths howled in thousands of voices, their large soft bodies easy marks for the explosives. One behemoth, struck by three mortar rounds directly, quivered and stumbled before bursting like a water balloon, molten fat and pus raining down over the ruined cinders of the creature's once towering frame.

Davis noticed with a frown that bedding had started growing from the fallen monstrosity, spreading wherever the fatty tissue fell. He fired another shot, blasting a tentacle at its base off a Child crossing the thirty-yard marker, before swiveling his gun to a larger one. Firing into its mouth as it stretched in a horrible yawn, Davis blew a foot-wide hole through the back of the upper torso. Slipping another bullet into his rifle, Davis fired at the closing wound, blasting apart the stretching flesh as its body attempted to mend the tear. A wave of bullets rained on the giant Child, the automatic rifles ripping a line of wounds across the chest and into the mouth. A tentacle fell while another slithered from the multiple injuries, the behemoth slowing down as its body slowly began to convert into something else, mass shifting back from its forelimbs and into its rear ones, a thick talon stretching out from the foot to maintain balance. The shrunken arms turned into tentacles that slid along the greasy creature to join several more that were growing from the pallid flesh, forming a ring around a flexible "head" that was little more than a mouth with small tendrils acting as teeth, waving from within.

Several of the soldiers let out cries as smaller Children appeared in front of them, using the darkness to shift through the ether to close the distance. Now sporting new tentacles and five legs, one instantly slammed three soldiers with the thick appendages, knocking them to the ground. One of the soldiers, firing from the ground, turned the automatic rifle onto the Child and began unloading his clip, tearing bloodless holes through the body that seemed to only push the pagan beast back a few inches rather than kill it. It lashed three tentacles down, one crushing the soldier's arms as it silenced the gunfire while the other two scooped beneath the man's armpits, pulling him up and into the maw, head first.

Wu's drone shone down over the soldiers, revealing a wide circle of land and allowing the soldiers to better see the combatants as they came into close range. Davis shot one soldier in the neck with his buffalo gun, severing his head as he was lifted by a behemoth and dropped into the widened maw. Small chunks of meaty flesh flew off the behemoth, Huan and James doing their best to stall the creature from its meal.

It only grew worse as the mortar team fell to four smaller Children, the multi-legged horrors lashing out and swallowing four soldiers in as many seconds. The mortar teams drew pistols and fired into the resilient hides of the creatures as they feasted, but they failed to even draw a line of bubbling fat.

A thermite grenade went off, a loud sizzling noise overwhelming the howling of the creatures, a behemoth holding one man in a tentacle while the upper body erupted into white-hot flames, the smell of searing flesh and fat making its way up the hill in seconds. The creature, still on fire and slowly collapsing in on itself, turned and trampled a soldier as it attempted to run back to the overgrown village.

It didn't make it ten feet before it fell, bursting like a watermelon as the flames ate the creature to ash. The soldier trapped in the tentacle stood up and shouted in Cantonese. "The grenades! Use the grenades!"

Davis smirked. They hadn't thought his "gift" would prove useful apparently, but now as several other sizzling eruptions took place, the howling slowly shifted to screeches. In less than a minute the Children of Flesh were retreating to the village, many sporting burn wounds from splashes of thermite that had seared through them like burning logs through snow.

The remaining men, three mortar team members and four infantrymen cheered. They walked along, using the grenades to clear away the bedding that had formed during the battle. Davis shook his head at the waste, but consoled himself that they'd have flame throwers soon. Turning to Huan, he was startled to see her flushed face and hazy eyes.

"Huan?" Davis said, breaking her reverie. She looked at Davis with what looked like a hint of scorn before schooling her features.

"Yes, professor? What is it?" Huan asked breathlessly.

"Are you okay? You seem… flustered." Davis asked, eyeing her as she caressed her rifle.

"I'm fine, I'll just need to… to work off some tension after all of this… maybe spar with one of the soldiers down there," Huan said, eyes lingering on the cheering soldiers and their lieutenant.

"You practice martial arts?" James asked, clearly surprised.

Her eyes snapped to him and grew thick with some emotion that Davis didn't recognize. "Yeah… professor, do we have anything to do now?"

"I was going to listen to some more of Lawrence's notes, but I was expecting you all to need to rest. I didn't think that this would go over as smoothly as it did." Davis replied.

Huan stood up and grabbed James by the collar, pulling him up with her. "I'm going to teach you some…. things. You're skinny so you could use something to fall back on if you ever find yourself alone."

"Okay—ah! I can walk on my own!" James grunted as she pulled him out from the sandbag gunners nest that Davis had requested be built for him and his students. Smiling as he watched them go, Davis shook his head.

"Hope she doesn't hurt him…" Davis said as he shouldered his rifle and walked out the other side and slowly down the hill.

The lieutenant spotted him first. The young man shifted nervously, obviously not very used to how battles were waged. He looked a little green at the various parts of his men being piled up on remaining bedding to be burned. Turning as Davis approached, the lieutenant greeted him in Mandarin.

"Honored elder! You were a valuable ally in our fight against the shui gui tonight! We were able to repel the enemy forces thanks to your efforts," the man said, bowing low in thanks. "My name is Sei Heng, Lieutenant Second Class."

"Never seen combat like this have you, lieutenant?" Davis chuckled, earning a wan smile from the officer.

"No, I've only been with the department for a year or so. We get called out when a contained entity breaks free or when one is found lurking around a village. This… this was something else!"

"Well, expect it to get worse," Davis said. He motioned to the men beside him, who were building a fire. "I would keep feeding that fire for the night; these creatures abhor fire and are uncomfortable in light, daylight in particular."

"So you've studied them professor?" Lieutenant Sei said, hope in his voice.

Davis chuckled. "Call me Davis, and yes. I have a researcher back home testing one in a controlled environment."

"If I may call you Davis then I demand you call me Heng, as it would be dishonorable to speak to an elder such as yourself with airs of superiority," Heng said. "I watched our mortar team try and use small arms against them… it did nothing!"

"Yeah, they're all resilient. While they're formed of nothing but muscle and fat, they can form hard armor from callouses and layers of keratin," Davis explained. "The reason they were eating your men, just so you know, wasn't for nutrition."

"Oh? What else would it be for?" Heng asked, clearly interested.

"I would be remiss not informing your department about this, but all of those creatures were once human. They get infected with the parasitic growth of what my researcher calls the Flesh, and they slowly become one of the monsters. The reason I requested goggles and gas masks is because I had no idea if the Flesh parasite could be transmitted through the air."

Heng looked over at the pile of burning limbs and slippery sections of monster. Davis raised a hand before the officer could speak. "The fire kills the infection, I assure you, but one of your survivors might be infected. How many soldiers are coming in with the flame throwers tomorrow?"

"Twenty experienced soldiers. They've dealt with old gods before and have all come away relatively sane and intact," Heng joked before falling silent. He looked down at Davis, head tilted to the side. "Their screech… why were we not informed of that?"

"Because we didn't know they could do that. Maybe they can manage that form of attack in large numbers, but for the most part they move silently and with purpose," Davis said, thinking of the two he'd encountered in Austin.

"What should we do? You seem to think one of my men is infected. How can you tell?" Heng asked, voice tinged with worry.

"You can't. The process is slow and speeds up at one point to where you must terminate the subject. Even then we're not certain that a Child of Flesh will not rise from the host," Davis said, the lieutenant's face growing grim. "What we'll do is send your men back and order quarantine on them with guards using flame throwers. I'm sure you have containment cells to house the supernatural entities native to China."

"Yes, we have the facilities. Thank you for the warning..." Heng said, bowing once more.

"Let's hope it's just an old man being paranoid Heng..." Davis said, bowing as well.

# Chapter Eighteen

Davis crept up the hill, his weapons slung over his back, his spear acting as a walking stick. The hill was crumbling; it was all dried grass and sandy earth, something that was strange for this area.

Exhaustion weighed on him, and the recent battle and trans-Pacific flight did not help matters. Normally he got off a plane and spent a week organizing his dig before setting out for the remote locale he would be pillaging for ill-gotten gains. His helpers, graduate students who needed a better grade, always aided him in fending off the defenses these tombs always seemed to have.

This time around he'd been dropped off in a temporary military base where he'd been briefed on the monsters he would be facing, the information proving less than helpful. Judging by how many soldiers had been taken by the Children, there could be many more of them now than before. He watched to make certain the paltry number of soldiers left over were taking up posts around their enclosure and the camp where the scientists and researchers slept.

Creeping along the darkened courtyard where the computers were set up, noting how Wu seemed to still be up watching the creatures via his drone, Davis slipped past the computer engineer's paranoid glances and walked into the area where his crew had tents set up for them. That was when he heard it.

Crack!

Spinning around, dropping the tethered guns to the ground as he brandished his spear, Davis peered through the darkness. This plateau was scoured of any detritus, so a breaking twig was something to note. Eyes peering down the alley that separated a set of communal tents from the storage tent, Davis heaved a sigh.

And that was when he saw the figure race across the path intersecting the aisle, moving quick as possible, far faster than a human. Davis ducked into the supply tent, walking around the stacked crates to get to the entrance. In the pitch darkness of the tent, Davis could see perhaps twenty feet in front of him thanks to his advanced senses. This only allowed him to see labeled boxes of ammunition and rations.

Those senses were what saved his life when a barb shot across the tent, Davis deftly dodging the half-foot of keratin that became embedded in a wooden crate, fat sliding from the end of the sharpened nail.

"So there *are* sneaky versions of you out here," Davis said low enough that nobody would hear him. The Children had dispatched one, if not several, subjects to gather intelligence. This meant that they weren't mindless beasts like one would think at first blush. The ones from America weren't aberrant, but a different type it would seem.

They plotted.

They planned.

Stepping around a stack of crates, Davis saw a laptop sitting open. The screen was locked with a password prompt. Greasy imprints over the keys showed that whatever was lurking in the camp was trying to access the technology. For what reason, Davis couldn't fathom. Old gods rarely paid attention to the technology of man, viewing it as something beneath their notice. Obviously, the Father of Flesh, whether he was asleep, imprisoned, or free took the stance that the abilities of man were something to keep an eye on.

Walking up to the laptop, Davis frowned at the lines of fat that had pooled atop the keys and crate, fresh bedding growing from the wood. Davis pulled his trench knife and scraped a bit from the enter key, looking at the jiggling slime on the end of the blade. It moved slightly, as if it were seeking something… maybe it sensed heat?

Hearing a creak of wood, Davis looked up and studied the stacks of crates lining the large tent. A single light hung over the laptop at a makeshift desk, wavering slightly back and forth. Davis reached out and grabbed the light, bringing it to a halt before pulling his fingers back, the sticky residue of… *something* coming off the hot light onto his gloves. He wiped the goo off his knife with an oil-stained washcloth. Looking across the shadowy room, Davis could feel the eyes on him, the darkness practically glaring at him, daring him to investigate the shadows.

A faint scent of smoke made Davis leery of just returning to his tent for a well-deserved rest. Something was in here and whatever it was had used movement that the Children took advantage of. Strange though… it wasn't like a Child to wait in the darkness, let alone access a computer. Davis stepped towards the central aisle, his eyes adjusting to the inky blackness caressing his skin. The chill of the night seemed to sink further into his skin than it had when he stood outside, something that was odd if you didn't understand how the creatures of darkness worked.

When one was stalking you, you would grow colder; the very attention of an old god's minion was enough to send chills down even a battle-hardened marine's back. The fact that Davis, blessed with powers from a forgotten god and more than a century of experience under his belt, still felt the chill meant that something was pondering on how it would work out if it lashed out now.

"I know you're there," Davis said to the darkness, picturing the hunched form of a Child, the blind creature standing behind a crate. "You might as well come out and let me see you. Who knows? I may find you, and then we might get to dance!"

"I don't think so, *professor*," Pho drawled from behind him, forcing Davis to whirl around, his spear held at the ready.

The elderly secretary was dressed in his traditional garb and little else apart from socks with slippers. He stared at Davis, then pointedly at the spear leveled at his chest. "Planning something, are we?"

"No," Davis panted, his heart going a mile a minute. "I just thought one of the creatures got past the quarantine… however secure it is now."

"Wu has been observing the beasts regurgitating captured soldiers and sliding them down the well one at a time. The smallest ones, which we've dubbed *workers*, are still dismantling the village while the others are digging into the pulpy mass..."

"Bedding," Davis interrupted.

"Bedding?" Pho repeated, obviously confused.

"I have a researcher with a captured Child, who has been doing experiments to better understand their physiology. The bedding, the pulpy flesh that builds up on the ground, is a separate organism."

"Ah," Pho said, clearly unimpressed. "Well, as I said, Wu has informed me that tunnels are being dug into this *bedding* for the creatures to presumably dwell in during daytime hours. The ash cloud over them only blocks out so much sunlight."

Davis decided not to correct him that the material was composed of spores. Instead he lowered his spear and relaxed his stance. Allowing half a smile to grace his features, he nodded to the laptop.

"There's some fatty tissue on the keys, and bedding growing on a crate," Davis said, causing the old man to turn and look, wincing at the bare bulb shining brightly over the workstation. "How do you explain that?"

"I have no clue... maybe there is a monster in our base," Pho said, his voice low.

"I smelled smoke, and they demonstrated on the battlefield tonight the ability to slip through space and time to jump forward distances, leaving nothing but a trail of smoke behind," Davis explained, motioning with his spear up at the bulb. "I knocked my head against the hot bulb and found some damaged tissue sticking to it."

Pho hummed a bit before crossing his arms. "I don't know what to tell you. I was worried you were... up to something when you came in here. The laptop is off limits, you know."

"I actually didn't even know it was here," Davis replied, eyeing Pho carefully. He didn't mention the attack for fear that Pho would rouse the camp and scare away the spy. "Well, I'm going to go to bed here soon. Since I have you here, what do you think the plan will be for tomorrow?"

Pho looked stunned at the question before he took on a pensive face. "I suppose we'll use mortar fire to hold off any encroaching *bedding,* as you put it, and then allow the lieutenant and his remaining men to be replaced by the incoming troops that are bringing supplies, including your precious flamethrowers."

"And these men are skilled?" Davis asked.

Pho snorted. "This is our Beta regiment, second best in the department with the highest kill ratio among our expanded military. They're also the best unit to bring underwater as they're all accomplished swimmers. Just what you requested, if I recall correctly."

"Yes, that'll do nicely," Davis agreed. They stood in silence for a few moments, both staring at each other before Davis coughed into his hand. "Well, I guess I'll head to bed now."

"You do that professor," Pho said, turning to walk to the laptop. "You do that."

* * *

Davis's dreams that night were plagued by the images of fleshy monsters craving bodies for the propagation of their kind. He woke up before dawn, his bladder protesting the few cups of water he'd drunk the night before while taking his medication. Walking out of his tent in just a pair of black silk boxers and his spear, Davis spied a most unusual thing.

James's tent, not five feet from his own, was rustling. He could hear grunts and groans, not unlike what he'd heard when he was struggling with the beast that appeared on his balcony. Walking softly over to the tent, he listened and heard a loud slapping noise followed by a cry of pain. Remembering the scent of smoke he'd encountered in the supply tent, he decided to investigate.

Grabbing the flaps of the tent, he whipped them back, peering into the darkness… right into Huan's eyes, closed in rapture as she knelt on the cold ground, James's pale form behind her ramming into her core with the vigor of a man possessed. The whole tent smelled of debauchery and sweat. Both students were covered in a sheen of perspiration despite the cool morning air, grunting as they rutted like pigs. Davis could see the mark of Pazuzu on James's chest, burning brightly before the aged professor's eyes. The scar tissue was raised and defined, and seemed to have an unearthly glow about it that lit the tent well enough for Davis to see Huan's perky breasts sway in front of him, one of James's hands gripping onto one from behind. Realizing this was something he should not be witnessing, Davis backed away from the tent.

Walking past the supply tent to some of the shrubs, he caught sight of a shadow moving within the darkened tent. The light was off but thanks to his enhanced senses, he could detect the mind lurking within the temporary structure. It was old, and twisted; it had a purpose and was driven to find something out. Beyond that, he couldn't tell anything about it. Deciding to hold his bladder for a few minutes, Davis walked into the large tent, poking ahead with his spear, obsidian point aimed ahead of him. The mind within the tent calmed, trying to hide its presence.

*This isn't some Child here… this is something crafty,* Davis thought, moving down one aisle. The whole tent smelled of stale sweat and smoke, as if one of the creatures had been moving through the ether to get in here.

"Hello?" Davis said aloud.

The mind panicked and began to fade from his senses.

"No! There's no reason to go, is there?" said Davis. "I just want to talk if you're up to it."

The mind resurfaced before… *shifting* into a more human frame, one full of curiosity and hope. Hope for what, Davis couldn't tell; the mind was well-guarded.

"Chosen of Fa'theli… you seem to be an inquisitive one," a silky voice crept through the crisp morning air.

Davis took a few steps down the aisle of crates. "I've been told that before. I'm curious how you know of my association with the Knowledge-Bearer, seeing as I haven't associated with anyone bearing his mark for over eighty years."

The voice chuckled. "Once chosen, always chosen. I heard your follower question your loyalties. The way you handled it shows your cunning. You are fit to bear the title of chosen, that I will freely admit."

"Where are you?" Davis asked, turning as he heard shuffling behind him.

Nothing.

"I can be anywhere I want to be, so finding me will be very difficult, chosen one," it said. "I'm impressed how you handled the shui gui today."

"They're not water demons," Davis snapped.

"True, but the people of this region called them that for the centuries they lay dormant. Now that they've returned, the name has resurfaced. I rather like it."

"So you're one of them?" Davis guessed, twirling around as he felt hot breath on his neck.

Again, nothing, save for a heady scent of smoke.

"In a way… I'm an extension of the Father. Don't worry, he still slumbers. For how long, I wouldn't be able to say," it mused aloud, a row over.

Davis didn't rush to try and locate the voice. He knew that was what it wanted, it wanted him to panic. "Wouldn't or won't? You seem to know a lot about me, why not share a little about yourself?"

"You've got me there. I suppose telling you a story would keep your mind busy for the next few days…" it said, as if deciding whether to say anything more.

"I'm all ears," Davis replied.

"All right. Long ago, when the Father was first laid to rest, the people of this land built a temple over him, along with several gates to a pocket world, where they moved him to. These gates were magically sealed and kept the Father asleep. But his dreams, they've grown… troubled over the past few centuries. He remembers when he was a greater being, and he yearns to join his brothers and sister. And so, the hidden conclaves of his flesh stirred, allowing the shui gui to resurface and begin working on unsealing the gates."

"I've heard of the gates," Davis said, thinking once more of the monster on his balcony. His words rang through his mind, saying he couldn't stop the gates from opening.

"Yes, I'm aware," the sibilant voice cooed. "There are four in total. One for each piece of the great one. The Singers worked with the Followers of Rewa to seal the Brother of Bone, while the Sister was buried beneath the layered stone of the Bashkir strongholds. The slippery one, our dear Mother, was the last to be entombed and the first to be rediscovered."

"Rediscovered? You mean by Grimlocke?" Davis asked.

"Yesss…" the voice hissed. "The man thought himself mighty and wielded magics that even he could not fathom. We turned him away, multiple times. You are the first we've spoken to since our Father was put to rest."

"How lucky of me," Davis groused.

"Yes," the voice murmured in the hollow of his ear, a slippery tongue licking his neck. "You could have died ten times over tonight and yet I've let you live. Think on that while I watch your group fall to the might of the Father. Know that you will lead them to despair and that we will succeed only by your actions."

Davis swung around, his spear slashing through a cloud of smoke and echoing laughter that seemed to haunt the tent, as well as Davis's very mind.

On the plus side, his bladder was empty.

On the down side, there was an enemy amongst the ranks of the Chinese. One that was watching Davis and his crew with interest.

# CHAPTER NINETEEN

Davis was sitting on a flat rock, enjoying the cool morning in the mountains. The new regiment had arrived via three helicopters, each one carrying ten to fifteen troops and extra crates of supplies. Pho oversaw them as they carried the heavy crates into the supply tent. Each of the soldiers was short but thick, built like a wrestler, with padded armor covering their skin and hoods with gas masks covering their faces. Slung over their backs were long rifles that had canisters on them, each canister marked with Mandarin lettering and the international sign of danger, a yellow triangle with a skull superimposed over it. Davis sipped his tea as he watched all of this, spear resting in his lap.

He was intent on finding out who could be the monster, the Child of Flesh amidst their ranks. He hadn't spent much time on it as he'd gone back to sleep, too tired to worry over the matter.

If the creature wanted Davis dead, it would have killed him.

Now, he watched the members of the camp moving about. The remaining soldiers, all tired looking, were trudging up to the unmarked helicopters, Lieutenant Heng walking slower with bags under his eyes that were evident even from a distance. He gave a sharp salute to an armored soldier, apparently, his replacement, and spoke to him for a minute or two. Davis shifted his attentions to the ether, trying to trace down any sign of a creature slipping through space around their base camp.

The ether was chaotic, as always, but around the base it was in tatters. The swirling currents of magical energy were draining into pits torn through the ether by a being capable of teleportation, but one either not aware of how to hide its tracks, or simply too lazy to care. There were pools of swirling ether all over the camp, forcing Davis to take the time to undo the snarls and snaps in the currents, allowing them to flow correctly through the air. Tracing the tunnels carved through the camp was nearly impossible, as they intersected randomly, as if the creature preferred teleporting to walking!

Pulling himself from the ether, Davis shook his head. Glancing at his phone, he found that twenty minutes had passed while he was attending to otherworldly energies. The helicopters were fully unloaded; crates being carried into the supply tent one at a time by teams of soldiers with Pho overseeing the whole project.

He looked as aloof as ever and when he met Davis's eyes he merely nodded. Confused, Davis gently probed at Pho's mind, finding it secure from years of training, yet spotty in locations where he allowed thoughts to drift out. Like a prison cell with a grate opening, some information could be gleaned if you just slid the cover over and shined a light inside.

*Fear,* Davis thought, the first emotion to come across the channel. Images and fragmented thoughts of the Children of Flesh breaking the line yesterday, and how quickly they would have consumed the camp if all the soldiers had fallen.

The fear was backed up by a great deal of curiosity, enough to make the fear seem inconsequential. This was Pho's first excursion where he was in charge. He wanted to please the minister with good results, hopefully by ending the menace of the shui gui once and for all.

Davis pulled back, fearing that he might be sensed within such an organized mind. The fact that Pho was frightened by the "water spirits" was good. Davis didn't need some overconfident blowhard leading the expedition, sending soldiers to die pointless deaths with minimal results.

The curiosity had Davis wondering of Pho's tenure as a researcher. Even the most banal of intellects could see the creatures' aversion to light, and the villagers set up within the camp had told stories of how fire drove the original shui gui off, back down into the well.

"That well," Davis muttered, jumping when a pair of hands slapped his flat rock, Huan slipping up next to him in a tank top and thick pajama pants, Chinese slippers on her dainty feet.

"That well, eh? I thought it was fantastic myself!" Huan said, leaning over to nudge Davis. "Don't worry you old perv, I'm not going to tell James you saw us going at it!"

Davis fought down the images of the torrid act from his mind. "I didn't mean to burst in like that, I just detected something paranormal around the camp."

"Yeah well, look around professor," Huan said, motioning down the hill to the shrouded village. "Not exactly the picture of nature at its finest, now is it?"

"I wasn't referring to that!" Davis snapped.

Huan smirked. "Then what were you following, if you weren't peeping on me and James?"

"I met someone in the supply tent, someone that spoke to me. It knew… things about me, things no one alive would know," Davis explained. "Just now I tapped into the ether and found tunnels and holes all over the ethereal plane. I spent twenty minutes fixing the damage, which is sure to rouse the attention of the creature."

"Creature?" Huan repeated, sounding mildly interested.

"There's one in our base. I knew they could change into human guise, but I never thought to try and determine if everyone here is human. I figured the creatures to be dimwitted dullards. Now I'm not sure who can be trusted."

"Well, James and I can be trusted, right?" Huan asked, pulling her feet off the ground, wrapping her arms around her knees.

"For now," Davis said. "James can *feel* the ether but you can't; it would be easy for it to get the drop on you and take you before we could even notice you were missing."

"Then I guess I'll be bunking with James for the next few nights," Huan purred.

"Yes," Davis stared at her, wondering why she was taking all of this in so easily. He didn't dare enter her mind as she'd already shown… erratic behavior before. He didn't want to try and sort out a whirlwind of images and thoughts all at once.

Huan hopped off the rock, her floral tattoo shining in the morning light against her tanned skin. "I guess I'll check in with James!"

"Try to keep the noise down," Davis sighed, running a hand through his hair.

"That's for prudes. If you don't like what you're hearing, walk away!" Huan called out over her shoulder as she walked the twenty feet back into camp and towards James's tent. Davis just sighed.

"They're going to be fucking, aren't they?" a voice close by asked in Mandarin, clear and crisp in the morning air.

Davis tried not to act surprised and looked over at one of the displaced villagers, a teenage boy with lanky arms and legs, and a head of long black hair. He was looking at Davis with a hint of curiosity mixed with fear.

Davis chuckled. "I imagine so. The fight seems to have riled our female compatriot's… nature, and she's taking it out on someone she trusts."

"That's good, I suppose," the boy said, walking through the grass and over to Davis. "May I sit with you?"

"Of course," Davis replied, patting a flat expanse of rock. "Pull up some sedimentary my fine fellow."

The boy smiled and sat down gingerly, as if injured. Davis raised an eyebrow and noticed beneath his vest he bore bandages, stained brown with dried blood. "Your injury, how did you get it?"

"Oh, you noticed…" the boy said, sounding disheartened. He moved to get up, but Davis's sudden grip on his shoulder slowed him down. The boy looked at him, frowning. "You don't want to be near me… one of the Spirits struck me, cursing me with ill-fortune."

"Ill-fortune, eh?" Davis said, dipping slightly into the ether to stare at the boy before him. His aura was slightly out of tune with that of a normal human, and seemed darker than others, but only by a few shades. He slipped back to gazing at the real world and shook his head. "I don't fear curses of ill-fortune. I know it can be bested with holistic medicines and simple rituals that can halt, even reverse, the effects the curse has performed upon you."

"Are you serious?" the boy asked, his eyes shining bright.

Davis nodded. "I could rid you of this curse for a small fee. You see, I need to know more about these creatures. This last attack wasn't the first time the shui gui have come to your village, was it?"

The boy flinched. "How did you know? We haven't told anyone of our shame!"

"There is no shame in being a victim. Now tell me what I want to know," Davis said, pulling a pipe from his vest pocket and packing it with a bit of Afghani hash.

"Well, it started before I was born, maybe twenty, thirty years ago. Women giving birth… attracts the shui gui, who slip into the village from sources of water. They swallow the woman and child whole before slipping away, always under cover of darkness."

"And?" Davis asked, lighting his pipe.

"And… well, we know they don't like light. And you know fire hurts them!" the boy exclaimed.

"I meant to ask how you got injured," Davis asked.

"Oh," the boy said, raising a hand to the wound on the side of his stomach. "One of the beasts, I think Kwan, stabbed me with a tendril while claiming my father for his endless hunger."

"What did this do?" Davis asked as he blew smoke rings out.

"It caused terrible pain, and something was stuck in the wound, wriggling. I ran from the village with the others and reported to our town physician as soon as we were safe."

The boy looked down at his feet. "He pulled the wriggling creature from my side and washed out my wound with cold river water and then sewed me shut. The wound hasn't been healing well and often leaks, but it hasn't turned me into one of them, thank the gods!"

"Hmmm… interesting," Davis replied, pulling out his cell phone and scrolling through the e-mails from Lawrence. "I have a researcher studying the shui gui under controlled circumstances, and he's reported being attacked by one usually leads to a complete infection in a short amount of time. It's been days for you."

"Maybe the doctor got the worm out from inside me quick enough?" the boy offered.

Davis shook his head. "No, they spread like a toxin or fungal infection, not like a parasite. I'll have to look more into it. In the meantime, take some danshen and da huang and have them ground into a fine powder before mixing them with flour and river water. Apply as a poultice over the wound and it should extract the curse while also fighting infection and scarring."

"Oh, thank you, honored elder, thank you!" the boy said, standing up to bow to Davis, wincing as he did so. Davis rapped his knuckles over the boy's brow, forcing him to flinch back.

"Don't go bending and flexing and take it easy on any activity for at least a week. That wound needs time to close, and all your motion keeps aggravating it!" Davis barked. "What is your name boy?"

"Nian Zhou," the boy said, eyes never leaving his feet. "How can I repay you for the advice?"

"Ask amongst the villagers," Davis said after a moment. "I need to know where a shui gui cave is."

* * *

Davis sat in his tent brooding. So far the messages on Lawrence's progress hadn't turned up anything groundbreaking. Mostly he just went on about the physiology of the creatures, along with their seemingly random caste system.

"Event date number eighty-seven..." Davis read the e-mail aloud for James and Huan. "Mortimer has grown nodules along his underside and taken to walking on his hind legs. Daisy has split into two lesser versions of herself, which then split into quarter pieces, each forming a single tentacle and three stumpy legs."

He cleared his throat and went on. "I've deposited their cage in a large observation chamber, reinforced concrete walls with seamless steel plating and three observational windows made of three-inch thick bulletproof glass. I then used a remotely controlled detonator and a four black powder charges to blow the cage apart, releasing them into the room."

"Why is Lawrence doing all of this? We just need to kill them, right?" Huan said, still clad in a tank top and pajamas while shooting glances at James, who looked exhausted.

Davis looked down his glasses at her. "Have you learned nothing from class? The ancient civilizations that first created these legends based them on real entities! The shui gui themselves are what inspired the stories behind people disappearing around rivers. These creatures can obviously swim, and I spoke with a boy today who survived an infection from one."

"So there's one lucky soul that the creatures couldn't contaminate, doesn't mean we should be sitting around waiting for another attack!"

James cleared his throat. "I have to side with Huan on this; we have the firepower and the manpower, let's go cleanse the old village and be done with it."

"If you're sitting by a river and see clumps of shit floating down it, do you just fish them out or do you go and look for what's crapping in the water?" Davis said rolling his eyes at the pair. "You seriously think that this won't happen again, but on a broader scale? What if they happen to connect to a tributary that leads them into urban areas? How will they hunt then? We need to find out *why* they're hunting and stop it at its source."

"So what more does Lawrence have to say?" James said, cutting Huan off.

"Let's see… ah! Event date number eighty-eight… Mortimer and what I've dubbed D-One to D-Eight have begun work on materials I have deposited in the room. I have deposited through the chute the following: four pounds of liver cooked medium rare, four pounds of liver raw, five pounds of broken pieces of wood, five pounds of gravel, five pounds of human waste, and five pounds of blessed objects. The blessed objects consist of a crucifix blessed by a cardinal, a reliquary of the late Buddhist monk Lao-Te, and seven Maori shark teeth that have been confirmed to be blessed by a shaman."

Davis cleared his throat and leaned back on his cot. "The D class of Flesh show signs of exploring beyond the bedding, the growth of which has stalled due to lack of organic material. Mortimer seems to have gained more mass since his last weigh-in, and I dare not touch him now. The eyes growing on the bedding track my movement behind the glass… it's strange, but I feel like they know something about me."

"Well that's helpful," Huan groused, folding her arms around her knees.

"And creepy…" James added.

"Well I want to take a crack at wherever the central nest of the shui gui happens to be, as I imagine Pho will declare this situation closed once his soldiers burn through the village with the flamethrowers I asked him to bring."

"Nice move, that." Huan chuckled.

"Shut it," Davis said, whacking her knee with the shaft of his spear. "Now I've asked the villagers to help me find a cave the shui gui use to enter our world from, as they believe them to be cursed spirits who drown their victims."

"So what do they make of all the slime covering their homes and the monsters stomping around devouring people?" Huan asked, idly playing with a knife she'd pulled from a sheath beneath her tank top. Davis ignored the urge to grab the trench knife balancing point-first off her finger, choosing to move on.

"The boy I spoke to, Zhou, said that the villagers are frightened right now and don't know what to believe. They've made him a pariah as he was cut open by one of the Children when the village was being taken over. The village doctor survived and, while stitching him up, found a talon stuck in his arm. Ever since they've been convinced he's going to become one of the shui gui."

"So why haven't they killed him?" James asked. Huan snorted.

"In Chinese mythology you can't kill a spirit," she said. "The spirit can become enraged from such an attempt however. The people are probably waiting for one of us to do him in, and have the ill-fortune fall upon us."

"From my experiences Huan is right," Davis said, looking back down at his phone. "The rural people of China, of any country really, are prone to superstition and fairy tales. Going against the grain, so to speak, would be against their nature. There are modern people here, soldiers!"

"So?" James asked.

"So let them try and take down a spirit and see what that gets them. At best, they'll be cursed, at worst they'll be dead. Either way, these people will be ready to move on to another village once Pho and his cronies release them."

"You really think so professor?" Huan asked, flipping the knife in the air, catching it with an audible slap with her off-hand.

Davis knew better but lied. "Yes, I believe he'll set them free. Do you have a different theory?"

"I have a feeling his Department of Paranormal Events just picked up some new guards, clerks, or test subjects," Huan said, leaning forward, studying the knife intently. "People that see this kind of stuff… the professionals don't want them going public. We already have vampires, ghosts, and zombies out as real-world threats… what would the world say if they knew about *this*?"

Davis nodded grimly. "I can see your point, but I will do everything in my power to have the villagers freed."

Even to the two students it sounded like a bittersweet lie, though neither one had the gall to admit it. After all, who would want innocent bystanders like these villagers pressganged into the workforce of the Chinese government in who-knew-what kind of role?

Davis nodded gravely. There was a good chance that they would become test subjects on gathered materials. After all, wasn't Lawrence testing on mice back in the States? Human subjects would be even more pertinent for testing...

Davis cleared his throat, looking up at the two students. "Let's focus on the task at hand. We can worry about the fallout later, assuming we survive."

## CHAPTER TWENTY

Ten e-mails later and they'd learned a lot about the Flesh that they hadn't known before. Lawrence had investigated and discovered many things, mostly through trial and error, that seemed to have adverse effects on the creatures.

He'd been able to watch the remainders of Daisy dismantle the broken workbench and bring it to the bedding, laying it out so the fleshy slime could extend and grow. The warm meat attracted Mortimer, confirming that the creatures could sense heat. The strange part was that he dragged the chopped pieces of warm meat over to the bedding, swallowing up chunks that the Daisy drones hacked up before burrowing a tentacle into the bedding, pumping digested meat into the sweaty flesh, which sped up its growth dramatically.

The rest of the meat was dissected by the workers and brought back and laid in small cubes over the bedding, where the half-inch thick Flesh began to attack and pull down the biological matter into the goo itself.

The gravel and human waste were gathered and set to task before four drones, who began breaking the substances apart in pits the bedding made, which filled with bubbling fat to help create a paste that, Lawrence described, looked like diarrhea, but was used in the most amazing discovery that the study had yielded. The workers began creating a solid base for a structure, lathering the mixture into bricks that they then carried and placed atop one another.

"The work is slow and Mortimer seems to have no interest in aiding Daisy's drones. The buds on his body have grown larger and, from a thermal scan of the room, show that they are radiating heat on their own. While I cannot weigh Mortimer anymore, he does seem to have grown close to the size of a tabby cat now."

The holy items had been largely ignored, save for the bedding's attempts at pulling them under. The mere touch of the blessed shark teeth seemed to burn the bedding like a branding iron, while the reliquary seemed to ward the glop away. The crucifix, having landed next to the reliquary, had not been tested.

"It would seem Eastern religions have a negative effect on the Flesh at the very least," Lawrence had written. "Something good to note: I took a piece of obsidian I'd chipped away from the spears you all are carrying, and dropped it down the chute. It grew red hot when the bedding came within a foot of it, and has so far kept the growth at bay. How long this will last, I cannot say."

Huan had, upon hearing this, decided to go and get dressed to prepare for the day. She'd left Davis's tent, but not before giving James a searing kiss and pressing something into his hands, whispering words into his ear that made his face flush with embarrassment. She sauntered out of the tent without a look back, leaving a speechless Davis staring at the frilly red panties hanging from his hand.

"P-P-Professor?" James had stuttered.

"Yes, m'boy?" Davis had replied after swallowing a lump in his throat.

"How do you handle a woman as..." James said, his mind drawing a blank.

"I think the word you're looking for is *aggressive*, and I am hardly the person to ask." Davis replied, turning to load thermite grenades onto a bandolier.

"Were you ever married, sir?" James had asked.

Davis hadn't spoken since then, other than a few words. "I have much to prepare for, as do you. Go on, James, and leave an old man to his thoughts."

Now Davis stood in the dim glow of his tent, eyes focused on his spear but seemingly distant. The question had caught him off guard; his wife was a sore point for Davis. They'd gotten along famously, bringing five wonderful children into the world before a palsy took her, snuffing out the candle that was her life with but a single gust of wind. His surviving children distanced themselves from their grieving father who, now Davis could admit, had not been kind to them when they needed him most. Instead he'd pushed them away, purchasing Blackmore Manor for a hefty sum, to house his growing collection of haunted items.

He pulled his pocket watch and flipped it open, ignoring the hands which were ticking closer to the final mark. Instead he chose to stare at the clipping of a photo, black and white, of his wife when they visited Galveston in the summer of eighteen ninety-seven. Her face was radiant, her eyes filled with hope. He saw his wife's eyes whenever he stared at Lawrence… probably the only reason he'd decided to keep him on as his assistant for so long. The university had taken exception to their rising star of a professor taking on some no-name apprentice, so Davis had paid to have forgeries made of Lawrence's diplomas from Greek universities.

The fact that he didn't speak a lick of Greek never seemed to have caught anyone's attention.

Now, Lawrence was the son he'd never cared for, a new chance at forming a family that could step into his shoes when something finally claimed his life. True, he was blessed by an old god, but Davis knew that provided only so much protection. His patron, a forgotten god of knowledge, had no followers save for him, and slept in a locked away cavern in Georgetown, Texas. He would slip away every few years to the hidden chamber deep beneath the earth to visit the bones of the cultists he'd slain over a century ago. The demon that they'd summoned, a Curator of Fa'theli, was the centerpiece of the cult. The blue skinned creature was a walking encyclopedia of profane rites and occult knowledge that the cult was poised to use to perform greater acts of evil.

It had stood by as Davis mercilessly killed the twelve men and women with a cursed knife.

Davis could still remember how damp and cold the cave was, how still the slender blue creature was. Instead of a nose it had slits like that of a snake, and long arms with upside down hands, tattoos dancing over its limbs where they could be seen, as most of the tall creature had been swathed in black robes.

It had regarded Davis like a curious child. "Young one," it had said. "You seem uncertain as to what you are doing. Do wish counsel before you move on?"

"No counsel," Davis had said, eyeing the demon warily. "I have a plan for you."

The curator merely smiled and nodded, never moving from its spot. While not overly dangerous, it was still a demon; they were formidable combatants when pressed and this one had been connected to the ether, granting it the ability to cast spells. "What is it you want, Davis Nickels?"

"Knowledge," Davis had replied. "*Your* knowledge, to be precise."

"Ah," it had said with a hint of a grin. "You wish to become one with me. Are you sure that is wise? This is a path few take, and it would bind you to Fa'theli for the rest of your days. I can see you've learned a lot from visiting other sects. That would have to stop."

"I could still visit them to kill them, right?" Davis had asked, licking his lips.

The curator tipped his head as if listening. "That," it had said after a moment's pause, "would be acceptable. Will you try to bring Fa'theli back to the world of man?"

"No," Davis had replied. He'd learned from another cult that curators were rare demons, and they could tell if they were being lied to. They were known for becoming dangerously violent against anyone foolish enough to try to mislead them.

Davis had not had the nerve to try and combat the demon, but oh, how he wished he had.

"Fa'theli finds that answer... acceptable. You will gain my blessing and come to us once a decade, to share your acquired knowledge. This will be a process that takes three days and three nights. You must be clean and ready for immersion every time. Can you handle that?"

Immersion... that was a term that Davis had learned to loathe.

To immerse oneself with an old god was to send one's mind to its inner realm, where its thoughts echoed and otherworldly dreams took place. Dangerous to the extreme, many cultists who went ahead with such acts were driven mad.

"I can handle that," Davis had said.

"Then come forward, youngling… let us make a demonologist out of you," the curator had said.

The process was painful, to say the least. The curator had flayed open Davis's back and crawled into the wound before closing it up, the larger than life figure slipping in amidst organs and veins like a parasite before attaching itself to Davis's heart. It'd taken nearly a day of screaming his throat raw to adjust.

But upon awakening from the shock of it all, he found himself staring at the world with a new level of thought. It was as if his brain could run a mile a millisecond, complex math and sciences became easier than ever for him. Knowledge of forbidden arts and lost sites of antiquity flowed into his mind like warm jam from a jar. His body was stronger, more durable as well. He'd gathered the bodies of the cultists and laid them out against the walls after stealing their identification and money, along with any other valuables they might have had. Knowledge of where they kept their hidden treasures came to mind, and the desire to see what they considered so valuable as to store away from prying eyes was insatiable.

With the demon in his chest, he could read surface thoughts and access the ether like priests of old. He knew a little of everything, and absorbed knowledge like a sponge, becoming an expert at something in a matter of days when it would take others years.

With all his mental prowess, he still couldn't figure out why the Children of Flesh would be building anything. And now that they had new Children thanks to last night's brutal raid, what would they do next? Keep expanding, or release the smaller drones to collect materials to be taken back to a central location?

Davis threw back the flap of his tent and strode out into the midday sun, spear in hand with guns hanging off him as if he were an extra in a *Rambo* movie. Walking across the camp to the new military commander, he stopped in front of the man, who was busy speaking with Pho. The two men turned to look at Davis, Pho sneering at while the middle-aged soldier merely studied him.

"Yes?" they both asked at once.

"Greetings honorable commander," Davis said, bowing to the man while slipping into the Mandarin tongue. "My name is Professor Davis Nickels, and I was called upon by the Minister of Paranormal Events to oversee this venture and offer my professional opinion."

"My name is Captain Phae Lu, and I've been informed by the Secretary here that your grenades were most useful against the creatures last night," the broad-shouldered man said. "I thank you for donating them to the Republic."

"Oh, those are on loan. Any we don't use will be coming with me," Davis said with a false smile.

"And why would a professor need thermite?" the captain asked, eyebrow raised.

"Oh, for this and that," Davis said, ignoring the strange looks he was receiving. "I came over to suggest that your men hunt and *capture* a mammal. A deer or a wolf, something large and warm. A cow would work just as well… capture this creature and bury a homing device in its stomach."

"So that we can locate where the creatures go when they go down the well?" the captain asked.

"Yes and no," Davis replied. "Yes we could use the intelligence of where they go to better hunt them down, but since they are swimming in an underground river I'd have to say that your men would have to be ready to dive."

"They are," the captain laughed. "We brought amphibious gear with us."

"Did you bring any weapons that could be used underwater?"

"Small ballistics and harpoon guns, nets to slow an advancing monster down. We can handle this, professor," the captain said, casually dismissing him.

"As much as I hate to be a stickler, I must protest," Davis said, trying his best to sound like a friendly grandfather. "While these creatures are vulnerable to fire, harpoon guns will do little to no harm. The ballistics while underwater will pose almost no threat. These creatures don't have internal organs that can be hurt... frankly, I'm not certain they can feel pain. They exist solely to fulfill specific roles, like workers in an ant colony."

The captain turned and looked down at Davis, his eyes darting to the Aztec spear he was using as a walking cane. "And this? This would harm the shui gui?"

"Are you versed in paranormal properties and the nature of anomalous objects, captain?" Davis asked, eyes darting to Pho.

The captain nodded. "Yes, I've been with the department for fourteen years now. I've seen these things before and have driven them back into their lairs from whence they came. Trust me, after we spank them and use fire to clean out the slime they've layered over the ground, we can move on."

"If it's all the same to you, I'd like to borrow six men. A team that is comfortable working together during infiltration jobs, demolitions, with skills that would work well in a subterranean environment."

The captain looked back at Pho, who merely gave a small nod. Laughing to himself, he shook his head. "You scientists and your need to figure out everything. Fine, I'll have the men ready and armed in the morning. I'm using all my men in the push we're going to do in the next hour."

"You're going to attack them?" Davis asked, panicked. He scanned the captain's mind only to find protection around his innermost thoughts. Davis could pluck some names from surface thoughts, as well as his willingness to use napalm for the upcoming fight.

*He meditates daily...* Davis thought, picking up the man's daily regimen of mental discipline. *I'm too used to the west where almost nobody has mental defenses...*

In the seconds it took for Davis to scan the captain's mind, Pho had spoken up. "They're nocturnal, as you've been so kind as to point out. The cover from the sun comes from the clouds of smog—"

"Spores," Davis interrupted, causing both men to look at him, silently questioning how he knew this. "I have a researcher back home experimenting with the substance. That's how I learned the flesh growing across the ground is a separate organism. The vents are pumping spores into the air."

"What do the spores do?" the captain asked.

"It's too early in the research to tell, but the primary focus is to shield the Children of Flesh, the shui gui, from direct sunlight."

"Can sunlight harm them?" the captain stroked his chin in thought.

"No, they're not related to vampires, they just hiss and seem to dislike bright lights," Davis replied. "But I digress… your men will be walking into a slaughter if you allow them to move under those darkened skies."

"We have the drone to provide ample light, along with flares and spotlights from the M16's. You should be happy," the captain said with a smirk. "Each one of those weapons is equipped with a functioning grenade launcher that your thermite grenades fit well enough as ammunition. We'll be done in there within an hour and spend the rest of the day turning the goo on the ground to ashes."

"If it's all right…" Davis said, trailing off. "I'd like to watch from the drone station. Just to see your soldiers in action."

"Not used to effective soldiers, eh? Well we'll let you see what six thousand years of near constant war has produced!" the captain said before bowing stiffly to Pho and Davis. Once he was out of earshot, Davis looked at Pho and jabbed his foot with the butt of his spear.

"You're an idiot! Why did your Ministry send such a meathead into a delicate operation like this?"

Pho winced and hopped back on one foot. "I know, but his squadron has the highest success rate with the smallest mortality rate. They come away with good scores in land and aquatic combat and are all trained in the art of Wushu. I figured they would be perfect and ordered them to come in before the disaster last night!"

"Those men are going to go out on that battlefield and end up hurting each other with my grenades more than the actual Children! Fix this!" Davis growled.

Pho rubbed at his temples. "Would if I could, but I have stressed with the captain that the creatures are toxic to the extreme. This should at least have them cover up in heavy clothing and gas masks."

"At this point I would assume the air beneath the cloud would be toxic as hell," Davis replied, leaning heavily on his staff as pain wracked his body. *Oh, gods… not now!*

"I'm hoping that the flamethrowers and grenades will drive the beasts back, maybe even kill some… say, are you feeling okay? You look pale," Pho said, taking a step forward to look at Davis closely.

Davis's heart wrenched in his chest, the dull ache of the demon within now a sharp stabbing pain, demanding satisfaction. "I'll be fine…" Davis said, reaching into his vest pocket for his bottle of pills, shaking out four tablets and throwing them back to ease the pain.

The ache subsided quickly enough, the demon quickly latching onto the chemicals coming from the drugs. People often wondered if Davis was addicted to his painkillers. He always laughed when he said it wasn't him, but his inner demons that craved the sweet toxins that were in the morphine tablets. It was almost funny how the demon craved the sinful delights of drug addiction.

Davis smiled slowly. Before the day was over, he'd need a good laugh.

# Chapter Twenty-One

Come two o'clock, the platoon of soldiers, all dressed in hazmat rubber armor with gas masks and goggles, stood in lines of three, some ten men across. The captain had donned his armor and loaded up with his M16, and spoke over a communication link that crackled to life from the speakers at Wu's console. Huan, Pho and Davis stood around the paunchy computer technician, all quivering in anticipation.

"All right men, look sharp," the captain said in accented Mandarin. "Intel reports that fire kills them, light irritates them, so second rank, you blast the lamps so first rank can take on the little blighters as the emerge from the dark. Third rank, you fall in to first rank when they raise a weapon, taking their place while they reload. I want one continuous stream of fire and death here people, no moments of what if or could be."

Davis pointed at a monitor with a gnarled finger. "Look, they're gathering again."

Pho shook his head. "How do they see us coming? Is it vibration? Heat?"

"Could be a combination," Davis said off-handedly, eyes never leaving the screen. There were five larger quadrupeds, each with four impressive tentacles ending in hands and a mouth lined with human fingers. They swept their tentacles in front of them as the smaller tripods ran about, slicing small bits of matter from the ground with their lone tentacle before scuttling off towards the well.

What interested Davis was the newest soldier to the contingent: bipedal creatures, thin with wide shoulders supporting three tentacles stalks a piece, with human skulls turned upside down to reveal a tube into the interior of the body. Their bodies were thick, with low stomachs, but despite their ungainly size they looked quick on their feet. The behemoths were one thing, while the smaller three-to-five-legged variety were another—now there was something new, and roughly twenty of them, that Davis had not yet seen in action.

Their inverted legs made them lean back as they walked, their tentacles stretched out as if searching for something. The skull, pulled taut against a mound of muscle, was devoid of eyes or skin, seemingly useless except perhaps to frighten opponents.

Davis gave this some thought. If a seven-foot-tall monster made of greasy white and pink skin with tentacles didn't inspire fear, then you were either insane or blind.

*No,* he thought with a frown. *The skulls have a purpose. The Children of Flesh are all pinnacles of violent evolution… they normally break bone down or reject it outright. So why keep the skull?*

Staring at the screen, Davis allowed his eyes to dance over the gathered audience. Huan was leaning on a sweaty looking James, his sleeveless top showing how the chill of the mountain valley was affecting him. Pho was staring down the hill at the captain and his gathered men, flame units all lit and primed with the third rank holding their M16's shoulder high. Wu was typing commands into the keyboard, signaling the drone to turn and shine its spotlight down over the bedding surrounding the behemoths, one easily reaching fifteen feet high while weighing possibly a ton and half, maybe even two tons of near-solid muscle. The creatures were utterly silent, with movement only from the hounds and the man-sized addition to the Children's rapidly expanding family, all darting between the tree-trunk legs of the behemoths. A new geyser of black spores broke suddenly beneath the drone, offering a last glimpse down as a torrent of black spewed up into the sky.

Looking out into the darkness, Davis's enhanced eyesight could make out the silhouettes of the monsters standing in the shade of the spore clouds. The bright floodlight was swallowed up, and Wu was rapidly typing away commands for the drone while Pho was demanding to know what happened.

"I don't know, I don't know!" Wu shouted, looking over his shoulder at Pho. "The primary drone is out of commission for now as none of its turbines are spinning. Most likely it crashed somewhere in the village."

"And the secondary drone? How long until you can have it up and running?" Pho demanded. One hand gripped the back of Wu's chair and spun the fat man around. "How long?"

"Too long!" Wu replied. "You said you wanted the primary drone to have all the bells and whistles, you wanted it to be able to stream directly to our equipment. Because of you I devoted the bulk of the equipment to that *one* drone! Now you want me to set a spare up with the same qualities?"

"Just something that can give the soldiers light and allow us to watch what is going on," Pho spat, glaring at Wu.

Wu met the old man's stare and kept it. "It would take me an hour to assemble the drone, another two to program it to match the console. And that's assuming nothing goes wrong."

"And something always goes wrong," James added with a sardonic smile. Huan nodded while Davis merely looked at the two.

*Would it be wise for them to aid the soldiers?* Davis thought. *No... no, they would only get in the way.*

"Have Wu start preparing the new drone," Davis said to Pho, who looked back at him with a withering glance. "We need that drone by nightfall. For now, we lead the soldiers with flares from our flare guns. The civilians have several veterans among them, they're skilled enough to use the guns to light up the darkness."

Pho snorted. "And what if the monsters stamp out the lights? Or the *bedding* absorbs them?"

Davis ignored the slight at Lawrence's odd name for the flesh spreading over the ground. "We have over a dozen flare guns and several hundred flares! We just keep firing them ahead of the soldiers! Besides, the front rank is leading with gelled fire. They should be able to light up the dark well enough."

"I hope so..." Wu said as he stood up. "Because those soldiers are our first, last and only line of defense and the sun sets in four and a half hours."

"If it comes down to it, we back out and return at daybreak," Davis argued, wincing as Pho cried out as if burned.

"There is no leaving the contamination alone! It must be kept in check!" Pho declared. "We have to monitor the situation at all times and, if necessary, call in for an air strike."

"Then why didn't you have one called in already?" James asked, brow furrowed.

Pho fell silent at this, leaving Davis to puzzle for a few seconds before realizing what the problem was.

"Your boss wants to know as much as he can about this menace, and he's put your head on the chopping block," Davis said. "Aerial bombardment essentially means you're surrendering and that we can't learn anything from the shui gui. If that's the case, you're going to always have to play defense when it comes to these monsters, coming in to clean up after each strike, as well as each possible infection."

"And there's no way the military would allow you to bomb the motherland multiple times," Huan said, catching on. "Each time you do it that would call international attention, wouldn't it? All the other nations have their paranormal activity under control, it would look bad if China couldn't claim the same."

Pho looked away, muttering to Wu in Cantonese to get the second drone up and running before turning and marching off towards the supply tent. Davis's eyes lingered on the old man's slumped shoulders, ears perking at his mumbled curses. Looking over to James and Huan, Davis frowned.

"Gear up," he said with a wave over their rather casual attire. "If we're forced to do battle today I'd rather we do it in something more befitting than our nightwear."

"Got it," Huan said, darting off to her tent to change. James just rubbed his arm awkwardly, his tattoo rippling as he lifted his arm.

"I don't know, professor," James said. "Do you really think we could handle any of those things on our own?"

"The spears should help, plus I have enough grenades for each of us to render a Christmas Eve parking lot at your local mall nothing more than a smoldering field of melted iron." Davis ground out before snapping his fingers. "*Vamonos*! Get moving and quit complaining!"

James turned and jogged off, looking around as he made his way to his tent, as though he were lost.

Davis rolled his eyes. "Great... Huan fucked his brains out. Perfect..."

* * *

While Wu was busy assembling the second drone, Davis walked down the hill towards the captain, leaning heavily on his spear as if the trek was difficult for him.

He had to keep up the act of being as ancient as he seemed.

The demon within his chest, coiling listlessly around his heart, seemed to purr in agreement. It would be a while yet before he had to down another morphine tablet, though if he learned something particularly interesting he would have to down a pill or two. The curator got excited when exposed to new knowledge, which led to pain unimaginable for Davis. Stopping at a gentle slope, he waved to catch the captain's attention. The solidly built soldier took a few moments to acknowledge Davis, barking orders to his men to stay alert and ready.

Turning, he marched up until he was a few feet from Davis, his face calm. "Yes?"

"I'm sure you've noticed, but the light source within the village has gone dim. It fell prey to what I can only assume was a trap from one of the spore vents, and the technician is getting another up and running as we speak."

"How long until I have light over the targets?" the captain demanded.

Davis tilted his head to the side while shrugging. "A few hours. But I figured we could help you with several dozen flare guns raining light down over the battlefield for you. It's not like the light actually hurts them, you just need it to be able to see."

"Light by flare is hardly light at all..." the captain grumbled.

"Well it's the best you're going to get for now," Davis snapped. "I've just come down here to let you know I'm recruiting the villagers into aiding you in this endeavor, and would suggest a few of your soldiers make use of the mortars left behind. I witnessed a well-placed mortar round cripple one of the larger ones yesterday, forcing it to retreat."

"They retreat?" the captain repeated, apparently hearing this for the first time.

"They're more intelligent than you'd assume. I was attacked by two in America that were capable of speech, and I still assumed these things were simple monsters," Davis explained. "The creatures are disturbed beyond human comprehension and have unique mindsets that allow them to think in ways we can only imagine."

"So use mortars while flares rain from the sky?" the captain asked as if seeking permission.

Davis nodded. "And use those grenades at a decent range, no closer than three feet. I designed them myself to douse a wide area in the burning alloy. The creature itself will be crippled or mortally wounded from a single grenade, making them vulnerable to gunfire. Gunfire beforehand just make them create smaller mouths and tendrils. Aim for their legs to sever the narrow joints if you must use gunfire. Body shots are pointless."

"Why wasn't I informed of this?" Captain Phae asked.

"Because this is all I've observed from the encounter yesterday and gleaned from my assistant's work with a captive creature back home," Davis replied. "I have a half-dozen e-mails full of pages of research material on the creatures. I can tell you the Children over there will try and take you and your men alive, to create more of themselves."

"Well," Captain Phae said, looking over his shoulder towards the shadowy village. "I suppose we can hold off on our charge for an hour or so. Fighting them on that bedding you spoke of might not be to our advantage..."

"Now that's thinking! Let me go over more of the research and I'll speak to you and Pho within the next hour."

Captain Phae bowed stiffly. "Thank you, honored elder, you've proven to be more than helpful when I was led to believe you were a typical western scientist."

Davis chuckled. "I'm hardly a typical anything. Now have your men stand down, but stay alert. I'll organize the villagers and arm them with rifles. Many of them are former soldiers from China's previous campaigns; might prove useful, you know?"

"I suppose... just don't pass them anything too advanced," Captain Phae replied.

"Simple .243 carbines that the first group left behind, that's all." Davis assured him.

Captain Phae nodded before turning to shout at his men, ordering them to stand down. Davis turned and began his slow ascent up the hill. Closing his eyes as he walked, he tapped into the ether for a moment, dipping his toe in the pond so to speak. Across the field were violent storms of souls and foul energy. The souls were weak while the energy seemed to be overflowing from the bodies… these Children would be able to jump through the ether multiple times in short bursts. He noted that there was a tunnel formed through the ether leading into the supply tent, with several paths opening off over tents all over the impromptu village.

"It's covering its tracks…" Davis muttered. "This is going to be a headache; I can already tell…"

Cresting the hill, Davis found his students standing together, chatting with a few of the villagers, dressed in their combat gear and ready for war. Huan and James looked warm beneath the leathers, both sweating despite the cool mountain air. The villager was an older man, hunched over with a cane. His hand had obviously been broken multiple times, his teeth brown or knocked out. He looked as if he'd been through the wringer a few times and always come out worse for it. Davis wondered if he would look as bad if he hadn't made the pact so many years ago.

His heart thrummed in some unknown meaning.

"Yes?" Davis asked as he approached, drawing everyone's attention. "Can I help you, sir?"

"You are the teacher these two have spoken of?" the man asked in a rough voice, waving his other hand minus two fingers at them. "They cannot answer my questions!"

"Well maybe I can. My name is Professor Davis Nickels." Davis bowed slightly.

The man bowed crisply in return. "And I am Doctor Lon, the current mayor of what is left of the village you see beneath the shadows over there."

"Well, mayor," Davis said, "how can I help you?"

"You asked one of my boys to find where the shui gui come from, for a cave that would lead to their lair, did you not?" Doctor Lon asked, tone neutral.

"That I did. Has he come up with anything?" Davis asked.

"No!" Doctor Lon grunted, shaking his head. "We will not help you in this. We have all suffered greatly from the attack by the shui gui. No more lives will be lost in some vain attempt to attack the home of the angered spirits!"

Huan looked as if she wanted to say something but James put a hand on her shoulder. Davis adjusted the glasses on his nose and smiled. "I can see how you would worry over your people's safety, especially after the events that have transpired. But your country needs you, and your people, to aid it once more. If you could lead me to where the creatures nest, then we could attack them where they breed and, maybe, stop them from attacking other villages. Isn't that something you would want to do?"

Doctor Lon scoffed. "You speak as if you can kill the shui gui … I watched the so-called battle yesterday. I've survived several wars and what I saw was nothing more than a controlled slaughter. The monsters suffered almost no losses while almost all the soldiers were spirited away. Now there are more monsters, just like what happened with Kwan! If you do not heed my words, you'll lead to all of our deaths!"

"I understand your frustration, but I need to know where the entrance to an underground river is. I've known many people who lived in the countryside; they always know where the odd cave is. I know some of your younger men know of a cave that has a river in it. I need them to take me and some soldiers to it. If you don't, then your government officials will be taking you back to their base to be used as human test subjects. Should you cooperate, I could intervene."

Doctor Lon's face grew red and Huan gasped, but Davis said it all with false cheer. He finally spun his spear around and placed the sharpened edge against Lon's throat. The older man stared at Davis as if he were mad, eyes darting over to where Pho was standing, watching the encounter with an uninterested eye.

"See? The soldiers are here to save face, not save you. Now I could kill you and speak with the next mayor and offer him the same proposition I just gave you, or you could just agree with me and lend me the young man you believe is cursed. I imagine with enough preparation, he can guide me to where I need to be."

Lon frowned, but he nodded slowly. "All right. You can have the infected child. I hope he turns on you the moment you need him."

"Let me worry about that," Davis said, pulling the spear back and leaning on it for a moment. "I'll trade your men some weapons so that you can defend yourselves if you provide some medicinal herbs to me. Opium would be fair, I think."

# Chapter Twenty-Two

Davis led eight villagers, the good doctor among them, to the supply tent and aided them in getting outfitted with flare guns and.243 rifles. The men all seemed to be familiar with how bolt-action rifles were used and rapidly loaded pouches with shells and thick orange flares. Doctor Lon had, under Davis's watchful eye, liberated an M16 with several spare clips.

"You know how to use that?" Davis asked, nodding to the weapon.

Doctor Lon slid a clip in with a savage smile. "It's like my old automatic, just lighter. I can make do."

"Be sure that you remember the nature of the shui gui. Bullets have little effect on anything larger than yourself," Huan chimed in, rifling through a crate loaded with sticks of dynamite. She'd taken one of the men's side satchels and was sliding the explosive sticks into it two at a time.

"I know enough, child," Doctor Lon said, looking over his gun. He threw a small cloth sack over to Davis, who snagged it before James could react. "Opium. Enough to render an ox unconscious for days."

"Perfect," Davis said, tucking the baggie into one of his vest pockets.

Turning to look over the villagers, Doctor Lon said, "Come! We must honor our agreement and share our knowledge with Nian so that we can be rid of the boy once and for all."

The other men nodded and, shouldering their rifles, they walked from the storage tent back towards their encampment. Davis turned to regard James and Huan. James was leaning against a post, arms crossed, his eyes never leaving Davis. Huan was bent at the waist, rooting through a crate that they'd pulled down, cooing over the weapons she had discovered.

"So what was that all about?" James asked.

Davis smiled softly; he had forgotten that James didn't speak a lick of Mandarin.

Huan grunted as she hefted a grenade launcher from one of the crates. "They have M203's! You have any idea how hard it is to get one of these?"

"Do you even know how to use one of those?" Davis asked, slightly concerned.

James backed up as Huan swung her carbine around her back. "It attaches easily enough to my M4, and the grenades you brought should fit in here."

"Yeah, I don't think my thermite grenades were what the combined militaries of the world were thinking when they made that monstrosity," Davis grunted, stalking over to the crate next to the straw-packed box of grenade launchers. He tapped it with his spear before looking at Huan. "There should be some grenades actually designed for that thing in here."

"The crate is labeled M403, professor, those are just your standard explosive round," Huan whined as James walked up to the crate with a crowbar, taking his time to crack it open.

"Huan," James said, giving her a sidelong look. "You need to tone down the violence. I can't do another round for a day or so…"

Huan smiled and leaned over to kiss him squarely on the lips. Breaking away, she winked at him. "We're getting a new guy, right? I can have him fill in for you if you want."

James waved his hands. "I didn't mean that! I just want you to try and control your… urges is all."

"Who are you to tell me to control my urges?" Huan growled, poking James in the shoulder hard enough to make the young man stumble backwards.

"Nobody, but I thought that you coming to my tent last night was a sign that you wanted to start something…" James said, running a hand through his bangs. His black leather body armor did little to block the harsh elbow to his solar plexus, dropping him to the ground with a wheeze.

Huan placed a foot atop James's crotch, pressing down slightly. "Now look! I love this piece of meat here, but that doesn't mean I love you! You want me, try flowers and a date. You want to fuck me, wait until we have a big fight. Otherwise you don't have any say in who goes in my pants or whose I pull down. Understood?"

James glared up at her before nodding once. She offered him a hand to get up, which he took. Once he dusted himself off, he turned and walked from the supply tent without uttering a word.

Davis watched him go with mild interest. "You know," he said, "he is going into a field of study that you just happen to be joining. You two would do well to at least stay on speaking terms if you both plan on becoming experts on the occult."

Huan looked over at Davis. "What, you're taking his side?"

"I'm taking the side that involves less beatings," Davis corrected her. "Remember we're all here with one goal in mind: push back the Children of Flesh to whatever hell hole is spawning them and place a seal over it. After that we'll look over the artifacts left behind before turning most of them to the Chinese government."

"I could always come and work for the Department of Paranormal Events when I graduate…" Huan said, sliding several explosive grenades to her satchel. Grabbing the grenade launcher attachment, she strolled out of the tent.

Davis snorted. "Like they'd accept a woman as a researcher… they're still stuck in the old ways over here…"

Davis began packing up the crates, brushing the fallen straw into a corner when he sensed the mind hiding a few rows over behind some large boxes. It was well-guarded, but human. Davis sniffed the air once, his face breaking into a wide smile. "Shang, what are you doing sneaking around an old man like me? You could give me a heart attack!"

Shang coughed before stepping around a corner, dressed in gray military garb, a heavy machine gun resting over his shoulder with several .45 caliber firearms tucked into a bandolier slung across his chest. He looked like a perfect agent of destruction, and considering who he worked for he very well could have been.

"My apologies, professor," Shang said, bowing low at the waist. "And I have given you permission to use my given name, if you recall?"

"I was wondering if that offer was still on the table after the failed attempts to gather intelligence on the village, Lao."

Shang smiled. "The failures of my countrymen are hardly a reflection of how helpful you will prove to be. I came here originally to tell you I will be one of the soldiers to go with you when you locate an entrance to a shui gui lair."

"Really?" Davis asked, surprised. "I would have imagined that Pho would prefer to keep you here. Does he know of this little change in personnel?"

"He was the one who suggested it," Shang said, walking forward to the laptop sitting against the tent wall between them. It'd been cleaned of any residue, with a replacement crate being moved in to serve as its table. "Let me show you something."

Shang logged in to the computer, the system taking a moment to load the black screen. Shang typed in a few commands that made Davis wonder how exactly Shang could keep track of what he was doing without an interface—it didn't seem to hinder him at all. A folder lit up on the screen with three video files inside.

"These were sent to us from one of our secure facilities. This is a man who we infected with a sample of the bedding," Shang explained, enlarging the video.

The feed showed a man in a large room, the camera up in the far corner. A narrow stream of water ran through the middle of the metal room. He was huddled beneath the camera, rubbing at one arm that seemed to be sloughing off skin, only to reveal rubbery flesh beneath.

Shang clicked a button to fast forward the feed. "Event One, the first stage of infection."

The man, dressed in a tattered orange jumpsuit, had a swollen right arm from which an eye socket had formed amidst the gained muscle mass. The man's legs had split apart at the knees into four muscled pillars of flesh that ended in wide, flat feet. The man was currently using his good arm to scrub at his flesh with handfuls of the water, peeling away growth of the Children's corruption.

Shang paused the video and set it to a still of the man, who now had his old legs back, and a remarkably smaller arm. The eye was still present, but it didn't seem to be looking around anymore. The man was filling a bucket with water from the stream and pouring it over his shoulder before taking a scrub brush and viciously tearing into the lumpy pink skin.

"He's fighting it," Davis said. "He found a way to fight it!"

"Indeed he did," Shang said, turning the video off. "Mineral water from certain mountain springs fights off the infection and can revert transformations that are not one hundred percent complete. After that you must destroy more than sixty-five percent of the body to guarantee a death. Upon death, they release a cloud of the black spores that have been hovering over the village."

"So have you figured out what they do?" Davis asked.

Shang nodded. "Yes, they absorb sunlight. They act in a manner similar to plants and photosynthesize the light, straining the gathered energy down to the bedding which will then spread."

"I'd wondered how that nasty mass of fat was growing…" Davis muttered. "Do you have any other intelligence on the creatures?"

Shang nodded before looking at Davis's spear. "They cannot absorb or contaminate anything with ethereal energy. We theorize that it is one of the more potent weapons we could wield against them, assuming we could convince any of the demonologists within our prisons to aid us in this endeavor."

Davis felt a thrum of energy within his chest, as if the demon were announcing itself for the first time. "Wish we had people with access to the ether who could actually channel it."

Shang stared at Davis for a moment before nodding. "It is a wise wish. Pointless, but wise."

* * *

Davis walked back to his tent, only to be surprised by James sitting on a small crate, waiting for him.

"Yes?" Davis asked, walking into the tent, waving his hands for James to move.

James stood up, watching Davis open the crate to fish out a few vials of amber fluid. He raised an eyebrow. "What're those?"

"Medicine," Davis replied absently, searching through the bottles. None bore labels, instead having raised bumps over a section where a label would be placed. "And don't think of messing with these, some of them could kill you."

"How do you tell them apart?" James asked, leaning over to look down at the stoppered containers.

"Braille," Davis said as he pocketed a bottle of clear fluid. "Now, what can I do for you?"

"I'm just curious," James started. "When Huan jumped me this morning, I was surprised."

"Women can be tricky bitches like that," Davis muttered. "My wife was a fan of morning sex. Never liked it, we both had morning breath and I need a cup of coffee to wake up and enjoy anything."

"No, I mean I was surprised she followed through with the promise to, well, *fuck* me," James said, rubbing his arm awkwardly. "I mean, last night she dragged me to my tent and said she'd be back after she freshened up, and I mean…"

"Nope! Don't want to hear it!" Davis declared, waving a hand at James in dismissal. "Your youthful shenanigans are your business. If you're confused why she decided to knock boots with you then I suggest you take it up with her."

"It's just… I've been think about her a lot," James admitted, ignoring Davis's order. "I think I may be falling in love with her."

"No, you're falling in lust with her. Remember, she's aroused by violence and bloodshed. That is not the basis of any stable relationship," Davis said, wagging a finger at James. "I'll tell you what I've told many a student: don't stick your dick in crazy. It'll only end in misery, and possibly a venereal disease."

"Oh God," James said, a realization dawning upon him. "We didn't use protection!"

"Well then," Davis reached into the crate and pulled out a small leather flask, tossing it to James. "Drink three gulps of that. It does wonders for the immune system and helps prevent any disease trying to take root within you. Think of it as an herbal Drain-O."

James pulled the cork off the top and shivered at the scent of sweetened rot and dirty socks. Davis tapped him with his spear, waving his hand to hurry him up. James winced and held his nose before bringing the flask to his lips, raising it so that he could swallow back three large gulps of the foul substance. Pulling away from the bottle, he made a retching noise as he sealed the flask.

"Don't vomit now, this stuff is hard to get!" Davis ordered, taking the flask away from James as the man sat down on Davis's cot. Placing the flask back in the crate, he looked over at the graduate student. "That should cleanse all toxins and diseases that aren't supernatural in nature from your body, and prevent any from infecting you for the next week."

"Joy," James rasped, his face dour. "Do you have anything to drink that can wash this taste from my mouth?"

Davis grumbled before motioning with his spear to his satchel next to the cot. "Outer pocket, there should be four bottles of water. Take one for yourself, I don't want your backwash even if it's guaranteed not to make me sick."

James fished the bottle out of the bag and quickly unscrewed the plastic cap, draining a third of the bottle in several deep glugs. He lowered the bottle, breathing heavily. "Ah... thank you professor. Up until five minutes ago I thought you were an egotistical ass, but you're all right."

"I'm overjoyed at the realization," Davis drawled, pointing a bony finger at the entrance of his tent. "Now get out and get ready. And check on Huan to make sure she isn't humping anything."

James chuckled, clapping Davis on the shoulder as he passed him. Davis just rolled his eyes and went back to his crate, loading his pockets and satchel with vials. Muttering the whole time, he said a silent prayer to Fa'theli that everything would go well on this excursion.

It had to.

A loud cry from outside his tent caused Davis to drop a vial full of powder, the glass clinking dangerously against other containers within the crate. Snatching the offending vial and stuffing it into his breast pocket, Davis grabbed his spear and slung his satchel over his side. There was a loud exchange of Cantonese going on, with Huan's voice amid the shouting.

Throwing back the cover of his tent, Davis walked out into the middle of a gathered mass of angry men. On one side four villagers, led by an irate Doctor Lon, were aiming their M16's at six infantrymen led by Shang. Huan was standing off to the side, her modified carbine in her hands, a grenade loaded into the barrel. A mad glint in her eye said she was waiting for fighting to break out.

"What is going on here?" Davis called out in Mandarin, gathering everyone's attention.

Shang turned and regarded Davis with a frigid glare. "These men say that you gave them the weapons they now carry. I'm telling them that you would never push us by doing something so foolish, and am demanding that they return our weapons."

"Well they're telling the truth!" Huan growled, all but ready to use her weapon on Shang despite his size and full suit of Kevlar covering. From how rigid the armor plates looked, Davis could tell that they had a metal base as well, to absorb heavy trauma without giving an inch.

Davis didn't want to test that in the middle of the base.

Not yet.

"I did give them the rifles, Shang, as well as flare guns," Davis said with a tone of finality.

Shang glowered. "When Secretary Pho finds out about this he'll have the military here to punish the villagers, you know that, right? They're not allowed military-grade weapons."

"I've just armed them in case we have some of the Children make their way up here," Davis said, motioning to one of the men, "these are hardened veterans of internal conflicts within China, all capable of being useful if given the chance. They can use the flare guns to light up the battlefield should the drone take longer than predicted."

"But these… civilians. They might *carry* the illness," Shang said as if he were disgusted by the men. "What if they begin to turn while we're away and they use the guns as a means of taking over the camp?"

"I doubt that would happen as the Children don't need guns, and these men have all gone days after exposure with no ill effects. If they were going to change, they would have started by now."

"That's right!" One of the villagers declared, lowering his rifle an inch.

"The only one injured by the shui gui is the one that will be leading us to the home of the flesh beasts. He may very well be immune as he was able to fight off the infection," Davis said, thinking of how the water had helped the one man in the video and how Nian had his wound cleaned out by river water.

Shang didn't seem pleased, but he ordered his men to stand down. "All right, keep the guns. But I want you to begin helping the soldiers with whatever they need. Flare gun duty should be enough."

Doctor Lon nodded and lowered his weapon, his fellows following suit. "Agreed. We would rather not get involved any more with your department than we already have."

A long silence hung in the air before the villagers turned and started towards their makeshift shantytown. Huan lowered her weapon and looked appraisingly at Shang. "So you're coming with us?"

"I'll be leading five men and protecting the three of you while you do what needs to be done," Shang confirmed.

"You're forgetting of our latest addition, Shang," Davis chuckled, watching as the young man jogged up the gentle slope towards the gathered soldiers. "Nian! Are you well versed in your village's folklore now?"

He smiled. "Yes, they proved most cooperative after they said you would be taking me. I think I may know where the shui gui's lair may lie. It's a few days' hike, but it should be easy enough to find."

"Then I say we get going," Davis said, loud enough for James to turn and look from his tent.

"Where are we going?" he called out.

"Hell, or more precisely the lair of the Children!" Davis called back.

"Okay. I'll bring a few extra grenades…" He ducked back into his tent, leaving Huan to heave a sigh. Davis looked at her with a raised eyebrow.

"I think I may be falling for that man," she said. "He says the sweetest things sometimes…"

# CHAPTER TWENTY-THREE

Nian proved to be a font of information, sharing numerous legends of monsters that resided in the mountains and caves.

"My village used to hold a festival," Nian explained as they walked away from camp, three soldiers in front with Shang and two others in the back. Huan and James were speaking in hushed tones with each other, though Davis didn't care what they were talking about.

Davis loved legends. They led to sites ready to be dug into, where treasure and cursed items lay ripe for the picking.

"When?" Davis asked.

"Oh, long before I was born," Nian replied. "Some forty or fifty years ago they stopped. Every change of the season they would take a sow and lower it into the well for the night, just to where it would splash and squeal. They would hold games that night, throw parties, and make feasts. In the morning, the pig would be gone."

"So why were they doing this?"

Nian shrugged. "Elder Lon said it was to stave off the shui gui and that many villages did this. We had monks come from the mountains sometimes, to bring us a pig. They never spoke with anyone but the mayor."

"Monks?" Davis repeated. Where there were monks there was generally a monastery. "Were they Buddhist?"

Nian shook his head. "They always wore great blades over their backs, and Soviet pistols at their hips. They would often trade silver with us for rice and grain. They always brought a wagon that was heavy with silver and pigs. They would visit several villages weeks before the festival."

Davis stared ahead, thinking. "So these monks were armed. Did this region have any problems with bandits?"

Nian shrugged. "I didn't ask."

"Of course not… well, no matter. A sect of monks willing to fight with modern technology as well as old seems a little too out of the ordinary."

"They were strange. All the silver they would bring would be in bars, which they would sell to the government for supplies we could use for winter." Nian pulled a hip flask and took a swig, the scent of sweet wine filling the air.

"So they were into metallurgy as well… not a common practice for monks, but they could be a sect I've never heard of. Do you know where they live, or lived?" Davis asked, holding out a hand for the flask.

Nian passed it, shaking his head. "No, the monks stopped coming down a few years after the festivals stopped. My parents spoke of them often, and would wonder what happened to them."

Sipping at the berry wine, Davis just hummed. Nian continued. "We never learned anything about them, and nobody ever went into the mountains to try and learn from them either. Elder Lon said that they killed men who ventured into their territory, often taking the bodies after death."

"Wait, they have a territory? Do you know where it is?" Davis asked, now interested.

"Roughly, yes. It's where we're headed, that's why I brought them up. We may get attacked if they're still around."

"Why are we headed into their territory if you knew of this chance, pray tell?" Davis asked.

Nian smiled. "Because that is where the caves are, the ones that lead deep into the mountains, where the spirit world is."

Davis shook his head. *Spirit world? That sounds promising… these monks might be dead if they lived so close to it, not knowing what they were sitting atop of.*

Sharp cracks echoed across the valley, gathering everyone's attention back toward the camp was. The black cloud spread across the sky ominously, like oil dripping into a pan of water. Gunshots and explosions rang through the air, as well as the horrible cries of the Children. Davis looked to Shang, who had a pensive look on his face.

"Do we go back?" Huan asked, sounding a little too eager to run headlong into a gunfight with monsters.

"No," Shang said, turning to look back up at Nian. "Keep guiding us, boy. The soldiers will not fail the department. They will not fail China."

The distant sound of gunfire reigned over the group as they marched up a steady slope, all conversations stopped as they wondered what was happening to the men down below, if the soldiers marching into the mountains were the last of their contingent.

A cold wind blew down from the mountain, whipping over them. No answers would come from the earth or the wind; not yet at least.

* * *

Night slowly crept over the group as they reached the rocky slopes of the mountains. Nian motioned to a clearing in the forest, and chores were quickly distributed. Nian and Huan would be sent to harvest wood while James and Shang dug the fire pit. The other soldiers dug two latrines and set up small traps along the edge of the glade, mostly for use in catching small game but to also act as an early warning system in case something tried to surprise them.

The entire time Davis sat on a rock, spear in one hand and pill bottle in the other. The curator within was coiling angrily, a serpent whose nest was being disturbed. Four morphine tablets swallowed dry on an empty stomach would hopefully calm the force for the rest of the night, though Davis somehow doubted it.

Huan walked over, dropping an armload of broken branches next to the fire pit. Turning, she smiled at Davis. "Time for your meds, grandpa?"

"Oh, ha-ha…" Davis sighed, screwing the top of the bottle back. Stuffing it in his jacket, he leaned back and fished out his pipe. Doctor Lon had come through and delivered some premium grade opium, which he planned on using to relax away his aches and pains. The curator gobbled up ingested drugs, draining the delicious chemicals from his blood to fuel its own hunger. Smoke drugs, however, were something the demon allowed Davis to have.

Lighting a match against his boot, he smiled around his pipe. *Thank the gods for small gifts…* Davis thought.

"How do you think the others fared, professor?" Huan asked, nodding back down the hills towards the base camp. The forest shrouded the lower reaches of the valley from view, preventing them from using binoculars to watch for activity. Shang had said, as they broke camp, that he'd radio in to see what had happened once they'd settled in.

Davis shrugged. "Hard to say. They had experienced soldiers on their side with effective equipment and instructions on what they would need to do to survive. But the Children are slippery, and they had one in their midst even before we left. Something bad could have happened."

"I hope not," James said. He walked up behind Huan, standing next to her with his hands on the small of his back. "It would be a bitch to find out that we came this far only for a bunch of monsters to crush our back-up."

"Quite," Davis nodded, puffing on his pipe thoughtfully. "I'm not really worried about them, seeing as the Children seemed reluctant to attack during the daylight hours. If we hear gunshots tonight, we'll know that they survived whatever it was that caused the ruckus earlier."

"So you don't think it was the Children who attacked? The village was swarming with them!" Huan exclaimed.

"I never said that," Davis replied. "I merely mentioned how they loathe the sunlight. And who says that the attackers came from the village? They could have easily been struck at by something else. We don't know the full extent of the Children of Flesh's abilities. I mean, some can be highly intelligent; what if they *all* are that way?"

Huan and James stood silently, both obviously uncomfortable with the idea. Davis let out a sigh before continuing. "I'm sure they're fine. You'll see, when Shang radios them they'll respond and say it was something simple."

"You really think so?" Huan asked, looking back towards the rest of camp. Nian seemed worried as he kept looking back through the forest they'd traversed. While the soldiers weren't saying anything, the tension in the air was palpable. They knew they might be the last surviving members of their group, and that was something that would shake anyone to the core.

Davis paused to let the smoke blow from his nose, clearing his lungs for another puff. "I won't lie and say I think that, but it is a distinct possibility. We'll see soon enough..."

Huan didn't seem to like that answer. She turned away in a huff, asking James to help her set up the campfire. He and Shang had already dug a sloped pit for the fire to rest, and Nian's supply of wood would be enough to start a roaring fire if given the proper attention. The branches she'd gathered would only serve as fodder for the flames long into the chilly night.

Davis shivered as the wind blew through the trees, the faint rustling of leaves an echoed sigh of nature as the temperature dropped lower and lower. It was still light enough to see, the low-light of the sun receding to the horizon bleeding into the sky an explosive fan of crimson that almost seemed like blood seeping into the ocean blue of the heavens.

*If I believed in them*, Davis thought, *I'd consider that a bad omen*.

The crackle and static spit across the camp, gathering everyone's attention as Shang, seated by the fire pit, adjusted the large radio. Three soldiers, along with Nian, gathered around him as he began speaking in rapid fire Cantonese. Huan and James watched for a moment before returning to the task of lighting the dry timber to chase away the encroaching cold and darkness. Davis, calmly smoking his pipe, looked on impassively at the unfolding drama. Shang didn't show it, but his tone was strained and his eyes were full of doubt; he was worried for the base camp in a way that he didn't want to let on.

"Wonder why?" Davis mused, closing his eyes and reaching out into the ether. In his relaxed state, it was easier to enter the mystical plane, allowing him to slip through the stream of energy flowing around them towards Shang's mind. In his worried state, he would no doubt be thinking of a few secrets that Davis could pull free.

Sure enough, his mind was on Wu, the paunchy technician. Apparently, he and Shang had a relationship, one that was frowned on by the department. They would meet in secret to share each other's company, had been doing so for years. A slip through Shang's mental barriers revealed that Pho knew of their relationship and while he didn't approve, he'd made certain that the two were on the same assignments since he'd caught them kissing in the dead of night. Pulling back before he could be noticed, Davis flittered over the minds of the soldiers, all of which were chaotic swirls of memories and disconnected thoughts.

*Untrained minds at their finest,* Davis thought. Taking a few seconds for each soldier, he created barricades within their thoughts, solidifying and calming their emotions, allowing them to be more logical and, best of all, resistant to mental attacks. The meager defenses would be a slight drain on Davis's ethereal reserves, but it was worth it to have men less likely to panic in the face of true horror.

Davis didn't know what lay hidden in the Nanling Mountains, but the mere fact that they were part of the Himalayas made the man wary. The large mountain chain sat perched between two of the oldest civilizations in the world, both known for mystics and monsters. While most of the old-world monsters had been reduced to legend, the six-inch claw hanging from a chain in his study at home was a testament that large creatures still roamed the wilds of the world. He knew for a fact that the fine specimen had been gathered from some nameless creature that dwelled in the regions they were about to traverse.

He'd bought it as it had supposedly been a lucky talisman for brave hunters.

"Always something good to have," Davis muttered through a haze of smoke. The opium had relaxed his muscles and was easing the aches in his joints and back. The curator had already absorbed the morphine from his stomach, falling into a deep sleep that allowed it to relax from its place affixed around Davis's heart. The tension he'd been carrying all day was gone and, upon checking his pocket watch, he smiled.

He caught Huan looking over at him, an eyebrow raised. He closed the golden clasp before slipping it back into a pocket, smiling at her with ease for the first time in days. Without the threat of some unholy doppelganger hiding amongst them, Davis was feeling downright cheerful, all things considered.

"Hello?" Shang said, switching to Mandarin as a voice crackled through. "Hello, Wu? Is that you?"

"Yeah… we… difficulty…" Wu said, his voice going in and out. Shang adjusted the dials on his portable radio, desperate to speak to the man on the other side.

"Hold on, we're getting some distortion," Shang replied. "Okay, try now."

"Can you hear me?" Wu asked, his voice coming through with a slight ring of static popping beneath it.

"Yes, I can! Report: what was the disturbance from earlier? I repeat, what was the disturbance?" Shang asked, a slight edge to his voice.

"You heard that? Oh my, we were worried something was attacking you too. You left just in time, several dozen flying creatures emerged from the cloud. They had wings like a bat and knobby limbs, one hanging low from the body that ended in a hard blade. They fell upon us screeching, causing panic among everyone."

"How many casualties?" Shang asked as the soldiers around him muttered dark thoughts.

"Five injured, three missing. The creatures were as large as tigers. They speared men, flying off with them even as the soldiers peppered them with bullets. The rest of the soldiers have retreated up to the top of the hill where we have lights. The villagers are using flares and torches to help in our struggle to watch over the village."

"Has Secretary Pho said anything? Is he there?" Shang asked.

"Negative," Wu answered after a few moments. "He is among the three that are missing. He's presumed dead."

"What are our orders, then?" Shang asked.

"The captain hasn't asked for you all to return, only for more fortifications to be built. The creatures have been massing in number, the new drone can see through its night vision lens that some rubbery humanoids have emerged from the well."

"How is that different from the others we've been facing?" Shang asked, holding the microphone close to his face. The rest of the soldiers had crowded around to listen to the two men speak.

They all looked worried.

"They have weapons, staves ending in pincers that are made from veiny wood. They have necks and heads, along with discernable anatomy. Some even appear to wear clothing made from skin and jewelry from bones. We haven't been able to count how many there are, but they're filling in the rank-and-file of the monstrous ones, tentacles from their backs extending out to connect with the others."

"Any idea why they're connecting?" Davis asked, earning a reproachful glare from Shang. He repeated the question nonetheless, and heard a frustrated sigh from Wu echo from the other side.

"Transference of material? Communication? Who knows?" he replied. "All we can tell is that a veritable army of these demons has gathered beneath a black cloud and are preparing to march. And we are in no way prepared…"

"Evacuation possible?" Shang asked, voice strained with worry.

Wu didn't respond right away. "No. No, we have to stand here and fight. Each of has taken a thermite grenade that we'll detonate as soon as we think we are being eaten. It may kill us, but if we can thin their ranks while halting their feeding process we might be able to last until morning. We need you to hurry and find out what you can in the mountains. I've called in for backup and the White Tiger squadron is being dispatched, with an ETA of six hours."

"Can you last that long?" Shang asked, panic creeping into his voice.

The sound of gunshots popped across the airwaves. Wu gave a defeated sigh before replying. "We have to," he said.

The radio went silent, Shang repeating Wu's name into the handheld set a few times to try and reach him. The soldiers all turned to resume their duties, none save Davis noticing the tears forming at the edges of Shang's eyes.

# Chapter Twenty-Four

A crescent moon hung low against a starry sky. The fact that the soldiers stood guard in shifts of two and the campfire was set at a low burn made the experience more comfortable. Nian had insisted on setting up the tents for Davis and his students, citing he was working for them now and as such he would be a dutiful servant. James had begun to argue but Huan had merely thanked him. Davis supposed this was a custom in rural China he was not used to, and merely nodded at the tent Nian had set for him, enjoying the fact that it was facing the fire.

Dinner was a mixture of wild game—mostly rabbits prepared by Huan and Nian—and dried fruits brought along by Shang. Water was passed around in small bottles, and the soldiers not on guard detail slept soundly while Shang continued to work with the radio, trying to get a response from base camp over the latest attack. Wu had gone silent after half an hour, leaving Shang speaking to the void for two hours before giving in to his rumbling stomach. Together, Davis and his students sat with Nian and Shang around the fire. A bottle of fermented rice wine was passed back and forth, the group doing their best to forget their worries while getting lost in the drink.

"So," James asked, his Mandarin slow and jarring. "What in mountains?"

Nian smiled, shaking his head as Huan offered him the bottle. "Many things," he said. "It is the place of myth for most of China, with sightings of fantastic beasts and creatures that have long since been thought extinct."

"Such as?" Davis asked.

Nian thought for a moment. "A large creature, scaled like a crocodile. Possesses a mottled hide, white in color, with a single twisting horn jutting from its forehead. Two great ears perch on the side of its head, and it flies silently save for when it screeches. The screeches are said to cause avalanches, and the sightless beast will dig through snow to find trapped prey. Other times it will swoop down and snatch someone right off the ground and bring them into the heavens as a hawk would a rat."

"That… I've never heard of anything like that before. Professor?" James asked, looking to Davis as he accepted the bottle.

"I admit I've never heard of anything like it. Cryptozoology is not my expertise, save for creatures that fall into occult circles."

"I've heard tales of such things," Shang said, breaking his long silence. "At the department headquarters, we have a skeleton of such a creature. It was killed more than a century ago and brought to our attention by some farmers north of here. It'd been coming down from the high mountains to carry away cattle. The militia took it out with a group of archers after throwing a net into its wings, grounding it. They ate from it and grew ill; that was when we became aware of the creature and moved in to take the body from the local populace."

"How old is your department?" Davis asked, curious.

Shang shrugged. "Even I don't know. Supposedly we date back to imperial times, using our combined military might and powers of the ether to put down any and all creatures that dared dwell within lands we claimed as our own."

"You have people who can access the ether in your department?" James asked.

Shang shrugged. "Some. Most of us know enough of it to guard our minds and break through illusions set up by dangerous creatures. We mostly deal with vampires these days, with the occasional zombie outbreak. I've helped put down eight vampires and over thirty zombies, not to mention a few ghouls and a lone diabolist."

"Ghouls? What are those?" Nian asked.

"Creatures that eat human flesh to survive, and become addicted to it. The Curse of Flesh overcomes them and they die, only to rise as a ravenous monster with a keen intellect. They prefer children above all else, and often form groups for protection," Davis explained as Shang drank deeply from the bottle.

"I've seen a few in New York," Huan offered. "Before I transferred down to Texas, I studied the occult at the University of Cheshire Hills. Not a big school, but it boasts a large population of hunters."

"Hunters of the dead?" Shang asked, passing the bottle to Huan.

She accepted it. "Yeah," she said. "After my dad died I served as a hunter for a few years, made a killing bringing in ghoul teeth and zombie heads. Never could hunt vampires again, don't know why..."

"Traumatic experiences can leave an imprint on a person longer than they realize," Davis offered. He rubbed at his chest through his jacket, thinking of the demon now dormant within his breast. "I cannot stand to be around creatures of darkness."

"You mean like the shui gui?" Shang asked.

"Yes," Davis said with a tight smile. "Like the shui gui."

"You seem to handle them just fine when they're close by," James said, feet by the crackling fire for warmth. "You were attacked by two of them back home."

"And I killed one while injuring another!" Davis laughed, earning a round of chuckles from the others enjoying the wine. "Lawrence sent me an e-mail, right before we left, stating that the monster had most likely survived and was forming a colony on its own in the sewers."

"More problems..." Huan chuckled, passing the wine to James. He just passed it to Davis, who smiled in thanks.

"You said that they have access to the ether and can move through it... can you do that, professor?" James asked.

Davis shrugged. "I can do an assortment of parlor tricks meant to dazzle and amaze. Short-range jumps are within my ability, though it is very draining."

James gazed at Davis as the man took a swig of wine. "To think: not one, but two crossed a vast ocean to reach you... why do you suppose that is? What makes you so special?"

Davis swallowed his wine and smacked his lips. "Knowledge, my dear boy, knowledge! I happen to know just about everything there is to know about the occult in the world. If the Father wants to rise and do whatever… he would want to do, he'll first have to clip any briars growing in his path."

"So you think that the Father knew of you by what, reading a textbook you published?" James chuckled, earning nervous laughs from everyone else.

Davis narrowed his eyes at James and pointed at him with a knobby finger, holding the bottle of wine all the while. "I have my theories but you best watch your mouth! I took you on as a student, and I won't have one demanding such answers from me. If, and when, I figure it out I'll share it with you if I deem it necessary. All right?"

James turned his gaze to the fire. "Yeah, I got it."

Huan stood up, stretching her arms high over her head, her thick shirt riding up to reveal her taut stomach. Davis rolled his eyes when he noticed Nian blushing and James begin drooling. She yawned loudly and turned, stopping when James jumped to his feet.

With a smile, he relaxed his palms behind his head. "You going to bed already?"

Huan nodded before catching his meaning. A wide smile graced her flawless features and she crooked a finger at him. "That I am, though with a night this cold I could use a bunk buddy. You interested?"

"With you? Always!" James exclaimed, stepping around the fire to link arms with her, both laughing as they made their way to the tents. Shang smiled after them while Nian blushed, staring into the fire. He held out a hand for the wine, which Davis graciously handed over, and took a long swig from it to soothe his nerves.

Davis noticed the bandages beneath Nian's shirt covering his wound were stained a dark brown. "Nian," he said, motioning for the boy to come closer. "Let me look at your wound."

"Oh, I don't want to be a trouble, sir…" Nian said, passing the wine to Shang who merely raised an eyebrow at the exchange.

"If you don't want trouble then let me look at the wound so I can make certain there's no infection taking root," Davis said with an edge to his tone.

Nian winced as he stood and pulled off his over shirt, a thick woolen sweater that had vest pockets, to reveal his upper torso wrapped in linens. The linen looked as if it'd crusted over where the wound sat, and Nian flinched when Davis pulled Nian down to his level where he sat to look at it better. Wrinkled hands moved with surprising speed as he unwound the bandages, baring Nian's chest and shoulder to him, the ragged wound green at the edges with paler than normal skin hanging limply from its sides. The hole was a mere two inches in diameter, but it sunk deep into the muscles and, if Davis was guessing right, grazed the bone.

"You're lucky to have walked away from this," Davis noted, pushing at the edges with his fingers. "I assume that it hurts to touch?"

"Yes," Nian replied, his face screwed up in pain. "I cannot lift with that arm and find my back aching on that side after standing for a long period of time."

"Sounds like you need some rest, Nian," Shang said from behind him, across the fire. "I'm surprised you're the one guiding us."

"Don't be," Nian grunted, flinching back as one of Davis's fingers dipped into the wound, his nail dragging lightly over the frayed muscles.

"Well you won't be guiding us for long with this injury if we don't treat you soon," Davis said. He reached into his pocket and pulled out a small orange bottle, offering it to Nian. "Here. Antibiotics, take one at every meal. That should stop any infection from growing. Now we just need to stuff the hole and disinfect it for the night."

"How are you going to do tha—" Nian asked, his sentence broken as Shang struck him in the back of the neck with his fist, dropping the injured teen to the ground. Davis smiled at the burly soldier.

"I was going to give him some painkillers, but that'll do for now," Davis said, earning a bark of laughter from Shang.

"If he's unconscious he won't squirm while you patch him up. Painkillers could take hours, and I have my own guard duty in an hour or so," Shang explained, kneeling to flip the teen over. "He isn't worse for wear, see?"

Davis held his hand over the wound, knobby digits shaking from age. Closing his eyes, he began picturing the growth of life, from seeds sprouting to eggs hatching. He tapped into the ether and let the energy well up within his arm, his thoughts on growth and life. Just as he knew Shang would say something to interrupt, he placed his hand over the tangelo sized hole, releasing the energy into Nian's body with a visible jolt.

Shang fell silent, looking down where hand met flesh; beneath Davis's splayed hand the wound was bubbling, blood seeping over the sides in unstoppable torrents.

"Tilt him to the side, would you?" Davis asked, catching his breath. "We need the poisoned blood to leave his body before we patch him up."

"Is that what you just did? Gave me Goosebumps just feeling it," Shang laughed, grabbing Nian by the shoulder and roughly turning him so the blood would gush across his chest to the grass below. "Are you sure this is okay for him? A lot is coming out…"

"It's all the infected pus and residual matter," Davis said. Grabbing the bottle of wine, he held it up to the light, frowning. "How alcoholic is this?"

"I'd say somewhere south of whiskey or—hey, what are you doing?" Shang asked, letting go of Nian as Davis placed the bottle into the wound and tilted it back. The boy groaned in his sleep as the potent wine sloshed about his insides, no doubt burning like an unruly fire underneath the skin.

Davis looked at Shang with a cocked eyebrow. "Disinfectant. The energies of the ether aren't mine to control so I wouldn't want to rely solely on my parlor tricks to save the lad. Now tilt him back so it can drain whatever pus and blood is coming out."

They spent the next ten minutes tending to Nian, from draining and packing his wound to redressing it with clean linen. Shang pulled the boy's thick coat over him before standing up, hefting Nian over his shoulder.

"I'll go put sleeping beauty here to bed. Can you tend to the fire for another hour or so?" Shang asked.

Davis waved him away. "Go ahead. And try and ring up Wu while you're at it, see if they're doing all right."

Shang stared at Davis for a moment, eyes slightly narrowed. "I'll do that," he said in an even voice, turning to walk off.

Davis shrugged and used a rag to wipe off the lip of the wine bottle. "Meh, it's antiseptic, I should be fine drinking it."

Taking a swig, Davis stared into the fire and thought about what was to come and how they would face it. In his experience, creatures created by old gods didn't stray far from their masters; they acted as guardians to prevent their masters from being bothered. If he was right, the Father of Flesh's physical form would be buried somewhere deep in the mountains, probably only accessible by a series of caves that were closely monitored by the Children. The foul creatures displayed a disproportionate amount of intelligence for creatures so haphazardly put together, a fact that left Davis worried.

If they could speak and reason, they could ambush. And if the one back at base camp knew where Nian was leading them, no doubt it had warned the others. They were looking at digging out entrenched monsters like pulling an ingrown toenail; it would be bloody, messy, and there would be a lot of pain and anguish over it in the end.

"If only there was something we could use in the tunnels that'd prove useful..." Davis grumbled.

The crackling fire dominated Davis's attention for minutes, his thoughts jumping from one option to the next. He didn't want to reveal his secrets to so many people, but he might very well have to open up to them if he wanted everyone to work together as a team. The smaller flame packs would serve as deterrents for any Children that reared their misshapen heads, while the automatic weapons would announce their presence for miles within the tunnels of the mountains.

Not a good thing.

Davis stared into the fire, eyes lulled by the fatigue of the day suddenly coming upon him. He'd marched some twenty-odd miles today and he knew his feet would be aching in the morning. The opium flushed into his system was doing its job by keeping him floating along through the rest of his time spent awake. He could barely feel his face, let alone the soreness in his feet and knees.

Grabbing his spear and using it to stir the campfire, Davis was surprised when he saw a shadow sitting across from him. Dark to the point that it almost faded into the night, the smoky figure sat with arms folded over its lap, a hood of night pulled over its head. The only bright spots were the hands, two luminescent hands that crossed over each other, their smooth features and tight skin making Davis sigh.

"Hello there," Davis said as cheerfully as he could. "And who might you be?"

"That is unimportant." The voice was distant, and dry as the sands of the Sahara. It lifted one hand, revealing a tattoo on its palm, an intricate line work forming a strange symbol akin to that of an anatomical heart crossed with a skull. It held its hand up for Davis to view for a few seconds before lowering it.

"Nice artwork," Davis commented, his mind racing. He didn't feel any pull of the ether, so that meant this was either an effect of the opium (unlikely) or a premonition. "Anything I can do to help you?"

"They come, hiding amidst the darkness from the stars and moon. They seek blood of the blessed and the child of man and monster," the figure said, bowing its head. "They will come when the time is right, striking hard and striking fast. They seek sustenance in the way the Children do. They will sup on misery and feast on dreams, ravenous for more. Beware and turn back now, while you still can."

"I'm afraid that's impossible," Davis replied. "Could you be more specific? Who is coming for us? What child are they seeking?"

The figure looked up and over its shoulder, turning and leaning forward quickly. "I have run out of time. Do as I have warned and death will pass over you without claiming any you care for."

And with that a gust of wind blew, as if the figure was blowing out a candle. The fire dimmed as the flames whipped against the bone-chilling breeze, forcing Davis to lazily toss another log onto the fire. As the flames grew, the light revealed the figure to be gone, vanished in that brief moment of confusion.

"Great," Davis muttered to no one. "First Joshua and now this guy. I swear I need to keep a journal of prophecies and riddles given to me by apparitions."

Davis reached into his bag and fished out a few mushrooms, tall slender ones he'd gathered while hiking through the forest. While they were largely unknown to the world at large, Nian had advised they were fine meals for those with troubled thoughts. Stabbing one on the tip of his spear, he held it over the flames and pondered his place in the universe.

Was he just a plaything to the old gods like he feared? Or was he making a difference by keeping them sealed away from the rest of the world? Perhaps he could let one free itself at a time the governments around the globe could marshal the forces necessary to combat them and their malign influence.

That was risky though. If even the weakest of the old gods proved too much for the militaries of the greatest nations, what would happen when an old one such as the Father of Flesh emerged? Could they contain it and prevent it from doing whatever it wanted? From what he could tell the Father desired to merge with its siblings and forge themselves into a gestalt being that the world had never seen in all of recorded history.

"What could have splintered a god in such a way, and more importantly, what kind of god was so powerful that its separate pieces were this potent?" Davis mused aloud.

His only answer came from the pops and cracks of the fire, along with the smothering silence of the chilly night beneath the stars.

# Chapter Twenty-Five

Davis woke when a ripple came from the ether. Eyes snapping open, his breath hitched when he felt it followed by several others, until there were over twenty shifts from one plane to the next. A group of creatures had emerged from the ether, and they'd surrounded the camp. Looking around his tent, he reached out and grabbed his pistol and spear. Checking to make sure the thing was loaded, he cocked the hammer back and stood up from his bedroll. Closing his eyes, he expanded his senses to try and locate the entities that had traveled via the ethereal plane.

What he found were the minds of his compatriots… and nothing else. Far off a deer was watching for predators, its base instincts warning it of some attack to come. Davis sucked in a breath when the creature's mind was snuffed out. Straining his ears, he didn't hear a sound.

No birds or crickets, no crackle of flame from the fire pit. It was as if they'd been overtaken by a void that refused to leave. Sniffing the air, he didn't detect any sulfur or smoke. He smelled the frost-rimmed grass and leaves of the trees, along with the charred remains of the wood from the fire pit… and a faint scent of oil.

Not motor oil or grease for a gun, though he smelled that too—no, this was an oil he hadn't smelled in some time. This was the kind you used on silver to keep it clean and free of tarnish.

"What's going on here?" he muttered to himself, walking towards the flaps of his tent. Unzipping the front slowly, he peeked out into the darkness in search of something, *anything*, that could be responsible for what had woken him from his deep slumber.

*It couldn't be a Child,* he thought to himself as he brought his pistol up to bear. *They tunnel through the ether like water sliding through a drain. Whatever these creatures are burst out of the ether in a violent way, as if they didn't care that they were announcing their presence. Or that they didn't know they were.*

Slipping from his tent, pistol up and spear low to the ground, Davis made his way over to Huan's tent, where he unzipped the front and darted inside. Doing his best to hide his revulsion, he found the girl spooning against James's nude form beneath a heavy blanket, both with a slick sheen of sweat on their bodies from the intense bout of lovemaking they'd been engaged in. Using the butt of his spear, he tapped James in the face twice, prompting the boy to jump and look around.

"Shhh..." Davis whispered. "It's me. Get dressed, we have some intruders that need to be dealt with."

James probed around the bedroll, reminding Davis of how pathetic a normal human's vision was without light. Huan began groaning, prompting Davis to step over James and slap a hand over her mouth. He instantly regretted this when her hand slapped up between his legs, fingers curled like the talons of an eagle which were now clasping Davis through his trousers. Davis let out a startled yelp, one that grew louder when he felt Huan bite into his hand, drawing blood.

"Huan, it's me! Stop biting and let me go, you lunatic!" Davis growled low, kicking her side so she'd let go. "And be quiet, we have guests!"

He pulled his hand back, wiping it on his night shirt with mumbled curses as Huan silently reached out to where her clothes were and began to dress. Davis handed James his pants, as well as his carbine, before tapping him in the gut.

"Stay low to the ground," he ordered as quietly as he could. "Whoever is here bypassed our soldiers' security measures."

"Not that they were much to begin with..." Huan muttered as she scooped up her M16. Looking around, she locked eyes with Davis, startling him. "Have you woken anyone else?"

Davis shook his head. "I came to you two first. I need you both alive as you're the only ones I trust."

"What about Shang?" Huan asked, loading a clip into her weapon. James fumbled with his carbine as he struggled to dress, using the rifle as a cane as he stepped into his pants.

"Shang is good but I'm certain he has an agenda of his own. Anyone who works for the government has an agenda."

"Even the Chinese government?" James whispered.

"*Especially* the Chinese government," Davis said, glaring at James through the darkness. "They have political prisoners that are used as organ donors for the highest bidder, and allow sweatshops so horrible that the workers would rather kill themselves than work."

"Okay," Huan whispered. "Do you know where they are, professor?"

Davis closed his eyes and expanded his senses once more, frowning as he sensed twelve new minds circling north of the camp. Of the six soldiers, one of the minds had been snuffed out, while Shang's mind stood as a fortress among the people within camp. Oddly enough, he couldn't sense James's mind within the tent; it was drowned out by Huan's chaotic, disjointed thoughts practically screaming as she fought the urge to rush out and kill whatever crossed her path.

"They're coming around the grove, away from where the snares were set up. One of the guards is dead, while the other doesn't seem to notice them," Davis whispered. "I figure if we sneak out we can surprise whoever is sneaking around and ambush them."

"Get the drop on the hit squad," Huan said, tongue dancing across her pink lips. "I like the sound of that. Let's go!"

Davis held open the flap and allowed James and Huan to sneak out into the night, the starlight shining down providing enough illumination that they could make out just outlines. Looking across the camp, Davis saw the other guard standing at attention with an M16 hanging off his hip. He wore goggles—night-vision, likely.

Davis choked back a shout of warning as a figure rose from behind the man, roping him around the neck with a garrote. The soldier struggled for a few moments before steaming blood spattered down to the frozen grass, bubbling into the earth to create a nasty mud that the body was slowly lowered into.

"Light 'em up," Davis said to Huan, stepping back as she took aim at the dark figure.

The sudden cracks of automatic fire broke the silence of the night, muzzle flashes illuminating the camp in short bursts. The person, a man in loose linen clothes with a vest that tapered off at the belt baring a tattooed chest, jerked back and forth as bullets riddled his body. He didn't cry out, instead dropping to the ground atop the dead soldier, twitching as the last vestiges of life ebbed from his brutalized form.

The air fell silent once again for but a moment before it was torn with war cries, shadowed figures disappearing in swirls of arcane energy only to appear in groups of three, brandishing long, thin blades drawn that seemed to possess an unearthly glow about them. Six surrounded Davis and his students, each hooping and cheering as they slapped their blades against metal bracers protecting their forearms. Gunfire filled the camp, along with the shouts of the soldiers and Shang. Davis would normally be pleased with how fast his compatriots responded to an attack, if not for the fact he was in the thick of the ambush.

Huan spun, opening fire in a wide arc with her weapon, a spray of bullets tearing through four of the attackers. One fell to the barrage while the others advanced, the bullets passing them by or merely grazing them.

James unloaded a shot from his carbine into the chest of a burly man who charged forward to get between Davis and the others. The man rocked backwards, falling onto his back as a spray of warm blood showered Davis's frigid cheeks.

Davis raised his spear just in time to block a downward swing from a slim attacker, a resounding clang issuing forth from the glowing metal as it bounced off the ancient wooden haft. The obsidian spear crackled to life, flames dancing over the razor's edge as Davis shunted the blade off to the left while slashing the spearhead up towards the man's face.

The man ducked back, dropping low to the ground so he could lash out with a leg sweep, catching Davis in the calves hard enough to send him toppling to the packed earth. Landing on his shoulder with a pop, Davis gritted his teeth as he leveled his .45 at the attacker from the ground. Before the man could close on James, Davis fired two shots; one catching the man in the left bicep while the other caught him in the chest. Gore rained down around him as the man shrieked, his glowing blade dropping to the grass with a dull thud.

Huan let out a cry of pain as one of the men slashed his sword across her side, drawing blood from her exposed stomach. Her tank top offered little in defense against the sharpened blade and she fell next to the downed attacker, clutching at the bleeding gash that was once her right side. James turned and cocked his carbine, firing at the man who had lad her low. He looked on in abject shock as the man whirled his blade in the air, deflecting the shot. The bullet whizzed past Davis, impacting the soil close to his leg.

The man now advanced with his two comrades, each twirling their luminescent blades with practiced ease.

"Huan!" Davis cried out, rolling out of the way of a thrust from one of the blades. "How are you? Can you fight?"

"No!" she gritted out.

Davis spared a glance at her and winced; silver fluid poured from a two-foot-long slash leading from her hip up to her breast, the moon reflecting in the blood in an almost hypnotic light. She was on her knees, holding her side together in a vain attempt at preventing it from tearing further. Her M16 was still slung partially over her shoulder, but the muzzle was grazing the ground, useless for the rest of the fight.

Davis's mind was moving a mile a minute, his thoughts calculating how well his chances were with just his one remaining student and himself. These three men were obviously well trained, and dangerous when in close quarters. They were closing fast and, despite James's continued efforts with his carbine, they deflected his bullets with hardly an effort.

Rolling onto his stomach, Davis gripped his pistol in both hands and aimed at the lead attacker, a tall man with tanned skin bearing the same tattoo he'd seen from earlier. Waiting until James fired another round, Davis squeezed the trigger at the same time. The man, predictably, knocked aside the shot from the carbine but was rewarded with a close-range gut shot from the .45, which blasted through him and out his back, severing his spinal column. Bursting like a water balloon, Davis closed his eyes as he was painted with the man's blood and grunted as the attacker fell on top of him, pinning him to the earth with his weight.

From beneath the warrior, Davis could hear the continued sounds of combat. James yelled out in pain before another thud hit the ground close by. Choking on the blood and bile drooling out from the man's wound, Davis coughed.

"James!" he cried. "James! What's happening?"

But James didn't respond. All Davis could hear were the continued war cries echoing throughout the forest and the ringing sounds of gunshots. Cursing his frail form, Davis struggled with the muscled torso pinning him. He panicked when the man, who he assumed to be dead, reached beneath him and grabbed Davis by the wrist, squeezing hard enough to make him drop his gun. Sitting up, the man with the hole blown through his torso dragged Davis along with him. With his advanced vision, he could only wince at the sight before him.

Another dozen attackers were rounding up the remainder of his group. Shang lay on the ground in a pool of blood, a sword sticking out of him like a branch growing up from the soil. Nian and three soldiers were stripped of weapons; all four were bruised and battered. Scattered around them were assorted rifles and guns, all bearing scratches and cuts deep into the metal. The attackers spoke in clipped sentences as they pulled cloth sacks over the heads of the surviving members of Davis's group, some moving behind the prisoners to tie their hands up with pearl-white rope.

Davis looked at the ground where James lay, his stomach bleeding from a long slash across his midsection. He and Huan were in bad shape, although Huan was worse off. She was pale, her side still leaking watery blood as she struggled to remain on her knees. Leaning heavily on her assault rifle, she looked at Davis and gave him a weak smile before being backhanded by one of the men. Once she'd been knocked to the ground, two men pinned her arms while the third brought his hands to her chest.

"No!" Davis cried, fighting against his captor to try and prevent these crude sexual advances upon his student. But his protests died quickly when he felt the ether spike, channeling like a drain pulled from a bathtub brimming with water. The draining energy rushed through the presumed molester's groping glowing hands as he ran two fingers along the gaping wound. Davis didn't understand, but he soon saw the effects of what the man was doing.

The blood flow stopped, and the wound scabbed over. While a far stretch from being in a safe condition, she was no longer bleeding to death, though by her deathly pallor she could drop at any minute. The man seemed to realize this and, barking at the men holding her arms down, pulled from a small belt pouch a roll of silk bandages. Hefting her upper body up, one of the men aided in the triage being performed to help keep the wound closed.

"Hey," James muttered, hands pressed over his own wound. "She'd better not die, or I'll kick your asses."

Davis couldn't help but snort at that. "I think," he said as he looked around camp, "that we are well beyond that now."

"Yeah," James sighed. "I think so too."

The man holding onto Davis quickly bound his hands together, slipping a cloth backpack over his shoulders which he loaded with clothes from his tent. Davis grumbled as he noticed his phone was left behind, but smiled as the gathered guns were shoved inside his makeshift pack. The spear he'd grown fond of was held up, examined closely by the man who seemed perfectly fine with a four-inch diameter hole running through his body.

Speaking in a tongue Davis didn't recognize, the man motioned at Davis with the spear. The man who'd started treating Huan, dressed in brown and who was apparently a leader, issued orders that made the other captors bow their heads.

Davis, standing on wobbly legs, watched as the medic administered first aid to his group. The soldiers were loaded down with gathered foodstuffs and weapons, clothes going to Nian. He was sporting three separate patches of silk bandages on his shoulder, which had started to bleed from the exertion of the fight. The men seemed unwilling to touch him.

Over the course of an hour, the camp was stripped of its weapons while Davis and the others were dressed in layered clothing, including foot-wrappings with the heavy silk padding. When Davis demanded to know what was going to happen to them, the man in brown looked over at him. It was only now that Davis noticed the man, in the dim light of dawn, was missing an eye. His left socket was dominated by a glint of silver, which seemed to have black lines engraved into it, forming complex patterns. The man smiled, his teeth long and stained.

"You the scholar amongst fighters, yes?" he asked in broken Mandarin.

Davis, surprised at hearing the tongue spoken after listening to the guttural language they'd been shouting since their appearance, merely nodded.

The man laughed, slapping his belly. "Is good. You fight well for *shi chatar*. Most not trained in way of war, but you hurt Yama good. He take many moon to heal from it."

The leader tapped his stomach, earning a round of chuckles from the other attackers. Yama, apparently the man Davis had shot a hole through, merely scowled while pulling brown sacks from his bag.

"No worry, *shi*, we take you home now," the leader said.

Davis wanted to reply, but suddenly a sack was thrown over his head and tightened around his neck until he could barely breathe. He heard James grunt and Huan whine as he assumed the same treatment was given to them. Davis scowled within his bag.

*This*, he thought to himself as he felt a beefy hand guide him by the shoulder, *is a setback*.

# Chapter Twenty-Six

With their heads covered and ropes linking their waists to each other, the six prisoners were forced to march up into the mountains at a steady pace, something that Davis didn't enjoy. The curator was slowly rousing from its drug-induced coma, causing slight pangs to radiate out from his chest. He could hear the others grunting and crying out in pain as their captors struck them to speed them up. Davis felt the flat of searing metal snap across his back numerous times that day, a stark contrast with the snowy mountains they were ascending.

How long, Davis couldn't say… he felt the sun on his shoulders warming him ever so slightly, making him guess it was some time in the afternoon. Their captors, at least nine men, were brutal and spoke in a mixture of Mandarin and Hindi, with some old Cantonese thrown in just to make the rapid-fire dialogue more confusing. Thanks to his demonic parasite, he was slowly learning the language.

It would be a while before he was fluent in it, and he doubted he would ever master it, given the time. For now, he was trying to come up with an idea of how to escape and continue with the mission. Not out of any loyalty to the Chinese government, no—he wanted to gather information on this old god and help seal it away permanently. The Children of Flesh were living proof that the Father's influence was extending beyond his sepulcher.

Stubbing his foot on another frigid rock, Davis cursed and slowed to a stop. Since he was at the front of the line this caused the train to pause, something his captors didn't seem too pleased about. Trying his luck, he began speaking in their blended dialect, ignoring the gasps of surprise behind him.

"We prisoners, yes? What you do with us? Why keep? Why attack?" Davis asked, moving his cloth-bound head around in a vain attempt to speak to anyone.

The gathered warriors murmured hushed whispers until one spoke up; it was the one-eyed man. "You speak as if you are a child yet this morning you could not even understand us. How can you speak our tongue so quickly?"

Davis shook his head. "Fast learner. Teacher from west, here to fix shui gui."

This earned a round of laughter from the men, one going so far as to clap Davis on his aching shoulder. The leader spoke up again, humor in his voice.

"You wish to fight the dreams when you have one in your presence? Why should we believe you?"

Davis stood there stunned, mind reeling at what the man had just said. *The Children of Flesh had a creature in our ranks? Dammit, I assumed it would have stayed with the base camp!*

"Who is dream?" Davis asked, his tone pleading.

"We will show you when we're safe at home, which is quite some ways away. Now start marching!" the leader barked, a harsh sting of heated metal striking Davis's back to punctuate the order.

Davis groaned within his hood, the stifling air from his smoke-laced breath filling the confined space to a point where it made him dizzy. But still, they marched on and up through the mountains, all the while slipping on snow covered stone and patches of ice that had formed over the forgotten trail. When they began walking into a thick carpet of snow, Davis cleared his throat. He could hear the leader's disgruntled sigh.

"Yes?" he asked, just close enough that Davis could feel the heat coming from his body. He was like a furnace.

"I am old, frail. Cannot wade through snow," Davis spat out, hating that he couldn't communicate better. "Need someone to make path ahead for me to follow, clear way."

A tense silence filled the air, broken only by a sneeze from somewhere behind him. The leader finally grunted.

"Yes, clear a path for the little one. Khul said we needed captives and that we needed to hurry," the leader ordered, clacking his sword against something metallic.

The warrior tromped through the calf deep snow and took hold of Davis's bound wrists. "You'd better be worth this," the man grumbled as he began kicking a path onward, deeper into the Nanling Mountains.

For another few hours, the travel was silent, with two brief stops to allow Davis and the others to relieve themselves before being bound up again. It was during this time that Davis slipped into the ether and scanned the warriors.

Each one had a mind like a sphere of iron; no thoughts coming or going. He could pick up the panicked thoughts of Nian and the grim visions the two remaining soldiers were conjuring up of torture and execution. Huan was worried as her side was hurting, her maelstrom of thoughts all focused on the pain she felt with every step. James was similar, though he was shielding his innermost thoughts from the brief touch Davis did on his mind. Had he the inclination, he could push into the guarded thoughts and find out what his student was so worried about, but he felt now was not the time. One of the soldiers, Jin, was contemplating on how he could escape. Kun, the other soldier, was thinking of his time in training where he learned how to resist torture.

Fun stuff.

Nian was a mystery as he was by far the most injured of everyone, having been nearly disemboweled, slashed across the chest, and stabbed in the back. All the wounds were sealed over using the strange execution of the ether, but it didn't stop the man from feeling the pain. His mind was a dull throb of depression and agony, simply begging to die so that he could finally be at peace.

Pulling his consciousness back, Davis had decided it would be best to see how all of this panned out. They were taken as prisoners for a reason, and the way the warriors struck Davis's group involved a heavy-handed lethality that didn't boast of slavers. More than likely these men were part of a drug cartel and they'd wandered into their territory. He knew Lawrence was cleared to use his funds to pay a ransom if such a demand ever were sent. The only thing that bothered him was that common thugs like thieves and bandits didn't tend to have such iron wills. They also rarely had anyone who even *knew* of the ether, let alone a dozen who could shift through it. While they were amateurs at best, they were skilled enough to be a threat.

This worried Davis.

* * *

Another few hours came and passed in deafening silence and frigid cold. The sack on Davis's head had begun to form ice crystals from the moisture in his breath. He could hear James speaking to Huan in English, something their captors didn't seem to notice or care about. He was promising her he would get them out of this, that he had a plan. Davis had piped up around then.

"Plan?" Davis had said. "You have a plan and you're just now mentioning this?"

"Look old man, they obviously want us alive for some reason," James had growled from somewhere behind him. "I say once they untie us we attack them; thumbs for the eyes and knees to 'nads. From there we can take their swords and fight our way out of whatever hell hole we're in."

"That's not a plan," Davis had snickered. "That's a course of action! And I imagine wherever we're being taken there will be more of them."

"And why do you say that?" James had challenged.

"Because I'm getting stronger as we go," Davis had replied as if that answered everything.

"Huh?" James and Huan had muttered at once.

With a heavy sigh, Davis said, "I can draw on ethereal energies, as can these fine gentlemen. The fact that I'm growing stronger as we move on means we're near a natural font of magical energy."

"A leyline?" James had asked, sounding unsure.

"Yes. My body is filling with ethereal energies even as we speak. While it might not mean much for us, it means a great deal for the warriors who can channel the ether at will."

"Oh," James had said, his voice resigned. "Then what's our plan?"

"I say we play it by ear until something solid comes up in our favor," Davis had answered, hoping to placate the young man. Everyone was injured and tired, and they didn't need to try a revolt when they were in the middle of the Nanling Mountains with a crippled guide. Nian was still radiating depressive thoughts and the thoughts of Jin and Kun revolved around outlasting whatever tortures they would undoubtedly face.

Not very heartwarming feelings to say the least.

The day was slowly growing dimmer, the sun filtering less and less through the linen cloth covering Davis's eyes. With a shudder, he stopped to stand against a blistering wind blowing down from *somewhere*, the cold biting into his exposed skin like a swarm of frozen locusts. He could hear the others complain of it as well, but oddly enough the warriors didn't seem fazed by it.

A sharp crack to the shoulder had Davis hissing in agony.

"Get moving, the winds pick up at night and we have a way to go yet," the leader said. "I have no plans of setting up camp while a blizzard is rolling in."

"Blizzard? Blizzard coming soon?" Davis asked, his native speech getting better by the hour.

Davis could sense the warrior nodding before he cleared his throat. "Yes, one is coming in from the north. We should miss it by a few hours if you keep a steady pace."

"What're they saying?" James asked over the howling wind.

Davis shook his head, despite knowing it wouldn't explain anything. "They want us to hurry."

James grumbled as they progressed, a warrior some distance ahead of Davis forging a path through the snow that was knee deep (waist deep for Davis). The howling wind, like a maddened spirit haunting the crags of some long forgotten valley, wailed ferociously, growing louder and louder. Eventually Davis lost feeling in his feet and hands, which he knew to be a bad sign. Frostbite was settling in.

Just as he was about to try and do something, the lead warrior shouted over the gale. "We're here! Sum, take them into the main hall so Khul can see what we've brought."

Another warrior grunted and grabbed hold of the line, tugging to drag the numbed captives across ice-slickened stone. A deep bell resonated in the distance and the almost painful warmth of crackling fires washed over them as they were led into a wooden building. Hundreds of voices slowly began to quiet, the clattering of metal on wood making Davis think of silverware being set down. He could just imagine how this must look; a haggard group of half-dead captives dragged in to meet someone in what Davis would guess to be a dining hall.

The curator twisted in Davis's chest, awake and spry from the rush of ethereal energies coursing through his body. Davis could sense it was curious, its mind pushed to the forefront of Davis's consciousness. It filled his head with knowledge long since forgotten, namely the language he'd been listening to for the past day. Davis winced as the infernal creature twisted within him, sliding a claw along the inside of his ribs.

It was hungry, and David didn't have anything to feed it. This would be a problem...

"Khul, we found outsiders coming up from the valley," Sum announced, his voice thick and rough. "They had a guide from one of the villages, a young man. We captured them for the greater glory of the sleeper."

"They appear tired, and many are in need of medical care," an elderly voice calmly stated, booming throughout the hall. "Take them to the holding cells and go fetch a healer for them, then warm yourself by the fire with some lychee wine."

"Thank you, honored Khul," Sum said before jerking on the ropes connected to Davis's wrists. Not bothering to struggle, Davis sluggishly walked from the warm room back out into the frigid cold, the slight feeling he'd been regaining in his feet falling to the wayside as he was led to a building, and then led down a flight of stairs. A door was unlocked, a brief few words exchanged with a woman, and then their ropes were cut free.

Davis instantly brought his hands to his head, yanking the dreadful sack off his face. Looking around in the dimly lit stone room, his stomach sank when he realized he was in an honest to goodness dungeon. The woman, dressed in similar garb to the warriors with silk wrappings covering her upper torso, held Davis's spear in one hand, testing the balance. She was young, perhaps twenty, and very muscular. She was clearly every bit as vicious as the men who had taken his camp down, and when her orange eyes glared at him, he didn't dare move.

Instead, he spoke. "Please, we're tired and hurt. We need warmth or we'll grow sick. We need food or we'll starve. We need water or we'll die of thirst."

She recoiled slightly before leaning in to stare at Davis, their noses almost touching. Davis noted that the tattoo prevalent on the male warriors was also marked upon her supple flesh, though half obscured by the bandages covering her breasts.

"You speak our language? Even the people of the valley don't know our tongue. How is it that you do, round-eye?" she asked, clearly impressed.

"Is it all right if we save that story for another day? My companions and I would prefer to be settled into our cells before Sum," Davis looked back at the tall, clean-shaven man, "fetches some healers to look us over. Do you have anything we could use to warm ourselves while we wait?"

The woman nodded. "This I can do, so long as none of you cause problems. Follow me."

Sum walked alongside Nian, who needed help to move his frozen legs, while the Jin and Kun studied the darkened chamber intently. Davis smiled. The cells were wide and open, each one containing a brazier and a chimney, with a spit installed over a brass bowl for the prisoners to roast whatever food they were given. Sum and the woman took everyone's outer clothes off, checking them for weapons as they laid their garments off to the side. The woman, using a set of tarnished keys, unlocked one large cell and ushered everyone inside. The bars were set into the floor and ceiling and, while old, looked sturdy.

"I'll fetch some wood and lantern oil for your fire; you should find the cots have wool blankets to keep the chill out," the woman explained, motioning to the back of the cell where twelve cots were lined up in the darkness, the few recessed torches in the large room offering dim lighting.

Davis entered the cell and turned to face the woman as the rest of his captives filed in behind him. "Thank you for your hospitality Madam…?"

"Brun. There is no madam here so please refrain from calling me such," Brun said, her tone growing as cold as the weather seeping in through the smokestack leading up from their cell.

"I'll remember that," Davis said, nodding. Turning around, he made his way stiffly to a cot where he pulled a blanket off and wrapped it around himself. Shuffling over to the massive brazier, he slumped down to look at his feet, wincing as he got his first true look at them.

The silk bandages had done wonders for a good while, but his toes were blue-tinged and veiny, with bloody cuts all over his numbed feet from rocks that had sliced through the protective wraps. Looking around at the others hobbling about, he saw most of them had similar injuries, with Jin missing a toe and Nian missing three. Fortunately James and Huan, who were now snuggling together beneath a blanket, seemed no worse for wear save for their blood-stained clothing and chattering teeth.

Jin accepted several thin logs through the bars from Brun, as well as a ceramic jug filled with lantern oil. Within minutes they had a roaring fire going to chase away the pervasive chill that had settled in their bones. They all huddled around the fire, blankets wrapped around them, silent as graves. Nobody asked Davis how he knew the language of these mountain monks, and nobody seemed to care about being captives.

All there was to them was the fire.

And that was enough for now.

## Chapter Twenty-Seven

The group huddled around the fire, blankets wound around them in a vain attempt to ward away the chill of the dungeon they'd been marched into. The dancing shadows on the hewn stone walls made it seem as if hundreds of tiny devils were hopping to and fro, something that made Davis smile. He knew everyone else was frightened beyond words, and understandably so. Their captors were the silver-ingot trading monks that Nian had spoken of, and they were just as violent as he'd warned.

Either way, they'd been subdued and captured, some outright slain. But he was alive, and to Davis, that meant there was a chance for him to come out of this. The only thing he needed was to find something that the leader of this group would want—something in exchange for their freedom. Knowledge would be a great place to start, as the curator was fully awake. It seemed curious about the current predicament that Davis had gotten into, and Davis felt a swell of amusement in the back of his mind, a familiar pressure within his skull that seemed to be asking "Well? Now what?"

Looking around, Davis winced when his eyes landed on Nian. Beaten and bruised, the Chinese guide had been on the receiving end of numerous blows to the head and several stab wounds that the monks had hastily poured ethereal energy into so they could take him back alive. He sat shivering on the ground, pale hands clutching his blanket over his head as he shook, as much from the bone-chilling cold as from pain.

Davis didn't need to peer into his mind to see what the boy was thinking: with a furtive glance from a swollen eye, Davis could see the loathing in the boy's haunted face.

They were all now dressed in wool pants and vests, while their torsos, hands, and feet were wrapped in linen bandages doused in a foul-smelling unguent that seemed to sooth their bruises and dull the aches. The bandages were holding Huan's wound closed, and keeping James from passing out. Davis looked back to Nian and the other two Chinese nationals, thinking about what he would need to do to survive.

If given the chance, Nian would sacrifice the group to save his own hide. He'd no doubt offer Davis and James, as they were foreigners. He might try and save Huan, but she'd be a bargaining chip for any monks that hadn't had a taste of a young woman in a while. And seeing as they lived atop a mountain in a secret monastery, they probably didn't get out nearly enough to vent pent-up sexual energy. Brun was most likely one of few female monks, and she didn't seem too keen on getting together with anyone.

Holding his hands out to the fire, Davis thought of Shang. He'd seemed the least likely to die in an attack, yet he'd fallen quickly. The only monks seriously harmed were the ones that Davis and the others had shot, and after seeing one take a hit from his .45 point blank like it was a swat from a rolled-up newspaper, he doubted the ones Huan shot were dead. No, the gunfire most likely had just slowed them down.

Pulling his blanket tight over his bones, Davis closed his eyes and began to meditate. He needed answers, and his link to the ether would be one way of getting them. He was surprised when, as he began the preparations for his ritual, his consciousness was pulled into the ether like getting pushed into a raging river.

Awash in the energies of the world, Davis fought for control, focusing on his breathing and keeping track of his heart. Slowing it down steadily, he gained control of his existence in the ethereal realm, clawing his way free of the flowing channel of energy. Looking around, a dense mist hung listlessly over the ground, the river of energy soaring up and over him towards a distant quasar of power, a low thrum echoing across the ether like a heartbeat. Davis just stared at it for a time, trying to understand what he was being shown.

"We're at a nexus point, my friend," a child's voice said from close by. Looking around, he blinked when a Chinese boy stepped out from behind seemingly nothing, arms folded behind his back. He wore the garb of the monks and had his head shaved save for a long trailing ponytail sprouting from his crown. It was adorned with small jewels, slivers of gleaming gold and silver twinkling merrily in the eerie twilight of the ethereal. Davis didn't say anything, choosing to instead stare at the boy with his forest green eyes.

Eyes he'd stared into many years before. The child smiled, green eyes calculating as the head tilted in wonder. "Even after all this time, I find your thoughts interesting, warlock. I once thought I would regret this, but you have proven to be far more entertaining than meager cultists fighting for scraps of power that they could barely handle. What is it you seek?"

Davis stood silent for a moment, eyes darting from the great source of energy where the river was gushing from (or into?) then back to the curator in human form. It'd never appeared to him before, merely choosing to communicate through surges of feelings and bursts of knowledge. This was uncharted territory for Davis.

For the first time since the expedition to China had begun, Davis felt a pang of unquenchable fear in his chest.

"Chosen, what is it you fear?" the curator asked, a deep baritone leaking through the childish tone for a moment. "You know I am with you until the bitter end and I am bound to aid you with my knowledge. Have I ever failed you?"

"No… it's just that I don't know where we are," Davis said, motioning towards the pulsing sun of energy. "You said a nexus, but what do you mean by that? True, we're on a natural leyline, but I've never felt this way before, or been pulled into the ether when I'm not having a vision."

The curator smiled. "Who says you're not having a vision now?"

Davis thought on that. "Visions… they're of things that are present or future, yes?"

"You know that to be the case," the curator confirmed.

"And this might be a vision," Davis muttered, looking down at his hands, which seemed to vibrate from the overwhelming energies flowing around him. "But I'm immersed in the ethereal right now. So, what is this?"

"That," the curator turned to gaze at the glowing star on the horizon, "I cannot say. There are many possibilities, but with as little knowledge as we have at this juncture anything would be little more than guesswork. And I'm not about to play in such fields of obscurity."

"So this could be the future," Davis said, working out a puzzle. "But I don't think it's the future of my world. I think it's the future of the ethereal."

"One of many possibilities," the curator agreed.

"But I'm being filled with power now, so this is real. If it's real then I'm standing in the presence of something, not seeing the future but the present."

"Another possibility."

Davis scowled. "I know you've been without your pills for a while but you could be a little more helpful right now. I'm in some serious shit, and need a way out of it as soon as possible."

"Hmmm... I think I've already helped you here, should you be wise enough to piece together the puzzle in time. Either way I'll be entertained."

"I'm glad to be of service," Davis sighed.

The curator turned, green eyes glowing faintly. "You should be. It takes a great deal of energy to visit you like this. Please don't make me do it again."

And with that Davis felt himself forcefully ejected back into his body, a wave of nausea overcoming him as his vision swam. Holding his throbbing head, he fought to stay awake, and ignored James's cry of alarm.

"I'm fine, I'm fine... I just need my medication is all," Davis assured him, eyes closed.

"Professor! Look!" James cried out again. Opening his eyes, he gasped as he saw what James and Huan were staring at.

Standing at the edge of the bars was a dead man, desiccated and hollowed from the sternum down to the hips. Engraved over every inch of his exposed bones were ancient glyphs that glowed a faint azure hue, the same glow that came from his eye sockets. Dressed in the monk's outfit, barring sandals, the creature was standing with a slack jaw, thin cheeks stretched taut, blue and black bits of frostbitten flesh showing on his lips and fingers.

Davis reached out to the creature with his mind and shuddered at what he felt. Tied together in a profane rite were the memories of two men and a woman, with a patchwork of lesser souls holding the entity together. The memories were fractured, but they all seemed to focus on the tasks one would be set to do when handling prisoners. In this case, he was checking on them to make sure they were alive.

"Relax," Davis said as Jin and Kun jumped from the sudden appearance of the dead man. "He's here to check on us."

"How do you know that?" Jin asked, eyes never leaving the dried-out corpse.

"Because it's a simulacrum, a shell of a human that necromancers use. This one is here to act as a guard. I imagine if we needed something it would provide it to us," Davis explained. Looking at the undead creature, Davis cleared his throat and spoke in the monks' choppy language. "Could we have some food? We are tired and hungry."

The cadaver clacked its gray teeth together, a horrid cracking noise, before rasping out over a dried tongue. "Meals will be delivered shortly, magus. You will be fed a meat broth with leeks and rice. Is this acceptable?"

"Yes... yes that should be fine so long as it's hot," Davis replied, curious over the name it gave him. "Why did you refer to me as magus?"

"Because you are connected to the celestial realm, where the gods dream and few men dare walk," the corpse hissed. Turning, it walked off into the darkness of the dungeon until the glow of its glyphs was smothered by the crushing darkness.

"What... what did it want?" Huan whispered.

Davis turned back to look at the group huddled around the crackling flames. All he saw was fear, fear and loss of all hope. Jin and Kun were staring at him with grim stares, expecting the worst. Nian had lowered his head to his knees, wrapping his arms around them as he began to sob. Huan and James looked concerned, but a flicker of fear darted in Huan's eyes, while James had panic written over his face.

Davis sighed. "It's going to bring us food. It asked what we eat and if what it is bringing would be suitable."

"What was it offering?" Jin asked, pulling his blanket up to his chin.

"A meat stew with leeks and rice, all hot." Davis smiled, trying to raise his compatriot's spirits somehow.

The thought of a warm meal brought several rumbling stomachs to life, earning a few chuckles from everyone. Davis scooted back into his spot, folding his blanket around him in a tight cocoon. He closed his eyes and peered into the ether again, this time focusing on the streams of energy heading through the rooms. Riding along one, he could track down and find the undead as it shambled through the raging blizzard howling over the monastery. The creature moved with unwavering dedication, glyphs glowing bright in the pitch black night. Looking them over, he could see they were in Hindi script with Mandarin lettering mixed in.

From what he could gather, there was a cluster of glyphs on the body, glowing through the threadbare monk's outfit on the creature's back. Davis recognized it almost immediately.

It was a reservoir, a complex set of old magic. What the soul jar back home had been born from, this ritual held and stored ethereal energy like living batteries. The problem with it was that it would cause the host intense pain. The glyphs running up the right arm showed animation and obedience runes, along with some very primitive runic arrays that gifted intelligence to a creature. The head rune was the strangest of all, as it held a one-sided scrying spell focused through the eyes, meaning there were gems embedded in the sockets.

All of this pointed to a skilled necromancer with masterful control over the fine strings one had to maintain to manage an undead of this complexity. The creature shuffled through the growing piles of snow, slowly descending a set of stairs that had been hidden from view before ducking into a heavily warded structure.

Following in, Davis was surprised to find that this was a slaughterhouse and kitchen rolled into one horrifying scene, with undead workers processing skinned animals, strange pigs hanging from hooks with their hooves and heads removed. At least five muscled pigs hung by their limbs from a pulley, blood draining from long slashes along their backs into a trough below where four skeletal dead ladled the fluid into ceramic jugs, stoppering them with corks once they were full. Full jugs were stacked together on a pallet, with two dead men waiting to haul the blood off when given the command.

The dead worked in silence, cooking large slices of ham while some were chopping the meat into chunks for use later. A large pot contained enough rice to feed a small army, and a boiling pot of water held hundreds of leeks within, several herbal roots resting in the water with them. Hopefully for flavor.

Hopefully.

Pulling back along a rushing stream of ether, Davis paused outside the dungeon. Two monks, living ones, stood guard in padded cold weather gear. They had pistols at their hips and swords over their backs. They were chatting in their rapid tongue, arguing it would seem.

Davis blanched when he heard the discussion.

A wiry man with a shaved head bearing ritualistic scaring sneered. "I want the woman. She'll be soft and supple, firm enough for my tastes while remaining juicy enough to really last."

"I was stuck with a child last time," the other one replied, "and I'll be damned if I'm stuck with one of the so-called warriors. They barely put up a fight, but did you see the muscles? Forcing them down would hurt. They'd be too tough for me to try and crack into in one session, it'd take me three or four before I made any headway."

"What about the old man?" Wiry asked.

The other man, equally bald but with a long scar over his cheek, shrugged. "I heard that Khul wants him, him and the albino."

"Do you think he's *touched*?" Wiry asked, sounding a tad worried.

Scar shrugged. "Could be. Hasn't made a peep all day and I haven't felt anyone trying to travel through the celestial realm, so I'd say if he is a magus, he's blessed by a minor one at most."

"Still, what an honor… I wish I knew their language so I could speak with him." Wiry shook his head before slumping against the wall. "And the boy! He's been touched by the dreams, but hasn't become one himself. He reeks of them!"

"I know," Scar agreed. "It seems strange, but who are we to question Khul?"

"I don't know; it just seems like he's going to be a waste to work over. He already looks half-starved and bloodied. While he'd give in easy, we can't work with one touched by a dream, it's too dangerous."

"So split the woman with me and we'll leave the others for the rest to squabble over," Scar offered. "You do that and I'll trade guns with you."

"Oh yeah? You sure about that?" Wiry smiled, leaning over to punch Scar in the arm. "I know how attached you are to that thing. All that for a woman?"

Scar leaned back. "I haven't had a woman in so long, the very thought makes me drool. If I must give up my old type fifty-nine, so be it."

"Deal!" Wiry crowed, taking a step over to grab at the gun at his friend's side.

Scar swatted Wiry's hands. "Wait until we have the girl ready, then you'll get your gun. Not a moment sooner."

Davis had heard enough. Disgusted, he retreated to his body, opening his eyes to realize he was staring at the ceiling. James and Huan stood over him looking down, and both broke into smiles when they saw him moving.

"You meditating again?" James asked, helping Davis up from the hard floor.

"Yes… I learned a few things about this monastery that trouble me. We'll need to speak to Khul as soon as possible." Davis said.

Kun raised an eyebrow. "Khul? That sounds familiar…"

Davis waved it off. "Their language is a mix of a dozen regional dialects that were blended together sometime in the distant past. They've secluded themselves up here and apparently only venture out when the Children are active. They're either guardians or cultists… I haven't decided which yet."

"Which would be better?" Jin asked.

Davis just shook his head. "At this point, I really couldn't say. And that's the least of my worries."

# Chapter Twenty-Eight

The dead man returned, a large silver pot with three legs being handled with ease as he approached the cell. He had Wiry and Scar with him, their swords drawn at their sides. Both had flecks of snow covering their frames, their leathers and furs keeping the chill of the blizzard from reaching into them. Wiry waved his sword, pointing it at Jin and Kun before pointing at the far wall, barking an order in his harsh tongue.

"He says he wants us at the back of the cage," Davis said, standing up despite his creaking joints. "If we want a warm meal we have to comply."

Everyone stood, Kun helping Nian up from the ground. The young man seemed to be fading in and out of consciousness, murmuring something about his mother as Kun walked him up against the stone wall of the cell.

Once everyone had their back to the wall, Scar unlocked the door, allowing the rune-covered dead to shuffle into the cell. Slowly lowering the steaming pot to the ground, it pulled four wooden ladles from a worn leather belt, tossing them idly to the floor.

"You'll have to share," it said, glowing eyes focusing on Davis. Davis merely nodded, gasping as his chest ached.

The slumped figure turned and began limping out of the cell, allowing Scar to close the door and lock it once more. Wiry stood there staring at Nian, dark eyes never leaving the panting boy. "He's going to turn," he said to Scar. "We need to go to Khul. Tell him that we have a dreamer in the cell with the prisoners."

Scar snorted. "And what would you have us do? You know as well as I that we can't contain a dreamer in our dungeon. It'd just slip through the bars to find a new meal."

"But what of the fate of the others? We need them alive, uninjured!" Wiry protested.

Scar sniffed, looking between Wiry and the group behind bars. "He's slowly changing, has a day or so to go at least. We'll speak to Khul; he'll know what to do."

Wiry didn't look pleased by this answer and, after casting a final glance at Huan, turned and followed the undead out of the bunker and out into the howling snowstorm. Scar remained behind, looking over everyone.

"I hate to be a bother," Davis said in their language, earning a raised eyebrow from the stout monk. "But among my clothes is a small orange bottle. It contains medicine for my pain, pain which can kill me if I don't take it. It's basically opium, and I need it. Could I please have it?"

"You speak out tongue?" Scar asked after a few moments. "How did you learn it?"

"You know how. I'm *touched*, after all. The albino is in a way as well, though his pale nature is due to an encounter with a cursed relic, not active practice in the darker aspects of the arcane."

Scar didn't seem fazed that Davis was quoting the conversation that had taken place outside in the cold. "You can travel the celestial realm without being detected? How is it one from the west can do such a thing?"

Davis smiled. "Meditation and the right tutors. Now, my medicine? I imagine the Khul will want me in good health when I'm brought before him."

The monk cracked a wry grin, turning to walk into the darkness, sheathing his sword. "It would be in the smallest outfit, yes? The one with many pockets?"

"Yes," Davis replied. "The bottle should be in the pocket on the inside, right above where your heart beats in your chest."

The others had begun muttering to themselves, walking away from the wall to investigate the steaming pot next to the brazier. Nian was lowered to the ground while Huan lifted the lid of the pot to reveal a brown broth, pink chunks of meat floating amid a variety of roots and tubers. Scar came back into the flickering light of the brazier, holding the bottle between his forefinger and his thumb. He rattled it once.

"Strange opium you have," the monk said.

Davis smiled at him. "The west has taken proper medicine and warped it into strange and exotic versions. It's quite potent and is the one thing that keeps these old bones moving."

"How do I know this isn't something that could help you escape?" Scar asked, tossing the bottle up in the air idly.

Davis shrugged. "You don't. But if we escaped, how far would we go? Would we run into the blizzard with just our blankets?"

"You have a point. Your friends would die of exposure in minutes. You, however, are in touch with the celestial realm. You might be able to travel through it like we do. What if I give you these pills and you gain the strength necessary to make a jump?"

Davis sighed. "You are right to worry. But I swear on my honor I won't try and escape. I need my companions, as we're on a mission to stop a great menace facing China."

Scar seemed to ponder the statement for a while before snatching the bottle with a snap of his wrist. He tossed it into the cell. It rolled until it bumped into James's foot, prompting him to look down. Davis smiled and bowed towards the monk.

"Don't make me regret it, old man," Scar said before turning to leave.

Davis heaved a sigh of relief and, slipping to English, hobbled closer to James. "Pick that up will you, and shake out four pills. I need them badly."

"Could you spare one for Nian? He looks like he's in a lot of pain..." Huan asked, looking over at the boy, who was leaning forward. His bandages were stained brown, as were the silk wraps over his feet. Tinges of blue lined the tips of his fingers and nose, while his face was slack from exhaustion. Davis thought on what Scar had said.

Davis said, in as cheery a voice he could muster, "No, I don't think so. He needs to eat and sleep, and per the guards he's beginning the change into one of the Children."

"Are you serious?" James asked, palming four of the pills before screwing the top back on. "How long do we have?"

Davis shrugged. "They said he would change in a day or two. We may have to kill him if we're trapped in here that long."

"That wouldn't go over well with the soldiers," Huan said, ladling broth up to her mouth. She frowned. "Ugh, pork. I hate pork!"

"Yeah, I saw a slaughterhouse they were operating while I was projecting," Davis said, accepting a ladle and his pills. Taking them with a quick swig of the stew, he smacked his lips. "Surprisingly salty… anyway, they seem to have a good deal of pork to prepare. I saw a few carcasses hanging, the blood draining out into a trough, where several dead bottled it."

"Wait, they were bottling blood?" James asked.

Davis nodded with a grim frown. "I know; they seem like cultists to me as well."

Switching to Mandarin as Davis caught Jin glaring at them, Davis smiled. "We're just discussing the possibility of our captors being cultists."

"That's kind of obvious, isn't it?" Kun said with a derisive snort. "They have the fucking dead up and about acting as servants. That means a necromancer is here at the very least… that's a Class II violation within the department."

"What does that mean?" Huan asked.

Jin patted Nian on the back as the teen began coughing uncontrollably, while Kun continued. "Quarantine and capture for study. Anything below a Class V is typically a capture issue. If these are cultists that are actively summoning or creating aberrations or extraplanar entities, then it's instantly a Class V."

"Seeing as we have no idea where we are and can't get in contact with your department, we'll have to do things on the fly, so to speak," Davis said, handing the ladle to Jin. "Help Nian if you would, the lad could use some food."

"He's ice cold, even with the fire and the blanket," Jin said, gripping Nian's sweaty forearm. "I don't think he'll survive the night unless we do something."

"What would you suggest?" Davis asked.

"One of us needs to lie under the covers with him, help raise his core body temperature with our own," Jin replied, looking pointedly at Huan. "She would be able to help him while also remaining still. Her wound is fresh and could open if she moves too much."

Davis waved a hand to stifle James. "She's not a bed warmer Jin, she has more of a purpose than serving as a plaything."

"Not saying she should fuck him, just that she should hold him and warm him up," Jin argued. Kun nodded, ladling broth up to his mouth.

"Then I suggest you hold him under the covers if you want him to live. You were tasked with keeping us safe, and you've been doing a stellar job so far," Davis shot back.

Jin threw himself bodily across the cell, a roar issuing forth from his lips. James stepped between Davis and the charging soldier while Huan lashed out with a snap kick into the man's side, sending him toppling to the ground with a meaty thud. He looked up from the floor, growling.

"You little whore! I'll kill you!" Jin growled.

Huan took up a defensive position, standing so her side was facing Jin with her hands raised. Davis, staring from behind James, eyed Kun. He was watching his friend fight with interest, his palm inching towards the back of his trousers.

"James," Davis whispered. "Kun has a weapon. We need to stop him before he can do anything, or else we could all die here in this wretched cell."

James nodded, shifting his gaze to the Chinese soldier as Huan blocked a right hook from Jin, twisting his arm until he cried out in pain. Kun leapt to his feet, brandishing a sharpened piece of wood, a stake that had been a leg to one of the cots. Davis cursed his inattention and was about to call out to Huan when James rushed forward, grabbing Jin and pushing him into his friend's path.

*Splorp!*

The impromptu knife sank into Jin's back, blood bubbling up from the wound as the man issued an agonized cry. Kun froze for a second, just long enough for James to punch him square in the face, a loud crunch letting everyone know the man's nose was broken. Jin fell to the ground in a fluid slumping motion, a whimper leaving his lips.

"Huan…?" Davis said, gathering her attention.

She looked up at him, her nose twitching and eyes darting back and forth. She didn't say anything, but the twitches over her body made her seem like she was about to break through her own skin. James was staring at her with wide eyes. Jin lay on his belly, his back caked in blood from the impaled stake. Kun was on his back, groaning.

"Huan," Davis said. "We only need the four of us to complete the task. We need Nian, myself, James, and you. Do you understand what I'm saying?"

Huan didn't acknowledge what he said, instead looking at James with a familiar hunger. James ignored it, pulling the stake from Jin's back. After receiving a nod from Davis, James stabbed Jin in the back of the head, driving the stake through the crown of the stocky man's head. Jin squeaked, his voice faltering as his body slowly realized that it was dying, before the light in his eyes finally gave out. Kun rolled on his back, holding his face in a vain attempt to keep the blood from streaming out of his nose.

Huan let go of Jin's arm, dropping the corpse to the ground. She knelt next to him and, before anyone could say anything, grabbed his lower jaw and yanked hard. A sucking pop had the mandible moving freely beneath the ruined skull. A slender hand slipped into his mouth and grabbed hold of something before pulling. She tugged for a few seconds, her hand finally jerking from the mouth with a torrent of blood, holding a canine tooth.

She stood back up, breathing heavily, and looked at James. James gave her a nervous smile, one that was returned with a savage grin. Davis chose to ignore the impending courtship and walked over Jin's body towards Kun. Reaching down, he punched the man's hands hard, causing them to slam down on his bloody nose, earning another howl of agony from him.

"You've lost this little revolt," Davis said in a low voice, looking down into Kun's eyes to try and emphasize the trouble the man was in. "I don't know what orders the department gave you regarding us, and frankly I don't care. But this… this was just an attempt to kill us. One you'd planned by making a weapon from one of the cot's legs. I should let Huan torture you before her blood lust gives in to more base desires."

"No!" Kun said, his voice distorted by his broken nose. "No, I'll behave!"

"Good," Davis pointed over at Nian, who hadn't moved an inch during the entire exchange. "Take him to a cot and wrap your arms around him. I'll tuck you two in and we can just let this incident go to the wayside… for now."

Kun complied without further urging, helping Nian to his feet and guiding him to a cot. It was a snug fit for the two men, but Davis smiled as he watched Kun's trembling form wrap around Nian's catatonic one. Throwing one of the wool blankets over them, Davis nodded.

"We'll save some stew for you both, but for now I think it would be for the best if you stayed out of sight," Davis said, nodding slowly to Kun in hopes the soldier understood.

"I'll be quiet," he said.

"You'd better, or your stake will go from Jin's head to your chest," Davis warned. Kun huddled deeper beneath the blanket, Nian wheezing slightly as Kun wrapped him in a hug. Davis leaned down so his face was inches from Nian's.

"Nian? Can you hear me?" Davis asked.

Nian mumbled something unintelligible, staring forward yet focusing on nothing. Davis leaned in closer, hoping to hear what Nian was saying.

What he heard he didn't like.

"...calling, soon he'll be free and we'll join. Then the days of glory will resume, washing this world in a new era of darkness and entropy," Nian muttered, his voice raspy and weak. Davis stared down at Nian with unblinking eyes. Slowly reaching forward, he laid the back of his hand against the boy's cheek.

He winced as the flesh stuck to his hand, peeling away like melted cheese as he pulled his hand back. Davis wiped his hand clean using the corner of the boy's blanket, watching as Nian's cheek slowly slithered and stretched back to its original shape. Nian's face broke into a wide grin, his face turning to look up at Davis.

Wide-eyed with teeth stained in blood, Nian spoke in a hoarse whisper. "He comes, Davis," Nian said in English, his voice a perfect match for Joshua's once-calm tones. "Soon, you'll face the Maker of Nightmares, and then you'll finally pay for what you've been doing all these years."

And with that, Nian's head went slack, his eyes slowly glazing over as the boy passed away, Kun panicking when he felt the lack of a heartbeat coming from Nian's body. Davis just stared at him, watching as his body slowly began to liquefy, first swelling as if it were being filled with water before melting like candlewax. Molten flesh reeking of decay filled the air. Kun leapt from the cot, wiping gore from his willowy clothing.

All Davis could do was wince as the demon within him twisted around his heart, fear blossoming from his chest in a way that Davis realized it wasn't his fear, but the curator's.

And despite the horrible scene before him, Davis smiled.

# Chapter Twenty-Nine

The bubbling mass of melted skin and putrefying organs were quickly wrapped up in Nian's ruined blanket, everyone taking extra care not to touch the mess. Davis removed the glove that had touched the boy's cheek, Kun using Jin's blanket to clean himself of the rot that had splashed over him while cradling the teen. The glove and blanket joined the putrid slime that was now tucked into a corner of the cell, neatly tied up like a Christmas present.

Not long after Nian's death did the servitor return, the glowing runes seemingly brighter than before. The creature stood at the edge of the cell, staring in at the group as they each took turns sampling salty broth. Davis sat atop Jin's corpse as if it were a divan. Huan was pressed close to James, spoon feeding him between periods of kissing and nibbling at his neck. Kun was just frightened, staring down at the broth, his hands visibly shaking as he ladled it up to his mouth.

"I see you've been busy," the servitor observed. "We'll have to take the corpses from the cell. I'm sure you understand..."

"Of course," Davis said. The curator's fear was now waylaid by the medication he'd swallowed, the creature falling dormant once again. "Back against the wall?"

"If you would..." the servitor said with a smile.

Everyone stood and walked back to the end of the large cell. The simulacrum unlocked the door and slowly dragged Jin's corpse out of the chamber. Two other dead men, these ones little more than lost souls at this point, were waiting with a wheelbarrow. The servitor walked back in while the two dead men loaded Jin.

"Pass me the remains of the dreamer," the servitor said, holding out a leathery hand.

Kun stared at him until Davis translated. His nose still dribbling blood, he cautiously lifted the soggy sack of blankets holding the rancid meat together. The servitor took it gently and carried it out of the cell, where another dead man emerged from the darkness with a bucket. The servitor dumped Nian's remains in the container as if it were slop to be fed to the pigs before rolling the blankets into a ball. The creature wordlessly took the blanket before carrying the bucket with the other two dead men pushing the wheelbarrow.

The servitor looked at them through the bars. "The Khul has demanded the presence of the three touched by the dreamers."

"Um, I only believe two of us have been touched by the so-called dreamers," Davis said.

The servitor pointed to James, then Davis, before finally pointing at Huan. "You three all bear the auras of ones blessed by the otherworldly powers of the dreamers. Come with me, or stay in the cell to be prepared for the coming ritual."

"We'll go with you!" Davis said, holding his hands up. Turning, he looked at Kun. "The Khul is asking for my students and me, so you'll have to stay here for a little while longer while we sort out this mess."

"Give me two of your pills and I'll be fine," Kun grunted, one hand moving to his nose. "This hurts like hell!"

Davis laughed and pulled his bottle from within his clothes, shaking out two tablets. Pressing them into Kun's hand, he leaned in and whispered, "Take them both. You'll be a little woozy, but you won't feel any pain."

"Thanks," Kun said.

Davis just nodded and turned to his students. "Let's go, the Khul wants to see us."

Huan looked unhappy that her ministrations on James would have to be held in check for the time being, while the pale youth seemed more curious than anything else. Despite the lack of ability to communicate, he was studying the servitor with a careful eye.

*Perhaps he's thinking of joining up with a group of occultists after this?* Davis mused, feeling the curator coiling around his heart in agreement. *He'd make a fine necromancer to be sure, but would James be able to handle the finer aspects of the ether?*

Davis walked ahead of the group, out of the cell a few feet but still within the servitor's sight. The creature turned and motioned for them to follow into the darkness, which Davis did without hesitation.

After all, he could see in the darkness, and all that he could find were empty cells and walls lined with clothing of all shapes and sizes. He smiled when he noticed his clothing folded in a neat pile in a low cupboard. The corpse stopped next to Huan's outfit, lifting it up to examine it. Her tank top was beyond useless now, torn and bloodied from where the sword had bit into her.

The servitor instead pulled down a leather vest and wool shirt, thrusting them into Huan's hands.

"Dress," it said with a tepid hiss, "the weather is not pleasant out and you may die from exposure if you are not suitably covered."

Huan stepped back from the undead and slowly, her wound beneath the bandages obviously still aching, began to remove her linen vest and leggings, slipping on the wool shirt and vest before pulling on a pair of woolen pants.

"We have a wide selection of padded shoes, all insulated," the servitor said while looking at Davis. "Gather some for your followers."

Davis nodded and walked over to a long row of stacked shoes. Grabbing a few larger pairs, he walked over to James and grabbed his leg. His student jumped in surprise, the darkness still too dim for his eyesight to adjust to.

"Here, try these on," Davis said.

"What are they?" James said, groping at the shoes in confusion.

"Moccasins, made from leather and insulated with fur. Find some that fit you while I get dressed," Davis said, advancing on his pile of clothing.

The servitor did nothing to stop him, merely raising an eyebrow as Davis shucked off his prisoner's garb, quickly donning his gear with speed that belied his age. Looking to the undead after he buttoned up his vest, he smiled.

"I came here with a walking stick, one that I need now more than ever thanks to the cold," Davis said, thinking of his precious spear. "Do you think you could wrangle something up for me that would prove sufficient?"

The servitor slowly nodded, turning to walk further down the row of clothes and shoes. He stopped and began sorting through what must have been canes, looking for one that would match Davis's miniature stature.

"Listen," Davis whispered. "I know you can't understand what's being said, but I need you to act as calm as possible while I speak. No quick movements, no frowns or grunts, and no talking back. If this is a cult, then we may very well be on the menu for a sacrifice. If these are just monks of some strange sect I may be able to talk them out of killing us."

"That'd be lovely," James drawled, earning a swat from Huan. "Ow! What was that for?"

"For not being able to help me out! I have an itch that needs scratching!" Huan hissed, her eyes mere slits as she bared her teeth.

"Hey, I'd love to help you but we're kind of captive in an artic climate! Plus, we're both wounded, we can't have a roll in the hay like this!"

"Can it, both of you!" Davis hissed as he watched the servitor pull a short, knobby staff with a leather grip, three iron rings piercing the top of the staff which made musical clinks when moved.

"Here," the servitor offered, walking closer with the staff. "This should do. Have you chosen shoes for yourself yet?"

"I'm afraid all I see are children's shoes," Davis replied, taking the walking stick and leaning on it with a sigh. "Could we just wrap my feet up further?"

"That's what the monks do," the servitor supplied, turning and reaching into a cupboard above the benches piled high with clothes. "Take a seat while I bind your feet. This shouldn't take long."

Davis plopped down onto a pile of folded shirts. While his students tried on shoes and dressed themselves, Davis was treated to a strange sort of wrap from a leathery material that the creature was sealing around his feet with a thick paste.

Davis couldn't help but notice that, while they were busy getting kitted out by the shambling butler, two monks had entered the prison, each armed with manacles and pistols.

They unlocked the cell housing Kun, who had climbed onto a cot to rest, and briskly marched up to him before savagely kicking him in the side of the head. He didn't make a noise, so Davis could only assume the blow had knocked the poor man unconscious. The two monks turned, and the light showed them both, their open vests highlighting their tattoos and an open sore on one's gut.

It took Davis a moment to realize that was the one he'd shot during the raid. He looked remarkably well, if not annoyed, and helped drag Kun out into the cold, not even bothering to close the cell door.

"There we are," the servitor said, patting Davis's foot.

Davis looked down at his feet, now doubled in size in hides and fabric, layered leathers held fast with a gummy gray goo.

"And this will hold?" Davis asked, curious about the dressings.

"Until it is cut off, yes," The servitor replied.

That gave Davis a moment of pause, but he just smiled and nodded. The servitor stood up and, after looking over James and Huan, ushered them towards the lit hall leading to the cells. There, Brun waited with two burly monks, each with their hands resting on the pommels of their sabers. Brun wasn't armed, merely dressed in furs and heavy clothing, the robes sweeping down to cover her legs. Her hands, bare of any covering, clasped together in front of her.

"Thank you for preparing them," she said to the undead, who merely turned and moved into the cell to begin cleaning. Turning to Davis, she smiled. "I'm sorry this has taken so long, but the Khul has been taxed as of late while communing with the spirits."

"That's all right," Davis lied. Because of how long they waited one of their men was killed in a burst of action that could have been avoided. "I'm pleased that we'll get to meet him. Is he expecting us?"

"Yes, he has a dinner prepared in a small chamber in his wing of the palace. He made certain the servants laid out food for all of you so you could eat your fill."

"You won't be joining us?" Davis asked, following behind her as she turned.

She chuckled. "No, I'm just a humble warrior-turned-warden of the prison. Whenever we have prisoners, I make certain they're taken care of."

She opened the door to the prison, the door pushing back with a bone-chilling wind, a flurry of snow whipping past them all. "Best hurry if you wish to meet the master on time!"

Davis waded out into the snow, which was hip deep for him. Pushing forward a few feet, he let out a surprised yelp when he was lifted by the back of his vest and placed on the shoulders of one of the monks. Tattoos following up his neck to encircle his right eye, this monk had the same metal armbands as the ones that had attacked them originally.

The other did not, and seemed to move with a fluid grace, as if his legs could part the snow instead of push it aside. Brun was following behind Tattoo, with James and Huan in between them.

The blizzard had died down to biting winds and frigid bursts of hail raining down upon them. This allowed Davis to look at the architecture of the palace, a giant building by any measure, constructed from smooth granite slabs, unadorned save for sconces for torches. Great doors barred entry from three directions, behind which were a large antechamber (Davis could only guess) with the rest of the palace being built into the mountain, scaling up to form a statue of a man standing with arms spread at his waist.

The founding monk perhaps?

Davis didn't get long to think on it as Tattoo closed the distance between them and the door in several powerful strides, pushing on the door to open it slowly. Peering inside, Davis could see a pair of jade Buddha statues standing with bowls, water dribbling from them into a fountain full of koi. The pond was flanked by two hallways, one with stairs. The stairs lead up while the hallway lead deeper into the mountain. The group slipped into the antechamber, easily sixty feet by sixty feet, with high vaulted ceilings and a balcony jutting out to overlook the pond, which dominated the room.

Once everyone was inside, the monks lowered their heads and muttered a prayer too faint for even Davis's enhanced hearing to pick up. Tattoo lifted Davis by the hips and placed him on the floor, jostling the older man slightly as he tried to right himself. Turning, he smiled up at the dour man.

"In my culture, we offer payment for those who go above and beyond in service to others," Davis said to him, earning a raised eyebrow. "Do you have any elderly family here at the monastery that suffer chronic pain?"

Tattoo seemed to consider Davis before nodding once. Davis pulled the orange bottle out and shook loose three tablets, passing them into the monk's gauze-wrapped hands.

"One each morning, these should give them three days in which they will feel no pain," Davis said. "Use them sparingly, and never within twelve hours of each other."

"The others spoke of your request for medicine, and witnessed you take four at once. Surely it cannot be that good if someone your size needs so much." Tattoo's voice was low and grating, as if he didn't speak much.

Davis shook his head and turned to Brun.

"Just make sure they use them responsibly," Davis said with a hint of worry. "The folly of youth is believing yourself to be invincible."

Brun cleared her throat, gathering everyone's attention. "That is enough of that. The Khul is waiting for you in his chambers upstairs. I am not permitted to visit his chambers, so you'll have to ascend into his holy sanctuary on your own."

Davis wondered what made them so special that they would be allowed into supposedly holy ground. Instead of asking, he merely bowed to Brun before waving to his students to follow him.

The stairs were made of smooth stone, well worn over centuries of use. The walls were adorned with silver branches, veins running along the walls leading up into the chambers of the monastery's leader. Davis frowned.

"This should be interesting," he muttered. "James, you and Huan won't understand what is being said, so be sure to stay silent while I negotiate our freedom."

"Not too different from how things have been going so far," Huan mumbled, earning a snort from James.

"I think I'll just enjoy sensing the energies swirling around this palace," James replied. "Huan and I will behave. Just make certain you can free us. I don't relish the idea of being trapped here for the rest of my days."

"I'll do my best," Davis huffed as they made their way up the stairs. They were wide steps, but his bones were aching from the cold; each step was difficult thanks to his arthritis. The curator within him twisted, hissing deep within his mind as it settled in to spectate the coming events.

It took them a few minutes to ascend the steps, the silver veins branching out, pulsing with ethereal energy that Davis didn't even need to try and sense.

*This must be an amazing sensation for James...* Davis thought. *The occult specialist is slowly gaining a foothold in the arcane arts. I just hope he doesn't descend into madness like so many others have before him.*

Davis's thoughts were broken by the wafting scent of warm food drifting down the stairwell. "It would seem we may be fed during our encounter..."

"I could use a meal," Huan said with a faint smile. "Our prison stew was only so filling..."

Ascending the final steps, they entered a massive chamber lined with columns. A long table dominated the center of the room while a massive fireplace sat across from the stairwell, roaring with flames. Dozens of jade statues of holy men stood in varying distances, all thin and frail looking, each with silver masks, rubies set into the eye sockets that glittered in the dancing light of the fire.

Standing at a balcony overlooking the room was a thin man, dressed in monk's vestments. His face, turned away from them, had silver horns sprouting from its sides.

*A mask like the ones on the statues?* Davis thought.

The man had bony arms, lithe with taut muscles that seemed to be pulsing with potent energies. Davis could tell from the curtain of silver hair descending his back that the man was old, the energies coursing through him marking him as someone who could be as old as Davis.

The group stopped at the landing, Davis holding his walking stick out to prevent the others from moving forward. Huan was staring hungrily at the table where a succulent looking seared pig, sans head and hooves, sat amid bowls of fruit and baskets of bread. Crystal decanters of dark drink sat among the various foodstuffs, begging to be opened and sampled.

Davis lowered his cane, waiting for the man to turn and acknowledge him and his students.

The man turned to gaze at them from behind his silver skull mask, eyes blazing red as he studied the group. In a voice stronger than one would suspect from the man's ancient frame, he said in a rich baritone, "So you are the magus and his chosen of the dreamers? What a strange entourage you make, climbing my mountain. I wonder what it is you could be looking for."

Davis bowed stiffly. "We are in search of a dreamer, one that may be slowly rousing from his slumber. We seek to ensure that it will remain asleep."

"Oh?" the man replied, stepping into the light. His exposed chest and arms were riddled with tattoos, swirling script that seemed to vibrate with channeled energies. The crackling red eyes bored into Davis's tired pair. "Why don't you take a seat at my table and we can discuss what you could possibly do to my charge. As the reigning Khul, I am most interested in what you think you could do to the Slumbering Ancient."

# CHAPTER THIRTY

Davis sat to the right of the Khul with Huan and James taking their spots down the table, each piling their silver plates with food. Davis's eyebrows bobbed when he laid eyes on Huan's plate—it was piled high with steaming slices of ham.

*Didn't she say she hated pork?* he mused, making a mental note but declining to comment on this at the moment.

The Khul looked on, hands folded beneath his chin.

"The chosen are hungry, are they not?" the Khul said. "I've known several that have housed a dreamer's child, and they've all shared common traits, insatiable hunger being chief among them."

Davis had cut a slice of ham and taken a small loaf of bread, which he was buttering with a silver knife. Without looking at the ancient monk, Davis smirked.

"I'm curious," Davis said with a careful tone. "You recognize the otherworldly power radiating from the lad, but also refer to the girl as a chosen. She, to my knowledge, does not have any external influences. I know she cannot access the celestial realm. Hell, she can't even *sense* it!"

The Khul speared a piece of ham he'd loaded onto his plate, bringing it up to his mouth to take a large bite, juices running down his chin. "She houses one of my charge's seeds, deep within her belly. I imagine she was bedded by one without her even realizing it."

Davis was stunned but stayed his trembling hands, forcing himself to take a bite of his bread. "You… you can sense she is with child?"

"In a fashion. After decades of dealing with the sleeper's dreams, I've grown accustomed to the unique energies that they radiate. Now that she is within the monastery it will begin to feed upon the power flowing along the celestial realm's currents, growing and consuming her from the inside out."

"Would you happen to know how to prevent her from dying to this infection?" Davis asked, doing his best to keep his eyes off Huan as she gobbled her third slice of ham.

"The blessed meats she eats will stave off the Dream-Child's hunger, though only for so long," the Khul smirked. "But, I do know of a way to contain the influence from the growing evil within her womb."

"How… how could she have been impregnated by one of the dreams?" Davis asked, wracking his mind.

The Khul shrugged. "She is coupled with the boy, correct? I imagine one of the craftier dreams took on his shape and had his way with her. The fact that she isn't distraught over her predicament means she is both unaware of her state and that she was a willing participant."

Davis frowned as he remembered James and his strange reaction to Huan being in his tent the morning after the first encounter with the Children of Flesh. Between that, and the Child lurking about the camp, it meant that she could have easily been bedded by the creature without her knowledge.

"You said you know of a way to contain the evil growing within her. What would this require?" asked Davis.

The Khul leaned across the table, gripping a decanter. "The tattoos we bear," he said as he poured himself the blood red wine, "are how we access the celestial realm. They also allow us to use the energies without being torn asunder."

"So she would need some of your tattoos?" Davis asked, following the Khul's logic.

He nodded. "Yes, the sooner the better. I can have her ready for the work to be done as soon as our meeting is concluded."

"That's most generous… I'm afraid you have me at a disadvantage, as I have no way of repaying you for this service."

The Khul waved the mention of payment aside. "You and I are cut from the same cloth—we are honor-bound to aid one another when needed. As for payment, you can assist me in my own problems with the Slumberer."

"Oh?" Davis asked after taking a bite of his bread. "If you'll pardon my assumption, I'd taken you and your followers as worshippers of the Slumberer."

"Oh no," the Khul laughed. "We are guardians, set here by Zhao so many years ago. He entrusted us with maintaining the seals holding the dreamer here after the armies of the Emperor Gong forced the entity deep beneath the stone of the mountains. Our order, long-forgotten forgotten in the sands of time, is trained to battle the dreams of the sleeper."

"Some of those dreams have been able to sneak out from beneath the mountain, invading villages and taking men and women at their leisure," Davis replied. "I've been told your order knew of this for years and offered pigs to keep the dreams from emerging from the underground rivers."

"Pigs?" the Khul repeated. "We have no pigs."

"Of course you do," Davis said. "I've seen your kitchen where the dead process slaughtered animals."

"Oh," the Khul said, taking a bite of his ham. "I would have thought you'd have senses what it is that you've been eating."

Davis looked down at the ham, reaching out with his senses to study the meat. Tainted with corrupted energies, the meat was fresh enough to still hold life energy.

Human energy.

Davis fought the bile rising in his gullet. "You… you eat people?"

"We eat captives that are of no consequence. This meal was prepared from the murdered man in your cell, his skull pierced by a wooden stake. His soul had yet to leave the body, allowing us to sup on his energies to replenish our own."

Davis stared at the Khul who set the decanter down, lifting his mug in a salute before tipping the drink back. He watched the fluid pulse with the essence of humanity—the fluid was anything but wine.

The corrupted monk was drinking blood from a prepared decanter, somehow enchanted to prevent the sanguine drink from coagulating. Davis looked at his own mug, filled to the brim with the soupy red beverage. The curator within him twisted painfully, sliding along his ribs as it too realized what they were eating.

It wanted the blood, the meat of man. Jin had died a traitor, but he was now serving in one final act: as a meal.

The curator sang within his body, absorbing the life energy that Davis was ingesting, his chewing slowing down as he realized that his meal was once someone he shared coffee with. True, he was an obnoxious ass who'd tried to kill them, but it was a horrible experience where tensions were high. To think that they were eating him now wasn't the *most* unpleasant thing Davis had ever done. Slowly resuming his chewing, Davis took another bite of the meat, savoring the salty taste. He'd often wondered what a human being might taste like... now he knew.

*We taste like pork...* Davis mused, staring at the growing smile on the Khul's face.

"You *are* a magus! Only one such as you and I would continue feasting on the flesh of man after learning of it," the Khul said. "How long have you been corrupted?"

"Decades... I absorbed a demon of knowledge some time ago," Davis replied. He found it strangely relaxing to speak so openly about his unholy patron.

"Each Khul is inhabited by the same dream, demon as you would put it. A fraction of the sleeper's power that we sheared from his frame when first containing him. It took dozens of warriors to subdue him, and several of the emperor's warlocks to bind him. It's how we first mastered the tattooing."

"So you've existed here for, what, twelve hundred years?" Davis guessed.

"Roughly. I'm the seventh Khul, and at the tail end of my regime. I have perhaps a decade to train a new Khul before my body is too weak to contain the monster's power. The transfer will kill me, but to keep the sleeper contained... it's worth it."

"But like I said, the sleeper isn't contained! His dreams, these shui gui, are slipping out and attacking villages! Your monastery used to deliver what the locals assumed to be pigs under orders to lower them into the town wells. You've known of this for nearly seventy years!"

The Khul chewed for a moment on a morsel of stringy meat. "I knew of this, but it doesn't mean that the sleeper is awakening. He stirs in his slumber, and his dreams venture out to feed. Nothing more."

"The Chinese government is going to investigate—*is* investigating—the emerging monsters. The man we're eating was a government official that we brought to help fight the dreams!"

"More's the pity, then," the Khul said with a savage grin. "His compatriot is being prepared for my next few meals. I assume he represents the modern government?"

"Yes, he does..." Davis said, shrinking back as the man barked out hoarse laughter.

"This will teach those bastards from coming into my mountains! I'll post their heads on pikes as a warning to all who would dare assail my home!"

"You don't understand, Khul—the modern government is far more lethal than the government of old. They have flying machines that can drop weapons of destruction that cannot be fought. They could level your palace without a second thought!"

"Impossible! Flight is something only the masters of the arcane can achieve, something the casual pig farmer can only dream of!" the Khul exclaimed.

"I swear to you, they have such weapons. And while they would be loath to use them due to your proximity to India, they would no doubt send in soldiers. They already have a group that knows we were sent to look specifically for you."

Davis knew this was a lie, and felt the curator twist within him as it feasted on the life energy.

The Khul seemed to buy it. "This may be true, but my warriors are the pinnacle of martial prowess backed up by the power of the celestial realm. We can defend ourselves..."

"Why take the chance? Allow my group, what's left of it at least, to investigate the lair of the sleeper. I know the incantations and rituals to keep one asleep, after all."

"You are skilled enough to perform such an act?" the Khul asked.

"I've done it before on several occasions. I have one that I do every ten years to maintain its continued slumber."

The Khul sampled his drink once more before asking, "With or without a sacrifice?"

"Both actually, though doing it with a sacrifice is far easier, let me assure you," Davis said with a slight chuckle.

"We do a sacrifice every fifty years to strengthen the wards holding the sleeper's body bound beneath the rock. From my texts, it was difficult building this palace atop him, but my order managed it."

"Wait," Davis said. "The sleeper is beneath the palace? As in, beneath where we're eating right now?"

"Of course," the Khul said. "Through the catacombs where we keep our honored dead, the dreams start and guard the sleeper as best they can."

Davis's mind raced a mile a moment. Finally, he turned and smiled at the Khul. "When is your next ward-strengthening due?"

"Eighteen years, why?" the Khul asked.

"Because I'd like to offer you a deal," Davis said. "Our freedom with the tattoos the girl will require to control her inner demon. In exchange, I'll add my own wards over yours for extra security, and we'll swear to never speak of this place to anyone who doesn't know of it."

"Hmmm… our plans to use you as fuel would bring ill fortune as you are all blessed by sleepers in your own way. What would these wards do, exactly?"

"They'd shore up your existing wards. I assume they're chiseled into stone, correct?" Davis asked.

The Khul nodded, prompting Davis to continue.

"My wards would be drawn in molten silver mixed with the girl's blood. That way it would target the creatures themselves, seal them within the chamber for a good while until you can come up with a method to keep them from swimming out to find meals on their own."

"And why would I expend effort in doing that?" the Khul asked.

"Because the more attacks made by the dreams, the more scrutiny your mountains will fall under. Hell, the only reason we bumped into you all is we had a guide that *knew* of you!"

"The one who was infested with the dream?" the Khul asked. When Davis nodded, the man shook his head. "Sorry, he had to go that way. We would have gladly contained the infection had we known about it, just as we'll contain the dream resting in your woman's womb."

"It's a failure on both our parts," Davis said. "Just let us do what we need to do so that nobody else is affected by the dreams of a sleeping god."

"And what would that be?" the Khul asked, sipping from his mug.

Davis leaned over his plate, hands folded in front of him. "We need to go into the catacombs of this palace so that we can make our way to the contained sleeper. I would love to take some of your martially-inclined monks with me, as I know there'll be some nasty business waiting for us down there."

"Said nasty business is there for a reason," the Khul said. "And I would be remiss in my duties in letting you go down into the mountain with the intent to perform a task that may very well awaken the sleeper. Your wards sound fascinating, in theory, but I would have to see them in action and see how they would interact with our protections."

"But surely you see the folly in letting the dreams run rampant across the countryside!" Davis said.

The Khul dismissed the idea with a wave of his bony hand, but Davis pressed on. "My group, when we were full and ready to deal with the problems that lay before us, has seen what the dreams do to the citizens living in the countryside. They infest the living creatures and plants, spreading contagion and hunger while consuming all raw materials in their wake. They grow into monstrosities that lash out at anything that lives, while changing the environment to make things more comfortable for them. This is not some fever dream or hyperbole, this is reality!"

The Khul's beady red eyes swiveled from Davis to Huan for a moment. He bowed his head slightly, lost in thought. Each passing moment seemed to stretch into chasms between the next, a yawning silence that was deafening. Finally, he lifted his head and let out a sharp whistle.

From the shadows between two jade statues against the far wall came a ripple in the ether, revealing two figures walking in from nothingness. Both were slinky young women, their revealing monk's outfits made decent by silk bindings over their chests and wrists. Both bore tattoos spiraling along their chests up the right side, curling up into the hollows of their neck. They both dropped to a knee, a fist resting on the smooth tile of the room.

"You called, honored one?" the woman on the left said, her voice light yet respectful.

"Yes," the Khul said with authority seeping into his jovial tone. "Take the woman here and place upon her the blessing of three ancient kings. Preferably on her right side, starting from her womb."

The women were silent, both exchanging worried glances between each other. Huan and James had stopped their dinner conversation upon the arrival of the two, their eyes lingering on the generous curves not often seen on a lady of China.

*Mixed heritage with tribes long lost to India, no doubt…* Davis thought as he cut a piece of human flesh and popped it into his mouth. The savory piece oozed with energy the likes of which he'd never consumed, which the curator desired more than the painkillers he was fed every few hours. Perhaps Davis had found something that could curb his patron's foul appetites?

His train of thought broken by the Khul's sudden movement, rising from the table with a high-pitched roar issuing from his cracked lips. Both women quailed under his fury, but the one on the left suffered far worse for as the Khul pointed a long-nailed finger at her, a slithering coil of green fire danced through the air at impossible speeds to wrap around her neck. The smell of burning flesh filled the air, though nobody moved to help her. Everyone was too stunned.

"I can see the questions in your eyes! You dare think of my demands as though they were simple requests?" the Khul thundered, his voice hollow as it bounced from the walls. "Do you wish to live?"

"Yes, please honored one, please, let me live!" the woman sobbed, in excruciating pain from the coil of flames cooking her neck. Blood and fat dribbled from the wound, staining her vestments. The other woman held still, knuckles on the tile and eyes cast forward.

The Khul held the position for a moment and Davis could swear he heard a faint echo of a whisper, a sibilant voice crooning for the woman's death. Looking around at the darkened corners of the room, Davis could find no other men or women to be muttering such things. It was only after the Khul dispersed the fire, snapping his hand closed fast enough for his nails to scratch together in a spine-tingling scrape, that Davis realized that the voice wasn't coming from anyone at the table.

It was coming from within the Khul. When he said all the leaders took on a bit of the sleeper, he meant each successive leader willingly allowed the demon to possess them, and slowly mastered the abilities granted by the foul denizen of the pit until they could keep it in check.

The curator coiled around Davis's heart merrily. It radiated feelings that were strange to Davis, that he could only interpret as a form of kinship. In the Khul was another like Davis who served as a host, but it was deeper than that, Davis knew, for the Khul was not just a necromancer or diabolist steeped in the black arts.

He was a demonologist, just like Davis.

# Chapter Thirty-One

Once Davis explained to his alarmed students what had just happened, and what Huan would have to undergo, they were understandably confused. Davis didn't feel it wise to disclose that she'd slept with one of the Children of Flesh, these dreams of the sleeper, especially in front of James. James was a normally level-headed person, but he clearly had feelings for Huan. The fact that she was pregnant with demon spawn was not something that could be explained easily, or tactfully.

The Khul didn't know English, so they stuck to that language; but he did understand the reticence that Huan felt going with the two women for a ritual tattoo session.

"Think nothing of it," Davis said, trying to assure her. "In this culture these markings are of the highest honor, and will lead to many of the monks respecting you. Not just anyone can have these markings you know…"

"Yeah? What do they mean?" Huan asked as she stood on shaking legs, staring between James and the two women patiently waiting to escort her elsewhere to begin the process.

"From what I understand they mark you as a warrior, and a mystic. They offer protections against the otherworldly and should allow you to tap into your inner abilities with greater ease. Who knows? You may be able to access the ether like I can, or better, as these monks can, after you receive their markings."

"So I might be able to teleport?" she said, sounding pleased suddenly.

"Or draw on mystical energy to ward away attacks," Davis nodded. The Khul remained seated, watching the conversation with interest. James merely sat in his seat and fumed.

"I don't like it," he said for the second time. "Separating us like this. They could be readying us for a ritual sacrifice for all we know."

Davis eyes darted to the partially dissected torso, the ribs missing from James's desire for the juicy pork he thought he'd been consuming. The fact that this was Jin they'd been eating was still lost on the two students, a secret that Davis might never share with the two for fear of how they might react.

*I don't need hot-heads this deep into an exploration*, Davis mused.

"Now go ahead and follow them Huan, attagirl!" Davis said, smiling as the women took Huan by her hands. Huan looked between them nervously before smiling wanly at the burned woman.

"The Khul… is he going to need me to do something after I get these markings?" Huan asked.

"Not that he's mentioned, though I imagine once we complete our mission we'll stay a while longer to peruse their texts and allow you to practice your newfound abilities, however they manifest."

"That'd be cool…" she muttered, nodded her head once, and then looked up and smiled at the women. "Let's do it!"

Davis translated. The women walked Huan to the wall they'd jumped through and opened a channel through the ether for them all to travel. It was a sight to behold the gray, twisting energies crackling with untold power, peeled back from the fabric of reality for the naked eye to observe. Huan let out a squeak of surprise as she was dragged in, the tunnel collapsing behind her with an audible crack that even made the Khul wince. Turning to James, Davis smiled.

"Don't worry," he said, "she'll be fine. The tattoos she'll be getting will be right up her alley, and from what I understand they shouldn't cause any discomfort like a normal tattoo. Once embedded, the markings sink into your soul."

James whistled low at that. "And what exactly is she trading for all this power?"

"Trading?" Davis repeated, doing his best to sound innocent. "This is merely a gift bestowed by the Khul to one he saw potential in."

"*I* have more potential for the arcane than Huan, and my recent encounter with the abnormal proves it!" James exclaimed, tossing his fork down onto his plate in a show of disgust.

"Don't be jealous, now tuck in and finish your meal. The Khul and I need to hammer out the details of our release, and what we can expect in our continued journey into the mountains."

"We're still doing that? But there's only four of us now! Kun is hardly in any shape to help us tackle any of the Children, and Huan is still cut up bad. I hate to say it professor, but we might need to throw in the towel on this excursion and call it a loss!"

Davis frowned at that. "I don't quit just because I'm presented with a few minor challenges. The Khul has informed me that the entrance to the Children's domain is beneath the palace. I'm negotiating with him to recruit some of his monks to help us clean out the area so I can perform the necessary rituals to help contain the Father of Flesh. If what the Khul is saying can be believed, his original bindings may just be growing weak. I'd have to examine them to be certain, but if that's the case the fix is pretty simple."

"How simple?" James asked, crossing his arms.

Davis glared at the graduate student. "Simple enough that some protection from some ether-wielding monks and a gun nut with her boy toy should prove capable in providing me the protection I need while setting it up."

"Wait, you'll need us to *protect* you?" James asked, sounding surprised by this. "What exactly does that entail?"

"Well first I'll need to examine the wards already in place. I plan on spending the next few days studying the Khul's library on all things demonic."

"But..." James said, eyes trailing off to the wall where Huan had been dragged through.

"But nothing. You continue eating while I hash out the deal that will grant us the freedom we need," Davis said, turning to smile at the Khul.

"Problem?" the Khul asked in his rough dialect.

"Just the complaints of youth, you know how they can be," Davis said.

"Ah," the Khul agreed. "To be young again. I remember the days before I took my role and accepted the dream. They're but a foggy memory now."

"Speaking of poor memory, I haven't studied ancient Song rituals in nearly thirty years. If I'm to provide any use in applying my own protections, I'll need to look over your writings on your wards."

The Khul eyed Davis for a moment. "And you know that we have these writings how?"

"Because it seems you and I are far too alike for our own good. I keep a terrible sleeper under wraps back home, and have his protections outlined at length in several books. If I've done it, so have you."

The Khul let out a hoarse bark of laughter. "Too true! You know me too well, magus. Let us finish with our meal and I'll bring you to my library. Your woman will be under the needle for the next four or five hours, and your pupil will be able to train with some of the acolytes if he wishes. I can sense he is on the cusp of understanding the celestial realm; perhaps some training with my people will give him the push he needs?"

"I'll let him know," Davis said. "Thank you for your hospitality."

The Khul shrugged. "It is rare I meet an equal in this region. To think that I get to share knowledge with one as obviously well-versed as you is a blessing; the least I can do is offer hospitality."

Davis nodded and pushed away from the table, his stomach full. The curator was, for once, solely focused on something other than Davis which left him with a degree of painless time that could be dedicated to the mission.

*It's a shame what will happen to Kun though,* Davis thought as the Khul stood, holding out a withered arm to guide Davis to a doorway obscured by shadows. *Then again, who knows what he was tasked to do with us once the mission was complete. The minister hates me, and Pho didn't seem pleased with me being around either. Just as well he was disposed of without me being forced to dirty my hands.*

* * *

Candlelight flickered in the side chambers leading away from the dining room. The halls opened above a massive room the size a small stadium, supported by numerous columns. Several small ponds gleamed by torchlight as monks practiced swordplay against wooden dummies, older instructors sporting faded tattoos instructing teens in proper fighting stances and striking methods.

Davis was amazed, as there were easily a hundred teenagers training, from swordplay to running laps around the cavern. He smiled as he watched Brun guide James into the chamber, pointing him to the sword trainers, his own sword hanging from his hip once again.

"I'm glad you trust us enough to return our weapons," Davis said.

The Khul snorted. "We trust your student, who is a novice in the arts of the body and mind. I would never allow you to be armed within my temple until I was sure you were an ally."

"And here you are taking me to your secret library," Davis smiled.

"Trust has been earned, however tenuous. The fact that you play host to a dream like I do means you have mastered its desires and have incorporated it into your lifestyle. That suggests a level of discipline I haven't been fortunate enough to see from those of the west for years."

"My people have become slaves to technology and advanced weapons of war. It's left our bodies weak, and our will soft," Davis said. "Even those within my country's military seem too fascinated with bigotry and abuses of power to prove useful in any prolonged engagement."

"Truly? That is a shame… a country is only as strong as its sword-bearing arm," the Khul said.

"Agreed. It would seem your forces here are well versed in swordplay, though I know I spotted some with modern weapons as well."

"Ah, you speak of the guns?"

Davis nodded, to which the Khul snorted. "They are an unwelcome addition in my opinion, but they've proven useful. Some encounters cannot be won with steel anymore, and require hot lead to finish the enemies who would stand against us."

"You speak as if you actually have enemies," Davis said. "Who even knows of your existence?"

"The Cult of the Broken God," the Khul growled. "A group of mad cultists that seek to awaken sleepers so that they can be bothered to rule over us as they once did. They have assailed our walls before, so we train to prevent them from disrupting our ordained commands."

"To protect the body of the… sleeper?" Davis asked.

The Khul nodded. "He has cast his mind into the celestial realm, allowing the flow of living energies to wash over him as he rests. He ordered his followers to protect him, which they did for centuries. Then the Song discovered what was here, and battled with the dreams, driving them deep within the mountain and placing the sleeper's followers in chains."

"Really?" Davis said.

"Yes, that was when their leader bargained with the emperor's advisors. Allow them to train some of the dynasty's mystics in the ways to protect the sleeper, in exchange for quick deaths. The dynasty accepted, and our order was formed."

"So, about your library?" Davis said, changing the subject.

"It's a combination of leather-bound books and scrolls made from tanned hide," the Khul said. "I've written around three myself, all detailing the dreams that lurk in the catacombs. They aren't as… volatile towards me, and allow me to observe them from a distance."

"The Father of Flesh—what the sleeper is called outside of your order—has some very aggressive dreams," Davis commented. "I find it surprising that you're allowed into their territory."

The Khul tapped his stomach. "I hold one of the dreams within my belly, kept in check by my tattoos. It makes me a unique case to the mindless dreams that are so common. The ones that plot and plan are capricious, and will often lure me into the dream's lair to ambush me."

"You seem to have fared well so far," Davis said.

The Khul snorted. "I bring my sword with me every time I go down, along with a host of mystical relics that make it easier to harm them. While they're intelligent, they are physically weak and don't enjoy hand-to-hand combat as much as the mindless laborers they oversee."

They entered a room with shelves, all stuffed haphazardly with nameless books and ornate scroll cases. Hanging from the ceiling were a half-dozen human skulls, each one bearing a luminescent stone in its mouth. The light from the oddly shaped rocks was enough to chase away the pervasive shadows, leaving the bare stone walls a slate gray. Another hallway led deeper into the mountain, though this one had a series of carved Chinese characters around the frameless opening.

While Davis wasn't an expert on ancient Chinese writing, he did consider himself an expert on traps.

Those words spelled out warnings of decidedly fatal traps ahead. Forcing a bit of himself into the ether, he whistled at the energy pouring off the characters, along with four large, previously invisible symbols marking the walls. They were all outside Davis's spectrum of knowledge and the curator didn't flood his mind with information, so perhaps even it didn't know what they were. Turning, Davis allowed his eyes to dim as he stared at the smiling Khul.

"Interesting set of protections you have over this room," Davis said. "What exactly do they do? I've never encountered those particular sigils before."

"That would be because they are all related to the sleeper beneath our feet," the Khul said, walking past Davis and through the open passageway lined with runes. "This leads to a room that I would not let any save the next Khul see, so you will be allowed to research as much as you need for the next few hours while I meditate on your requests."

Davis nodded and walked up to one of the shelves, fingers running over the spines of the nameless volumes. Closing his eyes, he probed his inner self to gather the curator's attention. The flash of pain surging up from his heart made it obvious it wasn't pleased with being disturbed.

*I need to know which books reference the Father of Flesh, as well as the weaknesses of the Children of Flesh,* Davis thought to the unruly demon. *Help me locate what I need and provide me the knowledge to read them, and I'll not bother you until you need your pills.*

The curator hissed in the back of his mind, funneling its energies into his eyes. Slowly the room fell into a green tint, with several books glowing a golden hue. Davis quickly gathered the tomes and dropped them onto the table, pulling up a chair for himself. The sight faded back to his normal vision, a light chuckle echoing in his mind as he could feel the coils of the demon tighten around his heart.

Grabbing the largest book, Davis opened it up and began studying what appeared to be a codex of known creations of the Father of Flesh. The words appeared to his aged eyes in English, though he knew that this was only the curator's doing.

Davis spent several hours by the light of skull-bound stones, poring over the various books. He learned that the dreams were just that—dreams that the Father of Flesh broadcast as a defensive mechanism. It'd started around the time of Christ, a time marked by earthquakes and fissures splitting through the province, with Children of Flesh flowing out to carry away as many living souls as possible.

One of the books detailed the seals over the sunken chamber, a ravine deep within the mountains filled with saltwater where the Father's body lay dormant. The entryway to the chamber was guarded by five seals, each interlocking with each other magically.

"If they're so intertwined, that means they're all decaying if his dreams are escaping…" Davis had muttered, finger going over the script depicting the seals. "Could just be the wear and tear of stone as time passes, but they need to be reconstructed."

Davis had devoted a good deal of time to memorizing the seals, and pondering how he would patch up any worn stone where the seals were chiseled in. The books were sketchy when it came to what they were etched with, or if they had to be done during a certain time of the month…

Davis didn't like that.

In his kit at the base of the mountain he had tools for this precise problem, along with weapons that would harm the dreams beyond their natural ability to repair themselves. The "thinking" dreams would be the most dangerous in this mission, as whatever they experienced was sent back into the Father's mind. Should they rouse him before the seals were repaired, he could awaken and burst from the Nanling Mountains like a maggot squirming from putrefying flesh.

Davis was interrupted by a bony hand resting on his shoulder. Turning, he spied an old man with glaring red eyes dressed in far more conservative leathers. Smiling, the figure set down a cup of red soup on the table before pulling a chair up to sit in. Only after spying a trailing bit of tattoo beneath his jerkin did Davis realize this was the Khul without his mask.

"What's this?" Davis asked, picking up the cup. It was smooth and light, yellowed with age. It had no handle, no markings, but Davis could *hear* the whispers of the damned hissing in his ear as he handled the cup.

"That," the Khul said as he settled into his chair, "is a relic from the cult that originally served the sleeper. There are only a few such relics left that have survived the years, and almost all of them are mystic in nature."

"Oh?" Davis said, mind racing at the strange turn of conversation.

"Oh yes," the Khul said. "I've decided that I'll allow some of my warriors to aid you in this endeavor. I imagine you'll want all of your tools?"

Davis nodded.

"Good, because we took everything from your camp before the blizzard hit. That spear you have is… unique, to say the least."

"I brought it to better battle the dreams of this god, knowing that the spear's powers caused them irreparable harm," Davis replied.

"Well I can tell you that should you approach the catacombs with it, the dreams will sense it instantly. It was made by a priest of an old one, designed to flense the muscle from the monsters that the gods created."

"So what would you suggest?" Davis asked.

The Khul nodded towards the cup. "That has a combined one thousand souls resting in its marrow. The fluid is my own blood, an admixture of mystic and profane. Drink, and you'll gain the experiences of the captured souls as well as a measure of control over the celestial realm."

The way he said it made Davis think he didn't have a choice in the matter. Staring down at the cup, he closed his eyes. "And of my spear?"

"I'll be keeping it, in case I'm one day called upon to battle the sleeper myself," the Khul replied. "Consider this a trade."

Davis felt an icy pit form in his stomach, the curator coiling around his heart painfully, declaring that it didn't want this action to take place. Davis clutched at his chest with one hand, surprising the Khul. Before he could do anything to help him, Davis brought the cup to his lips and guzzled the thick blood, the shrieks of the curator rattling within his skull as it was drowned in countless voices, one of which was much deeper than any Davis had ever heard.

## CHAPTER THIRTY-TWO

Hundreds of thoughts barraged Davis's mind. Dropping the cup to the table so that he could clutch his skull, Davis couldn't tell if he was screaming or if it was one of the many voices in his head. The constricting feeling around his heart loosened as the curator pulsed into his veins, rushing through his now polluted blood in search of… something.

The deep voice chuckled, a figure forming from thoughts in the forefront of Davis's imagination looming over him. "So you are the one I am to aid? I must say I'm not impressed…"

Davis squeezed his eyes shut, forcing himself to stare at the creature in his mind. It was pallid and waxy, with boneless arms that reached its feet. A lamprey mouth split its broad chest, a dozen eyes encircling the sucking mouth. Black markings, tattoos of some sort, covered nearly every inch of the pale, quivering flesh and seemed to twist along his skin as if they were snakes. As Davis listened to the roar of a hundred screaming voices, he could feel the curator entering his mind, sluicing through his veins to spread and seep into his wrinkled gray matter.

*Who are you?* Davis thought, fighting to stay awake despite the hammering his mind was taking.

*An echo of a fragment, a shadow of something greater… you know my whole form as the Father of Flesh. I am but a sliver of that mind, a piece to the puzzle. For now, you may call me Illias.*

Davis leaned down over the table, wincing as he felt a hand rubbing his back. The sensations were hot like fire, burning along his nerves as Illias spoke to him. Davis brought a shaky hand into his vest, reaching for his pocket watch. Opening his eyes with effort, he looked down at the face of the device as he flipped it open.

The longest arm was wavering between nine and ten, while the thinnest arm was spinning around madly. The shortest arm was resting on the number seven, with the background of the watch glowing a faint blue.

"You're... you're not as powerful as one would think!" Davis said through gritted teeth. "Only a seven... no problem for me to gain control of you!"

*Control was the point*, Illias said, settling into Davis's mind as if it were a comfortable chair. *I must say that is an ingenious device. Can it measure all of those touched by the divine?*

"So you can't read my thoughts, eh?" Davis asked, sweat rolling down the back of his neck. "What are you to me then?"

*My host, the man who sits across from you, is where I reside. As I am but a fraction of a fraction, I can only do one of two things: hinder or help. And I was given the impulse to help before I was separated from the rest of my consciousness. You can tell your other resident to calm himself, I'll be his next meal soon enough.*

The curator coiled within Davis's thoughts, the alien features lurking at the edges of Davis's every mental image. Davis studied Illias for what he was, scanning him as he'd done with magical trinkets for the past century.

What he found surprised him.

Still sweating, though his heart rate was slowing down, Davis looked over at the Khul, his features oddly normal for a man hosting such a strange entity. Save for his glowing red eyes, he looked like any man you might see sitting on a park bench, or in a Starbucks sipping coffee while perusing the Sunday newspaper. Reaching deep into his mind, Davis gripped the alien presence and pulled it towards his personal energies.

*And so, you realize what I am*, Illias said, not resisting as he was dragged deeper into Davis's mindscape, the curator floating close by as they grew close to Davis's gates housing his ethereal reserves.

While not a demonologist in the strictest sense, housing the curator for so long had given him access to his own pool of ethereal energy to draw upon. His core of energy was small compared to a practicing demonologist, but it was enough for him to do tricks such as read surface thoughts and scan the properties of relics. The gates that held it in check were enough to protect his mind as well, an added bonus to housing the curator.

Illias wasn't a gift of knowledge to aid Davis in his endeavors. He was a gift of power. Raw ethereal energy that he could pour into his own reserves, expanding them and pushing the boundaries of his own reservoirs until he could wield the energies in new ways.

Like teleportation.

*Exactly,* Illias thought. *Absorb my energies and allow the curator to feast on my shredded soul. You'll both grow stronger, strong enough to maybe face my ancestors' dreams.*

Davis concentrated as he drained Illias dry, squeezing his energy from him through his own ethereal gates, his veins vibrating with energy as his body began to hum in excitement. The Khul, sensing what was happening, smiled and clapped his hands together, drawing Davis's attention for a moment.

"Now you and I are bonded in servitude," the Khul said. "It was the only way I could allow you to enter the catacombs."

Davis was confused, his high from the influx of new energy muddling his thoughts. "What?"

"That energy," the Khul said with a broad smile, "is from the sleeper himself, however diluted. Now you have some of him within you. You cannot harm him, only work to contain him. I could not risk you doing anything that might harm my lord."

Davis thought on this as the last vestiges of Illias's energy sank into Davis's magical core. He tugged on it, pulling to try and regain control. Banned from harming the Father of Flesh? Unacceptable, as he might indeed need to in order to accomplish his aims. But the energy was like grappling with gallons of hot melted butter, streaming through his mental fingertips. The shredded thoughts held together with the barest of energies smirked at Davis.

*We can't allow you to harm the original,* Illias said as the curator coiled around him. *You'll thank me when you grasp the energy and process the knowledge you've been gifted.*

And with that the curator fully emerged from the subconscious, latching onto the thoughts with a maw filled with wispy fangs, tearing into the soul and gulping large chunks down in seconds. The soul didn't scream or cry, let alone whimper.

Instead it just smiled, radiating a happiness that Davis couldn't stand to feel. He mentally urged the curator to feed faster, cursing himself for accepting the energy so readily. His greed and desire for power had led to this trap, and now he had to live with it. Looking at the Khul, Davis brought up a shaky hand and wiped the perspiration from his face.

"You tricked me," he said to the Khul, earning a shrug in response. "I should be angry, but I haven't felt this alive in decades. Tell me, will I be able to battle the dreams?"

"Of course," the Khul said. "They will recognize you as something else however, and will be sluggish around you at first. The girl, Huan, she has taken to the tattooing well and is resting. She no longer carries the seed of a dream, instead she has the blood flow with her own. They will treat her in a similar fashion."

"And the boy? James?" Davis asked.

The Khul smiled. "The sword you gave him is proving quite deadly. I've had several injuries among my junior members, and a few among my senior ones. He's adapting well to our style of combat, and I imagine he could learn more than the basics if you stayed here with us for longer."

"Maybe after we see to the problem at hand," Davis said, standing from his chair. "You have my spear now, so I'll need a blade. Do you have any that'll work for someone my size?"

"Your spear will be returned to you for now," the Khul said with a laugh. "I'll have some brought up. What have you learned from the scrolls?"

"The way the protective wards were first laid down, for starters. I know what I have to do to fix what I assume the problem is," Davis said, twisting to pop his back and hip.

"And the problem would be?" the Khul asked, clearly interested.

Davis gave him an apathetic look after a satisfying crack of his shoulder blades. "Someone has damaged them, or at least attempted to."

* * *

Davis spent an hour in deep meditation, balancing his energies so that he could manage the new power added to his core. The Khul retreated down the hall guarded by the sigils, only to emerge with his mask back on, dressed once again in his revealing outfit, his chest practically glowing where the dark tattoos traced his skin.

After an hour, Davis opened his eyes and fished out his pill bottle, shaking out a single pill to take. His inner demon was full from the absorption of Illias's tattered soul, but Davis didn't want to rouse the beast when he was busy doing something important.

"I'll need my equipment from the tents," Davis said to the Khul.

"I've already had it assembled in the antechamber to the catacombs. Your students have been prepped and escorted to the chamber as well. The boy was hard to work with as we have no clue what he was saying, but we could tempt him with the girl. He seems to like her new markings."

Davis smiled. "He would. Will you lend us some of your warriors?"

"I've already asked Brun to go with you, bringing seven acolytes with her to engage the dreams as best they can. Please do your best to make sure they return alive. Their connection to the celestial realm is tenuous at best, so regeneration is out of their skill range."

"Brun can heal them? Like your men healed the girl when she was cut," Davis asked.

"Brun is not one of our best healers, but she has rudimentary skills in the art," the Khul said. "The acolytes can heal others to a limited degree, so do be careful. The girl *should* be able to use her newfound abilities to knit her own flesh back together, though I don't know to what extent."

"The dream she bore granted her abilities?" Davis asked.

"Could have," the Khul said as he guided Davis out of the library and back into the dining room, towards the stairs. "It's too soon to know what she was gifted with, if anything. Past women who've had this occurrence have been known to gain strength, stamina, the ability to regenerate, even access to the ether. She may manifest any ability, or none. Her sacred markings are there to contain and integrate the dream into her form, instead of allowing it to take over her."

"Will she be able to communicate with it?" Davis asked, thinking of his connection with the curator.

"I wouldn't think so, the dream was in a larval stage when we got to it, already attached to her soul but weak enough to contain with relative ease."

They walked in silence down the stairs until they reached the entry chamber. The Khul led Davis down the hall on the other side of the pond, noting that the fish swimming in the pool weren't koi, but some strange green fish that bore tentacles they used to propel through water. While curious, Davis said nothing.

The Khul walked down the corridor for a good while, passing the now-empty training hall, turning to an open doorway beneath the balcony above. Davis noted that the entryway was easily ten feet tall, the doors made from solid silver. Carved on the doors was the monstrous visage of a tentacle creature that was part squid, part hawk, bisected by the two massive doors.

The stairs led down into darkness with the scent and sounds of fresh water coming from below. The trickling of water, along with indistinguishable dialogue, echoed from beneath. Davis could recognize Huan and James's voices, as well as that of Brun. She sounded as if she were issuing orders, her barking harsh when bouncing off the smooth stone walls. The Khul walked slowly, his right-hand tracking the wall as he descended the carved steps.

"You'll find," he said softly, almost too soft for Davis to hear, "that respect is the true means to gain loyalty, but a healthy dose of fear will allow you to temporarily control any unruly group for short periods of time. With enough fear, you can move mountains."

"Know from experience?" Davis joked.

The Khul looked over at the smaller man. "I had to kill two others who wanted the title of Khul, and did so in as grisly a fashion as possible. I scared anyone else who would dare stand against me. I earned their respect through fear, and built upon that with years of disciplined leadership."

Davis fell silent at this, thinking on what this world must be like to those who dwelled in the monastery-palace. With all the effort this place put into training their young in the martial and arcane arts, it left them woefully unskilled in many other fields they would need to survive should this society ever collapse. Davis smiled at that.

*Like this place will ever fall,* Davis thought with a chuckle. *Hidden in the mountains beneath storms and border conflicts between India and China… nobody would dare approach these mountains in any way that could be a real threat.*

Upon descending the last step into a wide corridor, Davis was pleased to see his students in one piece, along with Brun and seven teenage boys, all bearing their silver blades in iron-fisted grips. James had his own sword out, the Persian scimitar glowing faintly in the pale light of the hallway. Huan was looking at the sword with interest, her AR-15 hanging from her shoulder. Resting on her hip was an old soviet pistol, and across her chest was a bandolier of Davis's thermite grenades. When she saw him she smiled, causing Davis to flinch slightly.

Her teeth, still white and unblemished, were more feral than they'd been hours ago. Her canines were longer and wider, while her incisors were narrow and flat. Davis frowned internally as her smile widened from his reaction.

She ran up to him, dropping to one knee to pull him into a tight hug, surprising him.

He chuckled, wrapping his arms around her and patting her back fondly. "Huan, I'm surprised! I didn't know you cared for me so!"

"I'm just like you now, professor," she whispered back to him, pulling back to look at him with luminescent eyes. "I have one too!"

Davis stared at her, confused, until he caught a strange scent. Taking a sniff, he paused and looked at her intently.

Sulfur.

She smelled like sulfur now, however faint, a trademark characteristic of a demonologist.

Like him.

"Oh Huan," he said. "I'm so sorry… if I'd known the infiltrator was that insidious I would have kept a closer eye on you."

"Don't blame yourself, professor," Huan purred, vibrations literally coming off her from the sound. "This was fate's hand at work. Just like what happened with my father, just like what happened to Nian. I was going to die, become one of them, but we just happened to be captured by the one group of people who could save me. It was divine guidance that this would happen."

Davis stared at her for a moment, about to say something. He paused when James slowly walked up, a frown marring his face.

"James?" Davis said, inquiring what was wrong with just a word.

"These people revere the Children of Flesh," James said in English. "I can't understand what they're saying, but they have murals of the monsters fighting *alongside* them in pitched battles. These are cultists, through and through."

"Yes," Davis said, casting a glance to the crimson eyes of the Khul, who was standing with his warriors, giving instructions in hushed tones. "I have a feeling we might have another item on our agenda, should we succeed in our mission."

"But these people saved me!" Huan exclaimed. "Why would they want us dead?"

"They may not want us dead," Davis replied, looking from Huan to James. "They may just want *us*."

"What do you mean?" James asked.

"What I mean is they have a sealed demon inside a healthy young woman whom they can breed with, a young man versed in occult arts that could be pressured into becoming a practitioner, and a so-called magus that could serve as a way of expanding their knowledge of the world as a whole."

"You think they would kidnap us like that?" Huan asked.

"Huan, they *have* kidnapped us like that," James chided. "They're just letting us do what we want to do… for some reason."

"They have protections in place to hold the Father of Flesh within his sepulcher," Davis said. "I may have been foolish and said I could strengthen said protections. The Khul even allowed me to study from his own collection of books the various ways the protections were made and how to interact with them."

"So you're saying he's just using us?" Huan asked, a low growl in her throat.

"No," Davis said after a moment. "I think he wants to use us but doesn't want to exert the effort unless we prove useful. This is a test."

"A test? He's gambling with people's lives to see if we can seal up the cracks in the dam?" James exclaimed, running a hand through his hair.

"Yes, and if we pass then the people of China, maybe even the world, will be safe," Davis said before heaving a sigh. "But we may not be allowed to leave this place."

"And if we fail?" Huan asked.

"Then it would all have been pointless, as we'll have sacrificed so much just to become food for an old god that is slowly rousing from his great slumber."

The three were silent for a moment before James let loose a sardonic giggle, surprising Huan and Davis. At their looks, he just shook his head. "Enslaved if you do, damned if you don't!"

# Chapter Thirty-Three

The room they stood in was large, carved from the stone of the mountain until the walls were polished and smooth. Two ponds bubbled in the chamber, filled by water flowing from the heads of monsters sculpted into the walls. Each had a long muzzle surrounded by six eyes. The muzzle opened at a tiny hole that served as a spout. Each eye was a different colored gem the size of a quarter, which flickered softly in the light of the torches the monks held. The water looked pure, and the ponds themselves could easily be mistaken for a koi pond if one wasn't versed in the ethereal arts like Davis was.

Carved into the stone floor in a ring around the ponds were interlocking runes, all giving off a faint amount of ether, just enough to feed the inhabitants of the pond. Seeing captured demons swimming freely in the clear water was something surreal, especially with how peaceful they seemed.

Shaped like fish, they had bony ridges along their spines that sprouted quills. Their long bodies made them more serpentine save for the fan-like fins that they lazily swept through the water, propelling them along the pool slowly. Each pool had three of these demon koi, each one bearing a brand upon their skulls.

The Khul cleared his throat, a smile gracing his aged features as his beady red eyes danced with mirth. "Those are spine fish, creatures pulled from the underwater tomb of the Brother of Bone. Each quill grows until it can be snapped off. We use them as tools for writing and for sewing."

Davis nodded, eyes traveling past the Khul to a large set of double doors, a heavy bar set over them to keep anyone from entering.

The doors were made of tarnished silver, covered in gruesome figures involved in horrid acts. Orgies of flesh combined with cannibalistic feasts made even more terrifying by the presence of sword-wielding men, all readying themselves for battle it would seem. The center of the doors, bisected between the two, was a writhing mass of tentacles and eyes that seemed to glow. It took Davis a few moments to realize that the demon effigy he was looking at was not only a seal in a physical sense, but in a spiritual sense as well. Small runes embossed into the silver hid in plain sight, each one charging a greater scheme of wards over the doors. Davis recognized the array as one from the Khul's books; it was a locking mechanism, one that relied heavily on the outside world to manipulate.

"Go ahead," the Khul said. "Try and open it. Use what has been gifted to you."

Davis glowered at the Khul for a moment before turning to James and Huan. Switching back to English, he sighed. "Are you two ready?"

"You know I am, professor!" Huan said, pulling her pistol from its holster.

"Better now than never," James said. His scimitar pulsed as if in agreement.

Turning, Davis eyed Brun and her initiates before walking closer to the gates.

Palpable energy radiated from the doors, like waves crashing into him. Davis found it difficult to walk any closer than a few feet. Holding out his hands, he began mumbling the incantation under his breath, allowing his mind to send out a slithering tendril of ether to connect with the locking mechanism. Twisting and churning, the lock was a vortex of ethereal energies that drew Davis in like a moth to a flame, feeding on his offering of ether as a suckling child would when offered a teat.

Feeding the hungering ward scheme, Davis slowly began to fill it up until it was to the bursting point. Just as it was about to overload and crack, he tugged back with his strand of energy, pulling all the gathered ether into himself with a mighty heave of mental fortitude. The lock, bereft of any energy, powered down to conserve the spell in place, causing the heavy beam over the door to slide off and into the stone walls as if they were water, the very rock rippling as if it were a disturbed lake.

Heaving from the exertion, Davis drew upon the foreign energies within himself and sorted them out, funneling them into the curator. The demented glee of the entity radiated out from Davis's chest, forcing a chuckle past his lips. He could hold back the barking laughter that threatened to spill from him by merely smiling. Turning, he nodded to the Khul, who merely gave an enigmatic smile in return.

"I will be locking the door behind you once you leave," the Khul said, sending out a wave of energy. "Descending into the tombs is strictly forbidden save for these circumstances, and as such I cannot leave the gateway unlocked. You can unlock it from inside so long as you perform the same rite you just did to the satisfaction of the wards."

"So what you're saying is that if I die, the rest of them will be stranded within the tomb?" Davis asked, frowning when the Khul nodded. "Great, no pressure or anything..."

Brun walked up to the doors, pushing them open silently. One of the initiates held a torch in the entryway, the flames flaring from a waft of pure rot escaping the tunnel leading down into the abyss. The tunnel walls bore no markings save for deep gouges where something with heavy claws had attempted to break through the protected passage. A distant howl echoed up from the cavernous tunnel, causing an involuntary shudder to climb up Davis's spine. Swallowing the lump in his throat, Davis thrust his spear forward, telling the monks to take point.

Scowling, Brun barked at the teenagers, ordering them to fall into ranks of two to lead down the wide tunnel, one student holding a torch while the other readied his blade. Brun pulled her own sword before jerking her head towards the entrance.

"After you, magus," she said.

Davis turned to James and Huan, once more switching to English. "Huan, you take up the rear with Brun, James you stay with me. Try and put the light coming off that sword to good use."

"Got it," James said while Huan nodded. Davis walked into the corridor, passing through a thin membrane of magic that hung lightly in the air. The sickly-sweet smell of decomposing flesh and sulfur pervaded his senses, assailing Davis in a way he hadn't anticipated. James retched, pulling to the side to empty his stomach of any food he'd eaten in the past few hours.

*Just as well,* Davis thought as Huan and Brun walked into the tunnel, the doors closing behind them. *He probably didn't want to be a cannibal anyway.*

The gentle slope of the tunnel became a sharp decline, the floor growing damp from some unseen liquid, the air warm and sticky. The flickering torchlight cast stark images along the walls, which slowly grew more veiny, long strands of pink muscle forming into intricate webbing made of the bedding, small toothless mouths framed by multi-hued eyes pockmarking the floor, walls and ceiling every dozen feet or so.

The bedding was slippery to the touch, yielding to footfalls like soft tofu gives in to a spoon. Davis allowed his mind to slip partially into the ether as he looked at the inquisitive eyes. He could sense thoughts, alien and disturbing, coming from behind them. Through his ether-enhanced sight he could see thick purple veins running underneath the bedding, leading deeper down the tunnel.

"Stop here," Davis called out. The monks looked back with raised eyebrows.

"Why?" one asked while the others murmured among themselves.

"Because he said to," Brun replied, stepping forward. "He's the magus, we listen to his orders while in the hall of the shapers."

Davis ignored the strange label given to the tunnel and instead lowered his spear to the ground, the fiery obsidian tip charring the bedding enough for a distant howl to echo up from below. Davis smiled. "Just what I thought..."

"What is it?" Huan asked in English.

"There's something down here that knows we're here, something that can feel pain. It's smart and it's waiting, watching us through those strange eyes."

James looked up to a malformed eye the size of bowl. Swinging up, he sliced through the organ, a slurry of colored goo sluicing out from the wound. The gash in the wall stopped about a foot above where the eye had been, perhaps six-inches below; all the remaining eyes sank back into the bedding, the soft muscle tissue knitting together over them as a means of protection.

"An oblique tactic, to be certain." Davis smiled. "I'm surprised it worked."

"Yeah, not going to lie, I only did that because it was staring right at me and freaking me out," James said, wiping off his blade with a scrap of cloth he had tacked into his belt. "The fact that it got the other ones to retreat is just gravy."

Brun snapped her head to the side, kneeling to place a gloved hand on the gooey flesh. Looking up at Davis, she hissed. "You fool! Something from below is coming up!"

"So?" Davis said, rolling his shoulders to work out the kinks. "We were going to have to fight them at one point anyway. Might as well do it sooner rather than later."

"We cannot slay one of the sacred!" a monk exclaimed, earning a chorus of agreement from his companions.

"Well we have to for me to be able to look over the wards. Would you rather slay a few now and secure them all or let them all loose where the nations of the world would just bomb them into oblivion?" Davis snapped, pointing down the tunnel with his spear. "Get ready and take no prisoners. That's an order!"

The men glared at Davis, looking to Brun for confirmation. She merely stared back, holding her sword down at her side. Seeing no support from their leader, they all turned and readied themselves for combat.

"They look ready to revolt and we haven't even come across anything yet. You're doing great, professor!" James joked, looking back at Huan. "What are you doing?"

Davis turned to look at Huan, who was running a hand over the wall, almost caressing the sweaty flesh. "I can sense them… they're scared…"

"Scared?" Davis asked, looking at her as if she were mad. "Scared of what?"

Her response was cut short by a deafening cry of a half-dozen behemoths climbing up from the abyss. Each had a long, sloping head that ended in three to five eyes. Their bodies, corpulent sacks of meat perched atop four legs ending in multiple human hands, were split down the middle to reveal maws filled with fleshy growths, all twitching and twisting as they sought to pull someone inside to create the most horrifying coffin imaginable.

The monks all stood petrified, causing one of their number to be struck down to the ground by a powerful forearm ending in snake-like fingers. His screams only grew in intensity when his bare flesh touched the bedding, which clung to him even as it began to dissolve the exposed sections of skin. The behemoth that struck the monk down stomped on his back, the hands digging through his clothes, blood welling and dribbling from the wounds the digging digits were inflicting.

"What are you doing?" Davis cried out, empowering his voice with a burst of ether. "Fight!"

The monks, their shock broken by the magically enhanced cry, dropped their torches and leapt into the fray, silver swords screaming through the air as they cleaved into the pliable bodies of the Children of Flesh.

Huan shot one of the Children in its drooping head, bursting the oblong limb like a plump zit. It flung its arms wildly about, seemingly blind, as pus drained from the deflating organ. A monk slid beneath its flailing arms and stabbed up into its chest, pulling down to cut through the buttery fat until he'd sawed off the left arm.

The limb fell to the ground, serving as enough of a nuisance to trip up one of the legs of another behemoth dueling with Brun, who was darting into its reach and coaxing it to swing at her, before cleaving off writhing digits and hands. Two monks were fighting another, slowly dissecting it as it bludgeoned them with hammer blows. The crippled monk being eaten by the bedding was silenced by one of his fellows, who swiftly sliced through the back of his neck before bringing the blade up into the attacking Child of Flesh, spearing a leg to the main body.

The maws of the Children were issuing forth cacophonous screeches, reverberations bouncing along the flesh covered tunnel hard enough to make Davis's ears bleed. Thrusting forward with his spear into the maw of one, he cried out as he burned away a section of grasping mouth.

James was darting back and forth in unison with two other monks, slowly dismantling another Child while the rapid staccato of automatic fire from Huan's AR-15 tore into the exposed hides of three of the gigantic monsters. Bubbling fat and pus oozed from wounds torn open by hot metal, wounds made wider by swords and spear to prevent them from healing over. The dribbling wounds and severed limbs that fell to the bedding quickly broke down, splitting and seeping into the floor as porous openings flitted open to drain the spilled fluid.

Within minutes, only one Child remained, head and arms removed via flaming scimitar and spear. Brun was allowing her initiates to end the creature's existence while one monk walked between Huan, James, and Davis.

"Are any of you injured?" the monk, a young man with a slash across his chest showing signs of infection, asked.

"No, but I think you are..." Davis said, pointing toward the wound.

The monk looked down and laughed. "I can feel the sacred one's attempting to change me. Normally we would allow this, or seal the infection as we did with your woman. But for now, I am needed as a strong sword arm and healer for my fellow warriors."

With that he dipped his hand into a belt pouch, pulling out a small jar of green cream. Unsealing the cap, he dabbed his fingers in it and rubbed them over his wound, which had begun to take on an angry red hue around the edges. The cream seemed to take immediate effect, chasing away the redness.

"What is that?" Davis asked.

The monk offered some. "A root we grow in the monastery that was used in a western country many centuries ago. They farmed it to extinction, using it to control when they would have children. We use it to purge spiritual energies from our bodies."

Davis declined. "Do you have anything for our ringing ears?"

The monk shook his head. "The cries of the blessed are meant to be heard, and can deafen those that have brought their ire. I have nothing that can help you, sadly."

Davis dismissed the monk, looking over as Brun finished off the remaining Child. A flash of silver in the flickering light of the torches followed by a squeal of pain marked the end of the unholy creature, the body slumping forward in on itself. She whipped her blade to rid it of the rotting flesh, watching with disdain as the bedding stretched up with veins to begin breaking down the body into composite parts to be absorbed. The various hunks of meat from the other Children were already half absorbed, as was the body of the monk who'd been summarily executed after being struck down by one of the behemoths.

"They'll return, you know," Brun said. Looking over at Davis with a glare. "The next time we encounter them they'll be angry from the pain we caused them."

"I think they're in a constant state of rage, truth be told," Davis quipped.

"That's not true," Huan said in a broken version of the monk's language. "Children hunger for meat, afraid of something."

"What do you mean by afraid?" Davis asked in English, Brun looking on with a raised eyebrow.

"I mean that I can feel their fear and confusion. They're scrambling to try and create a defense against us," Huan explained. "They know we have weapons that cause them pain."

Davis raised his spear, flames licking along the blackened volcanic glass. "James and I are the only ones with magical weapons to my knowledge. Is that enough to cause alarm?"

"No," Huan said, shaking her head. "It's the silver. They can't stand contact with it, especially when it's charged with ethereal energy the way the monks do with each weapon."

Davis turned and looked at Brun. "My student says that your weapons are causing the sacred ones' fear."

"That's not good… frightened animals are often the most dangerous, especially when cornered," Brun said, sparing a glance to the remains of her monk, the bones sizzling and popping as they broke down from the veins pulling them down into the squishy flesh.

"I agree," Davis said after a moment's thought. "We need to hurry if we want to capitalize on this advantage."

"Good, you understand how a warrior thinks." Brun smiled. "I was worried you were simply a magus in name only."

Davis gave her a wan smile as she turned to mobilize her monks. James scooped up one of the torches, a small hiss of steam coming from the scorched flesh where the flames had rested, bubbling fat brimming in a puddle that was rapidly sealing over with a thin membrane of skin.

"So what are we waiting for?" James asked, looking to Davis. "Huan says they're afraid, I say we take the fight to them and try to rout them while we can."

Davis nodded. "Have you been practicing tapping into the ether?"

James shrugged. "I tried it while we were in the prison cell with limited success. I have better luck with my blade; it seems to act as a focus for me."

"Makes sense I suppose," Davis mumbled. "The Persians were far more advanced in spiritual warfare than we give them credit for."

"I hate to cut your musings short," Brun interrupted. "But we should get moving, or do I have to reevaluate my opinion on whether the magus is well-versed in tactics?"

Davis nodded. "Lead the way my lady, we'll follow with torches raised high."

Brun snorted but said nothing, instead turning and marching forward, her remaining monks following her in an effort to keep up. Davis trailed her with a spring in his step, smiling as the curator roared within his chest.

It could sense other demons close by… and it didn't like the competition.

# CHAPTER THIRTY-FOUR

The trek further into the tunnel was met with little resistance besides dribbling goo coming from the ceiling and slickened, pulpy muscles flexing beneath every footfall. The tunnel branched off into three separate ways, each bearing a silver plaque above the extensions' entrance marked by an alien sigil. The only one Davis knew how to translate was the one to the left, which Davis understood to mean power, magic, and life.

Without saying a word, he motioned for Brun and her monks to lead the way, now only one of them relegated to torch duty. Huan had taken the fallen monk's sword and, in a display of unknown prowess, revealed she knew how to wield it when whipping it about to rid the shining blade of rot. When asked, she merely smiled and tapped the side of her head, nodding to Davis.

Davis had frowned at this, still uncertain of what to make of Huan's new passenger. True it was going to kill her from the inside out and make her into one of those… *things*, but the fact that she seemed pleased by her choice to retain the creature was disconcerting.

Davis had accepted the curator in a rare moment of desire, a brief flash of true knowledge before a student of the world. He'd grasped at what he could, the knowledge turning to smoke as his body became the fire. Now it was all he could do to try and feed the flickering flames while preventing them from overtaking him. Would she have the same troubles?

The curator curled deep within his chest, telling Davis it didn't like this line of thinking. Rubbing at his sternum, Davis marched on, James and Huan at his side as they marched down the tunnel.

After nearly five minutes of walking, they came upon a set of double doors made from squirming flesh and silver plates. The majority of the door, braces, and hinges were metal but what must have been wood originally had given in to the ravages of the Father of Flesh's dark nature. Now the rippling muscles, eyes blinking from unnatural spots with the split, multihued eyes of the Children themselves, sat in the way of the group's progress.

Brun turned towards Davis and inclined her head. He was half tempted to order the monks to cut away any flesh attached to the door, but checked himself. Instead, he reached over to Huan's bandolier and pulled a thermite grenade from her chest. She smiled, reaching over to grab James by the wrist.

"Come on, babe, over here," she said with a salacious grin.

James looked at her as though she were mad, but followed as she led him back down the tunnel and into the darkness. Davis blinked when he could still see her eyes, now radiant circles of silver. They locked onto his and winked, letting him know she could peer through the darkness with ease, just like him.

Brun sniffed once, looking at Huan with interest. "What is she doing?"

"I'm going to need all of you to back up," Davis said, hand on the explosive's pin. "While it doesn't splash much, this'll eat through metal fast enough to make a commotion. I'll need you to all be on the lookout in case this brings company."

"I don't understand..." Brun said, looking at the canister in Davis's hand with a puzzled expression.

"And you don't have to. Now, *vamonos!* Get back there with Huan and her squeeze toy while I open the door," Davis said.

Brun nodded and waved with her sword for the monks to follow. The one from earlier, the healer, stopped for a moment to spare a word.

"Be careful what you plan, for it could be the plan that gets you," he said. Davis wanted to ask what he meant, but Brun grabbed the monk by the shoulder and pushed him back down the tunnel. She stood by Davis, sword drawn and ready, most likely in case something came through the door.

Pulling the pin on the canister, Davis counted to two in his head before lobbing the explosive at the door. On four it exploded outward, spraying down the ten-foot tall, eight-foot wide double doors with the hissing scent of scalding rust and searing hydrogen. The liquid spattered across the pathway, the bedding stuck between the cracks and molding of the door instantly shriveling as the silver began to melt. The bedding surrounding the doorway popped and sizzled, some of it catching fire as it curled away from the toxic blaze. Davis pulled a cloth from Brun's belt to hold over his mouth as he watched smoke roil up to the ceiling, crawling along the red and purple network of veins and pink flesh.

"By the gods, you have dragon's fire at your disposal?" Brun asked, looking at Davis with newfound respect.

Not wanting to explain, he merely nodded. "Several more of them yes, just in case we encounter something… big."

Brun nodded. "When I was younger, my father was an honored vessel. He would come down into the catacombs without me, for days at a time, to commune with the sacred. Every time he would come back a little less like himself, a small piece broken away in favor of gaining respect from the sacred."

Davis didn't know what to say, so he just looked at Brun as she described what her father had been through, the brilliant flames bringing out the darkness in her cold eyes.

"Your woman is now an honored vessel, so I warn you now of what my father told me as a child. The honored vessels are servants of the sleeper and the sacred ones that roam these tunnels. There is no greater honor than being selected to become one, the honored vessel acting as a bridge between our two worlds. Eventually though, all succumb to the sleeper's call, and all become one with him in a blissful union that creates a vessel of unfathomable power. Most vessels cannot survive long off the ground they cover; nor can they suffer bright lights. These vessels can infect others with specialized tools, and can swim through the purity of water to fetch newborns to feed to the sleeper."

"So your father became one of these… enhanced vessels?" Davis asked, staring at the young woman intently.

She nodded. "You can recognize them as they have two additional limbs coming from their back, ending in thorny clubs that carry the essence of the sacred. They can reason, and speak! They're crafty and dangerous beyond reproach, save for when they meet an honored vessel."

"What happens then?" Davis asked, his voice a mere whisper.

"Then they see which is greater in the eyes of the sleeper," Brun said, motioning for the monks to come forward. "My father was deemed unworthy by one such being, and he was dispatched, from what I was told."

"Why are you telling me…?" Davis asked only to have Brun hold up her hand.

"Fall back into ranks men, we may have to deal with sacred that could be lurking within this area. That door looked as if it hadn't been opened in a while, and I'd rather not test our hands against fate today!" Brun cried out, leading her men through the burning hole in the door, jumping over a melting mound of silver that bubbled over the bedding with heavy splats.

Davis stared at the young woman as she jumped through the smoldering curtain, jumping slightly when James brushed up against him. "You coming?"

"Yes… yes, of course," Davis said, lost in thought.

Stepping through the muddy remains of the door proved difficult but manageable, the toxic fumes spreading fast enough to encourage them to hurry on.

Once on the other side of the doorway, Davis realized there wasn't as much reason to worry as he'd originally assumed. The room had three walls, the fourth wall being an open-air balcony over a dark pit leading down into the earth. The sound of rushing water filled the chamber, and the smoke rose high into the darkness dominating the high peaks of the cavern.

The room itself held two great sarcophagi, laid in such a way that the decorated heads of whoever was buried was flush with the far wall. The stone sarcophagi were devoid of any mutated flesh, though the bedding covered the floor, walls, and ceiling of the room. An open tunnel led down into the earth even further. A low groan, like the call of a whale, echoed from deep within the cavern, bringing everyone's attention to the outer edges of the room, where dark waters churned some forty feet below the edge.

"An open source of water... probably with channels going underground that lead to the villages." Davis said, motioning for the monk holding the torch to approach the twin stone coffins. "I need a little light, hurry boy!"

The monk didn't complain, instead he hurried at the order and brought the flickering fire closer to the stone, revealing colored etchings and pictograms of men serving platters of food to a massive tentacle covered monk sitting in the lotus position, three mouths dominating his lower face while four eyes stared out from the forehead.

"Freaky..." Huan said, looking over Davis's shoulder.

"Indeed. What we're looking at is most likely one of the first demonologists that the Father of Flesh took on after being separated from the entity it had once been," Davis replied.

"How do you know that?" James asked, shouldering his sword as he looked out over the bleak expanse of water.

Davis looked back at him and froze.

Floating some fifty feet away from the open-air balcony of the room on a tendril of red sinew was a creature unlike any they'd encountered so far. Face dominated by a lamprey mouth on an almond shaped head, it had a lone eye that peered through the darkness. A strand connected to the monster's back like an umbilical cord; it lowering the creature from high above. The being's arms were too long, ending in wide hands with oversized fingers. Its feet were atrophied and thin, dangling bits of muscle that looked as though they had never been used.

It just hung there in space, the sound of rushing water drowning out any sound it could possibly make while it stared at Davis and his compatriots. The strangest thing about the creature was its chest. Bare like the rest of the creature, it bore nipples as if it were a man, each one pierced by some unknown metal. Faded tattoos writhed and wriggled across the torso, dancing madly as the creature seemed to *breathe*, its chest rising and falling dramatically. What was even more startling was the fact that, despite the creature's humanoid shape and apparent markings over its skin, Davis could count the number of ribs poking against the taut flesh pulled over the torso.

*Ribs...* Davis thought. *It has bones... it's not a Child!*

Standing up fluidly, he grabbed the old pistol from Huan's holster, ignoring her cry of protest, and took aim at the creature. It cocked its head to the side like a curious child, allowing Davis to fire twice in rapid succession. The bullets soared over the short distance, one striking the creature in its thin neck while the other struck its eye.

An unearthly howl came from the creature, its oversized hands coming up to cradle its bleeding head. Thick, syrupy blood the color of neon green cake frosting spewed from it. Calling on the curator within, Davis pulled the demon up to look through his eyes.

It instantly hissed, curling painfully within his chest. Davis, wincing from the pain, took careful aim and fired another shot, this time missing by a few feet.

The dangling creature—no, the dangling *demonologist*—rose up into the darkness over the water, still howling in agony. Its cries echoed across the cavern like the wailing of a child, high and loud. Davis turned, tossing the pistol back to Huan who looked as if she was going to ask a question. She didn't get the chance as Davis walked over to Brun and struck out with two fingers, jabbing her in the diaphragm. Doubling over, she coughed for a few moments while the monks all brandished their blades, forming a circle around Davis and Brun.

She held up a hand, still coughing. "No need," she wheezed, "he saw what I warned him of… he just wishes he hadn't learned what the rest of you still don't know."

"What is that?" one of the monks asked.

Brun silenced him with a glance, but Davis took his spear and jabbed her foot with the butt of the weapon.

"Yes, Brun, do enlighten us! Tell us all how, for what I can only guess to be generations, your temple full of trained warriors would allow themselves to become infested with the spawn of the sleeper, before having it sealed away like you did with my friend over there."

Huan's ears perked at this. Davis continued, eyes narrowed at Brun as his voice got softer and softer.

"Tell them what we're to face in here the deeper we go. Tell them the *real* reason the wards have begun to fail."

"I don't know!" Brun exclaimed.

Davis snorted. "You're in charge of the prison, which is layered in wards itself. Who was in charge before you?"

"My father," Brun ventured.

Davis nodded. "And where is he?"

Brun fell silent, glaring at Davis to silence him as well. He was far from over though.

"Each of you is taught how to manage the ethereal, the spirit realm. Some, like Brun and her father, more than others. Then her father went and became an honored vessel," Davis said, the revelation bringing a share of murmuring from the monks, all of whom had lowered their blades. "He continued to venture down here, where other honored vessels went when they were unfit for society anymore. But he was still sane, still human enough at least, to see a way to weaken the seals holding the sleeper in the spirit realm."

"Magus…" Brun warned, but Davis merely moved his spear towards her throat.

"He came down here, I believe willingly, and allowed himself to be taken by one of the sacred. One thing I can tell you is that an honored vessel wouldn't be harmed by a simple sacred. They would view him as kin and treat him accordingly. What I can say is he may have rounded up some of the remaining honored vessels that hadn't fully given into their inner demons and put them to work."

"Doing what?" one the healer asked.

"By *undoing* what the Zhao did centuries ago. He's slowly stripping the bindings from this place so that the Father of Flesh will wake up. What I just shot was an honored vessel, a demonologist. I know this because… because I am one. So is Huan."

James couldn't understand what was being said, but by the way everyone shifted, Davis had little reason to believe his secret would remain one for long. "I house a curator, a demon bound in service to the old god of knowledge. And I know a demonologist when I encounter one."

Brun scowled at Davis, her sword arm inching slowly back so she could try and bat at the spear. Davis didn't give her the chance, instead pulling the weapon from the hollow of her throat. She glared at him for a moment before looking at her monks.

"Kill them," she ordered with a whisper.

# CHAPTER THIRTY-FIVE

The monks didn't explode into action, though there was a loud bang that echoed across the stone, drowning out even the wailing of the demonologist high up in the cavern. Brun looked down at her chest, eyes growing wide at the hole just over her heart, broken visibly within the pulpy wound that was now gushing blood like an unattended water hose.

A smoking Russian pistol held tight in Huan's hand announced the culprit, the single shot fired enough to kill any normal man or woman walking the world. Davis smiled as Huan raised the pistol higher, placing it three feet from Brun's face.

*Guess Huan doesn't take risks either*, Davis thought as he watched Brun's face implode from a second shot, the back of her head blasting out like a rotten pumpkin, scattering chunks of brain and skull around the sarcophagi. All the monks stared in confusion, clutching their swords as they all tried to comprehend what had just happened.

Before anyone could make sense of anything, Davis cleared his throat. "James, please take Brun's sword and then dispose of her body over the side of the cliff."

James silently did so, grabbing her ceremonial silver blade in one hand and looping his other arm under her armpits to begin hauling her to the edge.

"Now," Davis said, snapping his fingers to gather the teenagers' gathered attention. "I assume you're all wondering why I just had one of your leaders killed."

All of them nodded, some faster than others.

"It's because the Khul himself gave me authority to do so," Davis lied. "I've been sent down here to fix the damage that's been caused and find the culprit. She was the daughter of the one behind all of this. She must have been complicit!"

"How… how do you know?" one of the monks asked.

"I'm a magus, I can delve into your mind with a thought," Davis replied. "Now, we need to go deeper into the catacombs to find a room that holds the physical manifestation of the leyline."

"Leyline?" another monk repeated.

"The spirit realm," Davis replied, waving off the question like an annoying insect. "There has to be a focus point, a point where the wards are built into the infrastructure."

"Well… if the Khul ordered it, then we'll help you," the healer offered, his smile genuine.

Davis nodded. "What's your name?"

"Bohai," he replied.

"All right, Bohai, you're the new leader of your group here. Make sure they stay in line and chop up anything bigger than a dog that tries to get close to us. Got it?"

Bohai nodded, turning to begin chattering with the four other monks while Davis returned to studying the pictograms on the stone coffins.

"They seem to be pointing out directions. There's a symbol that means 'hollow' next to one that means 'enlightenment' and 'earth'… really hate languages I don't know," Davis grumbled in English.

There was a distant splash, proof that Brun's body had been dragged over the side of the defile and hit the water below. James walked up, tying her scabbard around his belt with a colored sash. "Nice sword, think I'll keep it!"

"You do that," Davis replied without looking up. "Okay! I think I know where we need to go. Down this tunnel and underneath a section that is labeled as 'beneath the currents', whatever that means…"

"All right!" Huan said. She was busy reloading her pistol while looking down the fleshy tunnel, the womb of the cavern humid and dripping with slime.

"Bohai!" Davis said, gathering the young healer's attention. "We're ready to head out."

"Okay," Bohai said, inclining his head. He turned to the other monks and ordered them to form a protective ring around the group, two in front, two in back, and Bohai in the middle.

Davis took hold of the torch from one of the monks. "I'd rather your sword arm be free. If we're crossing paths with honored vessels, then we're getting close."

"How do you know that?" Bohai asked.

Davis glared at the young man. "I've had this demon in my chest since before your father was born; every waking moment it battles me, trying to corrupt me into a more debauched version of myself. It whispers at the fringes of my mind, offering forbidden knowledge in exchange for human lives. So far I've resisted it, but I know if I ever gave in and started offering it sacrifices, I'd slowly warp into a version of myself that couldn't be trifled with. Then I'd seek out the old god that the demon served and seek to protect it, to serve it, and most of all, to feed it."

"So you think we're getting close?" Huan asked.

"I know we are," Davis said, pushing forward into the narrow tunnel, forcing everyone to rush to catch up to him.

They marched for an hour, maybe two, going down tunnels and steep drops, the entire time under the watchful gaze of eyes set deep in the walls and ceiling. The fleshy pulp underfoot squished with every step while toothless mouths formed into lipless slits murmuring wordless whispers as they pressed onwards.

Eventually they came upon what looked to be a bridge, twin waterfalls falling over a ridge branching out over the path. The walkway was maybe five feet wide, covered in greasy skin. The roar of the waterfalls drowned out any chance of calling out to each other, instantly making Davis worried.

*The perfect place for an ambush,* Davis thought. He had to relax his hand when he realized how hard he was gripping the spear's shaft, his arthritic fingers aching from the pressure.

"Bohai! Take your monks and cross the chasm first!" Davis called out, waving the young man forward. "We'll follow behind."

"Okay!" Bohai shouted, waving a hand to rally the remaining warriors.

James put a hand on Davis's shoulder, motioning to the dual waterfalls and the vast expanse they covered.

"I don't know how far the water falls, but it'll surely be a death sentence should we slip," Davis said in the young man's ear. "Tell Huan to walk carefully and have her eyes behind us. Use the AR-15, we should hear that if she starts using it."

Davis watched James relay the message, the glee of delight sparkling in the girl's eyes as she swung her semi-automatic rifle around to ready it. Huan flashed a thumbs-up at Davis, once again making him question her sanity in the face of all this.

*Need to keep an eye on her should we live through this shit,* Davis thought as he stepped out onto the bridge.

The water droplets and greasy skin made for a slick walkway, but by firmly pressing his feet into the bubbling meat, Davis could make certain he had a good foothold. Looking on ahead as the monks walked single file down the path, Davis shouted when he saw it, despite the fact the waterfalls were drowning out his call.

Bursting from the flesh of the bridge in a spray of sweat and pus, a malformed man crawled up while slashing at one of the monks' feet with a spiked tentacle. The raking tendril tore into the young man's ankles, breaking them both at the heel, sending him toppling to the ground, where the deformed creature leaned over with a hunched back to lower its drooping swathes of skin over the victim's face.

Davis stepped to the side and pointed his spear, waiting for Huan to shoot, cursing to himself as he noticed that the monks were unaware of the enemy rising from the sludge. Davis looked back when no gunfire sounded, and cursed once more when he saw another demon-infested woman standing behind them.

The woman was emaciated and nude, her lower body resembling an octopus. Twin limbs rose from her back, bony and flimsy looking, each ending in the dreaded bony club that Davis remembered being mentioned. Her face was that of an old Chinese woman, both eyes empty sockets. She had Huan by the leg, holding onto her with three tentacles and one oversized hand, all of which pulsed with unnatural light from veins beneath the translucent skin.

James turned to see what Davis was looking at and screamed. He pulled Brun's silver blade and his own Persian sword and swung at the old woman's extended arm.

Flesh sizzled as the Persian blade sliced deep into one of the beefy tentacles, severing a two-foot long section from the body. Packed meat flowed from the tentacle like sausage from the rind, churning out faster as Huan kicked her leg into the woman's lower belly to try and get some distance.

Davis turned, expecting something to be bursting up in front of him, pleased to find out he was wrong. Instead, he saw the malformed man now standing above a decapitated monk. The hunch in his back seemed to be a membrane designed to hold fluids; it quivered as the man raised his tentacle in the air. Black slime shot from the spiky tentacle in an arc, dousing the back of one of the monks with the jellied substance. The man started flailing about, screaming, as the jelly stretched over his frame, veins growing from the mass and sinking into his exposed skin.

The rest of the monks were now aware of the threat, and were beginning to try and handle the situation. Davis turned back at the sound of gunfire, watching as Huan unloaded part of her clip into the circular maw hidden beneath the tentacles, rotting flesh and gore falling from the woman and onto the ground.

The woman, now sporting a severed hand and two damaged tentacles, seemed more annoyed than hurt. She reached forward with her other hand to grab at James's swords, heedless of the flames coming off one, only to be stopped by the stream of bullets screaming from the AR-15.

Two oversized fingers blown off and a bullet-riddled palm forced the old woman to pull back, four more tentacles slithering forward to try and crush Huan. Davis lunged with his spear, stabbing into the floppy appendage while twisting, ripping the limb partially, forcing her to pull it back. Of her eight tentacles, she was now using three damaged ones to support herself while motioning with five others over Huan, trying to pull the young woman into her hidden mouth.

Screeching loud enough to be heard over the thundering cataracts of death flanking them, the woman swept out with one thick tentacle at James. Even as he stabbed into it with the silver blade, she punched him with her tendril, sending him stumbling back into Davis.

Davis, in an attempt not to spear his student, dropped his weapon and snatched the silver blade from the man's grip. James caught himself using Davis as leverage, forcing the old man to take a knee to the ground.

Davis stood up on shaky legs, gazing at the alien creature that was fighting them. No eyes were visible and yet she seemed capable of fighting just as well.

*It can't be echolocation or the vibrations, the waterfalls are too loud,* Davis thought. Branching his mind into the ether, he sent a probe out towards the attacking demonologist, only to find her already there, scanning the area with several mental probes.

Smiling, Davis stabbed his sword into the ground before starting a slow chant, not loud enough to be heard by anyone save himself. Using words from the time of the Vikings, Davis did something he swore he would never do in front of someone he wanted to live. Channeling the energy into his hands, Davis ignored the stinging sensation traveling through his arms as the ether became a tangible energy source on the earthly plane. With a pained cry, Davis threw out his hands, launching a twisting blot of azure lightning from blackened palms at the old woman, striking her straight between her sagging breasts.

The woman's howl of agony pealed louder than even the roar of the waterfalls, a horrid stench of roasting flesh filling the air as her sternum and ribs were illuminated beneath translucent skin. Her skin was now bursting as fluids boiled in seconds, forcing the woman back onto her tentacles to stay upright.

As the woman used her injured hand to push her innards back into her steaming wound, Davis palmed the spear into James's empty hand.

"Now boy!" Davis screamed, hoping James would do something wise with it.

He wasn't disappointed. James dropped his other sword and thrust the spear at the old woman, pinning her large hand into her breastbone with the fiery obsidian.

The woman shrieked, struggling against the ancient weapon as it burned her bones and muscle. James continued pushing the weapon home, slowly sinking it inch by disgusting inch into her chest cavity. Davis watched as the old woman tried to raise her tentacles, only for them to twitch and spasm from the effects of the electric shock.

The demon-infested woman slumped forward, a line of blood sliding from her mouth as she finally died. James pulled the spear from her chest, kneeling to help Huan to her feet. Whispering in her ear, she nodded with a feral smile before catching his lips with her own, her hand snaking around his head to clutch at his hair in a passionate display of lust.

Davis picked up the discarded swords and nudged James, forcing him to break the kiss. Passing the blades to him as he accepted his spear, he saw the distrust in James's eyes. Davis set his face in an impassive mask, but inside he was screaming.

*How could it have come to this?* he thought. *Now the boy won't trust me!*

Turning to check on the monks, Davis smiled as he watched Bohai push the headless body of the creature through the waterfall. The head, speared on another monk's sword, still seemed animate, mouthing foul words as it shook back and forth on the edge of the blade.

Just as Davis was about to do something, a pistol shot caused the head to burst like a ripe tomato. The monks, spattered with gore, looked over at Huan's steaming gun. She lowered it before kissing the tip, taking a slow sniff of the barrel.

The lust in her eyes only seemed to intensify.

Three monks beside Bohai remained; the living ones all sported numerous injuries, mostly deep slashes and gouges from the demonologist's spiky tentacles. Bohai walked between them, hands glowing a luminescent green as he massaged the bleeding wounds, pulling and stretching flesh as if it were putty to seal them.

Davis turned to James and waved for him to follow. The young scholar seemed displeased with the notion, but gave a curt nod in response.

Crossing the remainder of the bridge was simple enough, the waterfalls providing a disturbing curtain around them. Everyone was tense and ready for another assault, but none came. As they crossed the threshold into a small cavern, the fleshy bedding coating every surface shimmering beneath the torchlight, James finally addressed the issue at hand.

"What the fuck, Davis?" he said, cutting to the bone of his issue. "You lied to me!"

"No," Davis said with a wince, noting how the albino's knuckles grew whiter than usual from the strain he was putting on the handles of the swords. "I assured you I wasn't a diabolist and that I would have no part in harming you."

"Like there's a difference!" James spat.

Davis looked over at Huan, who nodded. "You feel that way about Huan as well? Those tattoos she's sporting beneath her vestments aren't just for show; they hold back a Child of Flesh deep within her body."

James turned, a look of utter revulsion marring his features. "What? When did this happen?"

Huan shrugged. "Apparently one of the smarter ones snuck up on me disguised as you. I don't know when, but it inserted itself into me and has begun slowly changing me. The professor negotiated a way for me to survive with it inside me."

James looked torn at the idea of his apparent girlfriend's life being saved by Davis. James looked at Huan for a moment before cursing under his breath.

"Fuck... I don't know what to make of this, Huan. I've hated anything to do with demons and fell creatures since..."

"Maybe you can share it with me someday," Huan said, placing a hand on his clenched fist. "I know you, James. You won't let something like this come between the first real relationship you've ever had."

Davis would have chuckled at the thought of how James had apparently been deflowered by a girl so bloodthirsty she could rival most demons. Instead, he nodded to Huan.

"She's right, James. You're better than this."

James glared at Davis. "Let's just get this over with."

Davis turned to Bohai, allowing James and Huan a moment to themselves. "How are your men?"

Bohai smiled. "Your cause for worry is unnecessary. We are trained how to resist the blessing early in our lives. We only allow ourselves to succumb should we feel it is the right moment."

"Please don't let that moment be any time during this foray," Davis ordered, earning the same smile from the teen.

Davis walked across the cavern, the squishing of fat beneath his heel now second nature, to examine their options for continuing their path. He was surprised when he discovered a darkened stairwell, along with a carved tunnel. The stairwell led both up into the caves and deeper into them.

"Well, since the cat's out of the bag," Davis said before holding his spear up to the wall, channeling ether into it to cause the flames to burn even brighter. Scorching bedding from the walls, he looked for any pictograms like he'd seen in the previous room.

After charring away some bedding, he found pictograms that he could only guess to say "life", "power", and "god". This was of course next to the stairwell, though it didn't describe any direction in which to go.

"Down it is, then!" Davis declared.

# Chapter Thirty-Six

Davis walked ahead of everyone else as they descended the stairs into a warmer, more humid section of the cavern. The walls were putrid purple and red, the veins running along them were thicker now, pumping into inflated hearts that jutted from the walls, each the size of an American football. The eyes were no longer present, though the mouths had begun whispering in a tongue so ancient that merely hearing it induced nausea in the group.

"Try to push past it," Davis said. "The old tongue isn't meant for mortal ears."

"Creepy," Huan said as she walked behind James, who merely nodded in agreement.

"That's what old gods are, my dear pupil," Davis said. "You'll find out soon enough, now that you have one of your own."

"Oh, I've already discovered some of the benefits," Huan said, causing Davis to stop and look.

Across Huan's belly there was a tear in her clothing, showing a scar that was rapidly shrinking. "The old woman cut me, deep too, and it closed up during the fight."

"My," Davis said. "Advanced regeneration… how helpful! It takes me a few hours to close up a wound or mend a broken bone. You won the demonic lottery with that gift."

"Yeah, I rule!" Huan chuckled.

James glared at Huan. "Can we keep going, please? We don't need to see your scars right now."

Huan looked as if she wanted to say something, but chose not to. Davis kept his face neutral as he wracked his brain for a way to earn the boy's trust once more.

*A worry for another day,* Davis thought. *Right now, we need to stay focused.*

Stopping at the entrance to a large cavern, Davis pushed more ether into his spear, causing the fiery obsidian to truly blaze, shining its dancing light even further into the chamber.

It was like the rest of the caverns that they'd seen, with one stark difference. The walls were contracting and expanding, causing blasts of wind to come in and out from what looked like a narrow entrance some eighty feet across the rounded chamber. A single pillar rose from the middle of the cavern, where five thick strands of bedding rose to meet the fleshy column, veins as thick as a man's thigh pumping fluid through the column and out of it. The entire room felt charged, a slight hint of ozone tickling Davis's nose.

"This is interesting," James said as he walked past Davis. Huan stopped at his shoulder while the monks fanned out, Bohai remaining behind to watch the stairs.

"Be careful in here. I can feel *something* in the air," Huan whispered, a noise which echoed across the chamber.

"That would be your inner demon attempting to connect to the ethereal through you. Sometime in the future I'll teach you meditation techniques that could help you," Davis replied absently, stepping further into the room. "Now let's examine the column, shall we?"

"You want my help?" Huan asked.

"You are my student, and I might need to make some changes to something in here," Davis replied. "You're right, this chamber has a purpose."

"The tissue on the walls looks different," James said. "Mind if I look?"

Davis nodded. "Don't touch it, but go ahead and examine it. If it's a new strain of the bedding we've been seeing I want to know about it."

Davis walked straight through the chamber, the bedding sinking beneath his feet as dusty clouds of *something* rose beneath his feet. Raising an eyebrow, he muttered a Sumerian prayer under his breath and, with a wave of his hand, aimed an invisible bolt of ether at James.

It struck his shoulder, shoving the man forward. He looked back at Davis, snarling. "What was that? I can sense the difference in ethereal energy around me?"

"An incantation that purifies air," Davis answered. "Wherever we walk, spores are being kicked up. I don't want to find one of us infected by this shit."

James didn't argue, instead choosing to walk closer to the wall to examine the folds of flesh.

Davis and Huan stopped at the column, both studying it carefully. It was cylindrical and seemed to thrum in tune with something unseen. The ground around it bubbled as if it were liquid, forcing the two to stand a foot from the protuberant veins that laced the pillar from the floor and ceiling.

"Huan, gather some of the bedding into an empty jar. Use a knife if you have to," Davis ordered, bringing the blade of his spear close to the putrid liquid. The heat from the fire made the fluid recoil, the pool growing thinner as the slime rose and slid to avoid the flames.

"Interesting," Huan said, squatting. Pulling her trench knife, she dipped it into the fluid and scooped up some of the jelly before dropping it into a partially full water skein. She dropped in another few globs before they all heard it.

The monks reacted first, charging their blades with energy and swiping at the tentacles that erupted from the walls. At least two feet thick, they were covered in whispering mouths, the words once more causing everyone to shiver. There were five total, two flanking the tunnel leading deeper with another two on the wall. The last one had emerged from where the stairwell was, whipping out and striking Bohai hard enough to toss him across the chamber.

The agile turn his uncontrolled flight into a tight tumble, whipping his sword along the wall as a means of slowing down. For the first time, Davis saw something other than fat dribbling from the bedding.

Thick and viscous as honey with the same coloring, ooze wept from the eight foot gash the sword had left in the wall.

"Attack! Go for the base!" Bohai shouted, and all the monks let up a war cry.

Davis, not knowing how to fight this threat, chose to try and press the offensive in a different way. "Huan! Cut the veins!"

Huan nodded and performed and uppercut into the vein closest to her, the six inches of sharpened carbon steel cutting deep into the vessel, which began to rapidly disgorge the honey ooze. The winds flowing through the chamber quickened, before a low and guttural moan echoed throughout the entire cavern.

Taking that as a positive note, Davis spun his spear, the fiery obsidian cutting a foot-deep gash in the floor before he plunged it into the column.

The swirl of ethereal energy began to manifest as more tentacles sprouted from the walls, the monks hacking away at the turgid base of the larger tendrils, their chants drowning out the whispers. James was using his Persian blade in conjunction with Brun's silver one to gouge deep into one of the large tentacles.

Pulling the spear from the column, Davis smiled as more ooze bled out from the seared-open wound. Huan was cutting deeper into the opening she'd made in the vein, slowly severing it from the main column.

As he watched the vein droop, gushing the ooze out onto the ground where it began to slush into a mound, Davis realized something.

"Start hacking through this wall!" Davis yelled, pointing at it. "Ignore that one and ignore the tentacles at the entrances!" he shouted his commands once in the monks' language and once more in English.

Bohai nodded and repeated the order. One of his monks jumped back from where an injured tentacle tried to grab him. The remaining three men shifted their attention to the two tentacles on the wall Davis had indicated, trimming back the smaller ones while James worked on the shaft of the other thick tentacle.

It swirled back, pressing in on itself as it moved to grab James. He turned and used the silver blade to hack off a foot and half section of the tentacle, which fell to the bedding with a loud *plop!* Spinning forward into the curling tentacle, he rammed the Persian sword into it before ripping upward, severing the sinew that held the massive limb together. The stalk of the appendage split and fell, strands of regenerative flesh stretching out around the steaming hole the blade had made, in a mad attempt to save the tentacle from falling apart entirely under its weight. James brought the Persian blade down upon the tentacle's open wound, fully severing the coil from the rest of the mass, leaving only a four-foot-long stump wriggling like a maggot.

Huan was on her third vein, cackling as she cut through the arteries into the now deflated pillar of flesh, which was trickling a small amount of ooze as opposed to the gushing torrent from earlier.

Davis grabbed a thermite grenade from Huan's bandolier. "Pardon me!" he said as he broke off in a sprint, pulling the pin on the grenade moments before he chucked it in an underhand toss. It struck the wall, sinking into the sticky mire of the flesh before detonating in a brilliant light show of magnesium and rust burning through a wall of tender flesh. The tentacles surrounding the area withered and died, their mouths letting out a wicked cry of pain as they burned away.

Bohai and his monks darted in and out, cutting away quivering masses of meat from the second tentacle sprouting from the wall, swarming like angry bees against an intrusive bear, their silver swords leaving stinging cuts that were slow to mend. Davis pulled raked the Aztec spear down the wall, shaving off a half dozen smaller tentacles while cutting into the folds of flesh. The walls' contractions were heavier now, telling everyone that their combined efforts were having an effect.

James rammed both swords hilt-deep into the wall, ooze pouring freely from the wound as he sawed the blades back and forth, higher and higher. When the blades met in a semicircle, he stepped back to admire his work. The stalk of the giant tentacle he'd cut through slammed into his side, the sticky ooze-blood capturing him like a mosquito in tree sap. He let out a scream as he flailed with his free arm.

"James!" Huan shouted, ripping a third vein in half before sprinting towards him. From the stubby stalk, more tentacles were sprouting, working to drag him into the mass on the wall. He hacked at them with his free arm, Brun's sword severing numerous sprouts before they could grip him. But for every one he severed three took its place, slapping onto him with an ever-tightening grip.

Huan slashed into the tentacles grappling his back, pulling a James's knife from his belt with her other hand. Heedless to her own safety she slid the blades in quickly yet carefully, severing the strands with surgical precision.

Davis paused from his assault on the wall, the thermite burning a crater that he'd been slicing into with wild strikes of his spear. Pulling on the ether surrounding them, he fought back the queasy feeling that suddenly overtook him and pushed forth a gout of freezing water from his outstretched hand, the pressure of a fire hose stripping the crawling flesh slowly consuming James as it was shorn away by the blast. Between Huan and Davis, James was free enough to use both arms to sever the remaining fusion of slime covering him. Falling to the ground with a splat of frigid water, James coughed and hacked, pushing himself up as tiny strands of bedding slinked through the water to try and take hold of him.

"James, are you okay?" Huan asked, stabbing and tearing into the recovering stump, in her tone heavy with worry.

"I'm fine," he said, his voice hoarse as he coughed up some water. "A little damp, but still fine. Thanks, babe!"

Pushing himself to his feet, James didn't see the look of delight cross Huan's face as she redoubled her efforts in cutting into the regenerating stump.

Davis turned back to the concave hollow of burning flesh that was extending out of the cavern, proving he was correct in his hypothesis.

"We're no longer in caverns at all," he said to himself. "We're inside a giant lung… the Father's lung!"

Looking over at Huan, Davis shouted out. "Go back to the pillar! Prevent it from healing!"

She looked reluctant, but when he barked the order again she obeyed, running through sloshy ooze to resume hacking into the veins.

"Keep going! If we keep this up, we'll get out of here!" Davis shouted.

James looked at him as he jumped back from the slab of tissue he'd been carving out of the wall. "What do you mean? We're just cutting into a wall!"

"And yet we haven't reached rock yet!" Davis called back with a cackle. "Keep going!"

James seemed to get the idea, choosing to dig deep cuts around the wall instead of cutting out sections. The walls were convulsing now, thunderous tremors showing that their work was causing an effect on the slumbering god.

Davis pulled back from the eight foot tunnel the thermite had burned through, taking a moment to get a breath of air that wasn't acrid smoke. Looking to the monks, he smiled on seeing they were in good shape, their chanting never ceasing, the large tentacle they fought now lying still, having been hacked into enough with blessed swords that the muscles couldn't reform. Now they were working like miners, digging into a section of wall in Bohai's direction. One of the monks, a whip-thin man who had pulled a silver dagger as well, was jumping in and carving wide X's into sections, leaving Bohai and the others to focus on that spot. The floor around them was ankle deep in translucent sludge, their fast footwork preventing it from hardening over them.

Huan had severed the last of the veins and was pulling her AR-15 around from her shoulder. Holding it steady, she filled the air with the sound of rapid gunfire, her target being the column itself. The high-caliber rounds blew meaty clods of muscle away from the column, more ooze pouring from the wounds even as they attempted to stitch themselves back together.

Davis grinned. *We might just be hurting this thing!*

Just then his heart sank. As if the old god had understood his thoughts, it sent defenders of its own. Thundering from between the massive tentacles were dozens of Children, their sickly pallor showing the fat pulsing through protuberant veins. They were easily seven feet tall, hunched over with four wormy appendages dangling from a tumorous growth covered in eyes. Each had a human arm sprouting from their sides, flapping about as it slapped their wet hides in excitement. Three stalky legs allowed the creatures to move much faster than normal. Among the pack, Davis spotted a relatively smaller individual, this one clad in tattered vestments of the monastic order above. It had obviously once been a woman, and had a pair of calloused swords growing from her arms, a third arm extending from its chest supporting a raking talon. The neckless creature's head was dominated by a hollow pit that led deeper into the body.

Davis readied his spear against the incoming demonologist. The monks and James abandoned their work on the walls and leapt into the fray against the beasts, while Huan turned her gunfire onto the oncoming herd's legs. The world seemed to fade into a haze of gunfire and chanting as Davis squared off against the charging beast, ready until he heard it calling at him in a familiar voice.

"Magus!" Brun screeched, her harridan tones reverberating within the slumbering god's lung, her third arm lashing out as she got close.

# Chapter Thirty-Seven

Davis parried a swing from the transformed Brun, catching her blow in the haft of his spear and turning it aside. What he at first thought were swords of toughened sinew and callouses struck like baseball bats—solid, bludgeoning blows that reverberated up his spine.

She hissed, a tongue snaking up from the hole where her head ought to have been. "Just die!" she shrieked.

Swinging with her clubs to try and clap him on both sides, Davis rolled forward through the slime and swept the shaft of his spear behind her inverted legs, dropping her hard to the lung's floor. She dropped one of the bats in the process, though it stayed connected to her via a thin cord of sinew. Davis stood up and kicked her in the side as hard as he could, feeling something within her burst as he pulled his foot away.

Swinging her bat up to try and club the side of his head, Davis ducked and raised his spear, fiery obsidian edge aimed at her chest. She sank through the floor as he stabbed, the muscle now a pool of murky, flesh-colored slime. Tapping into the ethereal, Davis jumped to the left. She burst from the ground not a second later, both clubs in hand.

"Damn you, magus! I wasn't supposed to become a sacred!" she hissed. "Father promised me a greater place by his side, so long as I delivered you to him!"

"So when you ordered your monks to kill us, what did you expect to happen?" Davis asked, feinting to the right with his spear. "I mean, I'm not much use to him dead, am I?"

"My father is the direct conduit of our lord, a union of spirit and flesh that raises him to a status none could hope to achieve!" she snarled, striking Davis in the thigh with her left club. He rolled with the blow before chambering a kick, which he lashed out at the joints of her fragile legs.

His maneuver was countered by the leg lifting, pushing back the strike with a three-toed foot. He spun to avoid the lashing of her chest-claw, bringing the spear up into her side. The sound of sizzling meat filled the air, fat bubbling in her veiny abdomen. He would have been able to smell her burning if the smog from the still-smoldering thermite hadn't clogged his senses.

Channeling ether into his spear, Davis sawed into her side, cleaving away two inches of body mass just below her left armpit. Her arm seemed to move with a wilder rotation now, tearing at the wound which quickly knitted back together where it had been ripped apart. The burns were superficial, at best, but it was a hit.

"Why betray humanity, Brun?" Davis asked as he got to his feet, twirling the spear like a bo staff in his hands. "You must know what will happen should the Father awaken."

"Oh, I know all right! He'll seek out his missing pieces to join with them, rousing them from their own prisons. Once he's complete, the dynasties of old will be renewed, and those that serve will be exalted above all others!"

Brun was about to say something else when several bullets tore through her body as if it were a meat balloon. Huan was standing by the ruined column, reloading her gun as she eyed Brun with a special level of hatred.

"Whore! You dare harm one of your fellows?" Brun screamed, turning at the waist, droplets of sweat flying from her frame.

"I'm not one of your fellows, your miserable bitch!" Huan called back, before unloading a fresh spray of bullets into Brun's body. Davis backed off, taking the spare moment to catch his breath.

*She's a demon now, just like the other Children,* Davis thought as he rubbed his leg, trying to shake the pain away. *That only confirms Lawrence's tests that the Children were all once human beings.*

"Brun!" Davis shouted over the sounds of battle, charging her at her with his spear aimed low. With a pockmarked arm raised to block the bullets, she readied her other arm to try and prepare for the assault.

Huan's pressure proved to be too much as a few well-placed bursts severed the left arm, leaving Brun to stumble into the oncoming salvo. Davis stopped a few feet from Brun and swept his charged spear through her midsection, cleaving her in half with holy fire. A keening wail whistled from the hollow pit as her legs collapsed under her, slowly breaking down into the lung like butter in a heated saucepan. She waved her club at Davis as Huan turned her wrath at other targets.

"You'll pay for this, magus! My father has been feeding directly from our lord for decades! He's risen to a state no honored vessel has before! He is a power great enough to paint the dreaded sun ebon with but a wave of his hand, severing your precious light from you forever!"

Davis chose not to reply, instead ramming the spear down through the pit, her voice wavering as she seemed to thrash in death, though he could sense her spirit clawing its way out of the physical form and into the ethereal. Giving a grim smile, he opened his mind and allowed the curator access to his body, the greedy demon lashing out through the invisible plane of energy to grapple the loose soul. Distant cries fell on deaf ears as the curator dragged her into Davis, feasting on her just as she'd feasted on so many men and women before.

The pain in his chest that had been present for so long faded, the demonic entity pleased now that it'd been fed something hearty enough to keep it sated. Davis plunged into his mental landscape, watching the curator's pulsing black energy subsuming her tainted pink and fuchsia aura.

*I need to know where the central ward scheme is located,* Davis projected the thought into Brun's struggling soul.

He felt panic, fear, and... pride? Delving deeper into her frenzied mind, he saw the chamber was in fact five chambers with thin membranes as walls, veins running through and along the walls and ceiling like thick piping. A central pillar, untouched by the bedding, glowed with a spectral light. A shadow passed over the vision he was receiving before he was thrown from her mind as if struck by a charging rhinoceros.

Wincing as he returned to the battle, he held a hand to his head to try and interpret the information he'd gleaned before *something* pushed him away.

*It must have been her father,* Davis thought as he rolled his shoulders. *If he's as strong as Brun claims, then he can fend me away from one of his charges, even if it was in the process of being absorbed by a greater demon.*

Davis rushed into the melee, twisting at the waist as he came up under one of the behemoth Children that was sparring with Bohai in a game of tag with swords and tentacles. Stabbing up into the midsection of the three-legged Child, Davis stepped away as he twisted the burring obsidian, tearing a long stretch of muscle and sinew apart. Bubbling fat oozed from with the creature as it howled in rage.

Davis cursed as one of the tentacles swung low and struck him across the head, looping quickly around his neck with a slime that quickly adhered to his skin. Reaching up with his hand, he pulled on the fleshy appendage, panicking slightly as it lifted him bodily from the floor and up towards a hidden slit between the overhanging tumor, which peeled back to reveal a hollow pit lined with writing tongues.

With one hand glued fast to the tentacle, he swung his spear into the creature's upper torso, the fires sizzling the skin but doing little else. Bohai leapt forward, slicing with his sword into the creature's flank. Davis glared at the monk, choking out a low gurgle that was supposed to be a plea for help.

All he could do was spit and hiss.

The tentacle curled, bringing him up into the cavernous maw, the tongues wiggling against his skin in a horrid parody of speech, leaving behind cold trails of hardening slime. The tentacle broke off from the section around his neck, leaving him barely able to breathe, now hanging by dozens of tongues that were looping around his wrists and legs.

The maw closed, sealing Davis alive inside the dank cocoon. It was only by the light of the spear's flames that he could see the tongues split open, dribbling a greasy oil into the maw as muscles contracted and pulled, the throat pulling him deeper into the creature.

Screwing his eyes shut, he concentrated as best he could on the ethereal stream around him, pulling on it to try and wrest his soul from his body so that he could project himself away to see what was going on around him.

It proved too difficult to ignore the slick tongues caressing his wrinkled flesh, the oils staining his clothes, and the overall stench of rot and foul breath coming up from the bellows of the monster's torso.

As he felt the world go upside down, his back aching from the sudden turn, he shrieked as a sword pierced the throat of the creature inches from his face, cutting down to allow Davis a chance to see the determined face of Bohai.

"Sorry, magus!" Bohai shouted before continuing his chant.

Davis could barely reply as the hardened bit of meat surrounding his throat was barely allowing him breath, his one hand trapped by the substance and his other gripping onto the spear for dear life. Seeing this as an opportunity, he used his free hand to tug the spear down a bit, the fiery edge singing the tongues where they crossed paths.

Bringing the fiery edge up close, Davis winced and leaned into the sharpened edge of the fiery weapon. Despite cutting his right cheek and the top of his hand, he managed to slice off the hardened tentacle, the heat from the spear tip proving to be too much for it.

Gasping for air, Davis reached through the hole with his free hand and held it out to Bohai. "Grab on!"

Bohai didn't look certain, finally withering beneath Davis's withering glare. He reached up and grabbed the slick hand, only to be pulled into the opened throat of the creature, the neck expanding to hold the two people in tight quarters.

"How are we doing out there?" Davis asked as he rubbed Bohai's arms with the greasy residue still being pumped by the tongues.

"Roshe has been consumed, as you were, but together we've killed all but six of the beasts," Bohai replied. "Why did you pull me in here?"

"Slide down, get in the stomach!" Davis ordered, pushing Bohai's shaved head down the canal before him. "And don't you dare lose grip of that sword!"

Bohai followed orders while Davis poked his head out of the hole to look around. James and the last monk were dueling with one of the Children while Huan was doing strafing runs on two of the abominations. That left a few wandering around.

"Everyone!" Davis said, channeling ethereal energy into his voice. "Allow them to eat you! Just hold onto your weapons and when you hear screams, cut your way out!"

"What?" James cried, looking over at Davis with incredulity. "You *want* us to die?"

"No! I want us to live! This is the quickest way, so just do it! And keep hold of your damn weapons!"

With that he pulled his head back into the dimly lit chamber of the Child's throat and allowed himself to be forced deeper into the distended stomach. It was there he was almost impaled by Bohai, who at least gave him a sheepish smile as they adjusted with their respective knees to their chests.

"So what now, magus?" Bohai asked, no fear in his voice.

"Now," Davis said with a sigh. "We go for a ride."

# Chapter Thirty-Eight

The sounds of battle reverberating through the fleshy womb Davis shared with the monk slowly died down, the final sounds being Huan's curses and the torrential spitting of her semi-automatic weapon. The spear poked through the side of the membrane holding them within the belly, the flames now a mere flicker as Davis had let go of his weapon.

Instead, he was focusing on weaving himself into the ethereal, all while being toted around by a rotting, greasy transport.

*I'll be the one to seal this deal,* he thought back on all his encounters with Children willing to speak. *They referred to me as chosen – hell, one was reciting a prophecy before I interrupted it. And the curator knows something... What could that last vision mean?*

Thinking on the pulsing center of ethereal energy, the various rivers flowing to and from it, Davis could only wonder what it meant. He remembered how full of energy he was then, like never...

Wait...

*I've used ethereal energy since I've been down here, numerous times now,* he thought as the body he hid inside of sloshed down a gentle slope. Looking at Bohai, Davis poked him in the dim light. "Can you sense the sprit realm?"

Bohai looked at him for a moment, casting an odd glance. "Yes," he said as if Davis were missing something important. "The area is saturated by the souls of our ancestors, willing to aid us when we call upon them."

*That's it!* Davis crowed internally, a smile playing on his face. "Okay Bohai, when we get to where we're going, get ready to start the chanting again. I have a feeling we'll need it."

"You have an idea then?" Bohai asked.

“A half-formed one, yes. It’s missing a few key pieces but it should work, assuming I’m right,” Davis said, slicing through the membrane a little more to peek out of their demonic conveyance. The walls were now a vibrant red, with thin sheets of membrane hanging like silk curtains. Small, hand-sized Children crawled over the walls in swarms, mending veins and reconnecting leathery vessels to sections of throbbing walls. Streaks of red leaked from the thrumming walls, syrup draining from numerous wounds the spidery creatures moved in a constant wave to seal up.

“I think we’re where we need to be,” Davis whispered to Bohai. “Now prepare for something wholly unpleasant.”

“I’ve been swallowed by a creature that is constantly basting me in grease and fat. Wholly unpleasant seems to be my state of being right now.”

“Yeah, well… don’t say I didn’t warn you!” Davis said as he felt the contractions begin. Undulating muscles pushed the two together, their weapons clattering against each other as they were slowly being pushed up via minute three-fingered arms, which were sprouting along the throat of the creature as they went.

Davis held his breath and sent a silent prayer to Fa’theli that his assumption was correct. The hanging tendrils from the monster’s oversized tumor grabbed onto Davis’s bony wrist, hauling him out of the greasy sepulcher and into the dim light of a chamber draped by veils of veiny-red membranes. Pallid hand-spiders skittered along the ceiling, knitting the flesh back together. The splits in the contracting walls were forming just as fast as the hands could seal them, oozing a constant drip of viscous red jam from cracked veins as thick as torsos. These veins channeled into a bulbous mass in the ceiling at the center of the room, held aloft by a pillar of blue-green stone covered in faded etchings.

“I see you’ve made it, chosen one,” a sibilant voice hissed, bringing Davis’s attention up to the domed building.

Dangling from what could only be described as a muscular umbilical cord was a tar-black humanoid, legs curled and atrophied beyond use. The arms were long and frail, each finger ending in a pus-filled nodule that seemed to dribble the yellow cream continuously. The frame was skeletal, telling Davis this had once been a man, judging by the deformed genitals dangling from its ruined hips. The most disturbing feature was the head, which was dominated by a single eye, split three ways in the brilliant colors the other Children of Flesh had. It descended from the ceiling, arms stretched wide, its hissing voice slipping through a lipless beak.

"Yes, warden, I've made certain I'd make it," Davis said, pushing himself to his feet with spear in hand. He could hear the other Children regurgitating his friends, Bohai making a disgusted retching noise as he slid from the pallid mouth.

"So you know me, then?" the warden said, not sounding surprised at all. "Astounding. The visions I had were true—you are a magnificent specimen to behold."

"You managed to keep us from ruining the lungs completely," Davis said, switching to English. "So I imagine you've got something to either regenerate the wounds or put out the fires."

"That is but one of four sets. It is trivial in the greater game we play." The warden chuckled, its voice rising in tenor as it did so.

Huan stood up, woozy from the lack of air in her carrier. "Professor, what the fuck is that?" she asked, glaring at the blackened effigy that was once a man.

"That would be Brun's father, the current warden of the Father of Flesh," Davis said with a smirk, the warden's laughter dying in seconds upon hearing the words.

"What did you say?" The warden lowered itself to where its eye could roll about in the massive socket, glistening teeth now visible beneath the beak. "What did you say, chosen?"

"I said you're the *actual* means of keeping the Father from rousing," Davis said confidently. "I figured it out just moments ago, so don't worry. I've also had help along the way by my own inner demons."

The warden's eye narrowed, his mouth a mere slit as he balled his fists at his sides.

"What was it the *real* Father of Flesh sent to me?" Davis said. "What did it say? 'Nowhere to hide, chosen; the gate must be opened, cannot allow you to stop. Six must, blessed they be, will defeat'… defeat what, I wonder?"

"You cannot hope to defeat the Father, Nickels!" the warden growled.

"Oh, I wouldn't dream of it. Just curious how the ones to come at me in America seemed to spur me on to get over here quicker. It's almost as if the Father of Flesh was seeking help from someone who handles the occult on a regular basis; maybe someone who takes the necessary steps to keep one sealed away so that the draining nature of the physical realm doesn't bother its rest."

The warden switched to English with little hesitation. "You know nothing, chosen! I've brought you here to bleed so that my lord will be able to venture back into his body. The mountains will crumble as he rises, sending you mewling ants back into your corrals where you belong!"

"I think you're bluffing!" Davis said, picking up his spear and spinning it to stab Bohai with the hardened edge, the monk letting out a cry…

*Splortch!*

…as the Child that'd swallowed them pushed Bohai away, allowing the blade to sink into its chest instead. Bohai looked on, oblivious to what was being said, a look of distrust marring his features. Davis gave him a wink before pulling his spear from the child, which sighed as it moved to protect Bohai from any more attacks.

"You *need* me, just as you need all of us," Davis said. "Your little messenger in the States was there to lure me here like a hound tracking a fox. But you didn't do enough to cover your tracks. You had your trickster slip in and drop the information just when I needed it."

"Nian?" Huan said, thinking back on how helpful the infected villager had been.

"Yes, Huan, the boy that suddenly grew ill when we came close to the monastery. The reason the little cutthroat started degenerating was because of the wards over this place. They're designed to weaken any of the Children when they're away from the bedding. The bedding isn't invasive slime like we thought—it's the Father's own body growing out. What we've been fighting have been white blood cells."

James looked sick at the thought and scowled at the shriveled demonologist hovering before them. "Huan being violated?"

"A necessity," Davis answered before the warden could spin a lie. "He knew the monks could fold the demon within her to her will, and he knew we would need her to make it down this far. She knew things even I didn't, and if we waited too long, then something bad would happen."

"Like what?" James asked.

Davis pointed at the warden. "Like that. Look at him, he's a stillborn abomination suckling off the tainted souls the Children reap. He's in pain and can't do anything about it, so he instead urges forth some of the Children to bring in fresh material. He must've struck village after village, hoping to get attention from the outside world."

"Silence!" the warden cried, waving a hand at Davis, a sickly wave of energy the color of fresh vomit rushing forth from his hands.

Davis took a step back, hoping he was right—

—and as the Child of Flesh protecting Bohai pushed him out of the way to absorb the release of energy, he knew he was. The energy flensed flesh from the Child, severing the tumors and tentacles to the ground with a meaty splat. The creature itself appeared unfazed.

"Face it, warden, you're through!" Davis taunted. "You're a cancer to this creature's body, directing its real guardians to do your bidding, all while sapping the wards to try and reawaken the sleeping old god. Problem is, it doesn't want to wake up!"

"Of course he does!" the warden screamed, clenching his fists at his sides. "The Father desires to be joined with its siblings, it's in all the writings! The Blood Mother, the Brother of Bone, the Sister of Soul… they *need* to become one again. The world needs them!"

"No," Davis said. "The world doesn't. And the Father is content to sleep away the eons until it does need to feed. What you want is the old world when we all served beneath the priests of the old gods. I imagine you came up with this once your inner demon began clawing away at your humanity. You gave yourself to a servant of an old one. You knew what you were doing when you did this."

"No!" the warden screamed, rising higher into the air. "I won't let you do this! If I must mingle all your blood myself, then so be it!"

Davis leapt to the side as a blast of flames roasted the headless Child in a burst of ethereal heat. "Bohai, you start chanting and provide us cover. The sacred should act as friends now!"

Bohai nodded and, after looking over at his saliva-soaked monks, began initiated the chant.

A wave of force surged from the warden which the Child of Flesh rammed into head on. A disgusting shower of gore burst from the creature and yet still it kept its footing, showing it could take more than its fair share of abuse.

Huan opened fire with her AR-15, bullets pinging off an invisible barrier the warden erected around his lithe frame. James ran up to the wall and jumped off it to swing at the atrophied legs, severing an elongated foot with Brun's sword.

The warden let out a howl at the injury, spinning to glare at James. The bedding James landed on erupted upward, strands of flesh lashing out to grasp the man where he landed. James fought back, surprised that he could slip through the bonds easily. He stood up and smiled at the warden.

"No… no, this can't be happening!" the warden cried, clutching his head with both hands.

Huan pulled a thermite grenade from her bandolier, one of her last. "Professor!" she shouted, looking to Davis for half a moment.

"Got it!" Davis said, pulling in as much ethereal energy he could muster while focusing on his breathing. Sweeping one foot along the sweaty ground, he paused and held his hands up, fingers splayed.

Huan pulled the pin and threw it at the warden, where it struck the ethereal shield with a crack, exploding in a gout of sticky flames that coated the warden's body.

Davis clenched his fingers as the flames blossomed, mimicking the warden's shield to form a bubble around him, trapping the burning essence in a pool with the writhing monster. The Children of Flesh in the chamber paused, moving to face the warden.

The umbilical cord coming from the ceiling twisted and writhed, splitting off at a stalk from the bubble of force. Dark red jelly surged forth in a frothy mess, prompting the Children to shriek in tones unheard by mortal ears. Hundreds of the skittering hands crawled forward like fire ants, quickly moving to spin and smooth flesh to seal the wound, even as the warden screamed within his fiery orb.

Davis held it for a solid eight seconds before dropping to his knees, the fire extinguished from lack of oxygen, a roiling cloud of smoke falling like a pall over the chamber. The only sign the warden was there was the light thud of his body impacting the ground. Bohai and his monks advanced, swords drawn and angled down, arms outstretched to ward off any last-minute surprises.

Davis, gasping for breath, pulled once more on the ether and waved his hand, banishing the smoke with a gust of wind. As the smog cleared, all that was left was the charred remains of the warden, eye bubbling within its socket while leaking fluids like an endless stream of tears. Twisted and cracked, the warden's frame was broken.

Huan helped Davis to his feet, smiling at her for her aid. "I think," he said. "That it's time I examine the wards now."

A hissing gurgle sputtered from the warden's charred husk. Head creaking up just enough to stare with a sightless orb towards Davis, he uttered a phrase in the old tongue, causing the monks to back away as their ears bled.

Davis felt a pulse of ether go off around him, a sudden chill as if someone poured a bucket of ice water over him. Quickly opening his senses, he could feel the ethereal form of the warden trying to force its way into Davis's body.

Panicked, he opened his mind up for the curator to try and tackle the warden's desperate attempt at possession, only to find that the curator wasn't responding to his mental cries. Cut off from his personal protector that'd been with him for so long, Davis found himself under assault by a focused mind that drove spikes of pain through his subconscious, a headache quickly blistering forth behind his eyes.

"Not so nice, is it, chosen one?" the warden whispered, his voice bouncing within Davis's skull like a loose marble clattering around in an empty bathtub.

Asserting control over his mindscape, Davis began to hastily erect walls to protect his mind, ethereal shielding sliding into place at a pace that was faster than thought.

Yet the warden tore into them at an equally furious pace, long blackened limbs ripping the shielding asunder, his single eye growing closer to Davis's mind by the millisecond. Running out of ideas, Davis decided to attack.

Hurling waves of mental fire and chunks of ice, he buffeted the warden with winds that forced him to slow his advance. The fire seared into the unholy creature while the ice battered his form. Calling upon the ancient spells he'd learned over his century of life, he accelerated time over himself, allowing him to cast spells in a chain rather than one at a time. Spears of pure force and darts of ether pierced the warden's body, slowing him to a crawl, his elongated fingers still prying the fortifications away at a slow but steady pace.

"You can't keep this up forever, chosen one," the warden chuckled. "Soon enough you'll be exhausted, your thoughts strained. I may be nothing but smoke in the ether, but I will never tire! Soon you will be mine, and then the ritual will be complete. The prophecy you were so quick to cite spoke of this moment!"

Davis, thinking in a blind panic, threw up another barrier to buy himself some time.

His mind raced. *"Nowhere to hide, chosen; the gate must be opened, cannot allow you to stop. Six must blessed they be will defeat…" What did it mean by that? There isn't a gate and we've already bested him! We can't just let him possess me, the others will be tricked into thinking I'm doing the correct ritual!*

Davis shuddered as the warden hammered on his barrier, a mad leer on the demon's face as it stared Davis's mental form down.

*Wait... demon! He's a demon now!* The thought hit him like a runaway train. *He's made of pure ether!*

Opening the barrier, Davis opened the floodgates of his ethereal reserves. Pulling the last vestiges of energy from within himself he bound the warden in ethereal chains. Just as he'd done with Illias, Davis tapped into the warden and began draining him of his energies, taking the tainted ether while also forming the beginnings of a spell he'd used on several demonologists in the past.

"What are you doing? Release me at once, whelp!" the warden cried, struggling against the mental chains. The more he struggled, the faster Davis bled him through his mental gates, refilling his core. As he continued murmuring in ancient Sumerian, the warden began to realize something was wrong.

"Wait! No, you can't do this! My lord must be freed!" the warden screeched, breaking an arm free to lash out at Davis, ripping into his soul with venomous claws.

Davis focused on pulling the warden deeper into himself while finishing the spell that would keep external energies from pouring in. All he would have for a good while would be the demonic energies of the warden to sate the curator and keep him alive. Hopefully, that would be enough.

Focusing on the gates to his own reserves, he closed them around the warden, sealing the creature within him permanently. With a final shriek of indignant rage, the warden was locked away. Davis pulled some of the foul energy from himself and put a seal over his own core, limiting the amount of power that could be drawn upon at any given time.

A simple enough task, but one that could very well cost him his life.

# Chapter Thirty-Nine

Davis slumped in Huan's arms, his legs too frail to hold him up. He just now realized that the battle that had lasted what felt like hours had transpired in less than a second. Looking up into the girl's worried expression, he gave her a smile.

"Don't worry, just overexerted myself there," Davis said. "Be a dear and grab my spear for me? I feel like I need a cane now."

James walked up, scooping the spear from the repugnant slime that had slowly been devouring it. The bedding had left it greasy, but Davis held fast to it as he limped away from Huan and towards the stone pillar.

"This," he said with no small amount of aplomb, "is what we came for. The ritual I originally had in mind would have made the wards around this place last for another fifty years. The wards I now plan on doing require six willing subjects who've been touched by an old one's influence."

Bohai and his monks all looked at each other while Davis repeated the directions to them in their language.

"We have been gifted by the spiritual realm, this is true, but none of us are honored vessels, magus," Bohai said.

"Oh, I would disagree with you there, Bohai. What you've been tapping into all this time while in your home was, in fact, the closest thing to blood the Father of Flesh has."

The monks looked surprised while Bohai was pensive. "You believe we have been harming the lord?"

"No," Davis laughed, causing all three to glare. "Hardly! You've been suffusing yourselves in his essence since you were taught to walk. I don't know if you have, but I've witnessed some of you healing fatal wounds, jumping through the spirit realm, and shrugging off the effects of ill weather with almost no effort. You've all been touched by the divine in such a way that I don't think anyone else would be as worthy as you three to finally give your lord the rest he deserves."

"We… we were told by Lady Brun that he wished to be free, and that we were to kill you during the heat of a pitched battle," Bohai said with some reluctance. "We never got a chance, and when we learned of her duplicity, we didn't know what to do. How do we know you are not going to trick us like one of our own did?"

"Because, unlike Brun, I've spoken with agents of your god. They warned me of what would happen here today, and thanks to his warning I have survived. I think he knows he could emerge now, but he *chooses* not to. Why, I can't say for certain."

"The sacred joined us in combat, Bohai," one of the monks, a man in his mid-twenties, said.

"I know that, Liu. I also know that risking you and Duyi is something I'm not willing to undertake, especially given the chance that this might be a trick."

"You must listen to me Bohai," Davis said, coughing a few times into his fist, "the fate of your world, of *our* world, hangs in the balance here. If your lord is forced into his physical form, he will not be able to return to the spirit realm for quite some time. There, he can rest, and offer the protections you and your families rely upon. You venerate and honor him, and in exchange you are trained in ways that none could ever imagine. I'm not asking you to give up your lives, just your willing participation in a ritual that will soothe your lord's pain."

"He's in pain?" Duyi asked, his sword still drawn at his side, a deep gouge running across his chest that was already a mere scar.

Davis nodded. "Transferring between the physical and the spirit realm is wholly unpleasant, but for a mere mortal it takes a fraction of a second. For someone as immense as your god, it takes years. The warden had been slowly pulling the Father of Flesh into our realm by weakening the wards a little at a time. Brun learned of this, and chose to aid her father in this pursuit."

Bohai looked to Liu, then Duyi, both giving a silent nod to Bohai. He sighed and sheathed his sword. "What would you have us do?"

"Stand by the pillar there, while I get everything ready. Your part should be the easiest," Davis said.

Turning as the monks headed to the pillar, Davis motioned for James and Huan to come close. "We haven't much time. I've convinced the monks to offer their services in the ritual, but I need to teach you both how to add your abilities as well."

"Whoa, what abilities? I'm just a scholar!" James declared.

"You know what I'm talking about, boy. Don't make me say it," Davis warned.

James's eyes darted to Huan, fear evident on his face.

"Now," Davis began, "what I need you both to do is to place your right hands on the stone when I tell you to. You'll feel a pulling sensation coming from your belly. Don't fight it! Just allow it to pull through and travel into the rock."

"Why?" Huan asked.

"Because if you do, I'll give each of you a relic from my collection," Davis said, not wanting to argue further.

"Even the… you know?" James asked.

"Yes," Davis sighed. "But I'll want Lawrence to go over the details about it with you before you so much as lay a finger on it."

James nodded. "I'll help."

"Me too," Huan said, reaching out to grab onto James's hand. "Maybe we can finish this problem together. I'd been worried that I might lose one of you. You're the first two people I've shared my past with who haven't rejected me."

"Huan, you are a certifiable psychotic. But I'm hardly one to judge," Davis said, earning a chuckle from his students. "Now, let's finish this."

Bringing his students over, he arranged all five of them in a loose circle around the stone, and instructed them to take out a blade. "I'll put my hand on the stone first and offer myself to the Father before cutting myself. The wards need blood of the willing to seal them back up, so be sure to bleed onto the stone no matter what."

And with that Davis began a chant akin to the chirping of birds, swallows dancing in the water of a stream on a morning sunrise. The monks looked on in surprise, as did James. Huan stood ready with her knife and, once he looked at her, she sliced her palm and placed it on the stone.

One by one the others followed suit, the blood spilling onto the rock and sliding into the carved symbols, leaving nary a trace of where they'd been. Davis held up his hand and, with tenacity that drained him still, bit into his palm hard enough to draw blood.

Slapping his palm onto the rock, he spat out his own skin to continue the song, now taking on a lyrical quality like a lullaby. The few Children that were still in the room seemed to fall under the sway of the incantations as they walked toward the walls, splitting apart to sink into the flesh, sealing the cracks in the gigantic heart they were all standing in. The red ooze stopped dripping, and the membranes grew so thick enough that they were no longer translucent. The thrumming of the muscled walls slowly began to settle down, thumping once every few minutes.

Davis could feel his stored energy being carried away into the stone, charging the ancient wards to their fullest. Gasping as he continued to sing, his vision faded in and out, everything growing blurry for a few moments before he went silent, collapsing with a smile.

The wards were mended.

* * *

"I should be mad at you, old man," Joshua said, arms crossed as he leaned against a tree outside the temple, the glowing pulsar that was the Father of Flesh now a faded, comfortable indigo.

Davis stood there, staring up at the marvel before him. "I've never *helped* one before… I've always viewed them as dark and malevolent, the source of nightmares. But to see it now, I can only wonder what the Father dreams of."

"Who knows? The old one you left me with hasn't been feasting on me enough to make my visits uncomfortable," Joshua said.

Davis looked at him, surprised. "What?"

Joshua shrugged. "Yeah, I know. I think it knew you would need me here to keep you grounded, to remind you of the path you've chosen. I don't like the role, but it beats the alternative."

"For what it's worth, Joshua," Davis said, looking away from the mass of energy. "I'm sorry."

"I know you are, professor. I don't forgive you, nor do I think I ever will. But it's nice to hear you say it with actual conviction now."

"So what's happening to me?" Davis asked.

"Oh, your body is giving up on you. The spell that the warden threw on you bound your inner demon, and it's not able to keep you alive."

"Oh," Davis said, not sure how he should take the news. "So I'm dying then?"

"Yes and no." Joshua said with a smile. "There's work you've yet to do, Davis Nickels, and lessons yet to teach. Let me show you the light and guide you back to your body."

Joshua began walking toward the quasar, Davis following earnestly. They walked around a section of snow-covered rocks to reveal the monastery in all its glory. Walking to, and through, the doors, the two spirits made their way through the halls until they reached what looked like a hospital. Cots lined the walls, pails of water next to each one with shelves holding bandages and spools of thread. Sharpened needles lay in boxes, and yellowed parchments hung from the walls showing the perfect acupuncture points.

There, standing beside the last cot in the hospital, was Bohai. He was stooped over an old man, the feeble thing looking like a wrinkled child that was taking slow, shallow breaths. But inside Davis could sense two forces struggling for freedom, both dark and sinister.

He looked to Joshua, who pulled the relic of a sword from his hip, the light coming off it powerful enough to make Davis wince.

"Know this, Nickels," Joshua said. "I'm only doing this for two reasons. One, the world needs you."

"And the other?" Davis asked.

Joshua gave a twisted smile. "Because this is going to *hurt*!"

Joshua swung the blade like one would a sledgehammer into concrete, hammering the frail body. While the physical form didn't so much as twitch, both dark forces swirled within him, commingling in a whirl of violent waves. Davis felt himself being pulled into the undertow, the energy white hot as it first submerged his hands and knees, and then the rest of his body.

He found himself in a twisted mindscape, his carefully made defenses torn asunder as the warden grappled with the curator, both shouting obscenities in languages Davis couldn't comprehend. The curator was the first to take notice of him.

"Nickels! Help me with this soul you trapped!" it screamed, its normally calm tones urgent and, oddly enough, scared.

"Coming!" Davis shouted, looking around for anything that could prove useful. Closing his eyes and expanding his senses, he could feel ethereal energy being poured into him. Latching onto it, he tugged it down hard enough to drain an ample supply. He fired off a set of ethereal chains, these gold in color and gleam.

They struck the warden from behind, coiling around his emaciated torso before snapping his right arm. The warden howled as the chain bent his arm into his body, binding it there with a sharp snapping noise. Then the warden looked over his shoulder, mouth wide as it screeched. Davis smiled as he felt a tug at what energy he had left, allowing it to be lifted from him without a fight.

"You pest!" the warden yelled. "You insignificant flea! I won't stand for this; nor will I allow myself to be consumed by some relic of a sacred!"

"You don't have a choice, warden," Davis said. "That's not my energy I used. That's someone else's, someone who's trying to draw it back out."

"What?" the warden cawed before screaming. The chains grew in brilliance, their intensity shining through with enough force to sear mottled flesh from tortured bone. Slowly, link by link, the chains popped off the warden, tearing away a gob of tar, the strands breaking away to reveal the man the warden had been.

Tall and noble, he had a shaved head and bore the same tattoos as the rest of his monastic order. He was nude, his muscles visibly tense as he fought against the chains, grabbing at the tar as it peeled away. His broken arm was pulled away, leaving a smoky trail of energy rising from a stump of an elbow.

"Wait, no! Not like this! I can't end like this!" the warden cried. "Please, don't take him away! I'll serve him for an eternity so long as he wills it!"

"It's no longer his will guiding this chain of events," Davis said, looking over the warden's shoulder.

The warden shrieked as an arm burst through his chest, followed by another. Soon the curator's whole torso pulled through, ripping the man in half, the demon's pale blue skin absorbing the life energy of the soul left behind in the wake of the chaos.

The warden never made a final cry, or threat, or even a plea. Instead, his head was stomped into the mindscape, wisps of ethereal smoke floating up and into the curator's leg.

Smiling, Davis allowed himself to pull away from his mindscape, back to the real world where his friends were waiting for him.

## Chapter Forty

Davis gave a jolt when he opened his eyes, as his gaze was met by twin embers set back in a skull mask. Said skull mask began cackling as it backed up, revealing the withered form of the Khul standing over him. Davis could sense the dark energies roiling within the Khul's form, settling within his core. His long-fingered hands settled over his stomach as he issued deep belly laughs, earning chuckles from those around him.

He saw Bohai and Duyi, with Liu leaning against a wall. Everyone seemed to have been patched up, bandages wrapped over their injuries. Bohai seemed to be in good spirits as he clapped his hands together.

"Magus, you are awake!" Bohai exclaimed. "I was trying to coax you from the hands of death when I suddenly felt the violent energies within you. I asked Khul to aid me, and he was able to bring harmony to your body once more."

"It was my pleasure," the Khul said as he rubbed his stomach.

"Where are my students?" Davis asked. He looked down at himself and raised an eyebrow. "And why am I naked?"

"Medical reasons," the Khul replied calmly.

"I'm sure," Davis said, glaring at the old fiend. "And my students?"

"We heard the woman screaming to the gods in the private bedroom we gave to her and the swordsman. They've been together in there for two days, only partaking in meals when they come to visit you."

"I've been out for two days?" Davis exclaimed, sitting up.

"Careful," Bohai was instantly at his side, resting a hand on Davis's withered shoulder. "You are still very weak."

"He isn't," the Khul said, red eyes gleaming.

Bohai looked at his master and sighed. "I guess I worry too much then." He looked to Davis. "Your clothes have been cleaned."

Liu walked over with his folded jacket, shirt, and pants. Duyi had his boots, which must have been retrieved from the camp as the Khul had promised. Duyi also held a sack, which looked quite heavy.

"All of your devices are here, safe and sound!" Duyi proclaimed.

"Here, get dressed, old man," Liu said with a smile as he tossed the clothes onto Davis. "I've grown tired of standing guard over a shriveled old corpse."

"I can feel the love," Davis muttered in English as he stood from his cot. As Davis got dressed, the Khul explained what had transpired while Davis was unconscious.

After the ritual, Davis had fallen over into a stupor. The various sacred had walked into the walls and bedding, sinking into it to better protect the catacombs. The remaining five in Davis's group had rushed up to the surface, where they had to pound on the door for nearly an hour before the three monks could muster the energy to perform the unlocking mechanism.

The Khul had been waiting for them, and he quickly ushered them all to the hospital wing.

After bee's wax and honey had been applied to their open wounds, Bohai had told the Khul of Brun's betrayal and how her father had been trying to free the sleeper. The Khul had been angry, and ordered a vigil be held over Davis with strict instructions to fetch him if Davis so much as blinked.

"And now comes the time where I shall listen to what you must say," the Khul ended his spiel. "What was this you performed, and how did you know it would work?"

"My friend," Davis replied, tapping his chest, "has taught me many rituals. This one fit the bill, following what the sleeper had told me through a messenger back home. Now that it's sealed correctly, you and your followers should train harder to access the spiritual realm, but will find it easier to master."

"Fascinating," the Khul remarked. "I imagine we won't need to send anyone down to check on the wards for many seasons. For this, I think we'll have a feast!"

"If it's all the same, I think my students and I should leave," Davis said, looking at the Khul with steady eyes.

The Khul stared back for what seemed like the longest moment of Davis's life. "I had intended for you to stay and learn our ways; have your honored vessel master her abilities like ours have, while your student could learn a better method of using the sword he seems to favor. I would also like to see him master charging the sword that he took from one of my students."

"That was Brun's blade, and I would like to think he earned it," Davis said as he pulled his jacket on.

"Oh, I had no intention of taking it away," the Khul said, shaking his head. "I merely want him to know how to use it. I would also like for you to teach my students how to better access the spirit realm."

"Really?" Davis was surprised. "And why can't one of your masters do this? Or you?"

"Well, the main instructor was shot, I believe by your honored vessel," the Khul said, smiling. "And I am training a new Khul, so my time is not as easily shared as it should be."

Davis thought for a moment, an idea popping in his head. "How long would you like us to stay?"

"Ideally? Until the end of days. But I know a man like you has things that must be done in your homeland, so I propose a bargain: we shall provide continued training for your students, and bring you on as a shifu for one year. I will allow you three access to my library and permit you to keep anything you earn. All this, so long as you also take a vow to never reveal our location to anyone who doesn't already know it."

Davis thought it over. *Lawrence is still working in my absence, and I told the dean that I was on an extended leave. I'm not needed for anything pressing for the next few years and Huan and James could use the training.*

"Well, honored Khul," said Davis, "I guess I'll be referred to as Shifu Nickels for a while."

The Khul gave a wicked smile, wide enough for his teeth to glisten. "Excellent!"

## THE END

# The Adventure Continues In Book Two: Travails For Teyuna

*"How does something as big as an elder god get misplaced?"*

Professor Davis's greatest adventure has only just begun. The journey continues in *Travails for Teyuna,* book two of the *Broken Gods* series.

After a year trapped in a Chinese monastery, world-traveling occult Professor Nickels and his students escape, only to brave bigger and deadlier challenges. A slumbering elder god known as the Brother of Bone has gone missing. Meanwhile, sinister forces are hard at work ferreting out the god's resting place, seeking to claim its mighty powers for themselves.

Knowing the catastrophic danger that would ensue if the Brother of Bone fell into the wrong hands, Nickels and his students set off to find answers. All signs point to Teyuna—an ancient city not on any map, inhabited solely by vampires and the humans who serve as their livestock.

Finding a city that shouldn't exist is only half the problem, because getting there alive is a completely different matter. With their path beset by assassins, deranged demonologists, undead hordes and mystical serpent women with horrific powers, Nickels and his group will need nothing short of a miracle to reach Teyuna in one piece.

## Discover Other Books Available Through Darkwater Syndicate

*A Moon Called Sun*
*By: Christopher F. Cobb*

> *"This is intriguingly different science fiction/fantasy/horror, wildly ranging, sometimes hard-hitting, not for maiden aunts."*
> **—Piers Anthony, New York Times bestselling author**

A botched alien abduction sends modern-day Trace Jackson to north Florida in the year 1818, where he meets a beautiful Seminole woman, and the two strike up a relationship. Unfortunately, Trace's distant ancestor, General Andrew Jackson, is hell-bent on driving out the Seminoles by whatever means necessary. Can Trace survive to fulfill his destiny in another dimension where time no longer has meaning, on a moon called Sun?

*The Gullwing Odyssey*
*By: Antonio Simon, Jr.*

> *"**The Gullwing Odyssey** rests solidly on the shaking shoulders of a good laugh—and that's what sets it apart from ninety percent of fantasies on the market."*
> **—Midwest Book Review**

A four-time award winning fantasy/comedy adventure. When an unusual assignment sends Marco overseas, he finds himself dodging pirates and a hummingbird with an appetite for human brains. Little does he know the fate of a civilization may rest upon his shoulders. In spite of himself, Marco becomes the hero he strives not to be.

*Slasher Sam*
*By: Simon Petersen*

Slasher Sam writes a killer blog. When Sam isn't gutting victims, the serial killer/blogger is posting it to the Internet for the world to see, putting readers so close to the action that they're practically in the splash zone when the blood and guts go flying.

*Postcards From The Void*
*By: Various Authors*

The places in this book are shunned, abandoned and forgotten. They do not exist, and yet here you will find the stories of people who have gone and survived to tell their tales, complete with photographs. These are the postcards from the void, frightful evidence of places that should not be, and yet exist in our nightmares. Should you dare to venture into these blighted places, remember: don't talk to strangers; don't stray far from home; and never, ever go in alone.

*Shadows And Teeth, Volume One*
*Ten Terrifying Tales Of Horror And Suspense*
*By: Various Authors*

> *"I highly recommend* ***Shadows And Teeth*** *for fans of horror… Each story is uniquely written by a talented author, and the writing styles varied so that each story stood out on its own… I really look forward to future volumes in this fantastic series."*
>
> **—Reader Views Reviews**

Prepare for extreme horror. This collection of ten stories features a range of international talent, award-winning authors and new voices in the genre. Take care as you reach into these dark places, for the things here bite, and you may withdraw a hand short of a few fingers.

*Holy*
*By: Abbie Krupnick*

Gus Stevens has the worst of both worlds. By night, he resides in the Dream World, a place steeped in magic and chock full of exotic dangers, with hardly a way to defend himself. By day, a giant snow-lizard, the ravenous personification of Winter, stalks him in the Real World, looking to make Gus its next meal. Author Abbie Krupnick blends the magical and the mundane in this avant-garde dark fantasy where nothing is as it seems.

*Chasing Blood*
*By: R. Perez de Pereda*

A briefcase full of money lies on the floor. Would you take it? What if the money belonged to a crime lord, and taking it set you running for your life? Still sound good? It did to Ryan, who had nothing to lose.

Born a child of the streets, Ryan Cantril learned early on to fight for his keep, and sometimes just to keep what he earned. Now in his thirties, the self-proclaimed king of the sucker punch fights to keep the cash he rightfully stole from a powerful crime syndicate—and if he's lucky, his life.

# About The Author

Born and raised in Texas, Nicholas Paschall started his career in writing at an early age, jotting down stories on scraps of paper when he could and saving them to read aloud at lunch to all his friends at school. The teachers, upon learning this, asked him to stop as the stories weren't exactly school-friendly, but this only spurred him on to continue his career as a writer.

After a stint as a journalist and editor, he started his career as a horror author. It was brought on by reading a book he found dull and listless, which, after lending it to a coworker, he was informed it was terrifying. He thought he could do better, and has been publishing ever since. He's been published in nineteen different printed anthologies and magazines, served two years as a recurring columnist for *Dark Eclipse Magazine*, and is a current columnist for *The London Horror Society*. His work can be found across the web, where he spins new yarns for all to enjoy on a daily basis.

## About Darkwater Syndicate

We are Darkwater Syndicate. We're the publishing company with a defense contractor's name, and that sums up our approach to books. Our mission is to be your source for uncommonly good reading.

We refuse to be mainstream. Our authors are not afraid to push boundaries and buck trends. Pick up one of our books and see why we call them "uncommonly good" reading.

We are headquartered in Miami Lakes, Florida.

Visit us at www.DarkwaterSyndicate.com.

Follow Darkwater Syndicate on Facebook and Twitter.

CPSIA information can be obtained
at www.ICGtesting.com
Printed in the USA
BVHW04s2159240618
519940BV00013B/96/P